STORMSWORN

Also by Eric R. Asher

Shop ebooks, audiobooks, and paperbacks at ericrasherstore.com

The Theme Park at the End of the World

The Steamborn Series

Steamborn

Steamforged

Steamsworn

Skyborn

Skyforged

Skysworn

Stormborn

Stormforged

Stormsworn

The Vesik Series
(Recommended for Ages 17+)

Days Gone Bad

Wolves and the River of Stone

Winter's Demon

This Broken World

Destroyer Rising

Rattle the Bones

Witch Queen's War

Forgotten Ghosts

The Book of the Ghost

The Book of the Claw

The Book of the Sea

The Book of the Staff

The Book of the Rune

The Book of the Sails

The Book of the Wing

The Book of the Blade

The Book of the Fang

The Book of the Reaper

Dreams of the Forgotten Dead

Garden Gnome Graves

The Vesik Series Box Sets

Box Set One (Books 1-3)

Box Set Two (Books 4-6)

Box Set Three (Books 7-8)

Box Set Four: The Books of the Dead Part 1

Box Set Five: The Books of the Dead Part 2

Mason Dixon: Monster Hunter

Episode One

Episode Two

Episode Three

Episode Four

Want to receive an email when one of Eric's books releases?

Visit ericrasher.com to get started.

STORMSWORN

THE STEAMBORN SERIES, BOOK NINE

By

ERIC R. ASHER

Edited by Laura Matheson
Cover design by Murphy Rae
Cover artwork by Enggar Adirasa

Through the black, we ride once more

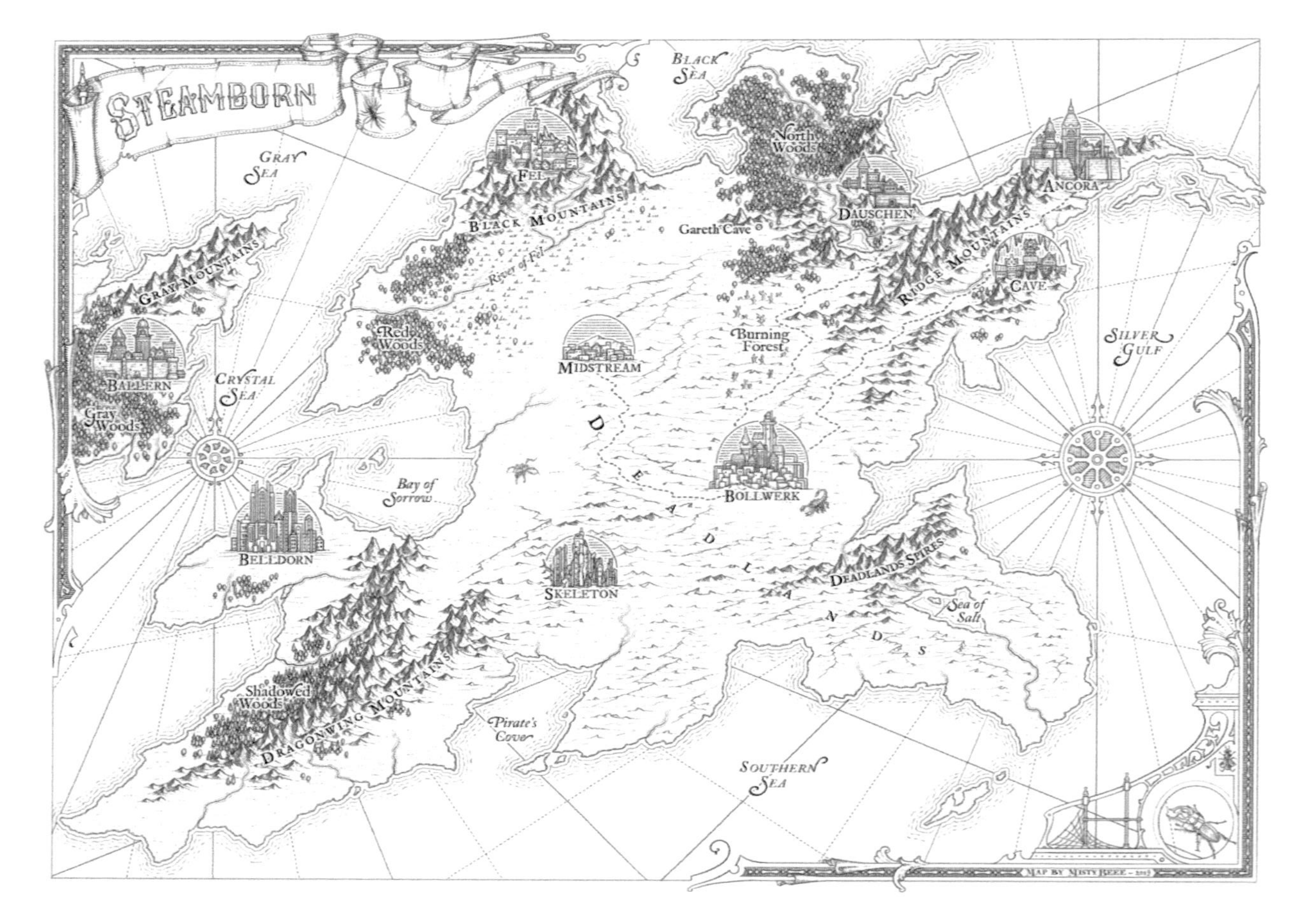

STEAMBORN
BLACK SEA
GRAY SEA
FEL
BLACK MOUNTAINS
North Woods
Gareth Cave
DAUSCHEN
ANCORA
RIDGE MOUNTAINS
CAVE
GRAY MOUNTAINS
River of Fel
Red Woods
Burning Forest
SILVER GULF
BALLERN
CRYSTAL SEA
Gray Woods
MIDSTREAM
DEADLANDS
BOLLWERK
Bay of Sorrow
BELLDORN
SKELETON
DEADLANDS SPIRES
Sea of Salt
Shadowed Woods
DRAGONWING MOUNTAINS
Pirate's Cove
SOUTHERN SEA
MAP BY MISTY BEEE - 2017

CHAPTER ONE

J ACOB GENTLY PULLED back on the reins of his Tree Killer, slowing the mount until she came to a stop beside their Karn guide. "Thank you for inviting us, Mali."

Mali glanced between him and Alice. "It is good of you to join me. We don't get many Ancorans in Karn, and that is something of an understatement."

"It's nice to be away from Ballern." Alice patted the head of her mount. "I'm glad we could help with the rescues, but after two weeks …"

"There isn't anyone else to rescue." Jacob stared off into the Gray Woods, his quiet words hanging in the air for a time.

"Don't tell Arun I quoted him, even though I am about to." Mali gave them both a meaningful look. "But he's told me a lot of things over the years. Some of them help me in the dark times. You gave what you could, and that is enough. You may feel like it never is, but know that for those who care about you, it is enough."

Jacob didn't miss the small smile that crossed Alice's face when she glanced at him. He knew why. It was close to what she'd been saying to him while he spent hours in the workshop, followed by hours climbing through stones and ruins in his exoskeleton.

He'd complained about changes he could have made that would have been better for a rescue, but he hadn't made them because he'd been too focused on what would be useful in a fight. And to that, Alice had told him he'd done enough. He *was* enough, and the simple fact he'd given so much effort was all anyone could ask of him.

But the truth of it was, he could do more. And he *would* do more. Wise words might be a salve in the moment, but they rarely pulled survivors from the rubble.

Jacob didn't speak any of those thoughts aloud. Instead, he focused on Mali, meeting her gaze. "Thank you."

"We have one more ridge." Mali gestured to the lightening shadows in the woods. Movement spread out around them, creatures large and small either avoiding the Tree Killers or contemplating them for a snack.

Whatever the case was, Jacob trusted Mali to know when danger was nearby. He might have known how to deal with Red Death and Widow Makers, but the creatures of the woods were another world entirely. Jacob patted his Tree Killer between the eyes, the many facets tilting back to study him like a thousand mirrors.

"We cross the ridge and climb the first Forest Giant, just there." She pointed to an expansive trunk with curls of peeling bark near the tangled roots. "The limbs are wide enough to support far more than the three of us, and the leaves aren't falling. We'll be all but invisible to anyone who might be watching."

Alice gestured to the ridge. "Lead the way."

"It's still a bit odd to be riding on a Tree Killer." Jacob pulled the reins to the side, and his mount followed without protest.

"They're no more dangerous than a Mantis, if you ask me." Mali stiffened and glanced back at Jacob. "Sorry, I know your experience with them has been different."

Jacob waved the thought away. "It's fine, honestly."

"Here, the Tree Killers are certainly dangerous, but they rarely attack people outright. And when they do, it's not for food. If they're cornered, or threatened, then they are one of the most dangerous creatures in the woods."

"The Acidwings are rather unsettling," Alice said, glancing up toward the canopy as they crested the ridge.

Mali nodded. "And they *will* happily feast on unsuspecting people. Best to be on your guard in the thicker parts of the Gray Woods."

It wasn't hard to identify the nearest Forest Giant. Far to the northwest, smoke crept through the scattered openings of the forest canopy, but they were well hidden behind the Forest Giant's trunk.

"Let me get my camera ready," Mali said. "I don't want to be trying to assemble it perched on the Forest Giant's branches."

She stopped halfway up the tangle of steep roots before pulling a slim rectangular box from her leather pack. Jacob assumed it was plates for the camera until Mali pulled out another small box, swinging open a door in the back before inserting the second box. She spun a dial on the side and removed the front of the assembly, revealing a round lens.

"What is that?" Jacob asked.

"My camera? I'm quite sure you have these in Ancora, don't you?"

Alice leaned forward. "Nothing so small. And I've really only seen the picture man's camera in the Wildhorse up close. Not many cameras in Ancora."

Mali blinked. "Truly?"

"Definitely," Jacob said. "Not only that, but Ancoran cameras are huge." He spread his hands to demonstrate that fact. "You need a tripod to keep them stable. How do you hold that one still?"

"It doesn't take that long, honestly. I usually rest it on a branch."

"And the smaller box is your plate?"

"The film?" Mali frowned before a broad grin crossed her face. "Oh, you're going to like this. That smaller box I inserted earlier? That holds the film. Think of it like multiple plates on a long strip. I can take almost fifty pictures on a single cartridge."

Jacob stared at Mali, remembering the huge plates the picture man had to slide in and out of the camera at the Wildhorse. How could fifty of those possibly be inside that tiny box? "I'd really like to see how that works on the inside."

Mali narrowed her eyes. "You're not taking apart my camera. Tinker or not."

Alice chuckled and grinned at Jacob. "Maybe Archibald will buy you one. You could tell him it's a necessary item for the new exoskeletons you've been working on."

Jacob started to reply, but trailed off. "That's … not a bad idea, actually. If you could have something that small mounted in the frame? Think of the reconnaissance someone could gather with that."

"You're talking about spies, aren't you?" Mali asked. "I think spies have enough to work with already."

"No … I mean yes, but not exactly."

Alice raised an eyebrow.

"No, no, think about it. The exoskeletons aren't going to be used by spies. They aren't quiet or stealthy. Compared to a Titan Mech, maybe, but they're still loud, especially armored. But if they were on the front lines, they could document what was happening. Send the photos back."

"They need to be developed." Mali tapped the side of her camera. "The film stays inside its cube, and that's all we need to get back to the city."

Jacob blinked at that. "It doesn't … I mean, it doesn't dispense like a plate on the bigger cameras?"

"Not at all."

He shook his head and let out a small laugh. "I have to know how that works. When this is over, do you think one of your tinkers could show me?"

Mali groaned. "Yes. And while they're doing that, Alice and I can move back to Ancora so I can try this Cocoa Crunch you two have been talking about these past few days." She turned to Alice. "Don't worry. I'm sure you'll see him again in nine or ten years."

"He is right, though, isn't he?" Alice rubbed the back of her neck. "It's not just the reconnaissance. Think of all the people and places that have been lost to history. Some we might have a few paintings of, but to have photographs would be … I don't know, more real? Like a book, but different."

Mali turned the camera over in her hands before securing it to her vest. "I never thought about it like that. Our tinkers are going to need to learn to make film a lot faster if we're going to start selling these to Ancorans. Now, let's focus, shall we? As soon as we reach the lowest branches, spread out along them. It won't be hard to see where the Great Machine is."

Jacob tapped on the center of his mount's head, the signal to follow its leader. He took the rear as Alice trailed Mali, guiding them over the rest of the roots before the Tree Killers' scythes cut into the bark itself. From there, the mounts moved something like the spiders, propping their riders up through training or instinct as they went.

A quick glance at the ground showed the forest floor vanishing below them far faster than it felt they were moving. It was disorienting at best. Jacob focused instead on his grip and the soaring branches of the Forest Giant. Every step of the Tree Killers above him sent small splinters and clouds of sawdust into the air, and for a short time, he wished he had goggles.

Soon enough, they reached the first branches. Calling them branches felt wrong, since Jacob was quite sure their Tree Killers could stand shoulder to shoulder across the width of the first branch.

Mali's mount scurried out a good distance before she stopped. Alice took the second branch, dismounting and sidestepping around the Forest Giant until her Tree Killer could follow. Jacob trailed behind them, watching each step of his mount before he caught sight of Alice, staring into the distance.

He was about to ask what she was looking at when the gap in the foliage opened before him, and he saw the rolling banks of fog. Heavy nearer the mountains, the thick fog broke as it left the valley, nearing the ocean and plains leading to the Gray Woods.

As much as it obscured, there was a great deal to see. A trapezoidal shadow lurked in the fog, spitting towering columns of smoke into the air, a dark contrast to the mountain fog. It served to frame the surrounding city, and a city it was. It could have been Ancora without the walls, but the lines were sharper, the roofs swept up like a wave, capping every home and structure he could see.

A burst of fire rose from a smokestack, leaving an echo of soot behind as if it were a dark flame in the sky. The ground surged with people and machines and creatures Jacob couldn't make out. But he'd seen something that looked similar before.

"It looks like a hive of Sky Needles. An impenetrable hive."

"Mordair is inside that thing," Alice said as the fog rolled back, revealing more and more of the Great Machine and what waited around it. Airships floated over the water and docked along a short, wide structure well past the Great Machine itself, and distant enough that the destroyers looked like little more than toys.

Warships continued along the shore and out into the bay, and suddenly Jacob understood why the ships Lady Katherine had sent in pursuit of Fel had never returned. Seeing what waited near the Great Machine, she'd been right to focus on the rescues. A direct attack on the forces before them would have been disastrous. They'd need more warships to break those lines, and even then, the Children of the Dark Fire had airships of their own. An attack here would require a fleet like nothing seen since the Deadlands War, and even then …

Jacob tried to shake the darker thoughts away.

Ranks formed to the southeast along the ground. A line of armored Walkers and crawlers.

"Are they marching on Ballern?" Jacob dismounted and walked out on the branch beside Mali.

Her camera clicked before she spun the side wheel and pressed the button for the shutter again. "Those Walkers aren't meant for a raid on Ballern. They're coming for Karn."

CHAPTER TWO

J ACOB RUBBED HIS forehead before taking a deep breath and trying to tie the Tree Killer's bridle on in the proper fashion. They'd only just returned, but Karn liked to keep its Tree Killers ready to deploy at a moment's notice. The bridle wasn't anything like the saddles the Spider Knights used, and getting the knots wrong could cut into even the thickest of their chitinous armor.

Alice peered over his shoulder before giving her appraisal. "Looks like it's not on backward this time."

"It wasn't *entirely* backward last time. I just fed the ties through the wrong side." He didn't keep the irritation out of his voice, but it had been a long couple weeks since the Battle of Ballern. "Sorry."

"You don't have to apologize." She patted his arm. "But thank you. It's been hard for all of us."

"I wish Tatsu and Rin were here. The dragonriders are all better at this than I am."

"Than *we* are," Alice said. "I've had quite a bit of trouble, too."

Jacob glanced at the perfectly flat bridle connected to the saddle of Alice's Tree Killer. "I can tell."

She grinned at him and squeezed his shoulder.

A tinker clad in black leather and shiny chitinous pauldrons pushed his way into the stables. "Mali, I have the photos you requested."

"How many were you able to finish?"

"You have fifteen there. The rest should be done in the next two hours, should you need them."

"Thank you." Mali took the offered envelope, tied closed with leather straps, before dismissing the man with a nod.

"How long have we been back?" Jacob asked. "Fifteen photographs already?"

"We have multiple rooms attached to the factory here. All of the rooms can be used to develop these photographs, but the chemicals to do that quickly are harder to come by. Perhaps you'd like to visit sometime? When this is done."

Jacob nodded, but Mali's words stuck in his mind. *When this is done.* What did that mean? When Mordair was dead? When the Children of the Dark Fire were no more? Was that even something that could happen?

"I must speak with Arun." Mali hesitated. "You two saw what is waiting at the Great Machines. Would you join me?"

"Of course," Alice said. "Anything we can do, Mali. Just ask."

"That's very kind of you. Come, please. He'll be in the Hall, I have no doubt."

✧   ✧   ✧

A SHORT TIME later, Jacob found himself standing beside Alice and Mali while Arun leaned over a wide map of the Gray Woods. Strewn across it were Mali's photos, and Arun slowly slid one on top of another, repositioning them as he went.

"I thought it would be easier to show you."

Arun glanced up at Mali. "The elders should be in attendance for this, Mali."

"No." A hint of anger bled into her response, softening as she continued. "They don't trust outsiders, Arun. It was a stroke of luck to get them to agree to let Lady Katherine use Karn as a waypoint."

"I like to think it had something to do with my skills as a negotiator."

Mali crossed her arms. "You know what I mean."

"Yes, that I do." Arun turned his focus back to the photographs. "Never have I seen so many vessels stationed around the Great Machines. Every bay of their airship docks must be occupied."

"It's the last photo I'm most worried about." Mali wrung her hands together.

Arun slid the photo to the center of the table, a clear view of the armored Walkers and crawlers, beasts and machines side by side along the main roads leading away from the Great Machine.

"Do you think I'm right?" Mali asked. "They're coming here? That's the road to Karn they're assembling at."

Arun pursed his lips and glanced between Mali and Alice. "I am afraid that may be the case." He pushed the photograph away and stood up straight. "We are not defenseless in Karn, but I would not wish to engage in a full-scale battle in the city proper. It would not take much for the oldest towers to fall, and we've seen what they're willing to do in Ballern."

"What *Mordair* is willing to do," Jacob muttered.

"A king cannot strike without a weapon." Arun's words soured. "He has bred loyalty, Jacob. As sickening a thought as that may be to you, we cannot discount it. His hand did not fire upon Ballern, though his orders may have been the cause."

Alice placed her hands on the table and leaned over the photos before meeting Arun's gaze. "You need to talk to Lady Katherine. You lent her help for the attack on Ballern, and she'll repay you for it. I know it."

"We have survived a long time here without the need for outside help." Arun blew out a long breath and studied the map again. "But I cannot discount the threat to Karn. It is certainly worth a conversation. I will discuss our situation with the Lady of Belldorn."

"The carrier is scheduled to be back in Karn in two days," Alice said. "You already know that, right?"

"I do, yes."

"Then talk to Kat now. If you ask for reinforcements, she's going to need time to get them on the carriers."

"I will. For the moment, we need outposts stationed along all the roads to the north and west. Should any of those forces move toward Karn, we must know. Mali, deploy our most skilled outlooks closer to the Great Machine. Seeing their defenses, I wonder if the control center may be our best option."

Alice leaned back and stepped close to Jacob. "If we can learn more about the functions of the Great Machines …"

"We may learn how to sabotage them." Arun gave a sharp nod. He eyed the trio before drawing a copper box from the interior of his vest. "Would you three remain here? I would like you to stay in case Lady Katherine has any questions I cannot answer."

"Of course," Jacob said. "Whatever we can do to help."

Arun set the transmitter on top of the map and pushed the button. "This is Karn."

Static came back before resolving into a familiar voice. "This isn't the best time, Karn. Might I contact you in an hour?"

"I fear the news is dire."

"A moment, please."

They couldn't hear Lady Katherine for a moment or two after her response, but Jacob suspected she was clearing out the room or bridge she was currently at. Her voice returned in short order.

"Continue. I am secure."

"Mali took your Ancorans into the Gray Woods. I'm afraid—"

Lady Katherine cut him off, her words sharp. "Are they well? Have they been harmed?"

Arun gestured to Alice.

She leaned toward the transmitter and clicked the button. "We're fine, Kat. It's what we saw that's the problem."

"Sorry I interrupted you. It's just … we've lost a lot of people the past few weeks."

Jacob gritted his teeth as memories of the battle bubbled in his mind. The screams and blood, and the terrifying crash of the Bones crushing the city below. He shivered and blew out a breath.

Arun continued his report. Most of it was a quick summary of what they'd already discussed, but instead of questioning whether or not the alliance of the Children of the Dark Fire and Mordair would be coming for Karn, Arun stated it as fact.

Jacob wasn't sure if he'd been trying not to worry their Ancoran guests, or if he hadn't decided if Mali was correct in her assessment until that moment, but it mattered little at that point.

"If you are able, we need your support, Lady Katherine."

"I do not turn my back on allies, Arun. Karn has our support in full. Whatever trials you face in this battle, Belldorn will be at your side. I can speak with Archibald about the possibility of his tinkers assisting you as well. The worst of the debris has been cleared from the eastern blocks of Ballern, and there will be little need for Titan Mechs until the reconstruction begins."

Arun hesitated before adding, "If any wish to fight, we will shelter and feed them in Karn."

"You may have more who wish to fight than you realize, Arun. Mordair has struck a blow against many cities, and our alliance against him runs deep. Prepare enough beds for a full company of fighters. Ballern raises capable soldiers, as I'm sure you know."

"Something I know all too well, my lady. It will be good to fight beside them."

"Any resources you need, send word to my commanders. I'll be sure you have them. With Archibald's warships and two Porcupines at Ballern, the city is well guarded. We will make certain blood is not shed in Karn."

"You speak of a battle in the woods. That is not something you or the Speaker of Bollwerk are familiar with, is it?"

Kat's words sounded heavy when she responded. "We have more familiarity with it than I would prefer, my friend. We can burn the forest to the ground, or we can be the wall that the Children of the Dark Fire die upon. It is your city."

Arun stared hard at the transmitter. "I've no wish to destroy the forest, Lady Katherine. Nor do my people. We will fight with you on the ground and in the woods. Karn is not defenseless, but we are stronger with you at our side."

"To lighter days for all in need," Kat said after a pause.

Arun tilted his head to the side. "And an end for all who war."

The transmitter went silent.

Mali stood up straighter. "How did she know that saying? I've never heard it outside of Karn."

A small smile crossed Alice's lips. "You should see her library."

CHAPTER THREE

GLADYS STOOD BESIDE the stage in the heart of Fel. Dozens, if not hundreds, of broken blades riddled the edge. An oath from the fisherfolk, and not one made lightly. She remembered working on a stage in Midstream when she was in school, one of her teachers always calling it the apron. Gladys flicked the cracked base of a blade, listening to the ring echoing around them in the oddly quiet city.

"Give them time, Princess."

She looked up at George, wondering if he had a few more wrinkles at the corners of his eyes, and perhaps a few extra strands of gray along his temples. "Are you sure we should wait here? We could have gone to their docks, or their pubs." Her voice darkened. "If I'd abandoned my people who were fighting a war across the Crystal Sea, I'd certainly be hiding in a pub."

George slowly raised an eyebrow.

"Sorry," Gladys muttered. "I'll be diplomatic."

"We are here to help them, Princess. They may be the least likely to fight physically against Mordair, but to abandon *them* would make it a certainty. We can invite them to Midstream, or spend more time here getting to know who remains. It would be in our best interest to court more allies."

Gladys rubbed her forehead. "I'm aware of that, George. It's just … the Children of the Dark Fire were here for so long. And look at what they did to Ballern, George."

The scrape of boots on cobblestone cut off the rest of their conversation. Gladys turned to find a small band of fisherfolk walking up the street not far from The Crooked Blade.

One figure stepped out in front, closing the distance to Gladys and George faster than the others, and it took a moment for Gladys to recognize the barkeep of that storied place.

"Speak your piece to these folks and let them be," the barkeep said. "They're a suspicious lot, and I can't say I blame them. What's been done to the fisherfolk in this city is vile."

Gladys nodded. "I appreciate you telling us. Have you seen any more of the Children of the Dark Fire in Fel?"

The barkeep shook his head. "Not a sign, and I tell you, almost every one of us has been looking for those tattoos. Not to say they don't have spies without them, but we do what we can."

The rest of the group caught up to him and spread out in front of the stage, as if waiting for Gladys to step onto it. That was something she avoided in Midstream when possible, and she intended to avoid it in Fel as well.

"How many of you broke blades here?" She projected her voice, catching several fisherfolk off guard with either her volume, or her question.

A few raised fists or shouted affirmations, but most focused on their hands, or feet, or anything other than Gladys.

"It's good to support your people." She waited a beat before continuing, seeking the moment where rising curiosity and rising anger brought more focus onto her. "But we are not all warriors."

"There is no *we!*" someone yelled from the back of the gathering group.

Gladys smiled and glanced at George. "There are times *we* are all we have. You may not know me. You may not know Midstream. But we have more in common than you might think. Fel has lived with threats inside its walls, while Midstream struggled with warlords for decades."

The barkeep from The Crooked Blade crossed his arms. "Heard stories you sold your city to Bollwerk. Bollwerk is no friend of the fisherfolk."

"Archibald is more friend to the fisherfolk than Mordair ever was." Gladys let the irritation bleed into her words. "Certainly more than the Children of the Dark Fire. Has he not brought supplies and guards to help reinforce your city? Are those not his airships that remain as a warning to any seeking to take advantage of your city's plight?"

"Plight?" a woman said with a laugh. "This is a bit more than a *plight*, child."

Gladys nodded and looked for the speaker but couldn't find her. That was okay. Being on level ground with the group gave them the confidence to speak up, which Gladys suspected was something they rarely did. Sometimes the most vocal was the most passive, but after a city was broken, Gladys found it was often the opposite.

"No one wants this war, but it's here, and it's ours, and the price is the blood of our friends and family. Midstream has seen it before. Many of you know the stories of the warlords, I'm sure. I almost died at Rana's hands before my Ancoran friend saved my life. I was there in Gareth Cave when he was cut down and his grasp on his people shattered.

"It didn't stop the war, though. Warlords still pester Midstream, though we have better defenses now. Better than the Speaker of Bollwerk provided. Friends from Ancora and Belldorn, Canopy and even Ballern. Allies from the ruined city of Dauschen, Pirates Cove, and the mighty Cave Guardians stand at our side. They will stand with *you* as well.

"Come to Midstream. *Ask* us for help if you have need. The only price I ask is a small one. I ask for your friendship, and a pledge that Mordair will *never* rule this city again."

"You can't understand what he did to us!" an old man in the front of the group shouted. "He broke us, Princess. He broke our friends and family. You can't understand." His gaze fell to the stage floor.

Gladys glanced at the blades cutting into the wood before she took a deep breath and walked to the steps, mounting the platform. She reached into her cloak and raised a broken wooden mask.

"This was my father's. A man of stern kindness and a warm heart. Murdered by warlords." Gladys's voice hardened as a cold anger boiled in her gut. "And do you know who gave the order to break my family? To murder those we called friends? Gregory Mordair. He is no more friend to you than he is to me."

The old man stared at the princess, eyes wide.

She held his gaze, her heart pounding at the mix of nerves and anger. "Should Mordair come to reclaim the throne, you run, or you fight. His return would be the death of us all. *This* was kept in his throne room like a grim trophy." Gladys ran her fingers along the stained crack in her father's mask. "You are welcome in Midstream, and you will be welcomed as friends. I hope one day, when Fel is returned to the hands of its people, you will welcome us inside your walls."

She offered a smile before taking her leave of the stage. Gladys grabbed George's hand, worried she might strangle the life from his fingers, before he escorted her away.

"Your parents would be proud, Princess," he whispered under his breath.

"I'd rather they were alive."

CHAPTER FOUR

J AKON SPUN THE ring on his middle finger, the band separating slightly to reveal the short blade hidden inside. It had saved his life more than once, but it wouldn't do a damn thing to help him if the Abernathys decided they wanted him dead.

The door banged open, throwing enough light into the warehouse to show the silhouette of a fit man who'd spent countless years as a loader on the docks. But Jakon had expected his brother, not Colt Abernathy himself.

"Where's Thomas?" The question left his lips before he could stop it.

Colt removed the tall hat from his head and ran his fingers through the damp hair underneath. "He didn't survive the collapse of the Bones."

A thousand things raced through Jakon's mind. Colt and Thomas had the full support of Viscount Allerton. They might have been his puppets, but the benefits of that were hard to resist. A good home in the wealthiest part of the docks, protection from the other guilds, a deterrent for the gangs roaming the lower levels … and a warehouse near the Bones.

Jakon cursed under his breath. "I'm sorry."

Colt tipped his head to the side, revealing a cauliflower ear and a close-cropped beard. "That didn't sound like a lie, Jakon. And I'm quite good at reading you. How long have we been on these docks together?"

"I have no idea." Jakon let out a sigh, ignoring the redness in Colt's eyes, a show of vulnerability he would have gleefully exploited not two weeks past. "At least twenty years now?"

Colt laughed quietly. "And what has it gotten us? More fights. More gangs calling themselves *guilds*."

"There's a pretty distinct difference there, Colt."

He waved a hand in dismissal. "It's all changed, Jakon. Allerton, Willett, hell, even *I* thought Mordair was a path to gold."

Jakon sat up straighter. "And now?"

"I owe him, Jakon." His words were a cold menace. "I owe him a great deal of pain. And I think you know folks who can deliver on that debt."

"We have pledges from almost every Skyborn guild and gang who support the Stormborn. They're fighting for people you don't like, Colt. The damned Speaker of Bollwerk is in this now. The Lady of Belldorn. The leaders of Cave and Canopy. Everyone."

Colt rubbed his hands, thick callouses grinding together with a sound like sandpaper. "All but one." He reached into a pocket and pulled out a length of satin. A red X stained the banner of Viscount Allerton, obscuring the brilliant emerald green of a Forest Giant's leaf. Colt turned it over and revealed the back side. The outline of a Shadowwing stained the cloth in curves and breaks as if the greatest of the dock's painters had applied it with care.

And maybe they had.

Colt dropped the banner into Jakon's hands. "A pledge I wouldn't have considered three weeks ago. But now there are a great many things I have reconsidered. Do not use this to cross me, smuggler. We may be allies against Mordair, but we are not friends."

Jakon folded the satin into a neat triangle and slid it into his pocket. "We'll need you to help maintain order on the upper levels. We've had more than a few skirmishes. Not everyone has had a change of perspective, Colt."

"You won't like my order." Colt's expression hardened.

"Reckon you're right, but I'll take what I can get. You know the upper levels better than most. Keep your spies on the watch for uprisings. Even if they aren't loyal to Mordair and his ilk, they may well be following the Children of the Dark Fire. We can't manage another fight on the docks if most of our fleet chases after Mordair."

"That is only half of our problems." Colt glanced at the door. "Several Ballern ships left with Mordair. It may not have been the bulk of the fleet, but I'm still surprised so many Skyborn would have supported it. It takes a lot of sailors to keep those warships running."

Jakon grimaced. "I know, Colt. There are likely a lot of sailors on those vessels who don't want to be there."

"Doesn't change the fact they made their choice." He dismissed them with a sharp flick of his hand. "There isn't time for rescues now, Jakon. The entire alliance should have thrown their fleet at Mordair the moment he fled. Our queen was soft too, and look where it got her."

Jakon bit back a dozen retorts. It wouldn't help to engage with Colt on any of those subjects. Colt didn't know everything that had happened, likely wasn't aware of the blockades to the west, or the missing ships from Belldorn. Mordair's tactics were brutal and layered, and it was going to take more than brute force to bring him down.

But when you were an enforcer like Colt, working for one of the most corrupt royals in all Ballern, Jakon supposed everything came down to brute force at that point.

"What of Allerton?" Jakon asked.

Colt spat on the ground. "Fled with Mordair. Should have seen his face when none of my boys followed. Damn fool is going to burn in the Dark Fire if I have anything to say about it."

"We don't have many royals left. Jonas died in his tower. The Baroness of Auxley is still here." Jakon tapped his chin. "Is she the highest-ranking survivor who didn't flee with Mordair?"

"She may be." Colt frowned, his brow crinkling as if it was counting something off silently. "Should we take care of her?"

It was a loaded question with two very different meanings. Jakon wasn't proud of how long he lingered on the darker meaning.

"Keep her alive. She could be useful."

Colt nodded. "We will. And should anything arise, I'll contact you." He turned to leave.

"Wait." Jakon slid a small copper box out of his vest and stood up. He held it out to Colt. "This is a transmitter. I'm not sure how much you know about them."

"I've heard rumors of the speaking boxes. Much smaller than anything Ballern has."

"Mordair knows about them too, so just remember not everything you say or hear on these is private. My frequency is on the back. You need me, you see something, reach out. Turn the dials until the numbers match and click the button."

Colt slid the transmitter into his pocket. "Strange days, smuggler. Very strange days." With that, he took his leave.

✦　✦　✦

JAKON STEPPED BACK into the light of the docks. It was odd being on the upper levels without the shade above him to cut down on the heat of the sun. Odd to be in another smuggler's den, because whatever Colt believed of himself, he was certainly a smuggler as well. That was half the Abernathys' business, after all.

He made his way down the street filled with small private warehouses, gilded and decorated as if they housed royals themselves. It wasn't too far from the truth, but it was a jarring reminder of how bare the Bones were, and how many hiding places had been lost with those lives when the docks fell.

The top level of Ballern's docks was too narrow to have been damaged in the destruction of the Bones. Not even the supports showed signs of stress, and if one didn't look over the edge, one might never know the tragedy that had befallen the Bones.

It wasn't all bad, though, Jakon had to admit. As many conflicts as he'd had with the nobles over the years, they'd been quick to take in refugees from the Bones. Worn Fleet uniforms and woven greenish gold jackets often seen only on the Bones were now commonplace on the higher levels. Perhaps it was from the goodness of their hearts, or maybe they had a better understanding of where their wealth originated than Jakon thought.

Power might have come from the crown, but the gold came from the backs of the Skyborn.

Jakon stepped into a lift with a small cluster of nobles and Skyborn. *Stormborn*, he silently corrected himself, as their jackets were emblazoned with ragged paintings of a Shadowwing.

The nobles didn't scowl or try to hide the purses at their waist. Instead, an older woman with graying hair offered coins to each of the Stormborn in turn, until her purse was empty and their company exited on the next level.

Jakon rode down two more levels before he reached the docks that felt more like home. They didn't look like home though as he stepped out of the lift after a nod to the nobles. The lower levels resembled a battlefield, the twisted metal of the Bones still signaling the sudden end to what had once been the warehouse district.

The more dangerous debris had been removed, nearly eliminating the risk that anything else would fall to the ground below. And with that done, the cleanup had begun in earnest. It was a hard thing to know the recovery effort had found as many survivors as they were going to, but it was time to move on. The city needed to heal. Leaving Mordair's ruin on display in the eastern districts was no way to do that.

Jakon's bootsteps echoed across the walkway as the solid metal transitioned to latticework. Where there had been sparse tents and bars, the area now swarmed with temporary dwellings and vendors who normally would have been in the market.

He nodded to a few in greeting, tempted to stop for a sandwich or a drink, but he had higher priorities. Closer to the edge, a handful of larger structures had survived. Most people understandably didn't want to go back inside of them, but a few did.

He pushed on the entrance to the nearest, a small one-story storage facility that would have easily fit within Kura's warehouse. Three figures waited there, huddled around a broken blackboard, a dozen books, and twice that number of maps.

Jakon raised his hand in greeting. "I have news."

FURI LOOKED UP when the door opened, not missing the fact Tatsu and Rin had both reached for a weapon when the hinges squeaked. Jakon stepped into the small storage space, and the room immediately felt crowded with one more person.

She missed the warehouse, the school, and most of all, she missed Kura. Furi pushed those thoughts aside. "What happened with the Abernathys?"

"They won't be a problem." Jakon adjusted the scarf around his neck as he stepped closer and sat down on a folding wooden chair. "They might actually be of some help."

"I'm surprised to hear that," Rin said. "Thomas has been a terrible person for as long as I can remember, even when we were young."

"Thomas is dead."

Rin muttered a curse under his breath.

Furi stood up a little straighter. "How?"

"When the Bones collapsed, he was in one of their warehouses. Colt wants blood, and I don't blame him. I wouldn't say he's our most dedicated ally, but our goals align. He also understands what's waiting with the Children of the Dark Fire. He's going to keep an eye on the upper levels, and if anything goes sideways, he'll contact me on a transmitter."

"You gave him our frequencies?" Furi wondered how smart that was.

Jakon shook his head. "Only one of mine. I'll have one tuned to that frequency for the duration. I don't trust him *that* far. For the right price, I'm sure he'd hand it over to some of my least favorite people. What about you three? Any news from the … reconstruction? Or a decision about coming to Karn?"

Furi exchanged a glance with Rin and Tatsu. "Tell him."

Tatsu clenched his fists and took a deep breath. "We cannot leave Ballern like this, Jakon. Until the rubble is cleared, and the dead are all burned, we will remain."

"I heard about the trouble with some of the Carrion Worms."

Tatsu nodded. "More trouble than you know, perhaps. They breached the north walls and pushed up through the cracked stone of the collapse."

"I understand." Jakon put his hands on the desk and leaned forward.

Rin spread his fingers out across the topmost map, near the Valley of the Roots. "We'll join you if we can, but we've left the Skyborn behind for too long. We may all be Stormborn now, but this place was our home for decades. Canopy is still in this fight. Many of the dragonriders will be with the Spider Knights."

Jakon bit his lip for a moment before focusing on Furi. "And you?"

"I'll fight." Her words came out as more of a snarl than she'd intended. "I'm not leaving Jacob and Alice to fight alone."

Rin's brow crinkled as he eyed Furi. "They won't be alone, Furi."

"You're right, because I'll be with them." She pushed back from the table, done having the same conversation over and over with Rin and Tatsu. They were correct in some regards. The survivors living on the docks needed help, but those same people wouldn't have a chance if Mordair returned to power. "Sacrifice now or sacrifice later. It's a rotten game of dice is what it is."

"I won't argue with that, kid." Jakon gave her a half smile.

"I'll be here until Jacob and Alice need me. After that, time will tell." She didn't know if it was what Jakon wanted to hear, but it was the truth.

"When the time comes, Furi, we'll fight together."

CHAPTER FIVE

Alice sat down in the corner of Karn's library. It wasn't so grand as anything she'd see in Belldorn, or even the bookstore in Ballern, if she was being honest, but she rather liked the low ceilings and packed shelves that deadened all the sound around her.

The quiet was an antithesis to the aftermath of what had happened in Ballern. There were no screams of horror here, no shouts of excitement when another survivor was found, nor were there muttered words for the dead as they were dragged to the pyres.

Here was the musty scent of old paper and the history of a city she didn't know. Alice knew she should focus on studying the Children of the Dark Fire, and while she told herself there might be some extra bits of information to be gleaned from the books about Karn, there probably wasn't enough to justify the distraction.

She sighed and turned the page, taking care not to crack or tear the dried-out tome where it rested on the book cradle on her lap. Echoes in Karn's history reminded her of Ancora, a city founded in a region that had been written off by the nobles of the time. Much as the Ancorans were believed to have immigrated from across the Silver Gulf, Karn's people had arrived from the far west.

The text *did* contain a few references to the control center Arun had mentioned, but there was no mention of the disease that had taken over that place. It sounded like a song one of the bards would sing in the Wildhorse. Tales of another time, or even another world.

The last book had shown her Karn around the Deadlands War. But the city hadn't been much involved across the Crystal Sea, instead mired in a more direct conflict with the Children of the Dark Fire. The stories reminded her of the dry writings Miss Penny had used to teach them about Ancora, and not nearly so engaging as Archibald's work in *The Dead Scourge.*

If more history books could be like his, though perhaps less tainted with the writer's opinions, Alice thought a good deal more kids would enjoy their classes.

The transmitter in her collar crackled and Alice turned the volume down, not wanting to disturb anyone who might be nearby.

"Alice, it's Eva. Are you there?"

"I am."

"Good, good. I'm here with Kat. Do you have a moment?"

Alice sat up straighter in her high-backed chair. "Of course. What's wrong?"

"Nothing so dramatic as that," Kat said, her voice growing louder. "Well, a great many things are wrong, but no more than usual."

That wasn't the greatest reassurance Alice had ever heard, but she smiled at Kat's effort.

The Lady of Belldorn continued. "I have Eva and two of my commanders here. Can you tell us more about what you saw by the Great Machine?"

"I ... yes, but what about talking to Mali or Arun?"

"But we want another perspective." Kat paused. "And if I'm being honest, from what Mary and Eva have told me, you're a bit more observant than Jacob is. At least when it doesn't involve gears and machinery."

Alice pursed her lips. "That's fair. I'm not sure what you want to hear?"

"Nothing, Alice. You tell me what you saw, and we can discuss things from there."

So she did. She told them of the forces gathered outside the Great Machine and woven between the city streets that surrounded the behemoth. She told them of the armored Walkers and crawlers facing the road through the Gray Woods that would take them to Karn. She told them of the fleet lining the sea to the north, a blockade to match their own, and the spread of maps in the Hall.

Alice didn't mention the strange camera or the thrill of riding on the back of a Tree Killer. She didn't tell Kat and Eva how worried she was for Jacob, taking a mount so similar to the one that took his leg. She didn't tell them how proud she was at how well Jacob handled riding a Tree Killer.

Instead, she waited as Kat and Eva spoke among themselves. Sometimes over the transmitter, and sometimes into silence, perhaps not wanting to expose their thoughts to anyone else who might be listening. When their voices returned, it was Kat who spoke.

"Karn had much the same to say. Though I appreciate the details on the airships. That gives us a better idea of what Mordair has stationed along the coast. This partial retreat shows a vicious strategy from Mordair. He's trying to splinter our alliances, and he *is* spreading us thin. We cannot attack with our full force and still protect our interests."

"Then we have to work to keep our allies safe as best we can," Eva said. "If we don't stop them here, the war will return to Belldorn."

"And beyond." Kat trailed off for a moment. "Alice, Mali is going to invite you to dinner with Arun this evening. Please be sure you and Jacob attend. We need the alliance with Karn to remain strong through this conflict."

Alice could understand *why* Kat would say that. To lose their alliance with Karn would put a strain on their deployment of the fleet and carriers. They could shift resources to Ballern, but that would leave Karn exposed to the Children of the Dark Fire and arguably weaken the entire front of the alliance.

Eva's voice sounded over the transmitter. "And Alice …"

"If you tell me to act natural, I'm going to tell Mary you're making plans with Kat without her."

Eva spluttered. "I wasn't! I mean, I'm not. Ancorans. I swear. Enjoy the dinner, would you? And try to keep Jacob's curiosity in check."

Alice glanced at the table stacked with books and the book cradle sprawled across her lap. She bit her lip before answering. "Of course. I'll keep the tinker out of trouble."

"Thank you, Alice," Kat said. "I would be there myself, but there is much to discuss with our friends from Bollwerk. Be well."

With that, the transmitter fell silent. Alice almost screamed when the voice sounded beside her.

"So, are you coming to dinner?"

She stared wide-eyed at Mali, who wore one of the largest grins Alice had ever seen. "How did you? Where did you? Yes."

✧   ✧   ✧

ALICE FOLLOWED MALI two blocks to the west until they reached a stretch of bars and restaurants lining the cobblestone street. Jacob had given them directions, but they were, frankly, terrible. He finally had to ask what the name of the place was, which told Mali exactly where he'd ended up.

"That's where all the tinkers end up. I should have known."

"And *I* should have known he'd find a workshop. If his head isn't in a book, he's working on something, or trying to learn from other tinkers."

"That's admirable."

"Sometimes." Alice smiled. "Sometimes it's annoying."

Mali pointed to a sign hanging out over the street. While a great many were copper or tin, this one was carved from wood. The irony wasn't lost on Alice as she read the looping scrawl for The Wooden Cog, which was literally written across a wooden cog.

She trailed Mali up three steps to the dark wood of the deck before following her through the copper-plated doors. The trail of tarnish around the rivets gave the place a weight, showing its age far more than the wooden sign above them and the brighter metal where countless hands had brushed by.

Inside, lit by bright lanterns and tall tubes of crackling lights, Alice found Jacob surrounded by four of Karn's tinkers. Two of them looked close to Smith's age, but not nearly so large, while the others had likely been around for the Deadlands War. She hesitated when she realized the older pair weren't just siblings, but clearly twins. The sister bore a scar across her forehead.

Jacob had his Biomech leg propped up on a stool, the panels opened to reveal the tubes and inner workings inside. A younger tinker traced the line of tubing to the fittings before nodding.

"It's such a simple design. Brilliant, really."

"And you say they installed this on a battlefield?" the older tinker asked before glancing up at the new arrivals. "Ah, and this must be your friend!"

Alice gave the group an awkward smile as they all turned to look at her at once.

"Quiet, Dinesh," the older woman said. "You're making the poor girl uncomfortable."

Dinesh blinked at his sister. "How could you possibly know that? She isn't a schematic to be read. Mali, is your friend uncomfortable?"

Mali slowly turned back to Alice before grinning. "Maybe a bit."

Dinesh grumbled under his voice. "Some days, I think you're a sorceress, Lata." He gestured to Jacob. "Best be getting yourself ready if Mali is here. She only comes to take folks away."

"That is *not* true, Dinesh." Mali scowled at him. "I was here for lunch not three weeks ago. But I do need Jacob. Arun wants to see the Ancorans."

"Bah." He waved them off.

Lata patted his shoulder. "His memory's a bit sparse at his age."

"Not as old as you."

"Two minutes. You're younger by *two minutes*."

Jacob snapped his leg closed and pulled the cuff of his pants down. "Thank you all again. I'd love to spend more time in the workshop."

"You're welcome anytime," Lata said.

Alice laced her fingers between Jacob's as he joined them, and Mali led the way back out into the street.

"What did I miss?" he asked.

She told him about the call with Eva and Kat, not sparing a single detail, including Mali's penchant for stealth. That part of the story put a wide smile on his lips.

"I'm also supposed to keep your curiosity in check." She flashed him a grin.

Jacob's eyebrow rose a hair. He stumbled over a cobblestone, catching himself before falling over completely.

"I didn't think it was *that* shocking …"

He scowled, but the expression broke almost as fast as it appeared. "What could I possibly say that would upset Arun? He's the one looking for us, right? I'm sure he's used to tinkers. Especially after talking to that lot." He hooked a thumb back the way they'd come.

"Jacob does have a fair point," Mali said.

Alice poked him in the arm. "I don't think it's so much a concern about your curiosity, as your ability to bring things up no one wants to talk about. Kat needs the alliance with Karn. We *all* need the alliance with Karn. Mali, would you kick him under the table if he goes off on a tangent or unwittingly starts an argument?"

"I would be happy to."

Jacob smacked his lips and looked between the pair. "I'll be on my best behavior. Even Miss Penny would think I was just sitting through another lecture."

Alice laughed under her breath. "Maybe don't fall asleep at the dinner table, though. If you can help it?"

Mali led them into the wide courtyard with the ornate fountains close to the hall. They didn't turn north at the intersection, as Alice expected, instead going farther east until the Forest Giants loomed over them. Only there, at the edge of the woods, did Mali change direction, heading south onto a short street with an almost immediate end.

But where the shadows were thickest, a small path angled off to the southwest. They followed it for a time, the path barely wide enough for them to stand shoulder to shoulder, until the outskirts of the city flanked them once more.

Mali walked to the iron-banded door of a cabin built of multi-colored stone. Smoke billowed out of the chimney on the second floor, casting odd shadows across the ground before it dissipated. Round windows gave them glimpses of what waited inside: a busy shuffle of chefs and servers.

"Is this a restaurant?" Jacob asked.

"Oh dear." Mali's lips drew down and she shook her head. "I'm afraid the alliance is done after failing to keep your curiosity in check."

Alice failed to choke back a laugh. She slapped Jacob's arm and grinned at him.

Mali reached out for the door and gestured for them to enter. "And yes, Jacob, it's a restaurant. Not one used every day, but a restaurant nonetheless."

Alice's amusement shifted. "Is this for diplomatic dinners and negotiations?" She peered through the doorway. "Mali, how underdressed are we?"

"You're fine. Arun usually shows up in riding leathers. The servers will be impeccable, but they're used to the rest of us. You'll fit in."

Those weren't the most reassuring words Alice could have imagined, as cotillion had taught her the idea of showing up to a formal dinner underdressed was akin to setting your home on fire. But cotillion was from another time, and some days she felt like Ancora was on a different world altogether.

Her worries almost evaporated when she saw a chef working a stewpot, dressed in the same kind of tunic she'd seen in the stables. Two of the chefs wore white jackets and hats like the staff at some of the finest restaurants in Ancora, but she'd never actually eaten inside one of those establishments. Sometimes, when they were lucky, the chefs would sneak leftovers out to the Lowlanders who had dared to enter the Highlands. She had good memories of those nights, a meal pilfered with Jacob's help in the late of night. Oh how angry her mom would have been had she known.

Jacob squeezed Alice's hand, drawing her attention back to the room. Something sizzled on a large flat grill near the corner of the room, steam and smoke rising into a hood that angled up into the chimney they'd seen outside.

One thing was for certain—there was far too much food for only four people. That brought another question to Alice's mind.

"Mali, how many people are joining us tonight?"

She glanced up as if counting to herself. "Four or five. And that's only if Arun brings a guest. He tends to do that. Sometimes I think he does it just to throw me off." She waved the thought off. "You know how politicians are. You prepare yourself for one thing, so they present something entirely different."

A chef harrumphed as she brought a cleaver down in a series of quick strikes through thick root vegetables. "You know better than that, Mali. Arun couldn't stick to a map to save his life, much less a plan so simple as dinner."

If the spread before them was a simple plan for dinner, Alice wasn't sure she wanted to know what a complicated plan for dinner was.

"You three take a seat. We have bread and spiced butter, if you'd like a snack."

They'd barely finished sliding into the chairs at the short rectangular table before a pile of rolls and butter thumped down in front of them. Alice didn't even get a chance to thank the server before he vanished, reappeared with a tray of water glasses, and disappeared again.

Mali reached for a roll and dropped it on her plate. "Don't wait. Get them while they're hot. You won't regret it."

Alice handed a roll to Jacob before grabbing one for herself. She watched Mali tear the steaming roll in half before using a wide spatula to smear butter across its face. Alice mimicked her, surprised at how soft the butter was, making it easy to feel the small lumps of spices embedded throughout.

When she heard the word "spiced," she'd thought it might be a festive thing, like they had in Ancora for special occasions. But most spiced Ancoran food ended up sweet and candy-like. This smelled rich and savory as the butter melted into the crusty bread.

Jacob stuffed nearly a quarter of the roll into his mouth at once, and Alice grinned when he sank back into the chair. "Oh, wow."

"I told you." Mali bit into her own.

Alice held the roll up to her nose, taking in the aroma with a deep breath before tasting it. There was a richness to the roll, a burst of yeast and rosemary and something earthier she couldn't quite place. To say it was delicious would be an insult, and that was before she'd fully enjoyed the chewy texture.

"Why don't we have this in Ancora?" Alice said before taking a drink of water. "These are amazing."

Mali was about to respond when the front door opened, and laughter preceded the new arrivals. Arun entered first, his dark eyes sweeping the room like Jacob had seen many soldiers and sailors do as the war escalated. Drakkar followed behind him, and Jacob blinked as the Cave Guardian's cloak fluttered in the breeze before the door closed behind him.

"Drakkar?" Alice asked. "What are you doing here?"

He gestured to Arun. "Our host invited me. We had a long discussion about the best feed for Walkers, which, of course, led to a detailed talk about the hatcheries in Karn."

Mali groaned. "Not another one."

"It is truly quite fascinating. Walkers in Cave are raised underground, which I believe may be why their eyesight is keener in dim light."

"Exactly." Arun walked to the far side of the table and gestured for Drakkar to take a seat. "Here in Karn, our hatcheries are all in the Gray Woods. They are in shade much of the time, but it certainly isn't as dark as the caverns beneath a mountain."

Drakkar slid into the chair opposite Jacob, and Arun sat at the end. "You would have to speak with some of the breeders to learn the finest details, but they optimized the light and heat for each egg clutch, depending on species."

"And it's truly controlled by the number of torches?"

"Or the size of them. That can also mean firepits as well. Once the Walkers are old enough, you need not worry about them wandering into the coals and injuring themselves."

Mali blinked at the pair. "Try the bread, Drakkar. I don't know if you have anything like it in Cave, but you should taste it."

Drakkar took the offered basket before passing it to Arun.

"Still warm. Excellent." Arun smiled at Mali. "I promise we won't discuss the raising of Walkers in captivity the *entire* meal." He turned his attention to Jacob. "I understand you were quite the attraction for our tinkers. Lata couldn't stop talking about the work on your leg or your understanding of biomechanics on our walk here."

"Is she joining us?" Mali asked.

Arun shook his head. "No, no. I wanted to spend time with our Ancoran friends. Drakkar was a happy encounter in the stables, so I invited him as well. His son is part of our alliance that has remained in Midstream."

Alice relaxed into her chair just a bit as Arun formally called Karn part of an alliance. Of course, that calm was shaken by his next comment.

"I understand Lady Katherine wishes to ensure our alliance is strong."

Alice glanced at Mali, who immediately put her hands in the air.

"I didn't say a word, Alice. Archibald might be famous for his spies, but don't underestimate the number of people listening to you in Karn. They're curious, and chatty."

Arun offered a warm smile. "It was only by accident you were overheard in the library, Alice. One of our older residents in a nearby aisle."

It was a convenient explanation, but it made a lot of sense, too. There were few people in Ancora who enjoyed gossiping more than the elders. And that was truly saying something when compared with the flurry of rumors that used to filter through her school every day.

"And Kat was worried it would be Jacob causing trouble," Alice said.

Drakkar chuckled. "To be fair, he does drag us all into trouble now and then."

Jacob stopped buttering his bread and blinked at the table. "Sorry?"

Arun smiled and gestured to the servers gathered by the large cooktop. "We are ready when the chef is, thank you."

"Arun, if I may?" Alice said. "You speak of us as though we've been friends for years. As though our alliance has always been here. What do you need from us? I don't mean the alliance, but why ask me and Jacob here?"

Arun sat half of his bread down and took a bite of the rest. "Selfish reasons, mostly, but there are some questions I have for you that would be considered … rude."

"I thought it was *Jacob's* questions we were supposed to worry about," Mali said under her breath.

Jacob spoke around a mouthful of bread. "Alice gets me into just as much trouble as I get her into."

"No, she does not," Drakkar said flatly.

It was blunt enough to stop Jacob in his tracks, and Arun let out a low laugh.

"As to your question, Alice, I wish to ask you about the Speaker of Bollwerk and the Lady of Belldorn. We have stories about each of them, but stories change over time. Spies report things with bias, and often a harmless comment is twisted into something malicious, or the reverse."

The first course of plates reached the table simultaneously, one server delivering a plate to each person, their movements synchronized as if they were playing a symphony. Or as if they were machinery like the tables in the Wildhorse.

"A round of acidwine for the group, please." Arun looked pointedly at Jacob and Alice. "Not too much. It can sour your stomach if you aren't used to it. And do let the pie rest. It needs to cool for a minute."

"What's acidwine?" Jacob asked.

"It's flavored by a spice harvested from the glands of an Acidwing.

Before it is old enough to cause harm, of course."

"Stronger than sake," Drakkar said. "So mind your portions."

Arun smiled at the Cave Guardian. "Too true, but perhaps easier for the hard conversations, yes? It can be difficult to tell the truth about your friends."

The phrase made Alice uncomfortable. And she wasn't entirely sure she'd call Archibald a friend. He was certainly an ally, and had done much good for Ancora, but his ambitions were lofty. Kat, on the other hand, felt like a friend. Mary had grown up with her, and Mary was more family than friend now. Even when the war was done, Mary was someone Alice wanted to keep in contact with.

She blew out her breath. "What do you want to know about Archibald?"

One server returned with five ornate glasses perched on narrow stems.

Arun tapped the side of his goblet when the server placed it in front of him. "I want to know if the offers he gives are true, or if he says only what needs to be heard in the moment. Can you tell me that? Has he betrayed your trust? Because if he has dishonored his word to a city that has suffered the likes of Ancora, I do not believe I can trust him."

Alice looked at Jacob. "You've had the most interactions with him."

"You're better at reading people." Jacob frowned and glanced between Drakkar and Mali. "I trust people too much sometimes."

"That isn't a bad trait to have," Mali said.

If Jacob wasn't going to answer such a direct question, she'd need to. Alice nodded to herself. "Archibald is trying to unite the continent from Ancora to Belldorn. Some cities, like Midstream, are loyal to him because of what he's done to help them stay safe, or defend themselves."

"And were these defenses necessary because of something he set into action?" Arun laced his fingers together, and his gaze bored into Alice's.

She realized this was the question that was the most important to Arun, and she was glad she didn't have to lie about it. "Never. I don't know of a single conflict that has involved Midstream or Ancora—or Dauschen, for that matter—that Archibald helped cause."

"He could have killed the Butcher in the Deadlands War, but he didn't." Jacob didn't raise his eyes from his goblet for a time. "I don't think that means his actions caused things directly, but they still had consequences."

Arun studied the Ancorans before raising his goblet, his voice quiet but firm. "We all have mistakes from our past. May we work to heal the damage they have wrought."

They all mimicked his gesture, but no one finished their acidwine in one gulp like Arun did. Alice sipped at hers, tentatively at first, until the rich flavors of a dark tea washed over her tongue and something sharp and spicy chased it.

Jacob coughed like he'd swallowed a Stone Dog spine, spluttering and immediately chasing his drink with a sloppy gulp of water. "It's so hot! How did you—it's so hot!"

"It reminds me of those sour candies we used to get at Festival." Alice swirled the contents of her goblet and took another sip. "I like it."

Jacob looked at her with absolute betrayal written across his face. "There is nothing sweet or crunchy about this. It's just fire!"

"An acquired taste, perhaps." Drakkar raised his glass, not hiding the grin on his lips.

"The pie should be cool enough to try the edges now." Mali picked up her spoon and paused. "We use spoons for just about everything, so don't expect the same range of utensils you see in Ballern."

Jacob scraped his tongue over his teeth and almost smirked as he turned to Alice.

Alice narrowed her eyes. "If you say one thing about memorizing all the silverware at cotillion, I'm going to hold you down and pour the rest of that acidwine in your mouth."

Jacob cleared his throat and leaned forward, focusing on Mali. "What about Sea Claw and grilled meats on the shell?"

"Hands. Well, for the Sea Claw, you smack it with the back of the spoon to loosen the shell, and it's easy to peel from there."

"That is why we have two sets of napkins," Arun said. "The left is traditionally for oily things, and the right for anything sticky."

Jacob looked down at his haphazard pile of napkins that he'd already balled up and stacked together like the remnants of an avalanche. "I see."

Arun smiled at him. "If you could enlighten me about Lady Katherine, I would be most appreciative. She spends a great deal of time with a known pirate. The rather *infamous* captain of the Skysworn."

There was a lot more to Mary's relationship with Kat and Archibald than Arun knew, or that Alice thought he *needed* to know. But there were a few key things she could share that might help Arun understand why a pirate might actually be one of the best allies Kat could ask for.

"Mary's not a bad person, Arun. She's made choices some of us might not agree with, but I've seen her go well out of her way to help her friends and allies. She has the same enemies as you. Losing Ballern as a trading hub would cause the Skysworn, and all the pirates, a good deal of trouble."

"Understandable. Buy why would a Lady of Belldorn welcome her as counsel?"

"They've been friends since they were kids. Since they were younger than me and Jacob. They grew up together in Belldorn."

Arun tapped his spoon on his pie, cracking open the crust as he listened to Alice. "So they were in the center of the reconstruction. Their parents would have fought in the Deadlands War, or perhaps their grandparents. Interesting."

"Do you know a lot about Ancora?" Alice asked.

Arun shrugged. "A bit. Some would say enough. I know it is a mountain city divided by a great wall, where the nobility is protected and those who serve them are left to die."

"It's … it wasn't quite that bad."

"It was in the Fall," Jacob said, not raising his eyes from his pie.

Alice grimaced. "We're working to change things. Jacob's parents, even, and my mother. It's … it will get better. But you know enough to understand. That kind of separation doesn't exist in Belldorn. They have wealthy areas and poor areas, like any city, but they mingle daily. They go to the same schools, have the same opportunities."

Mali let out a little huff. "I doubt that. Gold always buys more opportunities."

"Sometimes. But it doesn't stop kids from becoming friends, does it? Not all the time. They lived through trouble together, and the last Lady of Belldorn died when Kat was a teenager. Kat took the crown and had to live another life. But Mary was there with her until that happened, until she could change the way the city worked and see her friends again. But a lot can change in five years."

Arun raised an eyebrow. "She was separated from her friends for five years? That sounds somewhat extreme."

"I told you that," Mali said with a glance at Arun. "She was only a figurehead until she turned twenty."

"And she did what she could to make sure her friends were taken care of." There were stories Mary had told Alice of those dark days. Time spent in foster care and bouncing from family to family as the systems meant to protect the vulnerable of Belldorn failed them entirely. It wasn't her story to tell, but it was Kat who had stepped in to help Mary.

She raised her eyes to meet Arun's. "Lady Katherine tore down the system that let her friends down and rebuilt it to help everyone she could.

Mandatory fleet service, not so different from Ballern at one time, was eliminated and a truce was formed with anyone captured from Ballern. They were allowed to leave. Allowed to settle Canopy and have lives of their own. They weren't locked away or executed. Everything she did was the opposite of Mordair and the warlords."

"Generosity and kindness can get a monarch killed," Arun said.

"Helps when your best friends are pirates, tinkers, and pilots, doesn't it?"

Arun harrumphed and smiled. "A fair point."

"Something I can say about Archibald and Lady Katherine both: they won't leave you until Mordair is dead. And for Mordair to die, the Children of the Dark Fire will have to be thrown down."

"Then perhaps this alliance will be the stuff of legends, Alice. And you can write the story as you remember it, as Archibald once did in *The Dead Scourge*."

She blinked.

Jacob froze with a small mountain of pie on his spoon. "How did you know about his book?"

"I know many things about the Speaker of Bollwerk, but I also am wary of politicians."

"But you are one?"

Mali snickered into her bowl.

Alice leaned over and poked Jacob in the ribs. "What Jacob *means* to say is that you do an admirable job of separating your duty from yourself." She turned her focus to Arun. "Many who don't are quite unpleasant."

Arun picked up a second glass of acidwine after the server refilled it. "Small blessings, my friend, small blessings."

Alice needed food after that acidwine, already feeling the heat flow through her from the drink. She tapped the edge of her pie until the crust broke. Steam rose from the flaky pastry, overwhelming her with the scent of rich herbs and more of the butter they'd used on the bread.

The center was still too hot to eat, but the edges were far more favorable. She pulled some of the creamy broth onto the spoon, lumps of potatoes mixed with the white flesh of whatever meat they'd prepared.

Salt and heat and rosemary bloomed across her tongue as the delicate meat almost dissolved between her teeth. Alice sat back and smiled as Drakkar took a bite and his head dipped.

The Cave Guardian laughed. "I think Smith needs to come to Karn, considering his obsession with soup."

"Oh, this is nothing compared to our soups," Arun said. "Bring your friend. We will welcome them with open arms. Even if he is a pirate." The leader of Karn winked at Drakkar, and Alice almost sighed in relief.

Arun had been kind, but his questions were pointed. It spoke of either paranoia or extreme caution, either of which could harm their alliance. At least for now, Arun looked satisfied, Mali's posture had relaxed, and Jacob had turned his full attention to the stew.

For the moment, they had peace, and Alice liked to hope they had new friends as well. It was one thing to forge alliances, but quite another to call those allies friends.

CHAPTER SIX

THEY ONLY HAD one more night to stay in Karn. Then Mary and Smith would take Jacob to the carrier to work with Frederick, and Alice would continue to Ballern to strategize with Furi. But that would be in the morning. For now, they had an expansive view of the city at night. And that was something Jacob would miss when they left.

Karn surged with life when the sun went away. It wasn't the harsh city lights like the Highlands, or even Belldorn. Here it was the Fire-lights—huge beetles that glowed in the dark, attracted to the tallest towers as that was where Karn kept much of the smaller livestock.

"Do you think they built lifts big enough to pull cows up to the top?" Jacob asked.

Alice slowly turned and blinked at him. "Mali already told us they separate the mammals and the bugs, Jacob. The heaviest are always on the lowest floors."

That sounded vaguely familiar. Maybe it was the acidwine still trying to disintegrate his insides, or the excess amount of food they'd had at dinner, but he couldn't quite recall what Mali had said. "That does make sense."

"Brilliant, really. Having tiered farming in the towers lets them grow up instead of out. Keeps everything inside the city and gives them a smaller footprint to protect. Ancora could learn something from them."

Jacob blew out a small laugh. "It does sound a bit more convenient than running when a horde of Red Death is sighted in the foothills."

"Just a bit."

He watched two young Firelights circle around each other in the smoke from the fire, their wings disturbing the air like the turbines on the Skysworn, and rivaling the roar. Light in the firepit before him flickered as a log cracked and sent a spiral of embers into the sky.

Alice handed him another sticky bun. He could have mistaken it for one of Midstream's steamed buns, but it was rounder and denser. And after he bit into it, a little too sticky. The dough had lost much of its heat since they left the restaurant, but the honey still flowed, mixing with the crunchy center to form a wonderfully portable dessert.

Jacob cursed as the bun split, pouring honey over his palm. He didn't even get a chance to wipe it off before the nearest juvenile Firelights pounced, their buzzing wings no larger than his palm. "That's mine. Hey, hey!"

But by the time Jacob protested the bugs stealing chunks of his sticky bun, it was gone. They stayed on his hand for a second, hooked feet digging into his skin but not breaking it, until they were sure the sweets were no more. They vanished into the air as fast as they'd come, their orange glow trailing off toward the towers and their larger brethren.

"Thieves."

Alice laughed and held out the bag. "Mali also said to eat them in one bite, if you recall."

Jacob smacked his lips and narrowed his eyes. "I'm going to miss these riveting discussions when I leave for the carrier tomorrow."

Alice leaned forward and kissed him softly. "I know you will."

✧   ✧   ✧

To say Jacob wouldn't miss the bunk they'd been staying in near the hall in Karn would be much like calling the Skeleton well populated. He stretched his back and grumbled as he finished stowing his things in his pack.

"You can say that again." Alice rubbed her eyes and yawned. "This is why I packed everything last night."

The transmitter on Jacob's collar crackled to life. "This is the Skysworn. Are you two ready?"

"On our way, Skysworn."

"Where are we meeting them?" Alice asked.

Jacob hesitated. "I'm not sure." He clicked the button in his collar. "Skysworn, rendezvous point?"

"Southeast city limits. We'll be just inside the forest perimeter, close to where the carrier was docked."

"Give us fifteen minutes."

"From the barracks? How about thirty minutes just to be safe?"

Jacob frowned at that. He didn't think the walk to the far side of the city could possibly take thirty minutes. That would be like the full width of Bollwerk. Of course, arguing the point didn't make much difference. "We'll see you there."

"Here, drink this." Alice held out her canteen as they walked out the door and into the city proper. "It's full of that tea Mali made us yesterday."

Jacob hesitated, remembering the tea Mali had given them after finishing dinner. "Why do they love that tea so much? It tastes like dirt."

"With subtle notes of lavender." Alice grinned at him as he unscrewed the cap and took a drink. "It's better than I remembered. Try it."

He let it sit on his tongue for a moment before swallowing, and then frowned at the canteen. "Are you sure this is the same tea? It's almost … good?"

Alice snatched the canteen back and screwed the lid on. "I'm sure. You know, Drakkar said it probably didn't taste that good because the dessert had so much sugar in it."

"They could add sugar to the tea. It wouldn't be that terrible, would it?"

"They don't do that in Karn." Alice shrugged. "Some of our traditions in Ancora would seem odd to them too. I haven't seen anyone eating as much Pilly as we used to in the Lowlands. And if you want to talk about tasting dirt, you should try my dad's stew sometime." She shivered at the thought.

"I *have* tried your dad's stew, Alice. You know who needs to try that abomination? Jakon."

She let out a harsh laugh and slid her canteen into the straps on her glider pack. "Maybe Jakon knows how to make sticky buns. I think that should be my real focus when I get back to Ballern."

"I'll support you in your noble campaign."

They drew a few strange looks while choking down laughter as they made their way deeper into the city. It still felt odd, knowing what was going on around the world, yet finding some small parcel of peace among the chaos.

Jacob supposed that was the kind of thing Charles and even Targrove had tried to explain to him about the darker times. You had to find a way to step to the side, take care of yourself, and let things happen as they would … until you were ready to walk back into the fire.

"I don't think this is the right way." Jacob frowned at a broken fountain he hadn't seen before. "I don't remember seeing that."

"Trust me."

Apparently, Alice had already learned the layout of Karn better than Jacob, because before he knew it, they'd slid down two alleys framed by shorter towers, and when Alice turned left, the Gray Woods opened up at the end of the street.

"Have you been here before?" He glanced at Alice before turning his attention back to the cobblestones cluttered with dead leaves.

"No, but the city is laid out in squares. Haven't you noticed? The smaller streets and alleys run north to south, and all the side streets are east to west except for the outer roads."

"This is east? I could have sworn we were off to the southeast a bit."

"If we are, it isn't by much. Look." Alice pointed toward the canopy of the Gray Woods, where the Forest Giants stood sentinel over Karn. A shadow moved through the sky, slowly resolving into an airship as the Skysworn descended at the far end of the road.

A few people clearing leaves along the street took the time to comment on the busy skies being such an odd sight in Karn, but no one sounded angry about it. They only made observations, greeting everyone as they walked by with at least a nod, even the Ancorans.

While the Skysworn might have been in sight from their position on the street, it still took another ten minutes to reach the edge of the city, where the cobblestones started to break down and the ground changed. Mary had been right about giving them thirty minutes to get there. The relatively level terrain grew more and more hazardous where the fallen twigs and leaves and seeds had dropped from the forest itself.

It reminded Jacob of walking through the foothills, where it felt like every stone wanted to break his ankle. He stumbled a few times when leaves covered the round nuts and seeds that had fallen to the earth, some no larger than a Cork ball and others the size of his fist.

They reached the Skysworn soon enough, the ramp to the cargo hold open and waiting while Smith banged on a bent plate close to the gun pod.

"Leave it," Mary called from the top of the ramp.

"No! If I have to listen to that whistling the entire flight back to the carrier, I am going to lose my mind, Mary." He cracked the wrench against the plate three more times before heading up the ramp.

Once Jacob and Alice reached the ramp, he could see the end of a pry bar extending from the hull, grasping the edge of the plate, and bending it back into shape.

To get that kind of power, Jacob had little doubt Smith had engaged a much higher setting on his biomechanics. He waved to Mary, who stood under the gun pod with her arms crossed.

"You two settle in. I'll get Smith ready to go soon enough."

"How bad was the whistling?" Alice asked.

A small smirk flickered across Mary's lips. "Pretty bad, but don't tell Smith I said so. It wouldn't have slowed us down, but you know Smith. Everything needs to be perfect on this ship."

Jacob led the way up the ramp, stepping into the hall that connected the cargo hold, Smith's workshop, and access to the gun pod. He started down the corridor toward the ladder that would take them to the deck.

"Hey, Smith," Alice said.

"Be done in a minute." His voice echoed where he was leaning over into the gun pod. "Good to see you two."

They reached the ladder and made their way up before dropping their glider packs in the large lockers of the cabin. Jacob followed Alice out onto the deck and looked toward Karn.

He crossed his arms and propped himself up on the railing. "I hope this isn't the last time we see Karn. It's kind of nice, isn't it?"

"I do like it. Even if we don't make it back before the war is done, we'll come here when it's all over." Alice smiled and leaned against Jacob's arm.

✧　✧　✧

"What have you been doing?" Jacob asked.

"Repairs," Mary said as they rose above the canopy of the Forest Giants. "Smith's been working on the Skysworn nonstop since you two left for Karn. It didn't hurt that he had Frederick's help for a time."

"Did he use the Titan Mech to replace the gas chamber's cracked support?" Jacob couldn't tell from the deck, but he vividly recalled seeing it from above while the Skysworn was docked in Ballern.

"He did," Smith answered over the horn. "It was a good idea, Jacob. Likely would have been easier if you had been there to pilot the Mech, but Frederick got the job done."

Mary sighed. "Cracked the ship open like a roasted Pilly."

Her comment presented quite the visual for Jacob, as he imagined how that would have looked as they peeled back the gas chamber. It wouldn't have been such an ordeal if it weren't for the armored band that kept the gas chamber in such a low profile. But the way it was, they couldn't simply switch it out like an average airship.

Alice leaned toward Jacob as Mary pulled the ship around to the north. "Are you taking me all the way to Ballern?"

Mary shook her head. "I want to get to Kat. She's rotating her guard again, and there are a handful of faces I don't know. And if I don't know them—"

"I don't trust them," Smith finished with mild exasperation. "We will be back in plenty of time, Mary. The chances of assassins getting that close to her on the carrier are nearly zero with the new precautions in place."

"Nearly zero isn't zero, Smith." Mary's words were calm, but tension kept her shoulders tight as she eased the throttle forward. "Clear of the forest. Do you want to try the thrusters?"

Smith's voice echoed through the horn. "We do not need them at such a relatively short distance, but it would be a good test." Something clunked before the sound of metal striking metal reached them. "Thrusters are primed. Ready at your command."

"Then take your seat. We're jumping in ten."

Jacob double-checked his harness at that, as Alice did the same. Mary didn't count down, only rotated the safety off the lever for the thrusters and pushed the throttle to its limits.

There was nothing subtle about the power of the Skysworn. One moment, they were drifting through the sky, and the next, the lowest clouds raced forward to greet them. They punched through the cloudbank, and the world slowed as their points of reference were lost to the sky.

"How's it looking?" Mary asked.

"Pressure's steady. No leaks. Ask me again in half an hour."

Mary smiled and turned to Alice. "As to your next question, Eva will take you to Ballern. She's on the carrier with the surviving brig captains, and there's a whole squad of them itching to deploy."

"I was curious about that, yes," Alice said. "I'd like to talk to Eva. It's … we didn't talk much after the Battle of Ballern. And Jacob's still staying on the carrier?"

"For now," Mary said.

Jacob rubbed his hands together. "And I'll be assisting Frederick?"

"That was his price for helping us fix the Skysworn," Smith said. "A fair price, to be sure. I do not think we could have completed the repairs in a single week without his help."

Mary laughed at that. "More like a single month."

The banter between Smith and Mary loosened a knot in Jacob's gut. He didn't think he'd ever forget the look on Smith's face the first time he'd seen them in the aftermath of the Battle of Ballern. Smith had never looked so defeated, despite everything they'd been through. The Skysworn was broken, and part of Smith and Mary had broken with it.

Now they were back in the sky where they were supposed to be. Smith sounded more like himself than he had in weeks. And Mary didn't hesitate to poke him about every little detail.

"Did you hear that rattle?" Mary tapped on the horn. "Sounds like one of the intakes might have some debris in it."

Smith grunted. "Looking for it now. It is closer to the bow. I believe it may be something loose in the channels for the chainguns. I will have to open it up after we land. Try not to deploy them in the meantime."

Mary grinned at Jacob and Alice. "A few kinks to work out of the systems, but she's almost back to her old self."

"Mary, how big of a debt do you owe Jakon for saving you?" Alice asked.

Smith howled with laughter over the horn while Mary grumbled to herself. "That damn smuggler owed *us*. We're even now. Or as even as we've been in a decade. And if he says different, just remember he's a pirate."

No one pointed out the fact that Mary was one of the most notorious pirate captains in the skies, but that didn't stop her from complaining about pirates for the rest of the trip to the carrier.

CHAPTER SEVEN

A LARGE PART of Jacob had hoped Eva would be running late, which would give Alice and him more time to spend together. That idea fled when Mary contacted Eva as they approached the carrier. Ships crowded the skies, cycling in and out to the north toward Ballern while one of Archibald's enormous warships hovered to the west. The Skysworn landed by the brigs, and Eva was already waiting.

Jacob exchanged a brief goodbye with Alice, and their hug didn't last nearly long enough. But the smile she wore as she caught up with Eva lightened his mood. She was happy to be going to Ballern, and she'd be among friends, which was no small thing.

Smith had the panels pulled off the channels for the chainguns by the time Jacob had gathered up his pack and his air cannon.

"Sure you don't need any help?"

Smith shook his head and held up a sheared-off bolt. "I think we already have the problem well in hand, Jacob. I do appreciate the offer, though."

"Have you heard from Samuel?" Jacob asked.

"Saw him this morning, in fact. He has been working with the stable hands. They had some injured mounts come back from Ballern on the last supply ship."

"Thanks, Smith. I'll see you later!" Jacob clicked the transmitter in his collar as he started walking away. "Frederick, I'm on the carrier. Where do you need me?"

Static crackled over the transmitter before Frederick spoke. "Meet me in the workshop near the stern. We have some things to discuss."

Jacob frowned at that. Frederick was normally forthcoming with whatever tasks he needed done. It was one reason they'd been able to complete the carrier so quickly. Having the power of a Titan Mech at your disposal was one thing, but knowing how to strategically use it at speed was quite another. Frederick's direct instructions had been key in that.

Jacob turned and walked toward the stern, passing the Skysworn again and catching a glimpse of Smith with his legs already dangling out from beneath the hull. Apparently, he'd found more than a sheared-off screw rattling around in the channels.

The deck of the carrier wasn't as busy as Jacob had expected. At least not as busy as the traffic above it suggested. There were still lots of people moving across the ship with purpose, though none of the crawlers rocketed by at dangerous speeds for a change.

It was a lull in the conflict, he knew, and one they should use to rest and recoup as well as they could before the battle against Mordair resumed. A horn blared from a nearby crawler, and Jones waved as he drove by. Jacob raised his hand in greeting and continued on, passing several bays being used to repair brigs and clippers and a series of strikers.

The repair bays they'd originally designed for the carrier were almost comically inadequate when it came to capacity. Maybe four ships fit beneath the durable tents that shielded the crews from the relentless sun. The rest were exposed, and several workers had deep tans and sunburns to prove it.

Jacob's steps slowed near the last brig, trying to understand if his eyes were playing tricks on him. A small armored suit shifted under one of the gas chambers, taking the weight as the assembly was detached from the bridge. It wasn't a Titan Mech. It was an exoskeleton. Charles's design, repurposed with braces and attachments normally reserved for the cranes in the largest factories.

He shook his head and moved on. Frederick could tell him about it, he was sure. No one else was that deep in the designs … except Targrove. Jacob's lip quirked up in an unasked question. He increased his pace, hurrying past the restaurants and one of the few pubs that lined the carrier's deck.

The air smelled like hot oil and superheated metal the closer he got to the workshop. The scent of fried fish beckoned him to the last restaurant, but he stayed the course. The workshop might have been better called a factory now that Frederick had time to get his hands on it.

He walked through the towering bay doors, enough clearance to fly a brig into, but not so grand as to fit a Porcupine or destroyer. It was adequate for maintaining the Titan Mechs, and apparently large enough to reconfigure into a production line.

His steps slowed as he watched braces and gears moving down a conveyor belt. Tinkers stood to either side, sorting and clipping rods and cogs together as fast as they came, leaving the assembly back on the belt to move on to the next station. There, the braces became anchors for ratios he knew all too well, and somehow, he already knew he'd see the leg braces on another assembly line when he turned.

"Jacob!" Frederick called out, waving him over.

A smaller form stood hunched over the conveyor, his gnarled hands moving with more speed and dexterity than they had any right to.

Jacob stopped beside Frederick and smiled, exchanging grips before focusing on the old man behind the workstation. He leaned forward, looking past the stacks of lenses splayed out across the man's line of sight.

"Targrove?"

Targrove glanced up and smiled. "A moment, Jacob. We're almost done with this shift."

Jacob watched the tinker work, assembling the core for the controls of an exoskeleton in a matter of minutes before taking the parts of another and completing it as well before a low whistle sounded. The entire workshop breathed a collective sigh of relief.

Targrove raised the arm of every lens on his head until they all stood straight up. "Frederick mentioned you'd be back soon. Good to see you."

"You too." Jacob gestured to the room as a whole, catching sight of four upright exoskeletons at the far end of the line. "Is this all your doing?"

Targrove nodded. "The assembly line, yes. The factories in Bollwerk are admirable for their efficiencies, but let us say I have more experience with doing things under pressure."

Jacob knew he meant under the pressure of war. A time when speed was nearly as important as accuracy. A fine balance between things that could get you killed and things that could save your life. In many ways, Jacob thought, the same could be said about building any kind of weapon.

"No offense, of course." Targrove smiled.

Frederick held up his hand. "Of course not. It's like you said." He leaned in closer. "We do things different in Bollwerk."

"What about the exoskeleton on the dock?" Jacob asked. "I saw one helping with the construction of the brig. Who's piloting it?"

"We've trained about two dozen pilots in the past week."

Jacob blinked. "In a *week*? You have two dozen exoskeletons already built?"

"Not armored, but yes. The Titan Mechs aren't as deft as the exoskeletons in smaller spaces. We deployed several into Ballern to help with the reconstruction and several more on the carrier to assist with repairs."

Frederick hesitated. "Are you upset, Jacob?"

Jacob looked across the workshop, the pages of Charles's journal flipping through his mind, the pile of calculations, details, and tolerances. To get so many exoskeletons working in so short a time required a skill he could scarcely imagine. He slowly turned back, not to Frederick, but to Targrove.

"That was you too, wasn't it? You're the only one who knows Charles's designs so well. Who else could have broken down that exoskeleton so fast?"

Targrove tapped his fingers on the conveyor belt. "Yes, Jacob. Though, without you, we wouldn't have these magnificent creations, would we? Charles's lab would have stayed buried for years, even centuries, as the Lowlands slowly overtook it."

"What are those for?" He pointed to the cluster of exoskeletons at the far end of the workshop, four standing shoulder to shoulder. Jacob already knew the answer. He could see the armor as plain as his hand. What he wasn't sure of was if Targrove and Frederick would be honest.

"War," Targrove said. "They'll fight beside us. They'll protect our friends. And yes, Jacob, they will kill a great many people."

It should have infuriated him. He should have railed against Targrove, told Frederick that Charles wouldn't want his creation to be used in such a way. But that's why he buried it, wasn't it? It was Jacob who had dug it up. It was his friends, and Charles's, who needed those weapons now. To protect his family, sacrifices had to be made. Jacob faced the pair of tinkers.

"How can I help?"

✧　✧　✧

WORKING BESIDE TARGROVE wasn't like learning from Charles. Charles had hesitated to teach Jacob some of the darker parts of being a tinker until their situations had taken that choice away. Targrove, on the other hand, showed him how to build faster. How to think about the next tinker on the line, and to focus only on the task in front of him.

From wedging two pry bars into the conveyor belt housing to form a makeshift stand, to positioning a stool so his arms didn't get sore, commands rolled out from Targrove, and Jacob followed every last instruction.

There was only one cog in the control panel assembly whose position mattered. The rest were all reversible, sized the same, and stackable. The station before them sorted the cogs, so Targrove explained all they needed to pay attention to was the cog that allowed the pilot to select different gear patterns. Everything else should be muscle memory. So much so each tinker on the line became little more than a machine themselves.

It was a passionless approach, one that left Jacob with a hollow satisfaction. At the end of an hour-long shift, they walked down the assembly line to see what had been accomplished. Another exoskeleton stood beside the original four, and that feeling of accomplishment grew far more solid.

"That's enough for now," Frederick said. "Let's find dinner and you can regale us of your time in Karn."

"I do want to talk to you both. There's … a path forward, but it's not without risks. We were going to keep it between Lady Katherine and Archibald, but I'd like your opinions, too."

"I'll tell Natalia we're having a private dinner this evening," Frederick said.

Targrove waved the idea away. "Bring her. I trust that tinker more than I trust almost anyone in Archibald's fold."

Frederick paused before inclining his head. "I will. I know she would be grateful for that trust."

A short time later, Jacob found himself in a small bar unofficially reserved for officers of the carrier. In other words, when the crew needed a private place to talk, everyone cleared out.

The stools weren't the most comfortable thing Jacob had ever sat on, and he thought whoever designed them might be able to learn something from the artisans in Ballern or even Pirates Cove, from what Samuel had told him. That was all secondary.

Natalia sipped her drink before blowing out a breath and letting the metal stein crack against the table. "I miss sleep, Frederick."

"We all do." Frederick slowly spun his cup on the table. He looked small next to Natalia. Everyone looked small next to Natalia except Smith. From what Frederick had told Jacob, she outworked every tinker he'd ever known, which meant she needed extraordinary strength for some of her solo projects.

Natalia turned her attention to Jacob. "What did you think of those exoskeletons? We tweaked your design a little, made them more suited to specific tasks, but kept the essence intact, I think."

"Charles's design." Jacob took a sip of his Sweetwing Tea. It wasn't his favorite flavor, to say the least, but the earthy bitterness with a hint of honey reminded him of Alice. He swirled the ice with the shard of a translucent wing.

Natalia exchanged a look with Frederick and Targrove. Jacob pretended he didn't notice, but it would have been impossible to ignore in such tight quarters. "I didn't mean any disrespect, Jacob."

Targrove patted him on the back. "He likes to be sure Charles gets his due. Never mind the fact Jacob designed the ratchet for the waist, and the armor, and refined the ratios for the control panel. I saw an early version of these exoskeletons toward the end of the war, and I don't think Jacob gives himself enough credit. Charles would be proud to see what he's done with it."

Jacob didn't want the words to make him feel pride, but Targrove knew exactly what to say. The thought Charles might be proud of what Jacob had done with his teachings was a balm against the things Jacob *knew* Charles wouldn't be proud of.

"Have you spoken to Archibald?" Frederick asked.

Natalia leaned forward on her stool and sighed. "Constantly. You'd think he doesn't have a war to oversee the way he's trying to manage my workshop."

"We all need to get back to the workshops," Jacob said. "If those exoskeletons are really helping, we need to get more of them done."

"We will." Targrove rubbed the back of his hand. "Natalia's workshops are still dedicated to the Titan Mechs. We hope to have three more completed before the assault on the Great Machine begins."

Jacob blinked. "It's … planned? Have they settled on a strategy, then?"

Targrove nodded. "The only people who know are Lady Katherine and those sitting at this table. Archibald means to tear a hole through Fel's defenses from land and air."

"Has he seen what's waiting there?" Jacob glanced away and took a drink of his tea. "All he's going to do is get a lot of people killed." He clenched his fists. Had Archibald ignored everything they'd learned in Karn? Surely the evidence coming from Arun would mean *something*. A direct assault would cost countless lives. "People will die no matter how this goes."

"I'd rather it be Mordair," Natalia said.

Jacob looked around the group. They'd need to do more to offset any recklessness from Archibald. "I have an idea. Maybe it will help."

"What is it you know?" Targrove's words slowed as he asked the question. "You said you had a path forward."

"Maybe. It's not … it's still a risk. There's an old control center for the Great Machine far to the southeast of Karn."

Targrove's eyes narrowed. "How far?"

Jacob met his gaze. "Karn calls it a place of death and ghosts."

The expression on Targrove's face hardened. "No one goes into the Dead Woods, Jacob. No one."

"What the hell is the Dead Woods?" Natalia asked.

Frederick spun the fraying threads from his napkin between his fingers. "It's a place overrun with cordyceps."

"That doesn't answer my question." Natalia gestured with an open palm, asking for more details.

Targrove leaned forward and rested on his elbows. "Think of it like a mushroom in a way, but it kills anything it takes root in. Bugs are especially susceptible."

"It's easy enough to avoid poisonous plants, Targrove."

A dark smile crossed the old tinker's face. "It's not the poison itself that gets you. It's the bugs that are taken over by it. They don't die. They're absorbed by it, controlled by it, and anything seen as a threat will be dealt with violently and immediately." His smile darkened. "Have you ever seen a swarm, Natalia? One of the great desert clouds that devours everything in its path? Or a nest of Tail Swords when it's disturbed by an unsuspecting caravan?"

Natalia shivered at that question. "Yes."

"Imagine a creature so determined to protect itself that it would destroy itself in the process. No check on the power behind its blows. A Tree Killer striking hard enough to shatter its own scythe, a Sky Needle dying on impact as it dives with such force it could crush an armored crawler, a Walker breaking its legs as it stomps its perceived threat into oblivion. There is no reason left in those creatures. Their minds are lost, absorbed with the single purpose of protecting the cordyceps, even as it devours them from the inside out. It is a horror I would wish on no one."

Natalia slowly turned her gaze to Jacob. "And you want to *go* there?"

"Yes. Karn knows how to venture into the area without bringing any of the cordyceps back to the city." Jacob kept his voice as even as he could, meeting each of their gazes in turn. He'd learned to see confidence in people who met his eyes when they told him a half-insane plan. "I'm taking a small group. Don't let Archibald attack the Great Machine until we *know* what's waiting there."

"I don't know if I can support that idea," Frederick spoke quietly, but the words were heavy. "You're going to get yourselves killed."

"Maybe. If we march straight into Mordair's path, that's almost a certainty. Archibald should have the photographs from Karn by now. Ask him to see them. Look at what the Children of the Dark Fire and Mordair have. It's a nightmare."

Targrove snarled before throwing back the rest of his drink. The heavy stein thudded against the table as he eyed the group. "It's worth the risk. We know precious little about the Great Machines. Even if a sabotage causes no more than a distraction, that distraction could be all our fleet needs to break through Mordair's line."

Frederick slowly shook his head back and forth. "You're talking like this is the Deadlands War, Targrove." He leaned forward and gestured to Targrove. "We can't have that mindset."

"If we don't, you need to be ready to see Mordair bury your cities under the sands. What example would have more power than crushing Bollwerk to nothing? A strike against Belldorn? Strategic, yes, but those who live to the east have nothing to lose in Belldorn. Have no family in Belldorn. But raze Bollwerk to the ground. Burn Archibald's stronghold to ash. What then? He would have the attention of every soul on the continent."

Frederick closed his eyes and cursed.

"I'm with you." Natalia's words weren't loud, or zealous. They were a simple statement, or a concession.

"How long do you need?" Frederick's shoulders sagged.

"Alice is in Ballern," Jacob said. "I need to see when she can be back. Three days?"

"I'll try to clear you five. It would give us more time to complete additional exoskeletons."

"And Titan Mechs," Natalia said.

Targrove clenched his fists and closed his eyes for a moment. "It's too easy for memories of the dark times to return, my friends." He looked at all of them in turn. "I remember something Charles once said to me in the desert. 'This war will outlive us all.' In many ways, he was right. No one can know the darkness of the Deadlands War ever again. We have to end this."

CHAPTER EIGHT

ALICE STOOD AT Eva's side while they waited for Furi. It didn't quite feel real to see Jacob's exoskeletons carrying rubble from the reconstruction to a more open area for the Titan Mechs to sort into piles of waste and what could be reused. Worst were the carcasses of the Carrion Worms. Those meant there were still dead in the rubble, and the construction had grown far more dangerous for the workers.

"I thought Ballern sat on a bed of rock." Alice looked out toward the sea before turning back.

"From what I understand, it is," Eva said. "But rock breaks, Alice. And dropping a city on top of it is one way to crack stone."

Alice's gaze traveled up, away from the reconstruction, instead focusing on the docks far above them. The new unbalanced silhouette, where everything that had once stretched out toward the Crystal Sea now sat in ruin at her feet, had grown somewhat familiar.

She'd seen stone break in Ancora. It didn't need to fall from the sky. Even a home collapsing at the right angle could split cobblestones and barrier stones alike. She should have remembered that from the Fall. It had been enough to let far more Carrion Worms slip into the walled city. But some things she didn't want to remember.

"Alice!"

She turned toward her name and studied the surrounding crowd, fairly certain it was Furi calling out to her.

"Alice!" A hand waved in the air as two exoskeletons and a Titan

Mech strode by, and Alice caught a glimpse of Furi between the Mechs.

"Eva, Furi's here." She started across the street as the crowd's path cleared behind the Titan Mech.

"We could have come to you, Furi," Eva said as they reached the Skyborn.

Furi shook her head. "No, I needed to get out. I've been cramped up in headquarters with Jakon, Rin, and Tatsu. It was a lot more comfortable when we still had the school."

"How bad have the Carrion Worms gotten?" Alice hooked a thumb back at the destroyed district.

"Bad enough." Furi put her hands on her hips and turned toward the sea. "Natalia has a plan to seal the cracks in the foundation, but several of the surviving Ballern engineers are skeptical. They're still going to try it out, though." Her voice quieted. "What real choice do they have?"

Eva rubbed the back of her neck. "How, exactly?"

"Well, they're planning to set a new anchor for the docks close to where the old tower used to be."

"Willett's?"

Furi nodded. "The ground is broken up, so they should be able to drill far enough in for an anchor. But if they did that and left it, there would be too much space for bugs to come up from the sea caves and burrow deeper beneath the city."

"So they need a gasket or something?" Alice asked.

"Not exactly, but you aren't far off." Furi tilted her head to the side. "They're going to fill the anchor with a kind of grout. Like we use for the cobblestones." Furi tapped the stones at their feet with her toes.

"You mean mortar?" Alice narrowed her eyes. "They used quite a bit of that in the walls around Ancora." She pointed to the remaining archways and walls of Ballern. "The stones aren't so symmetrical back home, so the mortar creates a kind of stone itself."

"That's exactly it. Natalia thinks it will hold, even with gas chambers attached to it, as they rebuild the Bones."

"Natalia has Frederick and Targrove as her mentors, Furi." Eva huffed out a small laugh. "Maybe if your engineers knew that, they'd have more confidence in Natalia."

Furi shrugged. "They don't know her. That's just how it is in Ballern. Until you've proven yourself, they don't trust anything about you or your work. But she outranks them in the alliance, so they'll listen to her authority."

Alice gestured to the Titan Mechs and exoskeletons all around them. "She helped build all of these. And the carrier? How could they question her?"

"They just need time, Alice, and now isn't the time to wait for them," Furi said. "I'd rather them be skeptical and get it done than wait weeks to start while others try to convince them. Don't worry about it."

Apparently, Alice hadn't kept her expression as neutral as she'd been trying to. "I worry about everything these days, Furi."

"Don't we all. Natalia won't be back for another day. She's on the carrier with Frederick and Targrove right now, so for the time being, Rin and Tatsu are organizing a guard for the district. Are you two hungry?"

"Quite so," Eva said.

"Let's get some food. Most of the market vendors have set up in the old arena. I guess it's really the new marketplace until we can rebuild the sea docks. Follow me."

✧   ✧   ✧

THE IDEA OF doing any kind of critical thinking after the decadent meal Jakon had served them in the arena was almost laughable to Alice. But there they were, inside Ballern's sprawling arena, helping the chef cook for dozens of customers while they strategized about what to do against

Mordair.

Eva left to check on the brigs still stationed on the dock, but promised she'd meet up with them later. And even those words would once have been spoken with the utmost care and secrecy.

Alice found it to be a strange feeling, speaking so openly among strangers. Any one of them could be a spy, an ear listening for any information they could sell for a bit of coin. But in the aftermath of the Battle of Ballern, everyone felt like family. Perhaps a conversation wasn't so risk laden in that regard.

"The reconstruction is important." Furi handed Alice a round loaf of bread.

The exchange brought Alice's attention back to the simple job of slicing bread she'd been given behind Jakon's table. She'd taken to slicing it into cubes and lining the base of each bowl instead of leaving it in one large, unmanageable slice.

"I don't think anyone is arguing that, Furi," Alice said. "I think some people are arguing about what the priorities need to be."

"Protecting the city is first. Putting an end to Mordair is a close second. And part of protecting the city *is* the reconstruction. We lost a lot of homes when the Bones fell. On the docks, and on the ground."

A young child, not more than ten, wore the badge of a Shadowwing on her shoulder. Alice watched her take a bowl of bread over to Jakon, who ladled another portion out. She held out a handful of coin.

"No need, friend," the chef said. "Tell your guild their alliance is payment enough. Send them all to me, and they'll have food so long as I have it to serve."

The child looked at the coins in her hand before pocketing them. She hurried off, hesitated as she glanced back at the booth once, and then vanished into the crowds.

Jakon sorted through three tins of spice before dumping apparently random measurements into another stewpot. "Furi's right, you know, Alice? Protecting the city has to come first."

"What changed your mind?" Alice asked, and she barely managed not to cringe when she realized how blunt her question had been.

Jakon chuckled under his breath. "Not what, Alice. Who. I can't leave my friends to fight Mordair alone. Even the friends who annoy me."

"Mary," Alice and Furi said together before breaking down in a short laugh.

"Indeed. If the Skysworn fights for Ballern, well, I can't let my reputation be soiled by leaving, can I?"

Furi gave him a skeptical look. "Can we save some food for Rin and Tatsu? I can take it to them while they're on patrol tonight."

Jakon crouched down to look under the table before nodding. "I have a few more covered bowls. Why don't you two finish dicing the last few loaves of bread, and then you can head out?"

Alice's collar crackled before Jacob's voice came to life. He sounded muted in the cacophony of the market, and Alice was glad for it.

Jakon nodded toward the hall not far from the table. She laid her knife down and hurried over, getting away from the crowd so she could easily hear.

She was a little surprised when she turned to find Furi chasing after her. If there was anyone Alice trusted more than Furi in Ballern, she didn't know who it was. She clicked the transmitter.

"Jacob, I'm here."

"Wow, what's all that noise?"

"The market. We're helping Jakon. Well, we were. Now we're talking to you. Furi's here."

"Good, great, that's great. Furi, hi!"

Jacob's odd speech pattern sent Alice's hackles up. She'd known him long enough to know he was anxious to say something.

"Jacob, what's wrong?"

He paused. "Nothing, exactly. I just … I spent some time with the tinkers. You know, especially some of the older tinkers? About the control center?"

"Yes," Alice said, drawing out the word.

"They told us what's there, right? Arun and Mali, I mean, well, I talked to Smith and the others. And … Theo's assistant, of course, and they all think it's worth the risk. Smith has already discussed it with Mary."

"You're going to the control center?" Furi asked. "That's … I don't know if that's a great idea."

"Did you hear Furi, Jacob?"

"I did, and after everything we've heard, she might be right. But you saw the Great Machine, Alice. You saw what's waiting for us. We can't let our friends attack Mordair directly. The price … it's just …"

"I know, Jacob." She ran her hand through her hair. "When do we leave?" She glanced at Furi, finding the Skyborn's brow furrowed.

"Tomorrow. I know you just got to Ballern, but we need to do this."

Alice blew out a breath and rubbed her forehead. "Not the best timing. You couldn't have brought this up yesterday?"

Jacob laughed over the transmitter, his voice crackling with static. "I'm sorry. I know it's bad. Eva will bring you back if you want to go. Furi can come, too."

Furi glanced back at the market. "They need me here. I can't go anywhere yet. After Kura … they need me here."

"Did Mary already talk to Eva? We just saw her an hour ago."

"Yes, I contacted you as soon as I heard. It was either that, or Mary would have to fly up to get you and turn around to get back. Which might have been faster if Eva was still flying that old freighter."

Alice snorted a laugh. "I hope she didn't say that to Eva."

A small chuckle came back in a burst of static. "Alice, I have to go. There's a lot to get done tonight. We'll have all the supplies you'll need. Just bring your gloves, glider, and cannon."

"I will, Jacob."

"Good. See you soon. I love you."

"Love you too."

The crackle of the transmitter died as the broadcast stopped.

Alice bit her lips and met Furi's gaze. "What do you need from us? I have to leave tomorrow, and I don't want to leave you without help."

"We have help, Alice." Furi gestured to the entire arena. "I've never seen Ballern this unified. I only wish so many didn't have to die for it to happen."

"What can I do?"

Furi hesitated. "Tell me what you saw at the Great Machine." Her words grew hard, brittle. "Tell me why you don't want Archibald and Kat to force their way into our enemy's airspace and burn them to the ground."

"Jakon should hear this, too. Let's get him."

"You're right. Come on."

They made it back to Jakon's table as he started serving the last prepared stewpot.

"Perfect timing! I need more of that diced-up bread. Apparently, the locals like mutilated bread more than I expected."

"Mutilated?" Alice said. "I'd hardly call it mutilated."

Jakon grinned and ladled out another bowl of soup.

Furi stepped closer to him. "We have something we need to discuss with you. In private." She glanced around the thinning crowd.

"I doubt we've much to worry about here, Furi. Are you sure?"

She nodded, and he didn't argue any further.

"The market closes in half an hour. It's an early night as the theater troupe is putting on a show for anyone who wants to attend."

Alice stood a little straighter. "I'd like to attend." She hesitated. "After our talk, of course."

"Of course." Jakon didn't hide the skeptical note in his voice.

She walked back to the edge of the table and picked up the scalloped bread knife. She and Furi didn't speak much as they worked to prepare the bowls, and Alice had little doubt their conversation with Jacob was weighing on the Skyborn's mind as well.

But that distraction, and if she was being honest, the thrill of the idea of walking into the control center of a Great Machine, made the time fly past.

Jakon joked and plotted and traded drinks with a dozen more customers before the night ended, but as soon as the last walked away, his expression hardened. "Come. I'll be back at the table later to start preparing for breakfast. Let's discuss what we need to discuss. I've taken enough of your time."

They followed him out of the arena. It was one of the few places Alice felt she hadn't frequented inside the walls of Ballern. That was a ridiculous thought because she hadn't spent much time in the city at all. But she still knew the docks and the old market, the bookstore, and the hospital. It was a minor portion of the city, but it felt welcoming, and that was no small thing.

Jakon stepped into one of the smaller lifts closer to the hospital. The gate creaked closed, and with the throw of a switch, they rose into the air, leaving the towers and arena below them before they reached the lower levels of the docks.

They exited on the second, and Alice knew immediately where they were headed. Jakon took them past a couple bays to The Ray. Furi took the lead, opening a small panel in the stern that revealed a lock. Jakon joined them, unlocking it and pushing his way inside before locking the door behind them.

He didn't take them to the cabin, instead walking deeper into the cargo hold. A series of chairs waited there, and Jakon gestured for them to take a seat.

"Now, what did we need this kind of privacy for?" Curiosity was plain to hear in Jakon's question.

"Jacob contacted us," Alice said. "They have a plan that only a few know about. Archibald, Kat, Mary, Eva, and the tinkers."

"Which tinkers?"

Alice paused. "Targrove, Frederick, Natalia, and Smith."

"And you're telling *me* now?" He placed a hand over his heart. "A known smuggler and peddler of valuable information?"

"Of course!" Furi snapped. "What game are you playing?"

"I'm only enjoying the irony of it all, Furi." Jakon offered a bright smile. "Many thought I betrayed the crown, without knowing I was working *for* the crown. Spies and smugglers aren't so different in the end."

Alice met his gaze. "We trust you. Use that to your advantage with Archibald and Kat if you want, but for now, we need your help."

"I'll certainly use Archibald for a favor in the future, assuming he doesn't get his city annihilated in the meantime, of course. But I do appreciate your frankness about the idea, Alice."

Alice leaned forward and clasped her hands together. "You heard us talk about the photos of the Great Machine."

Jakon nodded. "An impenetrable defense, as it were. Or at least strong enough to inflict more losses than anyone wants."

"Yes, which is why we're trying to find another way in behind their lines. And that is taking us to an abandoned control center to the southeast of Karn."

Jakon's smile faltered. "The Dead Woods?"

"You know it?"

"I know anyone and anything that goes there doesn't come out alive." All jest left his words. "Who … why are you going there?"

"Arun doesn't think it was destroyed like the Great Machine in the desert. We might be able to get inside."

Jakon slowly looked from Furi to Alice and back. "And you're going with the Ancorans?"

Furi shook her head. "No. I can't leave Ballern. The Skyborn are looking to us, Jakon. I can't let them down. It sounds like Mary and Smith are going, though."

"They are," Alice said. "Arun and Mali provided a map to the control center. And ways to come back safely."

Jakon frowned. "They've actually been there, haven't they? Exploring the Dead Woods? They're mad." He grimaced and looked away for a moment. "Mary … always trying to upstage the rest of us, isn't she?"

Alice didn't quite hide her grin.

"How soon do you leave?"

"Eva's taking me back to the carrier in the morning."

"Unless you see a better way?" Furi said.

Jakon didn't so much as hesitate. "No. The defenses you described are formidable. We need a distraction, and while you may be looking for a way to slip into the Great Machine undetected, you won't get a substantial force inside without being discovered. I don't care how discreet the way inside is."

"What kind of distraction?" Alice asked.

"The bigger the better. Think like Mordair. He stopped the Battle of Ballern with one dropped tower and a collapsed gas chamber."

Alice almost recoiled at the idea. *Think like Mordair.* "That's something I hoped I'd never have to resort to."

Jakon glanced away. When he looked back, his expression wasn't so dark. "You two hungry?"

Alice and Furi both nodded.

"Follow me. I can at least get you a decent meal before you get yourself killed, Alice."

She didn't miss the smirk that crossed his face before he led the way off The Ray and took them deeper into the docks.

✦   ✦   ✦

MORNING CAME FASTER than Alice would have liked. Thankfully, Eva had no complaints about her going back to sleep as soon as they'd cleared Ballern's airspace. Sleeping hadn't come easy the night before. Alice wasn't new to resting in tight quarters, but the bunks in Furi's new headquarters might have been smaller than the beds on the Skysworn.

While space wasn't that much of an issue, it was still odd to sleep close to people you didn't know. Alice trusted Furi's inner circle a great deal, but she'd also seen people betrayed often enough. Sleeping beside strangers had never come easy.

"Alice."

She cracked an eye open, finding Eva tapping her shoulder as the windscreen on the brig filled with enormous trees.

"We're almost at the carrier."

Alice bolted upright. "I'm sorry. I didn't mean to sleep the entire way. And I've been in your chair." She stood up, glancing fondly at the padded captain's chair.

The ship angled toward the starboard side, and a view of the carrier opened up before them.

Eva smiled at Alice. "You want to ride the lines down, or you want us to land?"

"Neither."

Eva crossed her arms. "Are you going to do what I think you're going to do?"

"Just slow down a bit as we cross over the deck, would you?"

Eva grinned.

✦   ✦   ✦

ALICE STOOD ON the ramp to the loading bay of the brig. To call it windy would be understating things, but she was glad for her half-asleep idea. Sometimes, it took a while to wake up, but that wasn't a problem when you peered over the chilly precipice you intended to jump off.

One of the crew was still arguing with Eva as Alice started down the ramp. They, perhaps most sanely, thought jumping out of a moving airship with no more than a glider pack wasn't the brightest idea. She flashed the crew a huge smile.

"Bye, Eva!"

She heard the captain's laugh, and then the loading ramp ended. Alice clicked her transmitter before holding her arms out, stabilizing her fall as she prepared to deploy her wings.

"Where are you, Jacob?" she shouted into the wind.

Static came back before she could just make out his response. "What's wrong with your transmitter? I'm at the workshop near the stern. Mary and Smith are waiting for us, and I don't have much time."

Alice threw the lever and deployed her glider, the wind resistance pulling hard against her wings. She waved to the brig as it turned off to the west, looping back for its next destination.

"Come outside, and I'll show you."

"What? Outside? Outside where? You sound a little better now."

She didn't answer, only angled the glider to the south, and the stern. It was quite a view, seeing so many ships docked along the carrier. The quantity of them under repair was unsettling at best. The Battle of Ballern had cost more than lives.

But those darker thoughts were lost to the rush of the wind as it pulled at her hair and goggles, shifting her wings as she focused on her destination. There was a simple joy in the air, and she understood why Jacob enjoyed the gliders as much as he did. Sometimes it was easy to forget how much he'd influenced her.

One of Bollwerk's warships drifted to the east, a massive form eclipsed only by the carrier itself. Though the nearby Porcupine wasn't anything to scoff at.

As she grew closer to the deck, she could make out individual forms walking along the roads, keeping clear of the crawlers hurrying by. It was the clippers Alice needed to be careful of, as she was dangerously close to their flight path. And she doubted that gliders were something the pilots would be watching for.

Alice passed a bank of restaurants near the southern end of the carrier, and that gave way to a pair of storehouses before the looming form of the largest workshop came into view. She caught sight of Jacob well before he saw her, a perplexed look on his face as he held a hand over his eyes and scoured the area.

Everywhere but up.

"Nice apron!" Alice shouted when she was about fifteen feet away.

He looked up just in time to see her dive, pull up, and snap the wings closed. She only stumbled three steps before catching herself and pulling the goggles off her face.

"Did you jump off Eva's brig?"

"Yes." She grinned before wrapping him up in an awkward hug.

"I'm jealous! That had to be quite a flight." He tried to embrace her, but the partially collapsed wings kept getting in the way. Exasperated, he gave her a quick kiss and spun her around, packing away the wings and locking them in place, ready for their next flight.

That done, Alice enjoyed a much more functional hug.

"How soon are we leaving?" she asked. "It sounded like you were in quite the hurry over the transmitter."

"When I said Mary and Smith are waiting for us, I meant it. We need to get to the Skysworn. Let me return my apron. Lots of tools on here the tinkers will need." He patted a series of wrenches and ratchets before scratching his leg. It was odd to see him in shorts, though the shorts had certainly seen better days. Most places, it was still easier to hide his biomechanics than deal with the history of mistrust, but Alice supposed the carrier was likely the last place anyone would be worried about a Biomech.

She followed him into the workshop, her steps slowing as she tried to understand what she was looking at. If she didn't know otherwise, she'd think she'd wandered into a factory in one of the larger cities. Considering how much bronze and copper filled the space, it certainly looked like it would be at home in Belldorn, or perhaps Bollwerk.

"They're building Titan Mechs here?" Alice studied the towering form at the far end of the workshop. At its full height, it nearly touched the ceiling.

"Look lower."

She frowned at Jacob's response, but looked closer to the floor, standing a little straighter when she realized what the shorter forms were near the Titan Mech's legs. "Exoskeletons?"

"Guilty," an older voice said, drawing Alice's attention.

"Targrove!" She paused and turned toward the speaker. "Are we calling you 'Theo's assistant' here?"

Targrove shook his head. "No, no. The secret's out in the workshop. You get in one big argument with Frederick, and he lets your name slip in a roomful of tinkers. That was the end of that ruse. Bit of an open secret anyway these days, isn't it?"

Jacob handed Targrove the apron. "We have to go. I'll be back when I can."

"No, Jacob. Take the time you need. There is nothing more important here than what you're doing in the Dead Woods. Be careful, and listen to anything the folks from Karn tell you." He turned to Alice. "And *you* … try to make sure he's actually *listening*. Nearly crushed his foot in the hydraulics of that Titan Mech today."

"The fleshy one or the metal one?"

Targrove burst out laughing and patted Alice on the shoulder. "You two, just be careful."

With that, Jacob grabbed his own glider pack and air cannon. They left the workshop and hurried across the carrier, cutting between several repair bays on their trek to the Skysworn.

Steam rose from the ship's sides as they approached, and Alice could barely make out Mary's muttered words.

"Finally, they're here." Her next words weren't nearly so hard to hear. "Smith, prepare to launch. Jacob, Alice, untie us and get onboard. We have a stop to make near Karn. Mali will be joining us."

The thought of Mali coming with them lifted a weight from Alice's chest. It was one thing to venture into a dangerous place with no true idea of what you were going to face. It was quite another to go with a friend who had been there before, and survived.

CHAPTER NINE

"I'M TELLING YOU, these are the coordinates, but I don't see a thing," Mary almost growled at the horn.

They'd been searching for nearly fifteen minutes, and the conversation between Mary and Smith had grown more tense.

"I calibrated every instrument after the repairs, Mary. If they say we are in the correct location, I am confident we are. Give me a moment."

Something clanged belowdecks, and the sound of Smith's voice changed. "I have switched to the gun pod."

Jacob leaned toward the windscreen and saw nothing but trees. One of the Forest Giants loomed nearby, but the rest of the canopy remained dense, certainly too thick to land.

"This is the correct location." Smith's voice sounded louder from the gun pod. Either he was leaning closer to the horn, or the acoustics were simply different from the enclosed space.

"You already said that, Smith." Mary dragged his name out.

"I mean, start the landing sequence. Descend vertically."

"Descend vertically, he says." Mary threw the lever for the landing gear, the panels in the hull whisper quiet, before the gear unfolded beneath them with a thud. Their descent started as Mary pulled a wide lever toward the console's base, matching the movement with the throttle and smaller turbines to keep the nose of the ship level.

The canopy rose outside the windows, crossing into shadow and suddenly into darkness as the ship itself blocked out most of the remaining light. The Gray Woods opened around them, ancient trunks carefully cut down, but others showing jagged breaks that had eventually regrown into the canopy they saw now.

"What happened here?" Alice asked.

Jacob wondered that, too, as there weren't any signs of a nearby village or city that might have removed those trees.

The hatch to the gun pod banged closed below them. "You have a clearing in about fifty feet, directly ahead."

Mary held the Skysworn steady, a small cluster of Shadowwings flitting away from them as the wind from the ship disturbed their perch. A short time later, the Skysworn settled into a clearing covered by shadows and forest detritus.

Mali waited at the edge of the woods, perched on the back of an armored crawler that wouldn't have looked out of place in Belldorn. She waved when Mary leaned closer to the windscreen.

Mary glanced at the horn. "I guess you were right, Smith."

"Apology accepted."

Jacob couldn't quite make out what Mary said under her breath after that, but she pulled the levers down entirely for the throttle and locked several others to the side.

"Powering down. It may slow our departure, but it will conserve fuel to let the boilers go cold."

"We don't have a schedule on this, Smith, so I think it's for the best. Get changed into whatever you want to burn, and we'll meet you on the ground." Mary glanced back at Jacob and Alice. "You two have what you want to burn?"

Alice gestured to the torn gray dress she wore. The sides had been split and hemmed at the thigh for easier running, and it took a moment for Jacob to realize what it was.

"That's your dress from Ancora!"

She smiled. "It was. I guess it's changed a little."

It was a simple phrase, but it hit Jacob in the heart. "We all have." He chewed the inside of his cheek for a second before going on. "You know, these are the pants I had on in the Skeleton. Smith got most of the blood out." He traced the faded stains above the hem.

Mary's eyebrow slowly rose. "Grim, kid. I still say that's grim."

"They were already the right size, and we're just burning them, anyway. He had them in with the rags to clean up excess oil."

"They should burn very well, then." Alice bumped him with her shoulder and grinned.

"Bloody Ancorans," Mary muttered. "Make sure you have what you need. Let's go."

✧   ✧   ✧

"It's so … humid here." Jacob wiped sweat from his brow and glanced back at the Skysworn before focusing on the terrain again. He raised his hand in greeting as the three approached Mali. They were almost at the crawler before he realized Mali wasn't alone. Arun's Tree Killer sat on a branch above them, her rider nearly as invisible as she was.

"Welcome." Arun's voice sounded like deep thunder in the quiet of the clearing. "The mounts do not venture deeper. The remaining journey is up to your crawler, and your feet."

"Where do we need to burn our things?" Mary asked.

"Mali will show you. It is not a great distance into the woods."

Alice looked around the clearing, studying the same broken trunks and new growth that had caught Jacob's eye. "What happened here?"

"Old wars," Mali said, drawing everyone's attention. "You may see some of the wreckage as we make our way to the control center. There was a time more than Bollwerk flew monstrous airships."

"Older than the Deadlands War?" Alice asked.

Arun inclined his head. "I leave you in Mali's capable hands, friends. Drakkar sends his greetings. He is spending time in the stables, but I believe his bonding with the Tree Killers was a wise choice."

Smith reached out and squeezed Jacob's shoulder. "Still a little strange, is it not?"

"Yes," Jacob said, not hiding the hint of a nervous laugh. Even after riding on the backs of the silent beasts, the proximity could sometimes unnerve him.

Arun focused on Mary. "If you and your crew have need of a discreet place to hide, remember this clearing. Most from Karn avoid the borders of the Dead Woods, and no one outside of Karn knows of this place. Mali has food and water, but I suggest leaving the control center as soon as possible."

With that, they said a few informal goodbyes, and Arun ventured off to the northwest. The rest of them piled into the armored crawler with Mali, tucking their packs into the cargo bin between the rear treads.

She took the wheel, and Jacob tried hard not to laugh as Mary asked for the third time if she could drive.

"No," Mali said. "Maybe after you've seen the path. It's easy to get stuck if you don't know what to avoid."

Mary let out an exaggerated sigh. "Fine, be logical about it then."

"Was that … a joke?" Mali glanced at the trio in the back seat before blinking slowly.

Alice crossed her arms, barely fitting between Smith and Jacob as she met Mali's gaze. "I thought armored crawlers were supposed to have roofs."

Mali focused on the path ahead. "A few of them do, but I try to avoid them. Most people want them as protection from Acidwings."

"That would make good sense," Smith said.

"You might think so, but the roof gives the Acidwing a nice warm platform to stand on. You can probably guess what happens after that. So yes, I prefer no roof. They tend to avoid uneven perches like the seats and windscreen too. The Tree Killers will generally leave armored crawlers alone, and once we're inside the Dead Woods, well, you just don't need it after that."

Jacob leaned toward Alice and pointed to the south, focusing on a large clearing of the Gray Woods with ash and charcoal spread throughout. "What is that?"

"That's where we'll stop on our way back. There's a stream to run the crawler through if we get into anything, and a fire pit for the rest of our clothes. Hopefully, we won't run into any spores."

"Will you still take this crawler into the city?" Alice asked. "It seems like a risk, even if you submerge it in the water."

"I won't. The clearing where we met is as far as this crawler ever goes."

The armored crawler rattled across several ruts in the path before leveling out again. Mali concentrated on the narrowing path as the fire pit disappeared behind them.

Soon enough, the woods changed. The towering Forest Giants and their roots grew smaller, and the underbrush thicker. The bright greens and browns of the Gray Woods shifted into something more like their namesake—a grayish hue that sucked the color from the world.

"It's like everything is covered in ash." Alice leaned forward and held on to the back of the seat.

Mali pointed to the northeast, where sharp silhouettes towered from the forest floor. "Those are the remains of the old war."

Jacob couldn't make out much detail in the perpetual twilight of the forest, but the framework of a great airship was plain to see. A few tatters of cloth, or perhaps moss that had grown in sheets, fluttered slightly in the winds.

It reminded him of the Skeleton in some ways. Metal beams stretching toward the sky where they once glided through the air. Now, the Gray Woods were their tomb, and the old airship would never see outside of the shadows again.

"How old is it?" Alice asked.

"A hundred years or so," Mali said. "We aren't entirely sure, as the Dead Woods were already abandoned by the time that airship crashed here."

Mary studied the wreckage for a time before it was lost to the forest behind them. "We're in the Dead Woods now?"

Mali nodded.

"What's all the gray? Is it actually ash?"

"It may as well be. Dead spores and decay. You can't see it from the canopy. Some of our botanists believe that is because the wind prevents it from climbing higher."

Alice frowned at that. "You'd think if it was because of the wind, the spores would spread farther."

"The winds move southwest from the Gray Mountains and the Crystal Sea. Even if the spores rode the wind, they would be blown to sea. No spore survives the salt water."

Mali's gaze traveled up and away from the path. Jacob tried to follow, but only caught a glimpse of something pale and white in the canopy.

"We'll leave the crawler here." Mali centered the steering levers as the armored crawler slowed and eventually stopped. She powered the machine down and blew out a breath.

"How far is it?" Smith asked.

"Not far." Mali squinted into the distance. "Maybe a mile, at most. The path isn't even, so it may feel like more."

It felt wrong to leave their glider packs stowed on the armored crawler, but the less contamination they had to deal with from the spores, the better, according to Mali and Arun. There would be less exposure at the crawler, and it would be far easier to decontaminate them. And in regards to *that* particular issue, Jacob trusted them far more than anyone who wasn't from Karn.

But it meant he only had a small supply of Burners and Bangers, limited ammunition for the air cannon, and a handful of tools that fit in the pockets of his makeshift shorts and the leather bag strapped to his thigh.

"All I can think of is the Great Machine in the Deadlands." Alice adjusted the straps for the leather satchel on her hip. "Gliders were awfully helpful there."

"You won't need them here," Mali said.

"How can you be sure?"

Their guide looked back and smiled at Alice. "Great Machines are tall and imposing things. The control centers aren't. The tallest portion only has two levels."

"How many times have you been here?" Smith asked. "From what Arun told us, this area is restricted for almost everyone."

"It wasn't always, though." Mali gestured to the woods around her as she led the way past the gnarled roots of a Forest Giant. "And we've gotten much more thorough making sure we don't take spores back to the city."

Mary stepped over a tall knot in the roots at their feet. "Karn has been contaminated before?"

Mali nodded. "There have been a few instances. The worst required the burning of a farm and the surrounding woods, but it was eliminated. I'm glad I wasn't alive to see that."

She gestured to a sudden drop-off on their path. It wasn't a cliff, but the steep angle made the loose detritus of the forest floor quite treacherous.

Smith's steps slowed behind Mali. He let out a low whistle before pointing through a gap in the canopy of the valley.

"Almost there." Mali didn't slow down until she realized no one was following her. "You'll have a better view over the ridge."

Jacob studied the scene laid out before them. Even through the trees, the overgrown town was easy to pick out. The square buildings and squat structures had been overtaken by the forest, but more than the woods entombed the place. Gray carcasses stood sentinel along the trees and branches, more dense deeper in the canopy.

The crumbling exoskeletons of Tree Killers and Bombardiers, Sky Needles and Mantises, all frozen in time. Their bodies decaying as filaments of pale fungus shifted in the breeze above them. But it wasn't merely growing on the dead. It had penetrated them, broken them open like some jar of preserves that had gone bad and cracked its glass.

"That's why it's so quiet here?" Alice stepped ahead of Jacob and followed their guide down the second half of the incline.

Mali glanced up at the trees and dead bugs. "Yes. When they're close to dying, they climb. The few who have studied them believe they do that to spread the spores as far as possible. Like the fungus takes over the mind of its prey.

"Like a berserker," Smith said.

Mali's pace slowed for a moment. "The Biomechs from the Deadlands War? Yes, that's … that would be a good description. But here, the fungus ate everything it could. There are only the dead now."

Another few minutes of walking brought them into the small town. Every step sent up plumes of gray particles and dried leaves. The loudest sound was the breeze rustling the leaves above them, rivaled only by the crunch of each footstep.

Alice's voice, not much more than a whisper, sounded like a shout in the quiet. "This place is eerie."

Jacob shivered as they walked close to one of the desiccated husks of a Tree Killer. Two long fronds of yellow-gray fungus hung from its head where the eyes should have been. There was more color in that exoskeleton than the others he could see, and he carefully stepped away from it.

"Mali, some of these still have color." He pointed at the nearby Tree Killer.

She grimaced and looked around, but didn't slow her pace further. "It hasn't been dead as long as the others. A few weeks, if I had to guess."

"I thought this entire place was dead?"

"Apparently not."

Alice inspected the bolt cannon on her hip, removing the strip of ammunition before returning it and priming the slide. Next, she checked the bolt thrower on her wrist. It was an old model and couldn't carry as many bolts in a single bandolier, but it would do in a pinch.

Smith pulled the crossbow from his back while Mary did the same with a handheld bolt thrower. Mali only undid the straps on the long machetes she wore on either thigh, not drawing the blades.

Old brick peeked through the vines and growth encasing some of the small buildings. Dim light filtered through the canopy and reflected off dirty windows, startling Jacob on more than one occasion. Not all the city's buildings had survived. Piles of rubble formed irregular hills and barriers of broken debris.

The quiet followed them everywhere. They reached the next block, and there wasn't any question where they were going. At the end of the street, surrounded by the frozen forms of invaders and silent machinery alike, the largest structure in that place stood tall in the shadows of the Gray Woods.

If Jacob hadn't seen a Great Machine in person before, he could have mistaken the control center for one. It had the same shape, roughly a trapezoid with a few accents of metal protruding from the corners and tracing the lines of the roof.

A faint clicking echoed through the streets around them. Jacob turned to Mali with a question on his lips, but he wasn't the only one.

"What is that sound?" Smith asked.

Mali squinted at the canopy above them. "Bombardiers. Cannon Bugs, I think. They must be above the killing zone. I can't see them, but that's a pretty distinctive sound. Their mandibles click like that in warning. Let's get to the control center and out of their territory."

"How is any of this *their* territory?" Alice asked. "I thought everything was dead here."

"Eventually it is." Mali glanced back before increasing her pace toward the arched entryway of the control center. "And *eventually* doesn't always come as fast as we'd like. That's how the Dead Woods spread the most. Arun says it took years to destroy enough of the bugs on the border to contain it. Even now, it grows a little more each year. Let's get inside."

Mali led them to the front of the building. Crumpled metal sat before the door, long-rusted chains hanging from the top. Empty eyelets protruded from the wall above them, and Jacob figured it had once been a sign, something like what hung over The Fish Head in Bollwerk.

The wide door opened with a quiet squeak when Mali pulled on it. One thing that was far different about this control center from the Great Machine in the desert was the total lack of light. The open door illuminated a tiny slice of the interior. An old desk and coat rack waited beneath ages of dust, but the rest was left in darkness.

"Lanterns," Smith said. "It is black as pitch."

Jacob fumbled with the latch on his hip bag and pulled out the lantern and a vial of water. He unscrewed the lantern's top and poured the water in, waiting a moment to make sure it reacted as it should. Satisfied with the whisper-quiet bubbling, he screwed the top back on.

Alice already had her lantern ignited and was adjusting the reflector by the time Jacob finished clipping his to the strap for his air cannon. Smith was the last to join them, poking the hook for his own lantern through the fabric of his shirt so it swung loose as they walked.

Mali raised a different-looking lantern in her hand. It had a long handle, like a torch that belonged in a sconce, but Jacob was quite sure it would double as a weapon.

He swept his light across the room, focusing on the darker parts not touched by the others' lights, searching for anything useful. Old cabinets and decayed desks peppered the place, some overturned and broken, while a few looked as though they only needed a good dusting. On closer inspection, he realized those particular desks were metal.

The walls weren't overgrown like most of the town, but two dead Bombardiers lay crumbled in the corner of the room.

"Do you think the bugs overran the control center after it was abandoned?" Jacob asked. "Like they did with the Great Machine in the Deadlands?"

"There aren't many inside." Mali shined her lantern on the opposite wall, revealing a long stretch of a barren wall with little more than a broken corkboard and some rusted tools.

She guided the group forward, passing an empty stone pot as they approached another door.

"The Great Machine in the desert was raided and scavenged for decades." Smith leaned over a workbench beside the door. "It does not appear this facility succumbed to the same treatment."

Mali opened the door. Jacob expected the room to expand, to open into the full height of the trapezoid that formed the exterior. Instead, the hall ahead narrowed, lined with windowless doors and signs that had been broken or crumbled away.

A memory flashed through Jacob's mind: the old station beneath Ancora. Brittle flyers and postcards lining the walls of a place that had once been busy with life before it became a tomb. It was different here, to be sure, but it was almost worse in those cramped quarters of the control center.

Mali led them past door after door until they made it to the far end of the hall. Jacob and Alice both peered inside a few of the open doors. Nothing waited there but a bare ceiling and collapsed piles of what looked like little more than dust and splinters.

Beyond the hall, the room opened into a far wider space. Tiers of seats flowed out before them as if the place was a great theater or an arena. A stage of sorts waited at the opposite side, barely illuminated by the lanterns they carried, but it was enough to see it was no arena.

Each tier held desks and small booths lined with interconnected sockets and pins. Tubes like those Charles had designed as a smaller version of the city lights ran along several banks, some broken, some just dusty.

Jacob reached out and pulled one of the cables, the pin breaking off in the console and the wire's coating shattering, but the metal core was still pliable. "It's copper."

Smith disconnected another cable out and rubbed the coating off in his hand. He frowned and glanced around the room. "That is a great deal of wire. But why here?" He dropped the remnants on the table and started down the stairs, passing six tiers of desks before he reached the bottom.

Alice checked a drawer below the switchboard. "Paper. A lot of paper." She lifted a notebook with notes and symbols written across it in ink, carefully opening the front to reveal more of the same. "It's Standard and Mokuskrit mixed together. Reminds me of Yan Wu's manuscript, but different from what we saw in the Deadlands. It's holding together, too."

"Less exposure here," Mary said. "The ruins in the desert were open to the air for so long, it probably let in more moisture from the occasional desert rain."

Smith whistled, his gaze rising as he gestured for the others to join him. "Look at this. It is like an antenna for a transmitter. Just like the antenna Kura had in the school, in fact. But much taller, and much wider."

Mali stepped closer to it, studying the tightly wrapped and bundled wire where the outer coating had flaked away. "Do you think that's how they communicated with the Great Machine? Some kind of transmitter?"

Smith inclined his head. "It would appear so. I can hardly imagine wires long enough to reach past the Gray Woods and nearly to the northern seas. Look for manuals. They may be able to tell us more if they survived in this climate." He turned his attention to Mali. "Have you found any rooms here with maps on the wall? Maps made of metal?"

"Yes!" Mali's eyes brightened. "Follow me."

"Smith," Mary said as they started following Mali to the other side of the room. "The simple fact we found a manual in a map room at a different facility doesn't mean we're going to find one here."

"No, it doesn't." Mali pulled open the far door. "But there is a map room here. And there *are* more notebooks inside."

Smith grinned at Mary, who only narrowed her eyes in response.

The next hall looked like a photograph taken of another time. The dust and dirt so prevalent in the first hall and the adjoining rooms were minimal, the air stale like the deepest caves beneath Ancora. Jacob caught sight of a bookshelf in one of the rooms, filled nearly from floor to ceiling.

"Did you see that?" Alice asked. "There were books in that room."

"We can come back to it." Mali pushed her way through the door at the end of the hall and signaled for the others to follow.

Mary and Smith went first, followed by Alice and Jacob. They all froze inside that room.

Smith walked closer to the far wall as he spoke. "It is much like consoles at the Great Machine in the desert, yet different." He glanced at the wall, studying the small diagram etched into the metal. "And the map here is not nearly so grand."

Alice slowly turned, her light catching on banks of consoles filled with buttons and levers. "I'm rather fond of not having a thin glass wall separating us from a city's worth of sand and rock."

Mary tapped on a small black glass box set into a panel. "These what you were talking about, Smith?"

He stepped closer and pulled a bound manual from a shelf beneath the console. Age had yellowed the pages, but there was far more remaining than what had survived in the Deadlands.

Jacob hurried down the line of consoles, checking shelf after shelf and what few drawers there were set into the desks. More manuals turned up, but nothing else. Nothing but those same bound books over and over again.

"I hope those manuals have what we need," Jacob said. "If not … I don't see anything else." He frowned as Alice walked past him, dragging her fingers along the wall until she stopped and cast a smile over her shoulder.

She pulled on a recessed lever, and a door slid silently to the side, only shuddering slightly before clicking into place. "Your map room, Smith."

The older tinker abandoned the manual, instead hurrying across the room to join Alice.

"How did you know this was even here?" Mali asked. "There was nothing that *looked* like a handle. It took us ages to find it."

"It was the same in the Deadlands." Alice hurried to the console to the right of the map. It was nearly identical to the room they'd found the bodies in with Targrove. She pulled out a few folded pamphlets and one larger bound book.

"*Command Protocols.*" Alice said the title out loud as she set it on the corner of the console. She opened the book, the pages aged but still supple as she flipped through with purpose.

"What are you looking for?" Mary asked.

But Jacob knew what she was looking for. She wanted an answer about the Great Machines that no one had. And if this book was the same as what they'd found in the Deadlands …

Alice started to read aloud.

"The byproduct of removing the ore contaminants from bomb sites is an influx of oxygen. Studies have shown mutations in scavengers and a mass increase of nearly one hundred percent. If current trends continue, most vertebrates will be at risk of extinction as they are overtaken in the natural order of predator and prey.

"The alternative is unacceptable. There is risk with either approach, but inaction will cause the extinction of countless species. Should the toxins be allowed to age until they are no longer viable, estimated at several thousand years, far more than humans will die in the process. Enough that the toxins may cross the sea before they are fully neutralized.

"Our leaders are united in the decision to introduce new gases and compounds to eliminate the poison from our resources. The risks posed by the mutations are less severe than leaving the byproducts from the bomb sites to be nullified by age alone."

"There are photographs." Alice's voice was almost a whisper as she turned the pages for the others to see. A tiny Jumper, no bigger than a thumbnail in one, the size of a Cork ball in the next, and the palm of someone's hand in the last.

"The palm of your hand?" Smith said with wide eyes. "Those are the size of Jumper babies today. How fast did the world change after they built the Great Machines?"

"I don't know." Alice spun the book around and turned the page. Photos of Mantises and Giant Sticks gracing the pages. Past the photos waited another chapter. "The Great Machines in the sea are real." She leaned closer to Jacob and showed him the opening page. "At least one of them is."

He scanned it quickly, trying to absorb everything it said as fast as he could. There were few things as exhilarating as new discoveries in old books, and the feeling took him back beneath the streets of Ancora, back to Charles's old workshop, to the Crown Library in Belldorn, and even to William's shop in Ballern.

"The whirlpools are caused by the intake of water?" Jacob shook his head. "That's … how can that possibly be right? And if they're still operating under the sea, how long have they been there? Nothing can last centuries in salt water."

"Maybe they knew more than us," Mali said. "Maybe those machines aren't abandoned?"

Mary rubbed the back of her neck. "That's an unsettling thought. How could they live under the water all this time? The whirlpools aren't far from Ancora. Our fishing vessels would have seen something over the years."

"Mary's right." Smith blew out a breath. "Maybe we can learn more from these manuals, but it is possible the only manuals for the undersea Great Machines are buried beneath the water as well." His brow furrowed as Alice turned another page. "And it appears the last is across the Silver Gulf."

Mali ran her finger along the edge of the manual, slowly turning the pages when Alice pushed it toward her. "If the Great Machines were made to clean poison from the air, what happens if they stop working? I thought we were going to destroy it, but now I wonder if that could be worse."

Jacob walked down the console and started checking the low drawers and cabinets. "If they left one manual here, there might be more."

Alice stepped to the opposite side of the room and dug into the other workstations.

There wasn't much in the drawers except a few fountain pens that caught Jacob's attention. Some shone as if they were made of shells, while others felt dull and hard, like the gray stone they appeared to be. He pocketed six of them, curious if the old instruments had any insights to share, or possibly some value to take advantage of.

The last cabinet had what he was hoping to see. He pulled another copy of the manual out of the dark space and walked back to the center console. "Found another one."

But no one responded, and when he looked up, he understood why. Smith had one of the folded pamphlets opened, and at its full size, it spread some three feet wide by two feet high. The older tinker muttered to himself as his eyes raced across the expansive paper.

"It is a map of their entire system." Smith glanced between the etched metal on the wall and the map in his hand. "Look at the coordinates in the corner. This is a schematic detailing every system of the Great Machine from the Deadlands."

Jacob cursed and stepped closer, trying to comprehend every inch of the cramped diagram, but that would take hours of study. Maybe more.

Alice picked up another of the folded maps, this one a different color. Mary held one edge as Alice unfurled the other. The captain's finger traced the paper in the same place Smith had noted coordinates on the first map.

She frowned and looked to the side for a moment. "Smith, check these coordinates. I think this is in the Silver Gulf."

He leaned over and nodded. "It is. I suspect if we visit that exact location, we would be above one of the great whirlpools."

Alice abandoned the second map and grabbed another, only opening two of the folds to reveal the coordinates. She held it up to Mary. "What about this one?"

Mary's expression changed from a creased brow to a smile. "This is it. This is the map to the Great Machine of the Children of the Dark Fire." She folded the map of the Great Machine beneath the Silver Gulf back into a small pamphlet.

Jacob bounced on his heels. "Where do we start? We need to find every path in and out. If parts have collapsed like the Deadlands, we need alternatives. Those will be on this, right?"

"I do not yet know." Smith glanced at it and started folding his own map again. "There is more to the Great Machine in the Deadlands than I realized, and likely more to the home of the Children of the Dark Fire. Many resources buried under the sand that may be worth exploring. A wealth of copper, and if I am understanding their notations correctly, a large deposit of silver was being refined there. Along with several other compounds I do not recognize."

"Tell Jakon," Mary said. "He'll dig the place out with his bare hands."

"Perhaps when the war is done. Or if the factories need more resources before that happens."

Mary's lips flattened. "Smith, we're ending this war. If this conflict goes on long enough for us to establish a bloody mining operation, I expect we'll already be dead."

Smith made the last two folds in his map and sat it on top of Mary's. "A fair point, my friend. Let us not dwell on the darkest fates."

"Help me put it on the wall." Alice gestured for Jacob to follow her.

He wasn't sure what she meant by "put it on the wall" until she pulled some of the stubby gray cylinders off the metal etching and slid the map underneath. Jacob did the same, surprised at the power of the small magnets.

"What are these? Smith, we could use magnets like this as clasps on the exoskeletons. Feel these."

Alice almost huffed as the two tinkers huddled over a handful of the magnets. "Children, can I have your attention, please?"

Jacob blinked. "Oh, wow, you sounded like Miss Penny."

"That was the point." She gestured to the map as Smith grinned at both of them.

"Right, the map. Okay." Smith gave her his full attention.

With everyone gathered around it, the lanterns provided enough light to see every detail on the old paper. Smith traced a path with his finger, frowning when he reached a series of symbols before tracing the path back in the other direction.

"What is it?" Jacob asked.

"I am not sure." Smith tapped on another cluster of markings. "I believe we saw these same notations for one of the districts in the desert. Where much of the fuel was stored. But it would not make sense to have it contained next to corrosives, which I thought was this symbol."

"We don't know what's changed since these maps were made," Mali said. "How long has it been? A century? Two centuries?"

Smith grimaced. "You are correct, Mali. Even if we find an optimal path from these maps, there will likely be obstacles we cannot account for." He crossed his arms and leaned back, taking in a wider view of the schematics.

"Study it, see what you can find." Mary put her hand on Smith's shoulder. "You and Jacob know more about these symbols than the rest of us. Alice, Mali, look through the manuals. I'll check the other maps. We'll take everything with us when we're done."

"How many more maps are there?" Jacob asked.

"Two. One was nested inside another." Mary stepped away from the wall, and the light dimmed.

Jacob wasn't certain how long they should stay in the underground, but no one argued about it as the minutes grew into an hour, and they started to realize just how complex the construction of the Great Machines really was.

CHAPTER TEN

"ARE YOU SURE?" Jacob followed Smith's finger along the route he'd described.

"I am, yes. The only way these exhaust ports could be underneath the Great Machine is to be buried beneath it. But if they were surrounded by earth, any engine relying on them would overheat. Too much insulation. I am certain there are caves running under the Great Machines."

Jacob rubbed his chin. "You think Kat and Archibald could sneak forces in through the underground?"

"I highly doubt that, Jacob. Even if they could, it would only be infantry who could approach undetected. But for a small group to infiltrate the facility with the purpose of sabotage? It is a possibility."

"It's like Mali said, though, a lot has changed over the years since this map was made."

"We know some things." Smith tapped the lower right corner of the schematic. "There is no utility here for the town that has grown outside the Great Machine. They would need sewers at a minimum, and tinkers who are skilled enough to build the Great Machine likely incorporated water and any number of essential systems."

Jacob pointed to the lower left corner. "This was still woods, though. There was steam rising here, I'm sure of it."

"And if your memory is correct, then this vent is a probable source. It will need some kind of maintenance access. Whether that is from the ground, or from inside the machine, we cannot know."

"But we can find out." Jacob studied the topographic lines beneath the schematic, indicating a dip in the terrain, as if some massive sinkhole had swallowed a vast swath of land. "It shouldn't be too hard to find."

"Follow the steam."

Jacob took a deep breath. "I'm not excited at the idea of going underground again. This place is bad enough."

Mali cursed behind them and slammed her hand on the console beside the manual. "Here, look at this."

"What did you find?" Alice asked, hurrying over to Mali.

"The Great Machines were only supposed to run for fifty years to clean up the byproducts." Mali held her finger below the passage she'd been reading. "Fifty years? How long have they been running?"

"We don't know." Alice glanced up and met Jacob's eyes before focusing on the manual again. "Maybe shutting them down isn't as big a concern as we thought. We've found mention of them in manuscripts over a century old, and even then, no one seemed to know exactly when they started working."

"It's a shame we can't talk to the Children of the Dark Fire," Mary said. "Who knows how they've twisted the history of the Great Machine, but it's possible some of them know more than the rest of the world."

Smith grimaced and turned back to the map. "Possible, but they have sunk too far into their own rhetoric now."

Jacob tried to remember what they'd found in the Crown Library. "One of the Mokuskrit titles Furi translated, right?"

Alice nodded. "It wasn't a lot about it, but there was an interview with an old hermit in the woods who swore the Great Machine had been active his entire life."

"The book was almost a hundred years old, and if the hermit was anywhere close to that …"

"Exactly. The Great Machines have been running for centuries. Far longer than they were ever supposed to. But why didn't the mutations get worse? The invaders we know now have been the same for as long as anyone can remember. It's not like Sky Needles and Red Death and Widow Makers have gotten larger."

Smith slowly turned to the group. "It is possible that is because the Great Machine in the desert was destroyed. Or perhaps a saturation point was reached, and no matter how many of those facilities remain active, the world has found a different balance than the builders intended."

"We're just guessing." Jacob squeezed his forehead. "I don't think we'll ever know."

"We need to go." Mary pinched the bridge of her nose. "We need food, and I want to be back in Karn before nightfall."

Mali closed the manual and tucked it into a leather satchel. "Are you sure you don't want to explore the deeper levels?"

Smith shook his head. "Our cursory exploration was enough. If Alice wants to take a few more of the books we saw in the hallway, we should stop there."

"Yes." Alice beamed at Smith. "Just a few, if they're interesting, of course. It might just be some old tinker's journals, and who'd be interested in those?"

Mary chuckled and slapped Smith on the back, clearly amused with the stunned expression on his face.

ONE THING JACOB hadn't expected to find in the old bookshelf was a collection of flyers. Advertisements for what appeared to be some kind of traveling theater troupe, and another for musicians, illustrated with strange-looking lutes and drums.

He took one of the binders, as it was certainly an interesting piece of history, even if it wasn't the most revolutionary information they'd stumbled across in their research.

Alice was far more practical. Beside the collection of advertisements were a few children's schoolbooks, and she grabbed all three.

Smith crouched by the short bookcase and glanced at Alice. "You are taking after Mary."

Alice grinned as the tinker pulled two journals from a different shelf, flipping through the pages to reveal faded handwriting swarmed by diagrams and formulas. Smith handed them to Jacob, and he tucked them into the leather satchel with one copy of the manual.

Jacob wasn't exactly sure how much they'd taken, but the shelves were certainly less dense than when they'd first arrived, and their bags were far heavier. It wasn't until they exited the room and walked back into the cavernous space with the stage that the silence of the place fell around them again like a weight.

Smith's lantern flickered, and he shook it to stabilize the flame. "I do not have much more time on my lantern."

"Mine's already out." Mary shook hers and rolled the striker, but other than sparks, no light rose in the reflector. "Let's hurry. I have no desire to be trapped here in the dark."

They passed the tiers of consoles with wires and ports exposed to nothing but the dark. Smith took the lead at the top of the stairs, apparently confident enough in his memory of the path to the front of the facility. The thought almost made Jacob laugh when he remembered it was nearly a straight line, so long as they didn't turn through any of the flanking doors.

They were nearly back to the lobby when the first sound reached Jacob's ears. It wasn't loud, or shrill, but a faint scrape along a rough surface.

"Did you hear that?" Jacob asked.

Alice nodded and swept her lantern across the last two rooms. Nothing waited in the shadows but dust and the crumbling shells of the dead.

"Wait," Mali said. They stood silent for a minute, until Smith's lantern finally gave out, and the light in the hall dimmed a little more. "Don't worry. I have enough fuel for two days. You should all carry larger lanterns."

Mali stepped around Smith and took the lead. She reached out to open the door and paused. "You're going to see something when I go through the door. I need to check the rafters to make sure nothing followed us in. It's … it's pretty bad, okay? Just prepare yourself."

Jacob couldn't imagine what Mali was talking about. They'd come through the lobby. They'd seen what little was left to see, but had he ever looked up? Had any of them?

The moment Mali crossed through the doorway and raised her light, Jacob knew very well that none of them had glimpsed what waited in that place. Bugs weren't the only corpses in that tomb. The people were on the level above them, sprawled across a glass floor so their empty sockets could stare into the dark for all time.

Gray and white filaments spread all around them, some clearly the lifeless husks of invaders, swallowed by the fungus that had consumed the Dead Woods. But it didn't grow through the skeletons of the dead, only wrapped around them after devouring the bugs.

Frozen swords and makeshift clubs shone in Mali's light, some so rusted and corroded only an outline remained, like a stain flowing across the glass. Nothing moved but the darkness as Mali shifted her focus, tracing the full scope of horror that lingered above them.

She took a shallow breath and nodded, leading the way to the front door. Jacob glanced back once, realizing that the second floor had indeed been hidden behind an opaque wall when they'd first walked inside, a staircase in the far corner the only hint of what might wait above. Mali might have tried to spare them from the sight, but there was no forgetting that vision now.

The scraping grew louder as they regrouped outside, almost vibrating the air as they blinked in the filtered sunlight while their vision returned. It was then that he saw it. Not in the shadows of the lobby, but in the darkness of the path formed by a fallen tree and the wall of the control center.

Jacob's voice was almost a screech as he whipped the air cannon off his back, jostling his lantern so hard the light went out. "What is that!"

It moved like the larvae of a Shadowwing, its thick, wrinkly body compressing and expanding toward them, pudgy legs scraping the earth, but it wasn't alone. The jagged mandibles in the pale fleshy head writhed and scissored closed beside more of the graying worms.

Jacob counted five of the grotesque forms, three on the earth with two others piled on top of them, but the cluster moved as one, moved far faster than it should have been able to. A stuttering, grating cry echoed out from the ball of flesh before it crossed fully into the light, as if it had sighted them, or smelled them.

"Oh gods, they're ... *connected*," Alice hissed.

Gray and red columns grew from the sides of the worms, thick enough to be saplings until they twisted together, binding one life to another, while more tendrils dragged the dead behind it.

Jacob leveled his air cannon, and Mali almost tackled him.

"No! Acidwing larvae. You'll kill us all! Run!"

"Throw a Burner!" Smith shouted.

Jacob stowed the cannon and pulled out a pair of Burners in two quick motions. He tossed one to Smith before clicking the igniter on his own. They didn't stay to watch what happened, only hurled the orbs at the creatures stalking toward them, and ran.

It took everything he had not to look back when the shrill screeching rose in intensity. Jacob stayed with Alice as best he could, focusing on one step and then the next. So much that he missed the scythe of the Tree Killer striking from the shadowed alley nearby.

Mary didn't miss it. Her sword flashed up, breaking through a brittle carapace and sending an arc of greenish-blue blood against the rubble it was hidden on. Inertia kept the scythe moving, but its aim was wrong, grazing the thick leather of Jacob's sling instead of taking his arm off.

Mary dove to the side as another scythe reached for her, and Jacob's air cannon thundered through the Dead Woods. The sickly filaments growing from the Tree Killer's head exploded in a rain of chitinous gore.

They ran. They ran until it felt like their lungs might catch fire. Until their feet would collapse into nothing but blisters and worm flesh. Only when the thick gray coating of the Dead Woods thinned and the stream came into view did their pace slow.

"Wait." Mali gasped for breath and leaned against the roots of a Forest Giant. "Stop, can you hear anything?"

They stood in that place for a minute until they could listen past their own labored breathing. The woods were quiet once more. No sound followed nearby except the distant click of something in the dead city.

Mali started toward the crawler. "Get in. We get cleaned up, and we get away from this damned place."

No one argued. No one said a word as the visions of that place screamed through their memories. They rode in silence as the horror of the Dead Woods fell farther behind them. In time, Mali angled for a steep decline that ended in another stream.

"Anything you don't want wet, hold it up. We're going through the salt water to clear the spores."

Part of Jacob wondered if the boilers for the armored crawler were at risk in the shock of cold water, but he supposed the tinkers of Karn had long come up with a solution for that. He didn't focus on the question for much time, instead shivering as he remembered the sight of that cluster of larvae.

The nose of the armored crawler submerged entirely. Mary squeaked as the stream crested the door to the crawler, flooding the floor and seats with clear water. It certainly wasn't warm, and Jacob shivered as the crawler exited the opposite bank of the stream.

The trees immediately showed more color. Less of the gray ash and dead spores lingered on the trunks. More Forest Giants came into view, and around another bend in the stream, Mali slowed the armored crawler to a stop.

They were on the far side of the firepit now. Cold, wet, and Jacob couldn't wait to see a towering flame ignited in that pit.

"Fire, please." Alice's teeth chattered as she spoke.

Mali hopped out and grabbed one of the enormous dry leaves of a Forest Giant. She crumbled it into a pile of tinder as the others followed her. A short time later, she pulled a striker and flint from a patched pocket on her pants and threw sparks across the tinder.

Jacob was about to ask if she wanted a Burner to start the fire, but the pile of crumbled leaves started smoking before he could get the question out. Mali gathered a handful of the detritus in her hands and blew on the coals. The smoke twisted and thickened, obscuring her face entirely before flames burst out of the tinder.

She set it back into the brush as the rich scent of burning wood and leaves reached Jacob's nose. Once the flames grew larger, Mali gently pushed the rest into the firepit with her boot. The stack of wood and tinder below caught fire in seconds, and Mali brushed her hands off.

Jacob looked at Mary. "Thank you, for that."

She nodded. "And you. Fine shot with the air cannon."

"What was that thing?" Smith asked.

"I've heard stories." Mali rubbed her hands together. "The fungus gets into a nest and grows between whatever's living there. Takes longer to kill some of them. That's why they were dragging … well, you saw the rest."

Alice shook her head. "I wish I hadn't seen the rest."

"I know." Mali pointed to the stream running against the rear of the firepit. "The water slows down here. If you give it a few minutes, the stream will warm. Not like a hot spring, of course, but better than a mountain spring, I'm sure."

"How does the water kill the spores?" Smith asked.

"It flows through the old salt mines. There's a lake several miles to the southwest that is so dense with salt almost nothing lives in it."

"Inside the forest?" Alice asked. "I've heard of places like that in the desert, but not a forest."

"It used to be the forest, but it's not anymore. Everything's dead there. Even the trees. And those collapse from time to time. It's not a safe place to go." Mali paused. "Probably not as dangerous as today, though."

Jacob scratched the back of his head. "I've had enough visits to unsafe places for the day."

A small grin flashed across Mali's face. "When you're ready, place what you want to keep inside the hotbox." She pointed to the wide metal cube set in the edge of the firepit. "Any spores will be killed, but anything sensitive to heat may be damaged."

"Why don't you just place your clothes in it?" Alice asked. "That would seem less wasteful than burning everything."

Mali shook her head. "Too many accidents. We burn woven fabric because the heat of the box can be too much and cause a fire. Leather you can put in the hotbox, but everything else needs to burn."

Jacob stood in front of the open box with the manual from the control center and the leather satchel he'd worn into the Dead Woods. "Are you sure this isn't going to set the books on fire? I'd hate to lose these."

"You aren't the first one to bring a book out of the old city." Mali held up her own copy of the manual and placed it inside. "Keep the books and maps toward the front. I'm sure it wouldn't be good for them if you did this several times, but I've never seen anything catch fire myself."

Smith crouched and slid his own gear into the hotbox, careful to keep the crossbow close to the books so the string wouldn't come undone. "Maybe you should call it the lukewarm box."

Mali blinked slowly. "What?" It may have been a one-word response, but she dragged it out like a sentence.

"I am surprised it is not hotter."

"It will be."

Smith brushed his hands off as he stood up, making for the crawler, where he stripped out of his shirt and started unbuckling his pants.

Mary sighed and turned to Mali. "You get used to him. After a while." She put her leathers in the back of the hotbox, swords pointed toward the farthest end, and Jacob was surprised to see they had room to spare.

"Where should we put the air cannons?" Alice asked.

Jacob rubbed his chin before lifting the sling for his air cannon from his shoulders. "I don't think it should matter either way. Just make sure the chamber is vented so it doesn't overpressurize."

The metal on the far side of the gray box started to change color. Jacob checked the temperature on the hotbox. "Ten degrees to go yet."

"It should be good in less than a minute." Mali scratched at her wrist. "We're extra cautious with the spores, and that will be enough to kill them."

"A few more minutes will not harm any of us," Smith said. "We may be in a hurry, but we are not in so much of a rush that we will put your city at risk."

Jacob started to place the thigh bag inside, hesitated, and took out the last remaining Burner first. The Bangers had a high tolerance for heat, but Burners could be set off at far lower temperatures.

"Throw it in the fire," Smith called out.

Jacob made the mistake of looking toward the older tinker. "What are you *wearing?*"

Smith glanced down at the short leather briefs before shrugging. "Best to be prepared if you have to burn anything made from fibers. What did you wear?"

Jacob's eyes widened as the realization struck he hadn't brought *anything* to replace the clothes he had to burn. At least, not until he'd washed himself clean of any spores before retrieving the change of clothes in full.

Smith started to laugh, but the sound changed quickly to a cough when Mary shot him a glare.

"Are Ancorans uncomfortable with nudity?" Mali's brow furrowed. "We have public baths in Karn, so it is not so unusual. I hadn't thought to ask."

"We can take turns," Jacob said. "It's fine, really."

Mary scoffed. "We're in a hurry, kid. You want another giant ball of fungus-fused worms to catch us? Me neither. Get in the water."

Smith growled as he stepped down into the stream. "Do you have *any* idea what a pain it is to get saltwater out of biomechanics? My chest is going to be grinding and clicking for days. At least Jacob can simply soak his leg."

"I'll drop you in a nice lake." Mary grinned when Smith scowled at her.

Alice lifted the hem of her dress and pulled the entire garment off in two quick motions. Jacob's heart thudded in his chest and he started to turn away until he caught sight of the leather beneath. His jaw slackened as he realized he was the only one who hadn't thought to wear anything leather under his clothes.

"That's a fantastic bathing costume, Alice." Mary gave her a small clap and gestured to the stream. "Let's get in before Jacob gets any more uncomfortable."

He looked after the pair as they walked away. Both were clad in shorts and a wide top that would have passed for the standard apparel for a Cork tournament in the Lowlands, especially when the high summer heat threatened to roast anyone who dared step into the sun.

Mali, despite her declaration of comfort when it came to nudity, wore shorts of a fabric Jacob couldn't identify. She either *had* considered the rest of them might not be as comfortable, or it was custom to wear something into the stream. Regardless, her garment didn't look like leather, and he suspected it would hold up much better than his friends' clothes. At least he wouldn't have to worry about that. He blew out a breath and stared at the firepit.

Smith called out from the stream. "Come on, Jacob."

Jacob stepped behind the hotbox where no one would be able to see him directly. He sighed, stripped out of his clothes, and tossed them into the fire. He watched, somewhat longingly, as his only hope of modesty turned to ash in the flames.

With strategically placed hands, he wandered over to the bank of the stream, away from his friends.

"That's going to be cold!" Mali shouted, but the warning came a little too late.

He hit the water, and it leeched the warmth from his bones like ice. Needles of cold penetrated his skin, and he could already feel his teeth chattering by the time he remembered to swim. All thoughts of modesty gone, he swam as fast as he could to the small alcove with the others.

The change in the water temperature came immediately, heat flooding his limbs where ice had been moments before. He paddled his way past the others, as close to the metal wall of the firepit as he dared. Relief flowed through him before he heard Alice.

"Nice butt."

Jacob flailed as he spun around, laughter filling the woods nearby as the fire crackled behind them. The change in demeanor came so fast and so sudden he almost forgot how embarrassed he was in the moment. A laugh was all they needed as they escaped the horror of the Dead Woods. And embarrassment was a price he was willing to pay.

CHAPTER ELEVEN

BADDAWICK STOOD ATOP the Lowlands wall, the airship docks spread out before him as people moved in and out of the area. Cage had taken it upon himself to set up defenses around the docks, and while part of Baddawick thought it was a step too far, another part of him knew preparedness was often the best solution in any battle.

He turned away from the bustling docks, facing the mountain peaks to the east. The valleys stood wide enough to show the Silver Gulf at the height of the new walls, and the view beat anything the Highlands Walls could offer. The irony of it all amused Baddawick. He had little doubt there would be Highlanders building tall homes in the Lowlands soon.

Rough seas sent bursts of white into the air, and Baddawick could only imagine how large the waves on the rocky shore must be. Footsteps caught his attention a moment before a voice called out.

"Baddawick!"

He looked for the Speaker, finding Cage and Nora stepping onto the wall at the nearest stairs. Baddawick raised a hand in greeting before brushing the hair from his eyes in a sudden breeze.

"What news, Cage?"

"We need railings on all of these stairs if we're going to leave them exposed." Cage gestured to the narrow staircase they'd ascended. "One accident is enough."

Baddawick inclined his head. "I heard about the mason on the south wall. Is he recovering?"

"He has a long road ahead of him," Nora said. "But the outlook is good."

The old tinker rubbed his beard. "Take some of the dowels from the latest shipment. We won't need them for quite some time, and while they may be narrow, they'll make a better railing than nothing."

Cage turned against the wind, stepping closer to Baddawick. "That is appreciated. As to your question, I'm sure you weren't wondering about the railings."

"No, though that is good to hear it will be addressed. I was hoping we'd have the new spiral staircases built before anything happened, but that was a mistake."

"The meeting?" Cage asked after a brief pause.

"Yes."

Cage gestured to Nora. "She spoke to more families than I did."

"I don't see what difference that makes." Nora turned her attention to the old tinker. "Most of the families will be there tonight. Only a few were contrarian about it, but even they'll be attending. I'm sure they want their voices heard."

"Good, that's good." Baddawick crossed his arms. "I'll have the chefs make something nice. Easy, not too messy, as we may be short on dishes."

"You're sure about this?" Cage asked. "I don't think a nice snack is going to change many minds about being sure Biomechs are welcomed in Ancora."

"That's only part of it." Baddawick's posture relaxed, and his usual smile returned. "I know how to give people what they want. And I know how to make them *think* they want something. Combine the two, and, well, you can accomplish a great many things, can't you?"

"You should have been in politics, old man," Nora said.

"In another life, I was, Nora. A life I'd prefer not to see return. Hence, our meeting at the Wildhorse tonight. The new Parliament must forge its own path, but for the sake of all our friends and family, a little guidance is in order."

A small frown crossed Cage's face, but he didn't protest. Baddawick thought he might know why. Cage had seen firsthand the destruction of Dauschen, and the aftermath of the Fall of Ancora. Cage's own cousin, his family, from Fel. Should they be forced out of Ancora, Cage might not have a choice but to follow them to a new home. Loyalty was a complicated thing when it was stretched in multiple directions.

Nora pulled out a tarnished pocket watch to check the time. "You have two hours."

Baddawick bounced on his heels. "Well, we best be off then! Come, join me for a drink while we prepare for the evening's crowd."

Cage blew out a breath before raising an eyebrow and looking at Nora.

"It *has* been a long day." She closed her pocket watch and slid it home. "Let's go."

✧   ✧   ✧

TO SAY THE chefs were stressed when Baddawick had the brilliant idea to wrap hundreds of sausages inside thin pastries and bake them off would be discounting their panic. He had spent the better part of fifteen minutes convincing them they could get the food ready in the two-hour allotment he'd given them.

Those two hours had vanished faster than he would have liked. Baddawick made his way to the rear bar, not far from the piano. Cage and Nora chuckled with the bartender about something, and that was a welcome sight indeed.

Raucous laughter and loud conversations were the order of the evening in the Wildhorse. He'd given the people enough extra time to arrive, and if they weren't there yet, they likely weren't coming.

Baddawick raised his hand to attract the attention of the gathered families and leaders. He'd grown used to speaking in front of large gatherings long before he owned the Wildhorse. It was a matter of patience, or a matter of yelling louder than everyone else.

From time to time, he wasn't bothered by yelling or whistling to get a room's attention, but his throat was sore from the constant meetings and strategy sessions of the past week. Today called for patience for other reasons as well. Changing minds was a delicate thing. The front rows quieted first, one or two turning to silence the groups beside them until that quiet rolled out like a dropped jar of screws.

"Thank you all for attending today. There aren't a great deal of things to cover, but there *are* some essentials that even our new Parliament has been slow to address." Baddawick nodded to the Anders and Ms. Morrow, Alice's mother, seated in the first row. He'd spoken to them beforehand, during one of his many meetings that week, and they expected to be called upon.

Baddawick set his focus along the back row, filled with Spider Knights and City Knights alike, now united under a single banner. None of them wore armor at the Wildhorse, but something in their eyes told of the things they'd seen. It was a look, a stare of loss and hardship that he'd seen often in the Deadlands War. That he'd seen on the face of his brother before the end.

And that thought almost curled Baddawick's lip. That memory of the judgment handed down to his own blood because of what he was. And that was the reason Ancora had to change. His voice rose, and the pain in his throat mattered little against the purpose of what needed to be said.

"We've discussed a great many changes that must happen inside the walls of Ancora. Changes to help ensure no one like Newton ever rises to power again. The balance of power must remain checked, split between our organizations, reviewed by our people. It will be a long road, but we have more allies outside Ancora than we have ever had before."

A modest round of applause went up, and Baddawick silenced it with his next words.

"We owe a great deal to the Biomechs."

The clink of glass sounded like thunder in the silence as a bartender worked on loading one of the small trains that ran along the Wildhorse.

"Yes, consider that for a moment. Where would we be without them? Where would we be without Jacob Anders and his friends? Many of them are Biomechs themselves. Many more helped refine the Biomechs and knew berserkers in the Deadlands War."

"That's why they're a poison!" one of the City Knights shouted.

Baddawick didn't care who spoke. He'd been waiting for it, waiting to strike as the outrage swelled among some attendees.

"My brother Killian was a Biomech!" Baddawick roared, his throat burned like the searing heat of a boiler held to his flesh. "He died after the Deadlands War. After Targrove saved him. Yes, *that* Targrove. I see your faces. You know the stories of that legendary tinker. Killian died serving this city! He died saving lives in the fire brigades. Without him, half the water you enjoy in this city would be stagnant, and half the homes you live in would have long burned to ash."

Baddawick's voice quieted, the shout no longer needed in the stunned silence of the City Knights. "And if we had one single doctor we could have trusted, he might have survived the blasted infection that stole him from us. But my own family cast him out. Their only *favor* to him a promise not to reveal he was a Biomech. They never came to see him in the weeks leading up to his death. And I never spoke to them after that. Remember this story when you look down on Biomechs. Remember what they've done. Remember why we need them."

Jacob's dad stood, and the hairs along Baddawick's arms bristled with the thrill of it. It didn't matter that he knew the words to come. He knew the bravery it took to say what had to be said.

"My son is a Biomech." Many in the room knew that already, but gasps and a handful of exclamations still echoed out. "He designed the cranes that rebuilt our walls, that raised the Lowlands higher than they've been before. He saved our city in more ways than he will ever know. He has friends who are Biomechs, knows tinkers who build and maintain them, who keep his leg working.

"You all knew Charles. He worked with Biomechs from the Deadlands War and beyond, and it was only with his help that Jacob survived. He gave his *life* to save my boy! I will always treasure that old man because of it. Only with his help did Jacob rid us of the Butcher. Without him, we'd be nothing more than a shadow of Fel."

His lips quivered. "And without Jacob's thievery, I would have died! The mines didn't pay me enough for medicine. I looked away when he stole from some of you because to do otherwise was to let myself die. And what kind of life is that? Who of you wants that for your families? Steal or die. It's no way for anyone to live." His voice quieted. "It's no way for anyone to die."

"So we change!" Baddawick stepped forward and put his arm around the man he was proud to call a friend. "We change the balance between the Lowlands and the Highlands. We take care of our people. The citizens of Ancora are our *strength*. Without our neighbors, our walls will fall."

A rumble started in the audience, whispers of agreement. Whispers of anger.

"If the Speaker of Bollwerk and the Lady of Belldorn can form an alliance to chase Mordair across the Crystal Sea, then *we* can rebuild Ancora better than it's ever been." Baddawick gestured for the bartenders to start delivering drinks to the room.

"So I ask you to raise a glass. To stand with me. To stand with our Biomech brethren, our friends from Cave, our allies from Dauschen, and our refugees from Fel. Stand together, and we will prevail." Baddawick held his glass high in the air, and his voice cracked with anger. "Stand together until we stand on the grave of Gregory Mordair!"

The room shook with cries and shouts, with sworn oaths and pledges to do something, to be better. But Baddawick didn't miss the raised glasses and nods of Cage, Nora, and Ambrose near the back wall. Relief flowed through him even as the surge of adrenaline still racked his body. He had no doubt those three were also keys to the future of Ancora.

CHAPTER TWELVE

ALICE TRIED TO focus on the manual while they flew back to Ballern, but it was hard to concentrate after the chaos of the day before. They hadn't spent a single night in Karn after their journey through the Dead Woods, which meant Ballern wouldn't be in the windscreen until well after dark.

Jacob, on the other hand, snored beside her on their bed. She finally gave up, closed the book, and gently stepped over him, trying not to disturb the covers or the folded pillow he'd wedged under his head. Considering the snoring didn't change, she counted it as a success and padded over to the coat hooks by the hatch. Bundled up in a leather jacket, she opened the hatch just a hair and slipped through.

Alice made her way into the hall and followed the corridor down to Smith's workshop. The tinker had his head so far into the pipes she could barely see his waist. She didn't say anything, not wanting to startle him, and instead headed for the next corridor, past the gun pod, and up the ladder to the deck.

It wasn't as cold as she'd feared, but the wind still howled as she clipped onto the safety lines and closed the hatch behind her. She stood there for a time, listening to the gale in the dark and watching the pinpoints of light and great seas of stars float by overhead.

When the chill started to penetrate her jacket, she finished the trek across the deck, stepping inside the cabin and slamming the door as it fought the wind.

"Alice?" Mary raised an eyebrow. "What are you doing awake? And up here?"

"I don't know. I was trying to translate some more of the Mokuskrit, but I can't concentrate." She hesitated and then blurted out what had been gnawing at her. "Do you really think the photos of the maps Mali took will be enough for Karn?"

Mary turned back to the dark windscreen. "I'm sure Arun would have said something if they wouldn't be. Once we get them to Kat, she can have them replicated in short order. And Smith gave Mali another transmitter. She'll contact us if there's an issue."

"I guess."

"That's it? That's all that has you awake?"

"Jacob was snoring pretty loud."

Mary chuckled. "It's usually you who's snoring."

"I doubt that." She stared off out the starboard window. "Although my mom *does* snore, too."

Mary cast her a grin. "Don't worry about it. You can spend as much time in the cabin as you'd like."

Alice pulled up a jump seat and settled in. If she could get a few more passages translated, it might give them a better idea what some of the symbols on the maps meant. Or it might be up to Smith or Jacob to figure it out, since the tinkers used similar drawings in their schematics, and that gave them some context to start with.

"I keep thinking about what Smith said."

When she didn't elaborate, Mary turned to look at her. "About what?"

Alice glanced away from the string of characters that looked familiar but weren't quite Mokuskrit. "About the exhaust ports being something like the Great Machines would require. How there must be a cave system, or at least a tunnel carved out for maintenance."

Mary shrugged and focused on the Skysworn's controls. "Smith makes a lot of assumptions, Alice. Granted, he's right quite often, but he's also very, very wrong on occasion."

"We all are." Alice frowned and turned the page, finding another passage that was a blend of Standard and Mokuskrit she could actually read. She still needed to reference some of the translations from the Crown Library, but she could get through it.

Over the hours, Alice took to searching for specific words. Any mention of tunnels or caves she could find was where she stopped to translate the passages in the manual. It was slow going, and not every symbol had a match in her references, but she hoped Furi would be able to help with that.

She wasn't sure how much time had passed by the time her eyelids grew heavy, and she started to slouch in the jump seat, but being suddenly slammed into the harness certainly did the job of waking her up. Alice found the manual strapped onto the jump seat beside her, which she was quite sure hadn't been pulled up when she dozed off.

"Thrusters off, stowing them now," Smith called over the horn.

Alice blinked. If they were cooling and stowing the thrusters, that could only mean … "Are we at Ballern already?"

Mary glanced back. "We are indeed. I strapped the manual in before you could drop it. Or at least, I thought you might drop it. You had an iron grip on that book, even dead asleep."

Alice rubbed her eyes before wincing and taking some time to stretch her neck. She unbuckled her harness and stepped up beside Mary. Lights ran all along the docks, even in the dead of night. It gave Ballern a timeless glow, perhaps even more than Bollwerk. They didn't have much choice, she supposed. If there weren't lights of some sort there, airship travel could never continue throughout the night, and wayward vessels could crash into the sprawling docks' lines and supports.

The darkness on one half of the docks gave her their orientation. The absence of the Bones felt like a weight on her chest, and she could scarcely imagine how Furi and the other Skyborn felt. But there was a bond in that horror, a memory of the Fall, and an oath to stop a king's atrocities. It was a small light, a small thing to grasp in such terrible times, but Alice needed to hold onto it. They all did.

"What time is it?" Alice asked.

"Dawn soon. If Furi is anything like Jakon, I suspect they'll both be up and plotting by now. You could still get some sleep?"

Alice looked back at the manual. Thin strips of paper poked out the top, marking passages she thought might hold some promise. She needed Furi.

Apparently, that look told Mary all she wanted to know. "Smith, we're docking in the west, at Jakon's usual haunt."

"Understood."

"And wake Jacob up if he isn't already. I doubt he'll want to miss Alice's sudden departure when we land."

Alice grinned at Mary. "I'm going to shower. I still feel itchy from the salt water."

"Imagine how I feel," Smith grumbled over the horn. "I need someone to run a toothbrush over my biomechanics. They'll be gritty for days."

✧　✧　✧

SHOWERED, SOMEWHAT RESTED, and very excited, Alice practically dragged Jacob off the Skysworn the moment he finished tying his boots. She didn't give him a chance to do anything more than rinse off in the shower, and even then, she pestered him about how much longer he would be. Alice almost felt bad about that, given he was rinsing the salt out of his biomechanics again, but like Mary said, that would last a while.

Their boots hit the ramp, and they were back on Ballern's docks before the sun had fully risen. Alice kept the leather satchel with the manual and the maps held tight to her chest. Nothing was going to happen to those documents while they were in her care.

They passed The Ray, and she glanced at the windscreen to see if there was any sign of Jakon on the ship. Only darkness waited in the bay. She led Jacob to the lift, the lattice rattling closed behind them before Alice hit the switch for the second level.

It might have been a short ride, but that didn't stop her from tapping her foot.

Jacob rubbed at his eyes and yawned. "Alice, what are we doing?"

"Going to see Furi. I told you that." Maybe he wasn't quite as awake yet as Alice had thought.

"I know, but why?"

The lift stopped and Alice pulled the gate open, ushering Jacob out before leading the way into the district of small warehouses and storage flats. "I found some passages in the manual about the tunnels."

"Under the Great Machine?" Jacob suddenly sounded much more alert, which was typical, if Alice was being honest. The moment something interested him, his mind latched onto it, no matter the state of his sleep.

"Yes. But some passages are Mokuskrit, and others are that other language I don't recognize. Maybe she can help." Alice trailed off as they turned down the street that would take them to the small warehouse. "I hope she can help."

One more block put them in front of the door of the new Stormborn base. That's what it was now, Alice knew. Furi and Kura might have helped recruit the Skyborn to their cause, but they were all Stormborn now. With the risks and danger that came with it.

The thought caused her to flex her fists before grabbing the doorknob and twisting. She'd been worried it would be locked, that *this* would be the day Furi decided to sleep later than usual, and what if she wouldn't have her transmitter on, and what if that delay would give Mordair the upper hand he needed? But those thoughts crumbled away when the door opened onto a room bathed in lantern light.

Furi looked up from the small desk in the corner, her frown lightening into surprise and then a broad smile. "Alice, Jacob! What are you doing here?" She set her pen down and stepped from behind the desk, hurrying to embrace both of them.

Alice glanced around the room, surprised at how much larger the space felt than what Furi had described. "This is nice."

"After a lot of work, sure. There were boxes and crates for the school here that … well, we'll find a new place for them. It still isn't big enough for the kids. They're all attending classes with the earthers for now. William presented the idea and without the royals to protest, the kids were welcomed."

"That's a good problem for a lot of reasons," Jacob said. "Harder to hate an entire caste if you're friends with some of them."

Furi let out a long breath. "Yes, it is."

Alice walked over to the desk and started unpacking her satchel. "This is why we're here, Furi. I don't want to rush you or push you so early in the morning, but we found a manual and some maps in the control center for the Great Machine."

"You went into the Dead Woods?" Her voice rose as the surprise bled through into her words. "That place is … no one goes there."

"Karn does on occasion. Mali guided us."

Furi shivered. "No thank you. What about the spores?"

"Killed by heat and salt water. Something we wouldn't have known without Karn." Alice nodded as she set the manual on the desk, followed by the folded maps. "I looked for every section that mentioned tunnels. I could have missed some, but I skimmed it twice and took my time on a third read."

"You read that three times last night?" Jacob asked.

"It's not that long, really. And no, I read it on the way back to Karn, and waiting for you and Smith to finish checking over the Skysworn before we left. Then I read it again."

"And again, apparently." Furi opened the cover to the manual and gently turned a few of the pages. "It's not brittle. At all. How was this so well preserved?"

"We found it fairly deep in the compound. No moisture, no life I could see. I set bookmarks for each passage that mentions the tunnels. You know Mokuskrit so much better than I do. I hoped you could look it over."

"Of course." Furi skipped ahead to the first bookmark. "I wish William was here. He's probably more knowledgeable than any of us, but he's already in Belldorn, from what I understand. Took the rest of those manuscripts and the rarer books with him to donate to the Crown Library."

Jacob crossed his arms and leaned against a wooden shelf support. "I wish we could see his face when he sees *that* for the first time. The only books I've seen preserved that well were in the bookshop beneath Ancora."

"And this is probably a century older," Alice said. "If not more."

Furi read through a bookmarked passage and shook her head. "This one is making note of a maintenance hatch, but it's only to get inside an isolated section. It sounds like there is a gate separating sections of the exhaust ports."

"Of course there is," Jacob muttered. "That's just great."

"Then we go in with something that can break the gates down. Are you telling me you or Smith or Targrove can't come up with a tool to tear through a centuries-old gate?"

"Maybe? But we don't know what it's made out of, or how thick it is, or if there are even openings in it." His words tumbled out a little faster as he spoke.

"It's an exhaust port, Jacob." Alice raised an eyebrow.

He hesitated, frowned, and then sighed. "So it probably has openings."

Furi moved to one of the maps, unfolding it and tracing the southwest portion of the drawings with her index finger. She tapped the page three times. "These are identifiers of some sort. Look, the symbol on the map matches the symbol in the book. It follows the word for tunnel, so that's either a number or possibly a name."

Alice rubbed her fingers together and tried to think of where else she might have seen numbers in the manual. "The chapter headings. Go to the table of contents."

Furi stood up a little straighter before bending down and fanning through to the front of the book. "Right here." She flipped back to the passage, then to the front before a wide smile appeared on her lips. "Tunnel Eight."

"Seriously?" Alice scooted around the desk to stand by Furi.

The Skyborn picked up her pen again and started copying down every chapter number from the table of contents. Beside it, she wrote the Mokuskrit symbol for the same number, followed by its meaning in Standard.

"They're all numbers?" Jacob asked.

"I think so. Wait …" Furi frowned and flipped between the pages again. She unfolded part of the map and compared another line of symbols. "I could be wrong, but look at this. This symbol here with a slash through it?"

Jacob stepped closer and nodded. "I've seen that on schematics quite a bit. Not exactly like that, but especially on any of the old designs that required specific wiring."

Furi glanced at Alice before focusing on Jacob. "And those old schematics? Did it represent a connection?"

"Yes."

She laid her pen in the middle of the symbol. "Look at the left half of it compared to the right. They're entirely different, practically unrelated."

Alice traced the line of another, covering half as she inspected the exposed portion. She did the same again as Furi flipped to the table of contents, and Alice almost jumped in place.

"The numbers are combined. It's not a different symbol at all. They're overlapping!"

"Exactly!" Furi's words came out in a hurry. "The symbol is connecting them, like a hyphen or a dash. But it *is* a symbol too, like the schematics, notating a path. I think this is telling you where those tunnels are. But what I can't tell is how big they are. Can you walk through them? Crawl? Or is it just large enough to send a tool through?"

"We need to study more of it." Alice grabbed a chair and sat down, looking at the spread of symbols and characters with an entirely new eye.

Jacob grabbed a third chair from the corner and sat opposite Furi, excitedly unfolding another map.

Time escaped them as they sat and studied for hours, comparing the Mokuskrit lettering with Standard and again to the third language none of them really understood. It had characters in common with both Standard and Mokuskrit, but slashed lines and dots played a role as well, placing modifiers in the center of words in a way Alice had never seen.

She wanted to return to the Dead Woods and pull more books from the shelves. Even if it was a dead dialect, they might be able to pull enough out of it to help. For now, they could work with what they *had* taken, with the tiniest hope it would be adequate.

✧   ✧   ✧

ALICE WASN'T SURE how long it had been since they'd sat down with Furi and dug into the manual and maps, but when the door squeaked open, the sunlight nearly blinded them all.

"I can't see anything," Jacob grumbled.

"Good thing we aren't trying to kill you then," Mary said as she let the door fall closed behind her and Smith.

"Any news?" Alice asked.

"Not much." Smith paused before reaching into his collar and pulling out a few grains of white powder. "Salt. Everywhere." He made a disgusted noise before continuing. "We shared some of Mali's photos with Jakon and a few other, well, guild members, shall we say?"

Furi smiled at Smith's phrasing. "You know, Rin used to be a thief for hire. You don't have to be so subtle around me."

"Was he now?" Smith rubbed his chin. "That *is* interesting. It could be nice to speak with him about his time as a pirate. If he was with the guild?" Smith waved the idea away. "That can wait for less precarious times."

"What about the photos?" Alice asked.

Mary crossed her arms. "There's no getting through that blockade without a tremendous loss of life and ships. Even if we were to circle around them, the mountains on the opposite side of the Great Machine are well defended."

"We couldn't see that far." Alice glanced at Jacob before focusing on Mary again. "How do you know the mountains are defended?"

"We have some old friends who trade with the Children of the Dark Fire on occasion. They had some insights for us, but nothing encouraging. I passed the information along to Kat and Archibald."

Smith rested his hand on Mary's shoulder. "Essentially, as we understand it, Archibald could send his bombers across the Great Machine for a week and barely scratch the superstructure. It is armored far beyond what we found in the desert. To say nothing of those defending it."

Jacob pinched the bridge of his nose and cursed. "That has to be an exaggeration."

"To a degree, I am sure it is. It does not change the fact we are set against a force potentially equal to our own, and they are entrenched."

"Then we go underneath it." Alice spun the map to face Smith and Mary. "If the alternative is really that bad, we don't have a choice."

Smith smiled. "It would be futile without knowing where to go, Alice. We cannot simply … cannot …" He trailed off and leaned forward, placing a hand on either side of the map as he stared at the notes scribbled across them. His brow furrowed before rising, eyes widening."

"I told you Furi would be able to help with the Mokuskrit and the other symbols."

"Help?" Smith almost choked off the word. "This is like breaking a code. Furi, this is incredible. We can use this map for more than topography. This details the depth of the tunnels."

"Does it tell you how large they are?" Jacob asked.

Smith shook his head. "I do not believe so. But if it is like the venting systems for many of the larger airships, each connection point will result in a wider tunnel. Or possibly pipe. We will likely need reconnaissance to be sure."

"Underground …" Jacob traced the path of the underground tunnels.

Alice didn't miss the shiver that ran through him. She reached out and squeezed his arm. "What is it?"

He looked away from the map and met her eyes. "If we're going underground, we need to be prepared. Rope, cables, and a grappling cannon. Charles's design. I think I can build one without too much trouble if you can spare some wheels, Smith?"

"Whatever you need, Jacob. The workshop on the Skysworn is yours for the day."

"Thank you."

Furi raised her hand to draw everyone's attention. "If you would like to join us, Rin and Tatsu are coordinating a ceremony tonight to commemorate the fallen from the battle. They … *I* would like you all to be there."

Jacob glanced down at the map. "Do you think we have time for breakfast? I'm starving."

Furi burst into laughter as Alice swatted Jacob's arm.

CHAPTER THIRTEEN

J ACOB WANTED TO be there for the ceremony, but he also wanted to finish the grappling cannon. He'd stayed with Alice and Furi for a time after breakfast, but not much time passed before he had the itch to get started on the project.

Furi had noticed his fidgeting, and before long, he had a notebook and fountain pen in hand, scribbling away while Alice and Furi continued digging deeper into the manual from the control center. By the time lunch arrived, taking them to a small restaurant not far from the lift that would take him to the Skysworn, he'd made plans to do just that.

While he'd nearly finished the design on paper, that only gave him seven hours to build it out and test it. He laid the project out into three parts. So long as the first was completed, the grappling cannon would be functional. If the second was completed, a single cable could be fired, retrieved, and fired again.

Jacob wasn't sure how happy Smith would be when he realized a quarter of the hollow coil he had on board was gone, but if it meant the third part worked, well, Smith would probably understand. Using the same concept as the wheels they used to descend and race up landing lines, the cannon itself would be mounted to the cables with a quick release.

That also meant the Skysworn was now down two sets of wheels, but considering how many were in the locker by the landing lines, Jacob didn't think Smith would mind.

It took time to shape the mount for the barrel, but once the ports were cut to size, the top of the grappling cannon slid into place with a few taps from a rubber mallet. The question now was to either engage the hollow coil cartridge for the initial test or try something a little less valuable. It had taken nearly an hour to feed the hydraulic actuator through the narrow gap in the coil, and he didn't want to have to do that again.

But he also wanted to test the release he'd built from the magnets they'd brought back from the control center.

Jacob muttered to himself, debating before finally clicking the hollow coil cartridge into place. He closed the chamber, which levered it up into position inside the barrel. Under close inspection with a lantern, he could see the collapsed tips he'd added to the cable on either side, ready to deploy.

With the shape and fletching like that of a bolt thrower's ammunition, he hoped the aim would be true. It didn't have to be exact, really, but being able to hit a three-foot-square target would be helpful.

"How long is that cable?"

Jacob yelped and fumbled the grappling cannon, mercifully catching it before it fell. He didn't have any of the protective housing installed yet, and a drop could have been disastrous. He turned to find Smith peering over his shoulder.

"How long have you been standing there?"

Smith frowned before answering. "Perhaps five minutes. Not too long."

"Good thing you weren't an assassin."

"I suppose that depends on how much of my hollow coil you used." Smith laughed at Jacob's horrified expression before squeezing his shoulder. "I am joking, Jacob. That coil came from Frederick, and he has a great deal more, should we require it."

Jacob blew out a breath. "I *was* a bit worried about using it, but I didn't want to bother you on the transmitter."

"You made the right choice. Mary and I were with Jakon, and some of the guild leaders were there as well. From the docks, not the pirate guild, if that was your next question."

That *was* Jacob's next question, but he didn't feel a need to tell Smith that. "Do you have anything we can test this on? I don't want to fire it on the docks in case the accuracy isn't as good as I'm hoping."

"Well, that brings us back to my first question, does it not? How long is the cable?"

"Twenty-seven feet per side, but only twenty-five feet are functional. The rest are reserved for the locking mechanism and to make sure it doesn't tear itself apart."

"Is that what the magnets are for?" Smith stepped around to the side of the workbench and pointed to the stubby gray cylinders on either side.

In answer, Jacob pulled the secondary trigger that removed the shielding on the magnets. The actuator clicked inside the housing until he released the trigger.

Smith whistled. "That's a delicate design, Jacob. Are you sure it can handle the impact with stone if the tunnels are solid?"

"Definitely. The grapples are made from the same metal as the bolt glove. It's not as delicate as it looks. Stone, metal, wood, it'll hold."

"Get your glider pack. Let us give your grapple a *true* test. But then we need to hurry to the top deck. The feast is starting in half an hour, and I do not wish to suffer the wrath of Mary and Alice should I fail to get you there on time."

✧ ✧ ✧

Jacob wasn't entirely sure *why* Smith had asked him to grab his glider pack, but there were few people he trusted more than the older tinker. As he looked across the bay from the Skysworn to Jakon's ship and the metal plate Smith had set up as a target, he began to understand. Smith gave him a thumbs up and walked down the dock, going a bit farther, when Jacob gestured for him to stand back more.

While he felt confident in the grappling cannon's redesign, it was also the first time he planned to stretch the springs inside to their tolerances. If one of them broke or gave way, it could fail entirely. Jacob still thought this was a better plan than adding a pressurized chamber like the air cannons, but he supposed he'd find out soon enough.

Even with a tensioner, the springs had been hard to place. It gave him a new respect for the design of the wheels because no matter how heavy a load was attached to them, he doubted the devices would ever give way. At least not at a reasonable weight.

His transmitter crackled in his collar. "Everything ready?"

Jacob glanced at Smith and clicked his transmitter. "Ready."

"Area is clear. And remember, even if you miss, the cable does not have the length to reach the level below us."

Jacob frowned at that, trying to calculate how long the cables were, how far from the edge of the dock he was, and how much would remain if he missed. But he trusted Smith, and he was already tired from a day in the workshop.

He placed the grappling cannon on his shoulder. That motion released the safety in the metal arch he planned to add a bit of padding to. While it could be used on a forearm, or held in the hand, he liked the idea of the shoulder mount. It kept both ends of the barrel away from the user.

Aiming was another issue. He currently had a repurposed arm installed from a broken set of lenses under Smith's workbench. With that flipped out, he centered the steel plate across the dock, aiming a little high to compensate for the distance.

By raising the forward barrel, the rear angle lowered, creating a straight line to the wooden barrel behind him. Jacob took a deep breath and let it out slowly, pulling the trigger gently until the springs released, and the snap of the chamber was followed quickly by the whir of the coil.

The bolt hit the barrel first, but Jacob didn't check it. He waited until the forward bolt slammed through the metal plate, and the tension in the cartridge reversed, pulling the cable taut.

Only then did he turn to check on the barrel, the bolt stuck firmly inside. That done, he released the slide for the cartridge, effectively turning the launcher itself back into a pair of wheels. Only these wheels would coil as they went.

"Now, Jacob, only try this if you are feeling—"

He didn't wait for Smith to finish what likely would have been some good, practical advice. Instead, Jacob hurdled the railing of the docks and ground his teeth as the cable took all his weight. It dipped with the sudden change in tension, but it felt stable. He clicked the release for the second spring, and as it slowly decreased in tension, the grappling cannon carried him across the line, a bit faster than he'd expected.

The opposite railing came speeding toward him, the wind whipping through his hair. Jacob barely had time to get his legs up. The railing caught his glider pack and sent him tumbling onto the dock until he slammed into the metal plate that had been his target.

Smith whooped as he ran down the dock. "Are you okay?"

Jacob put two thumbs up and then brushed his hands together as he stood, checking the penetration on the plate before returning his attention to the grappling cannon.

"This is the real test, Smith. Let's see if I wasted your hollow coil."

He triggered the guard for the magnets, and the effect was immediate. The actuators closed the spikes of the grapple with a high-pitched squeak, and the hollow coil rocketed back around its modified wheel mounts.

It was the first time he'd held a grappling cannon since Dauschen. The first time he'd really thought about using one since that dark day beneath the city. Jacob's grip tightened on the housing, his knuckles whitening and pressure building behind his eyes as he tried to share Smith's excitement over the test.

But all he could remember in that moment was Charles.

✧   ✧   ✧

LATER THAT EVENING, and with a delicious feast in his stomach, Jacob stood at the railing near the top of Ballern's docks. It might as well have been the top of the world.

Alice leaned closer to him as a cool breeze rippled flags on the docks. "I think Furi is still upset that Rin and Tatsu didn't make it to dinner."

Jacob reached out and squeezed her hand. "They're working on the celebration, and it sounds like that's important to all the Skyborn. And we're all Stormborn now, Alice, so it's important to me, too."

"I think you should tell Furi that when she gets back. It's easy to forget sometimes, you know?"

"I heard it."

Jacob almost jumped when Furi spoke just behind them. The rush of adrenaline faded, and he smiled at Furi. "I meant it, too," Jacob said. "I'm glad you invited us."

"I'm glad you both came. And the pirates." Furi grinned as she looked across the gap in the docks. Mary and Smith stood by a large group of pilots and crew wearing a patchwork of colors from half a dozen different cities. The lack of uniformity was a dead giveaway for the usually disguised smugglers.

"It's quite a statement, isn't it?" Alice asked.

"It really is." Furi gestured to the railing ahead of them and the flags draped between the levels below. "Maybe not as big a statement as that."

The flags of Bollwerk and Belldorn rippled in the breeze beside those of Ballern and the Skyborn. But there were other colors in that space, a dark flag with the Bull's Horn emblazoned across it, a symbol Jacob had only seen in Cave. And another, a pale thing with a gridwork of stone and towers represented in the broken stripes.

"Ancora?" Jacob asked, the name of his city trailing away.

"And Midstream!" Furi said. "It was Drakkar's idea, and Tatsu ran with it."

"Where did they even find an Ancoran flag?"

"Ancora, I suspect," Furi said flatly.

Alice grinned at Jacob as he attempted to measure the full length of Furi's sarcasm.

The Skyborn didn't dive any further into it, instead pointing to the banner below them. "Did you see that one?"

Jacob leaned forward. It was hard to make out, though the blue looked familiar. The wind picked up just enough to ruffle the flags, revealing the outline of a Shadowwing embroidered in brilliant silver thread.

"I'm not sure if we got every flag from every city in the alliance, but the Stormborn flag might be my favorite. It wouldn't be here without Kura, you know?" Furi stared down through the opening in the docks. "It wouldn't be here without you two, either."

They stood there for a time, listening to the lively chatter around them while a bard played a solemn song on a lute at the northern end of the docks. It may have been difficult to hear amid the general buzz of the crowd, but it was welcome.

✧ ✧ ✧

JACOB TRIED NOT to laugh as Furi stared at Rin like he'd asked her to jump off a building.

"Come on, Furi. It won't be that bad. Just say a few words about Kura before we start the fireworks, will you?"

She looked back at Alice and Jacob as if they might save her from her impending discomfort from speaking onstage, but in the end, she took Rin's hand and followed him through the crowd.

"I'm glad they have the horn set up for this," Alice said. "I'd hate to miss it. Furi might be nervous, but she'll do great."

"Yeah, she will." Jacob laughed and nodded. "Remember that address she wrote to rally the Skyborn?"

"We wouldn't have the Stormborn without her."

They waited together while Furi and Rin wove past dozens of revelers. Jacob could see the platform to the north clearly now, the tarps pulled back to reveal various mortars for the upcoming fireworks.

Furi hopped onto the small platform where the bards had been playing throughout the night, hesitating when Rin gestured for her to take the horn. She finally did, and the crowd slowly quieted when she started to speak.

"Hi, everyone. I don't know all of you, and I'm sure there are quite a few of you who don't know me. I just wanted to say a few quick words about Kura. She took me when my living family wouldn't. I won't bore you with the details because this is about her, not me.

"She sheltered a lot of Skyborn over the years. More importantly, she founded the school so many attended on the Bones. We all lost people in the Battle of Ballern, but many of us lost our homes, our schools, and even our families."

Furi hesitated as a quiet rumbling worked its way through the crowd. She stood a little straighter and projected her voice more as she went on. "But Kura raised us not to give in to those who would throw us down. Not to bow before the corruption of the nobles. Not to bow before the corruption of a usurper.

"She taught us to learn from our mistakes. To learn from the mistakes of those who came before us. And to fight the poison in our city, no matter the cost. But she never told me how high the cost would be. A price of lives and homes and friendships broken. Now, some of those same people who would have called Kura a friend have joined with Mordair and the traitors. Have followed the Children of the Dark Fire to the west."

Furi turned and raised her arm, pointing away from the sea to the shadowed skies that led to the Great Machine. "But Kura taught me more than compassion and understanding for the mistakes of those who would leave us behind. She taught me that traitors often come home. And she taught me how to fight!"

She lowered her arm and turned back to the gathered crowd.

"I fight for her and everyone we lost on these docks and the city below. Remember that lesson. Kura's lesson. When a traitor returns, they are still a traitor. *We* are family now. *We* stand for Ballern." Her voice rose, nearing a scream. "*We* are the *Stormborn!*"

There was a moment of silence, of awe, of unity, before the crowd responded with a roar, and the docks shook beneath Jacob's feet. A moment before the first salvo and the fireworks exploded overhead, the shimmering silhouette of a Shadowwing in the sky, and the world was lost to the screams of a people united.

CHAPTER FOURTEEN

THE FIREWORKS LASTED for almost an hour, and Furi couldn't help the tears that came as she stood in that place with Rin and Tatsu. They were her family in every way that mattered. And now they had friends from across the sea. Jacob and Alice, Smith and Mary, so many more. She'd dined with the Lady of Belldorn and walked through the Crown Library.

There was darkness in the day, the loss of the Bones, the loss of lives, but there was a light around the edges. A way forward that might leave them all in better times. They only needed to keep pushing.

Furi leaned against the railing. "Do you remember bringing that pinecone to school, Rin?"

He bowed his head and laughed under his breath. "How could I forget? That wasn't just an unwelcome surprise for Kura, you know. I had another one stashed in my parents' house. How was I supposed to know there were eggs hidden in it?"

"We had bites from those Tree Killer hatchlings for weeks. I don't think I ever saw Kura quite that annoyed again."

"I can still remember the sound of notebooks swatting them. They used to echo in the warehouse before it was filled with crates. In the old days."

"It wasn't the brightest thing to do."

Rin smiled and stood up straighter. "No, it wasn't. But it wasn't on purpose, either. I don't know if *you* remember, but I was terrified of Tree

Killers when I was a kid. Even the littlest of them. For a good two weeks, my parents didn't need the bell on their alarm clock. They had me screaming every time I thought one had crawled under my sheets."

Tatsu stepped up behind them, laughing. "I remember that story. And yet you handled far more dangerous creatures regularly after we got to Canopy."

"I didn't know they were Stone Dogs." Rin closed his eyes and sighed before meeting Furi's gaze.

She was caught somewhere between laughter and disbelief. "What do you mean by *handled?*"

"He cleared out a nest of Stone Dogs in one of the rotting trees. Didn't want them to get crushed when the arborists cut it down. Carried them with no more than a gardener's glove on one hand."

Rin shrugged. "I should have worn leathers."

"It's a wonder any of us are still around." Furi hesitated, hearing distant shouts that no longer sounded like a celebration. Shrill notes of joy faded into cries of warning and the growls of a pub brawl. "Something's wrong."

Rin stepped up onto the first wrung of the railing, peering over the crowd before cursing. "Come on. I see cloaks in the northwest, close to the stage."

Furi didn't have to ask what Rin meant by cloaks. It was short for one of two things: the overdressed and under-burdened nobles or the Children of the Dark Fire. Considering the worst of the nobles had fled with Mordair, Furi made immediate assumptions, pulling a collapsed crossbow from the quiver on her calf. A second quiver held a dozen bolts. Not nearly enough for an extended engagement, and she hoped she wouldn't be forced to rely on knives.

"Clear out the area around the lifts. Give the people somewhere to run!" The top level of the docks only had four ladders, and ladders weren't a quick way to evacuate. They needed the lifts running, and Furi could already see the cloaks surrounding the nearest of them.

"Rin! Look. They have the lifts blocked off."

Rin cursed and grabbed Tatsu's shoulder. "Clear them out. I'll take the next lift. Rally the crowd if you can. If you can't, run."

It was a hollow feeling, almost a helpless one. Furi knew if they couldn't get through to the lift, there wouldn't be anywhere to run. Pushing through the crowd slowed them to an agonizing pace. There were too many people. Every minute that passed would end in more injured revelers, or worse.

"Alice!" Rin shouted.

Furi looked left and right, trying to see where Alice was. She found the Ancoran a second before a report sounded like cannon fire in the crush of people. Only it didn't merely *sound* like cannon fire. Jacob stood beside her, the small air cannon in Alice's hand as a cloak collapsed to the dock.

"Go!" Alice cried back to them. "Leader!"

Furi understood what that one word meant. The leader of the attackers was nearby. Alice pointed to the stage before another cloak took her from behind. The Ancoran didn't freeze at the sudden attack, didn't cry out. Instead, she ducked beneath the cloak and punched them in the back of the head.

Furi had seen Alice's bolt gloves before, but she'd never seen the devastation they could wreak on a life. The cultist was dead before they hit the ground.

A small gap in the crowd opened before them, and Furi slipped into it, Rin right on her heels. Jacob and Alice weren't the only ones fighting back. A rallying cry echoed up around them, and the masses that had been pulling away a moment before surged forward, closing on every lift.

Another minute passed, and Furi reached the stage. She hurdled over the edge, reaching the empty platform before realizing her mistake. The stage wasn't the only thing waiting beyond the platform. The gangway for an airship stood there, black as night and all but invisible in the darkness.

Crouched forms, armed with spears, scythes, and crossbows, waited in the shadows. She could strike at a handful, and they'd be on her. She could try to run into the crowd, but that would cost the lives of more Skyborn.

Furi raised her crossbow and the cartridge of bolts primed as she fired. It took an archer in the chest, but it didn't kill them. She pulled the lever to cock the crossbow and fired with a quick draw. The cloaked forms started to move then.

"Behind the stage!" Rin shouted.

Furi clicked the transmitter in her collar. She didn't know if anyone would hear her, *could* hear her, but she had to try. "Ambush behind the stage!"

She fired again before the first bolt took her in the thigh. She screamed as Rin pushed her to the side, out of the path of the next bolt. Rin dove across the stage, lashing out with his sword as blood flew over the dock. He sheltered by a crate, where the horn from the night before had been stored, before two bolts slammed into the wood.

From the corner, through little more than a peephole between the stage and the railing, Furi fired into the cloaks. Something grabbed her from behind and lifted her into the air.

The edge of the railing appeared in her vision, the lights of Ballern far below, and she realized what was about to happen. She realized how everything in her life had come to this moment. This end.

"Stop!" a woman roared from the cluster of cloaked forms. "Put her on the stage, you fool."

Whoever had spoken, the massive warrior obliged, sitting Furi on the platform with an odd amount of care.

"Stand down. Return to the ship. Now. Fools."

Furi blinked as she realized the speaker was walking down the ramp, crossing through the huddled cultists before they surged back onto the midnight ship.

"As you wish. We obey The Red Hand."

The Children of the Dark Fire echoed the statement from the huge warrior who had almost thrown Furi from the docks.

Furi froze as the speaker pulled her hood down and revealed a face she recognized. A woman she'd met in the bookstore, someone who had spoken against the Children of the Dark Fire. "Patrice?"

The Red Hand stared at Furi with hard eyes. "One time, child. If I see you again, it will be your end. Leave this battle."

"Two destroyers moving in, Commander," a voice said from the darkness.

Patrice studied Furi and Rin. "Do with our allies as you will. Abandon this war, Stormborn." She turned to leave.

Furi wanted to fire on The Red Hand, but instead, she only screamed. "I thought you didn't have a mind for that cult!"

Patrice stopped on the ramp, but she did not turn back to face Furi. After a moment, she finished boarding, and the gangway snapped up flush against the hull. As fast as they'd come, the Children of the Dark Fire were gone.

"She could have killed us," Rin said, flopping down on the stage by Furi. "Your leg!"

"It's okay." Furi flinched as she studied the bolt. "It's in the meat."

"That's ... not great?"

"I mean, it's all the way through. It's not too deep." She winced, turning so Rin could see. It was in the outside of her thigh, not much deeper than the skin. "Just a big splinter, really."

"Furi!"

She turned as best she could until she saw Alice, with Jacob trailing close behind. She worried at the sight of them, blood splattered across Alice's cheek and two cuts lining Jacob's forehead. Not cuts, she realized as he got closer. Something had hit him in the head, leaving a parallel scrape up into his hairline.

"We saw Tatsu by the lift. Are you okay?" Alice almost cringed when she saw Furi's leg. "How bad?"

Furi shrugged.

Rin let out an exasperated sigh. "She says it's not too bad, but we need to get her to the hospital. How are the docks?"

"A few bodies." Alice shook her head when Rin started to curse. "No, it's mostly the Children of the Dark Fire. Once the fighting erupted, the entirety of the docks just … overran them."

"How many Stormborn did we lose?" Furi asked.

"We won't know for a while," Jacob said. "I only saw two on the ground who weren't wearing those cloaks. I don't know if they were Stormborn or not."

Furi grimaced as the encounter played over and over in her head. "It was The Red Hand. Patrice is the Red Hand. Why didn't she kill me?"

Alice blinked at that. "What are you saying? She was *here*?"

"On the ship that just left." Rin gestured to the empty space at the edge of the docks. "I've never seen a ship painted so black. It vanished against the sky. If they'd opened fire with cannons, everyone on these docks would be dead."

Jacob's brow furrowed. He looked like he was about to speak, then his brow furrowed again. "The Red Hand is merciless. Why would she leave here like that?"

Furi glanced at the bolt in her thigh. "I think it was me. She remembered me from the bookstore. Alice and I had met her before. She … she didn't just let me live. She saved me."

Alice exchanged a glance with Jacob before looking back out at the crowd. "We need to tell everyone what's happened here. Find Smith and Mary. Jakon, too. Spread the word."

"You do it." Rin balled his fists. "I'm taking Furi to the hospital. If we don't get her there soon, we'll need to field dress this wound, and I'd rather have it cleaned out than subject to whatever filth is in the air."

"The baroness is dead!" A shout rose from the northeastern docks. "The Baroness of Auxley has been assassinated!"

Furi closed her eyes and cursed. "I guess we know why Patrice was here now. Petty revenge for Mordair."

"Likely more of a statement, Furi." Alice crouched down beside her. "No matter how guarded, or how dense the crowd, Mordair can reach into our cities and steal whatever lives he wants."

Jacob almost growled behind her. "It'll be harder to do that when he's dead."

Furi raised her hand to Rin. "Help me up. I'll go to the hospital with you, but then we need to work."

Rin blew out a long breath, and then obliged. "I could carry you."

"I'll take this bolt out and stab you if you try." Furi didn't miss the amused smirks that flitted across the Ancorans' faces.

CHAPTER FIFTEEN

RCHIBALD TAPPED HIS finger on the worn copper trim running the length of the conference table on the bridge of Warship One. The maps were nearly three inches thick now, and the fact he had to clip them together to group them by region irritated him to no end.

Some might call them foolish for their rendezvous, but there were times when nothing was more effective than a face-to-face meeting. And that felt especially true when the fates of far more cities than Bollwerk were being gambled in this new conflict.

Lady Katherine leaned over the map of the woods that surrounded the Great Machine. The forces of the Children of the Dark Fire had been laid out in detail, accompanied by photographs provided by Karn. She flipped between two of them, matching the photographs with descriptions from the only surveillance ship to make it back from the Great Machine.

She stood and turned to him, her words resigned. "They're right, you know? We may be able to prevail in a frontal assault, but the cost would be unthinkable."

"The force of your Porcupines, combined with our warships and bombers, could break them." He crossed his arms and leaned back in his chair.

"In time, yes. But at a price none of us wants."

"And what of the news from Ballern?" Archibald stood, walking to the opposite side of the table. "What of The Red Hand? How did that ship get through our blockades, Kat?" It still felt odd to use the shortened version of her name, but here, in private, it was what she'd asked.

"Without a sacrifice, there is no victory here, Archibald. I cannot argue that point. But I do wish to minimize the cost. The lives lost. As to The Red Hand's ship, I have little doubt how it passed our blockade. A ship black as pitch, a high enough altitude, and a sun fully set. Who would notice the dimming of a handful of stars?"

"More than a handful, from the description of that vessel."

Kat shook her head. "No. That ship was smaller than a destroyer. Have you set foot on the top levels of Ballern's docks? It wasn't larger than a supply ship, based on the description."

"They should have seen it in the fireworks. *Someone* should have noticed."

"Archibald, it is likely someone did. But who would have suspected a strike force? As busy as Ballern's docks are, even now. And if they did notice, could they have gotten word to those who needed to know?"

Archibald grimaced. "Perhaps not without a transmitter or the like, no. A fair point, Kat. A fair point."

"They struck one noble. A single noble in all of that chaos. The Red Hand could have done that on her own, Archibald. This was a statement from Mordair. He wants us to tighten the defenses around Ballern, and we know why."

"Karn."

"Indeed. And how do you gamble with a newly forged alliance like that? *Our* alliance is new, by most measures. But Karn, even more so."

"We split the fronts. Mordair wouldn't expect it. He'll expect me to create a fortress of defense around Ballern. That is all he knows of me, and we can leverage that expectation." Archibald wandered to the far side of the map where the western wall of Ballern stood, represented by a finely carved stone castle.

"Fel is moving on Karn. We can't leave them to face that alone."

"No, we can't. But we can turn Mordair's own strategy against him. We bolster the defenses of Ballern, but not with airships. Utilize the Stormborn. Arm them with Titan Mechs and armored crawlers for the ground defenses. Install ballistae and cannons on the docks themselves."

"Cannons? What sort of cannons, Archibald?"

A wicked grin crossed the Speaker's lips. It was only there for a moment, and then it was gone. "Did you bring replacements for the Porcupine's flanking cannons?"

Kat leaned away from the table. "You mean to mount airship cannons on the docks?"

"Yes. We'll need to clear it with the tinkers, of course. Anything fool enough to approach would be grounded before it could attack."

Kat rubbed her cheek as she studied the map. It all came back to the Great Machine, no matter what they did on the fronts. "We need people inside that blasted machine, and despite the discoveries made at the control center, it is very well guarded."

"We don't even know if those tunnels will take them far enough, Kat. But a war on two fronts …" He gestured across the map, from Karn to the northern sea.

"It gives us a chance. The fisherfolk from Fel may be willing to lend their strength as well. They fought side by side with the Skyborn in Ballern. And if Mordair can slip a single ship past our blockade …"

"Then let us return the favor."

✧   ✧   ✧

"SOME OF THIS can never be repeated." Kat flexed her fingers into a fist. "For our people to learn what we're planning, Archibald, it would ruin both of us. Fighting for Karn, risking more exposure in Ballern, all while …"

"I know, Kat. That's why we did this alone. It's time to let the others know what's been decided. Mary and Smith will need more than a few hours to make preparations. Reinforcements will need to be sent to Karn. Mordair will likely strike the moment he realizes what is happening. He'll want to do as much damage as he can before we can fully reinforce Karn."

Kat took a deep breath and leaned forward to click the button on the transmitter in the center of the table. "Mary, we must speak." She waited a short time before adding. "It's urgent, and we need privacy. Just your crew."

"A moment, Kat. We're leaving the hospital."

Lady Katherine drummed her fingers on the table. She had little doubt as to where Mary was going. "They'll probably head up to the Skysworn. Mary can be overly cautious about spies."

"Not a bad way to be, given the times, Kat."

She blew a quiet laugh out. "True." They waited what felt like days before the transmitter hissed with static, and Mary's voice returned.

"Sorry. The lift had quite a line. We're secure now."

"Who's with you?"

"My tinker and my Ancorans. Why?"

"I'm with Archibald, Mary. We have things to discuss. Specifically, about your group's idea to explore the tunnels."

"I don't think you're going to talk them out of it, Kat. If that's what you're trying to do?" It wasn't quite a question, but Kat didn't miss the confused tone in Mary's voice.

Archibald clicked the transmitter. "We are not. We agree it is the best way forward. What we do not agree on is how large of a distraction you need."

"Well, we'd thought it may be a good time to explore when they move against Karn. At least some of their defenses wouldn't be concentrated where we're scouting."

"Or you could go at night," Kat said.

Mary didn't answer immediately. When she did respond, she picked her words carefully. "What do you mean by that?"

"As the ship you described moved against the docks. Camouflage another to do the same."

"You want me to paint my ship?"

"Unless you have a better idea for it?" An edge of caution tainted Kat's question.

Amusement crept into Mary's voice when the captain responded. "Sometimes I forget you were never a pirate, Kat. We have better ways of masking the ship than paint."

"Prepare for it then, Mary. We may have need of it."

"We may not. Once some of the defenses disperse, there are two entry points that may be exposed. We go in on foot, far more stealthy than any airship can be."

Archibald leaned forward, bracing his arms on the table. "You mean to take mounts into the woods? To close the distance entirely from the ground?"

"If we can, yes. I'll make preparations for the camouflage in case the need arises. Paint. We're going to have a talk about this, Kat."

Kat pinched the bridge of her nose. "When you speak to Eva, tell her I am sorry for evading her. I didn't want anyone to know where we were meeting."

"Understood. Be safe, Kat. And you, Archibald."

With that, Mary disconnected.

Kat eyed Archibald. "I expected her to be more resistant to the idea."

He gave her a flat smile. "There was a time I would have, too. But I've learned over the years that once an enemy steps too far, resistance will often fall to the wayside. Mary is a fighter, as you well know. And she has a role to play in this war with Mordair."

"We all do, Archibald. We all do."

CHAPTER SIXTEEN

I T FELT WRONG to be leaving Ballern so soon after the attack, but Jacob knew they could do more good on the carrier. Mary remained focused on their path over the Gray Woods while he and Alice studied the maps for what felt like the fiftieth time.

Alice tapped on the far western edge of the map, where the jagged mountain peaks ended, and the forest diminished into wetlands. A massive lake waited beyond the swamp, but more importantly, several entrances to the tunnels peppered the area.

"I think this is our best chance. If we're going to do reconnaissance, the swamp is the farthest entrance from the Great Machine."

Mary glanced over her shoulder. "You really want to go into a swamp, Alice? Do you have any idea how nasty the swamplands are in the west?"

"What do you mean?" She hesitated. "Is quicksand a danger?"

Mary barked out a laugh and shook her head. "No, Alice, you've read too many adventure books, I'm afraid. You'll rarely find a dangerous patch of quicksand. Losing your boots to the mud is a concern, and some of the bugs aren't the friendliest."

"Worse than Tree Killers?"

"Probably not," Jacob muttered, rapping his knuckles on his leg.

"In some ways. The Dragonwings are more aggressive than those of Canopy; different altogether, honestly. They'll take a hand off just as easily as a Tree Killer."

Smith's voice echoed over the horn. "Water Beetles like the fresh water, but leave them alone, and they will leave you alone. The Shriekers are a bigger problem. Harmless unless they ruin your hearing, which is a real danger. Deafening this time of year."

"Harmless, but they'll deafen you?" Jacob tried to make sense of Smith's comment.

"Harmless in the way they will not bite your leg off, yes. They may be sleeping so long as the sun has not set. The true danger is they can be used as a warning system. They fall silent when startled. However, they do make an excellent stew."

Mary pinched the bridge of her nose. "I promise we'll get you a good stew soon, Smith. You should have asked Jakon while we were in Ballern."

"Not the time, Mary. I can be patient."

They continued bantering about the best stew in Bollwerk, while Jacob and Alice returned their attention to the map.

Alice pointed to another cluster of tunnel entrances. "We need to be prepared for anything. Multiple entry points in case we run into too many guards, and a clear way out if things go wrong. Despite the dangers, I think the swamps are our best chance of proving we translated the map correctly."

"I agree." Jacob hung his head. "I don't like the idea of underground rivers and lakes, though. Reminds me of Ancora. Last time I saw a Water Beetle, it didn't go well."

"You have a gift for understatement." Alice held his gaze for a moment before a small smile crossed her lips.

"Ten minutes from the carrier," Mary said.

They'd nearly closed the distance when Jacob thought of another question he wasn't sure he wanted the answer to. "Are there Widow Makers in the swamps?"

"Yes, but you won't see any of them."

Alice cocked an eyebrow. "How can you be sure?"

"Ember Needles feed on them. Those, on the other hand, those you'll see plenty of."

"Do you mean Emerald Needles?" Jacob tried not to cringe at the idea of Emerald Needles being an issue in the swamp. They were bad enough around Belldorn.

Mary shook her head. "No, Jacob. *Ember* Needles. At a distance, their wings look like fire in the right light. Stay away from them. They're more aggressive than Sky Needles, but not quite so deadly as Emerald Needles."

"They hate fire," Smith said. "Keep a torch with you."

Jacob rubbed at his eyes. "Why don't you two come with us if you know so much about the swamps?"

"Mali or one of the riders from Karn should go with you. Mary and I have spent time in the swamps, but not enough to go underground. We cannot begin to guess what you will actually encounter as you approach the tunnels."

"Get your harnesses on," Mary said. "Landing in one minute."

The transmitter buzzed with static before Arun's voice spoke. "The Children of the Dark Fire are moving against Karn. Multiple reports that forces have deployed. For those who would fight beside us, we ask for your help now."

Alice flopped onto her jump seat and strapped in, looking to Jacob. "First, we help Karn. Then we find the tunnels."

Jacob clicked his harness into place and nodded.

✧ ✧ ✧

"WE'LL BE BACK as soon as we speak to Frederick," Jacob said. "I promise."

Mary tapped her watch. "Two hours. We're in the air in two hours. That will give Smith enough time to refuel and check the systems over."

Alice grabbed Jacob's hand and pulled him away from the Skysworn. They wove between the crawlers as they crossed the street, heading toward the workshop near the stern of the carrier.

"It still feels strange, doesn't it?" Jacob asked as one of the pontoons rose in the west. "We're going about our day like nothing is out of the ordinary, but this entire carrier is about to deploy."

"Of all the things we've seen in the past week, *that* is what you think is strange?" Alice let out a little laugh and pulled him into an alley as they hurried on.

The next block held the bars and restaurants needed to feed the carrier's crew. It was only when the ship vibrated beneath their feet that Alice released Jacob's hand, instead holding tight to the railing that ran the length of the carrier.

They weren't lifting off quite yet. Jacob knew what that would sound like, but the dull roar filling the air in that moment wasn't anything more than the cycling of the furnaces. Once the boilers were well and truly at temperature, then they would be airborne. Of course, the loading ramps would be withdrawn before any of that happened.

Alice's steps slowed as they reached the warehouse. Jacob had been so busy thinking about the launch sequence for the carrier, he hadn't been paying much attention to what was in front of them, or why Alice might be slowing down.

"What is …" He didn't finish the question. He realized why she'd stopped. A line of Titan Mechs some twelve deep crouched at the edge of the carrier. These were not made for building. These looming giants bore long blades and axes, and two wielded enormous maces.

And before those, like some metallic family lined up for a photograph, stood a troop of exoskeletons. Two dozen on a quick count, bolt throwers mounted to their arms, and a miniature ballista on either shoulder.

"What is this?" Jacob started to walk toward the rows of Mechs, but turned for the workshop instead. "Come on, let's find Frederick."

The clang of metal on metal grew louder when they neared the doorway. Heat rolled out in waves from the small forge in the corner, the ventilation hood above it not nearly enough to normalize the temperature. Two tinkers worked on a hammer and anvil, dark glasses protecting their eyes similar to the way heavy gloves kept the worst of the heat from their flesh.

Inside the workshop, more Titan Mechs moved through the production line. They looked far from being ready to deploy, but that didn't slow the frantic pace of the tinkers on the second level.

Frederick faced a bulletin board in the corner, pulling down one set of schematics before placing another. He ran his fingers through his gray hair, catching sight of Jacob and Alice when they were nearly halfway across the floor.

"What is all that?" Jacob raised his voice and gestured to the towering bay doors where they would roll out the completed Titan Mechs.

"Ballern's new perimeter." Frederick's answer was almost a shout, speaking over the sheer volume of the workshop. "It wasn't supposed to be, originally. But things have changed, haven't they?" He gave them both a knowing look.

"You talked to Archibald." Alice wasn't asking.

"I did, yes."

Jacob pulled the conversation back to his previous question. "But the weapons? I saw bolt throwers that looked more like ballistae."

Frederick nodded and rubbed his neck. "That you did. Natalia's design. She's better than me with some of the delicate work. Well, if I'm being honest, she's better than me at some of the larger work, too."

"Where is she?"

"Back on the other carrier. Took a flight with Lady Katherine."

"How did you know about that?" Jacob asked as quietly as he could. They were close enough to Frederick now he didn't need to shout, but the workshop was still raucous. "Mary's done her best to make sure no one knows where Kat is."

"She told me herself when she left for the carrier. She'll likely rendez-vous with us closer to Karn." Frederick hesitated. "Don't, ah, don't mention that to Mary. Now that you remind me, Lady Katherine *did* say something about not mentioning any of it to Mary."

"We have a little less than two hours. How can we help?" Jacob looked around the workshop. In a matter of days, Frederick had reorganized it. The production lines were fully separated so the Titan Mech construction wouldn't slow down the exoskeletons, or the reverse.

Frederick studied the pair before nodding. "Some of my tinkers could use a break. If you wouldn't mind installing some of the bolt throwers on the exoskeletons, I can send that pair to lunch."

"Show me what to do," Alice said. "I've helped Jacob with far stranger things than that."

"As has anyone who dared to spend time with a tinker." Frederick laughed and patted Alice's shoulder. "Come, I'll walk you through the process. It's not too different from the one Jacob designed for Ancora, though it is made for a smaller target."

TWO HOURS WENT by in a flash, and while Jacob was happy they'd been able to give Frederick's tinkers a much-needed break, they were running late to get back to the Skysworn.

"I can't believe we lost track of time. Frederick should have told us our two hours were nearly over!" Alice almost growled when she said the older tinker's name.

Jacob laughed between strides, clicking his transmitter as he went. "Mary, we'll be there in a minute. I hope you waited."

Static hissed for a moment before Mary answered. "*I would have left you lot, but Smith is taking longer than expected with the repairs.*"

Smith's faint voice echoed over the transmitter. "*That is not entirely true! I needed a part I did not have on board, and I told you—*"

"*We'll be here,*" Mary said.

Alice's pace slowed a bit after that. She still hurried, and the impact of Jacob's Biomech leg on the hard metal of the carrier didn't exactly feel great, but they rounded the corner by the Skysworn soon enough.

Smith stood underneath the ship, ratcheting something in place on the opposite side of the foremost landing gear.

"Thanks for waiting for us!" Alice called out as she sprinted up the loading ramp.

Smith paused and leaned out from behind the doors that covered the landing gear. "You are most welcome. It was definitely my choice to wait and had nothing to do with whoever manufactured these blasted valves." He grumbled something else as Jacob passed by.

Alice grinned when he made it up the ramp and stepped inside. "Sounds like we missed a fun time on the Skysworn today."

"Right," Jacob said. "Absolutely that."

He followed her down the hall and up the ladder to the deck. It still felt strange to be boarding the Skysworn from below. The gangplank was such a wonderful little device, that Jacob almost missed using it.

Alice stopped just outside the cabin, pointing toward the forest in the west. "Look, they're raising the ramps."

Jacob had to squint, but between two hangar tents, he could see a Titan Mech twisting the ramps into place. A small crew trailed close behind, installing the railing and locking it down. It wouldn't be long before the engines would roar, and the carrier would take to the sky once more.

Taking her crew into another battle.

Jacob grimaced and followed Alice into the cabin.

$$\diamond \quad \diamond \quad \diamond$$

ONCE THE CARRIER was airborne, it was only a few hours to Karn. Jacob was surprised when Mary said they were going to stay on the carrier. It gave Smith more time to finish his last task, and Jacob wasn't complaining as it gave him and Alice more time to study the maps.

After a while, he turned to one of Charles's journals. He couldn't shake the vision of those Mechs and exoskeletons armed for battle. Jacob knew they'd be used in the war. He'd helped arm the Titan Mechs of Midstream, but he didn't have a hand in what had been done with his updated designs. It was like they weren't his anymore. But knowing the blood they spilled would still be on his hands was a thought he couldn't escape.

Jacob sighed and lowered the journal, placing his hand over Charles's words.

"What's wrong?" Alice asked as she leaned closer to him.

"I never want to lose myself, Alice. Not like the berserkers did. Not like Charles did."

"To the metals in your leg? You're safe, Jacob. Charles and Smith made sure of that."

"No, Alice, I mean like Charles lost himself to the war." He lifted his hand to reveal the passage underneath it.

Damned fools, the lot of them. Asking me to modify a soldier so they can't die. We've traded advancements for madness in this war. Archibald is pushing to expand research into biomechanics, but I fear what the addition of more berserkers would do to the war effort.

That's to say nothing of the psychological effect on their friends and fellow soldiers. A machine, powered by blood and a human heartbeat. There is little I consider heresy in the goal of our mission, but not allowing a dead man to die crosses a line.

"He knew. He knew it was wrong, but he still did it."

Alice reached out and gently turned his face to hers. "You aren't him."

"I'm close enough. Look what I've built, Alice. It's … I can't take it back."

Alice took his hand. "When the war is done, we can worry about making amends. When our families are safe, and it's not a question of either having enough food to live or bowing to a merciless king. We all fight, Jacob, and I'll fight with you until the world is better for it." She kissed his cheek.

Jacob closed his eyes. He didn't need Alice to see the tears threatening to fall.

CHAPTER SEVENTEEN

THE CARRIER HOVERED south of Karn, near enough that the smaller ships could remain docked in the air or reach the small landing areas with little expense of fuel or time. It was smart, in its way, but Samuel still wondered what good, if any, those ships were going to do in the tightest quarters of the Gray Woods.

Bessie paced from side to side, not far enough to break ranks from the other mounts, but enough to let Samuel know the spider knew what was happening. She got as anxious as he did when deployments started. He patted her on the top of her head and watched Drakkar at the far end of the stables.

The Cave Guardian spoke to Allie and Alana, both dressed in riding gear, and Samuel didn't hide his smile at the sheer level of irritation on Drakkar's face when he first saw them both. They may have been the leaders of Canopy and Cave, but they had no interest in sitting and watching, injured or not.

But when Mali walked through the front gates, Samuel couldn't sit back with Bessie any more, whether he wanted to or not. The spider almost dragged him across the hall, and he had to jog to keep up. Mali caught sight of the furry gray tank at the last moment and braced herself before Bessie yanked her in close with her pedipalps.

"Easy, girl!" Mali said between laughs. "I don't have any Sweet-Flies right now."

In their short stints in Karn, Bessie had grown particularly fond of the plump red Sweet-Flies that were native to the region. Samuel wasn't sure how he'd ever convince her Ancoran Sweet-Flies were just as good.

Bessie finally released Mali, and when the spider trotted back across the hall, Samuel found Drakkar, Allie, and Alana all staring at him.

"What?"

"I thought the Spider Knights had better trained their mounts," Alana said.

"Oh, did you?" Samuel put a hand on his hip. "I'll have you know I almost got mauled by a Walker in Cave. Not so well trained, that, was it?"

Allie burst into laughter and patted Drakkar's shoulder. "Did he?"

"Yes." Drakkar drew the word out as he crossed his arms. "Never step between a hungry Walker and its trough. That is common sense, Samuel."

He started to open his mouth with a snappy retort, but realized he didn't really have anything to say to that. It was one of the first things they learned when training their mounts in the Spider Knights. And he probably should have used more caution in the stables with that Walker.

Alana gestured to Mali. "Did you have something urgent before you were accosted by that well-trained mount?"

Samuel muttered under his breath.

"Bessie is great." Mali grinned at Samuel before turning her attention to Alana, but her smile faded as fast as it had come. "Arun sent me. The Children of the Dark Fire are moving faster than we expected. We need to have our ambushes set in the next four hours, or we risk losing ground."

"And the carrier?" Samuel asked. "What about the airships?"

"They can't do much in the woods themselves, but they'll be posted all along the city perimeter. Anything that gets through that isn't from Karn will be a target."

"So the woods are up to us." Samuel nodded to himself. "That's what we've been training for."

"Not just us." A wicked smile etched its way across Mali's face. "You should come to the landing zone before we deploy."

"Is it important for us to do so?" Alana asked. "We do need to be sure our mounts and soldiers are prepared."

Mali gestured to a stable hand. "Get the bridles set and feed the mounts. Add enough feed to the bags for two days. If the worst happens, we'll be ready for it."

The stable hand gave a short bow before turning away and shouting orders down the line.

"As to your question, Alana, yes. Your mounts will be prepared as best they can." With that, she led the group into the streets of Karn, heading to the northwest.

Samuel was somewhat surprised by that path, as he knew the carrier was stationed in the south, but when they turned the corner by the last of the towers near the entrance to the Gray Woods, he understood much better.

Supply ships swooped down, settling on the earth long enough to unload pallets and crawlers before taking to the skies again. In the time it took them to walk the distance from the soaring tower to the outskirts of the landing zone, two supply ships had unburdened themselves.

It wouldn't have been possible without the Titan Mechs waiting on the ground, and Samuel whistled when the next supply ship landed. Two more of the towering Mechs rolled off the ship, balanced on wheeled pallets. Once they reached the earth, the Mechs simply stepped away from the pallets.

Samuel had worked with metal pallets like that before. They weighed some five hundred pounds. Far too much for a single person to manipulate, but here, on the outskirts of Karn, that was exactly what was happening. Only it wasn't just a person. They wore a suit of bronze and steel, dulled and camouflaged to all but disappear against the backdrop of the woods.

He'd seen something like it before.

"Samuel! Drakkar!"

The Spider Knight frowned as his concentration broke when he heard his name. From a familiar voice, no less, but it didn't lessen the surprise when he saw two Ancorans running toward him.

Samuel grinned as he slammed his forearm against Jacob's, trading grips with the kid as he would a soldier with the Spider Knights. Only Jacob wasn't just a kid anymore. Samuel might think of him that way no matter how old they got, but Jacob was changing as fast as the world around them. Part of that made Samuel despair the life they'd lost in the war, but another part of him couldn't be prouder of the kid he called a friend.

Alice nearly tackled Drakkar as she embraced him.

"It hasn't been *that* long since we had dinner," the Cave Guardian said with a laugh. "But it is good to see you too, Alice." He squeezed her close before exchanging the greeting of the Steamsworn.

"You finished Charles's exoskeleton, didn't you?" Samuel asked. "It looks different from the one I saw in Ballern."

Jacob gestured to the small Mech suit walking back up onto the supply ship. "That's just one of them. Frederick started a production line. Some of them are closer to Charles's design, weapons and all. Others, he and Natalia gave more specialized functions. They had to change the ratios for some of the joints to manage the extra weight, but—"

"Whoa, kid, whoa. That's dangerously close to tinker speak and I don't want to fall asleep right now."

Jacob laughed and slapped Samuel's forearm.

Samuel flashed him a smile.

Drakkar stepped closer and held out his fist. Jacob wrapped his fingers around it. "Jacob, Alice, you remember Allie and Alana."

Alice gave a small bow. "Of course we do! We are so grateful for all the help you've given Ancora, and to our friends in Belldorn."

"It is what an alliance should do," Alana said. "And Ancora has shown our own people much grace in these times. It is a welcome thing to call you friends."

A shadow crossed the landing zone, and when Samuel looked up, he almost flinched at the looming Porcupine in the sky. Its cannons bristled along its flanks like the quills of a Stone Dog. A threat, and a promise of protection, in one titanic package.

The great warships of Bollwerk might have been awe-inspiring, but the Porcupines were *more.* It drifted over the woods before wheeling around and heading back toward the carrier.

"Are you going to be piloting the Titan Mechs?" Drakkar asked. "I have been told you are one of the best."

Jacob shook his head. "No, but I'd like to take an exoskeleton into the woods. It'd be a true test in the mud and roots."

"I don't know if a battle is the best time to test that." Samuel scratched the back of his head.

"Not for the battle!" Jacob's brow furrowed, and he leaned away from Samuel. "I'm not completely mad. But afterwards, to really test it on the terrain."

"Kid, you jumped off a building to test a glider."

Jacob opened his mouth to say something, hesitated, and Alice answered for him.

"Yes, he did. Twice. Let's not encourage him."

Alana smiled and gestured to Jacob. "Perhaps when this war is done, you would be willing to visit Cave again. Our tinkers could show you the value in more cautious methodologies, and you can share the benefit of being more aggressive."

"If you can get me a room at The Rock Inn, I'd be happy to visit anytime."

Alana raised an eyebrow and turned to Drakkar. "I sense *your* hand in this."

"I may have introduced him to the fine fare at the inn. In my defense, I believe it was more Charles's fault than mine."

"You can't blame Atlier for *everything*, Drakkar."

"Not anymore, anyway," Alice said under her breath.

Samuel didn't miss the grin that flashed across Drakkar's face.

Mali slipped a thin pocket watch from a pouch on her hip. "We deploy in just over two hours. Best make final preparations." She glanced at Jacob and Alice. "If you would like to join me with a company of Tree Killers, we have spare mounts."

Jacob nodded. "Thanks, Mali. We'd love to."

✧   ✧   ✧

JACOB TRIED NOT to laugh when Mali and Alice both looked at Samuel in horror as Bessie clambered over another outcropping of roots. They'd been debating how the airships could be utilized, and Samuel's latest suggestion was, admittedly, not the best Jacob could have thought of.

"You are failing to consider the land that surrounds you, Samuel." Drakkar offered a warm smile to the Spider Knight.

"I'm not saying to bomb the *entire* forest. But remember how Mordair bombed Midstream? If you did that, you could clear a path, make things more visible."

"And ruin every ambush we have set up for miles," Mali said for what had to be the third time, exasperation clear in her voice. "And that's before you even consider the fact much of our food comes from the forest. You're talking about bombing farms, Samuel."

The Spider Knight visibly sighed as Bessie returned to the ground. "I didn't know that. Okay, sorry, bad idea, I admit."

"How could you know?" Mali waved his apology away, her words less heated. "The best use of airships, other than killing ourselves as we fight our enemy, is to target the broad clearings in the Gray Woods. There are areas where the road runs through swaths of dead forest. It may only be a few hundred feet in any direction, but it's something.

"Other than those targets, the entry to the woods is the best place for an airship. It's half a mile from the northern edge of the city."

"A half mile isn't much," Alice said. "An armored crawler could cover that in well under a minute if it was moving at speed."

Drakkar inclined his head. "That is true, though the roads here are not paved like those of Bollwerk, or even the desert sands around Midstream.

"If the road was clear, they might be that fast." Mali gave her a knowing smile. "But the road is never clear, Alice. No matter how unguarded it may appear. With the shadow of the airships overhead, our enemies will pay a dire price to set foot inside Karn."

Jacob looked back, as if he could see through the woods they'd already traversed to catch a glimpse of Karn. "You don't even have walls, Mali. How can it be that well guarded?"

"We may not have the same technology as what you told us about in Midstream, or what brought down the walls of Ancora. But we do have farms in the towers, many of which you would not want to anger."

Jacob cursed under his breath. He'd seen what invaders could do on a rampage. The idea that Karn had trained some of the bugs they depended on for sustenance to be defenders of the city was both impressive and disturbing.

"Do you train them in the same way you train your mounts?" Samuel asked. "I'm curious because one of my old captains always thought we could train the Jumpers to be their own squad. No one to direct or control them, just train them to attack any invaders."

Mali tapped her chin. "In a way, the training is not so different than how we train our mounts. It's mostly reward based, giving them extra food and water when they strike at a predator that comes too close. Training the Needles, of any sort, is a difficult task. Dangerous, too. The Tree Killers are easier to work with, both mounted and not."

Jacob looked up at the branches and soaring trunks of the Forest Giants all around them. The idea that some of the Tree Killers surely hidden nearby had been trained to watch for invaders was mind-boggling. "How can you be sure they won't attack people from Karn?"

"We know the roads to avoid. Some of it is scent based. A cocktail of perfumes and organs from the dead indigenous wildlife that live around the city. Trainers will sometimes don the scent like hunters trying to blend in with their prey."

"What if it rains?" Samuel's brow furrowed.

Mali grinned at the question. "It is not so easy to wash away, Samuel. The roads only need to be doused once every few months, and though you may not smell anything, the bugs have keener senses than we do."

"That makes sense." Samuel patted Bessie's head. "I swear this girl can smell a trough of Sweet-Flies from a mile away."

"That's nothing." Alice glanced back for a moment. "Jacob can smell Cocoa Crunch from at least a mile away."

"That's … mostly not true." Jacob grinned at Alice. "I'd certainly walk a couple miles for a good Cocoa Crunch!"

Drakkar's Tree Killer sped forward when Mali's pulled ahead. They rode side by side, Jacob and Alice close behind as Bessie and Samuel scrambled over roots and fallen trunks just to their right.

Every so often, Jacob glanced back, checking on the next group of marchers. They didn't move in a column like they had when Allie and Alana had guided them toward Ballern. Now, they moved under the direction of Karn's commanders.

The smaller groups meant fewer of them could be ambushed in a single strike, but it also opened each squad to far more dire consequences should a strong enough attack befall them. But Tree Killers and spiders were not slow to react. The smallest hesitation in any attack would give them some space to retreat, scatter, or mount a counterstrike, but even a complete loss of a squad would leave the attackers to deal with what came before, and what came after.

And not all of their mounts were as obvious as those that traversed the ground. As plodding and imposing as the Tree Killers were on the forest floor, those closer to the canopy moved with a terrible grace, allowing their riders to hang upside down and nearly sideways as they walked in silence. It required a more robust harness, but it was something Jacob hadn't noticed the first few times they'd seen the mounted Tree Killers.

Drakkar held a hand to his side, and Jacob didn't miss the wince that crossed his face. Alice called out to the Cave Guardian before Jacob could.

"Are you okay?"

He cast a smile back in their direction. "Fine, my friend. A little sore, as I am still healing from Ballern. It will resolve in time."

Alice wore a flat expression that said, quite plainly, she didn't think Drakkar should be riding with them.

Apparently, Drakkar didn't think her expression showed any kind of agreement, either, as his voice took on a more confident tone. "If I can throw a spear, I can certainly ride on a Tree Killer."

"You've been throwing spears?" Alice shouted after him. "No wonder you're hurting again. Are you sure you aren't related to Samuel? He likes to do foolish things too, you know?"

"Hey!" Samuel yelled from the path's edge.

"Oh, don't try to act like you don't." Alice pointed a finger at the Spider Knight. "Remember when you broke your leg on patrol? Five years ago? I remember it because it was one of your first patrols and you were trying to impress a new recruit."

The sudden, and rather violent, blush on Samuel's face said all Jacob needed to know. He didn't remember Samuel breaking his leg, but the Spider Knight likely would have been cared for in the Highlands if it had been five years prior.

And if Jacob was being honest, five years felt like a lifetime ago.

"Everyone does what they can." Mali projected her voice, but she wasn't yelling. Her words still brought the banter between Alice and Samuel to a stop. "I saw Allie working through the pain of her burns. An injury from a Bombardier is no small thing." Her voice hardened. "We all fight on. We don't have a choice."

It was another way of looking at their injuries, to be sure. Jacob thought it applied to far more than the more recent incidents. Smith still moved forward regardless of the injuries he sustained in battle. Jacob still fought with his Biomech leg. He'd seen Charles fight to the bitter end, and read a hundred other tales of people fighting on in the Deadlands War. And it *was* people, despite the fact they weren't always soldiers.

They continued in silence for a time, listening to the woods around them, and deep in the forest, the basso buzz of some distant bug vibrated through the air.

CHAPTER EIGHTEEN

A STRANGE, HIGH-PITCHED squeal sounded through the woods. At first, Jacob wasn't sure what the sound was, but a break in the canopy showed a supply ship above them, two Titan Mechs dangling from a tangle of wires beneath it.

As quickly as the sight had come, it was gone, lost in the thicker clusters of branches and leaves.

"Where do you think they're taking them?" Samuel asked as the road widened, and Bessie sidled up closer to the Tree Killers.

"There are two clearings to the north." Mali pointed just to the left and right of the road. "They could be deployed to divert any infantry marching on Karn, but Arun may have other plans. Whatever the situation is, they are certainly not being stealthy about it."

Jacob still found himself looking at the canopy from time to time, trying to pierce the darkness and make sure no Acidwings were a threat above them. It was likely unnecessary, as he was certain Mali or the others from Karn would sound an alert if danger was imminent. Knowing that didn't stop his occasional focus on the shadows above them.

Another fifteen minutes passed before the echoes of a rapid staccato reached them. Faint at first, but the Tree Killers near the canopy repeated the sound until their mounts rubbed their hind legs together, and the staccato drumming threatened to overwhelm any attempt at communication.

Mali must have given a signal Jacob missed because their mounts gathered in a tight circle, backs toward the center so riders and bugs alike could wield their weapons. Jacob's heartbeat thudded in his ears as the cacophony of warnings faded, and they were left with the eerie stillness of a startled forest.

He could hear the rumble then, the distant churning of armored crawlers working their way through the Gray Woods. But even from their current position on the crest of a hill, he could see nothing but spiders and Tree Killers for nearly a quarter mile ahead.

"Mali," Alice hissed. "Something's in the tree closest to us. The bark moved."

Mali squinted, her knuckled whitening around the haft of a spear. She started to raise it, paused, and blew out a slow breath. "It is one of ours. An ambush in wait."

Jacob still didn't see a thing out of the ordinary, which had him questioning just how flawless Karn's camouflage was. Only when a section of bark opened like a door and someone exchanged a quick series of signs with Mali, could Jacob tell where they were positioned. Once the door closed, he lost them immediately.

"That's not good." Mali frowned and looked around them. "Scouts haven't seen anything coming this way. All those crawlers came into the woods on *this* road. Where did they go?" She pulled out a small map held in a bronze case with a floating compass embedded in the center.

"I still hear the crawlers." Jacob could make out the distant rumble. "If it's as far away as it sounds, I'd think they were a mile out at least."

Mali shook her head. "That's not possible. Another mile and we'll be in the territory of the Children of the Dark Fire." She frowned and peered into the woods. "We missed them somehow."

Alice's face fell and then she sat ramrod straight in her saddle. "Mali! Mali, are there tunnels under the Gray Woods?"

"Of course, the old rivers from the wetlands carved a vast cave system that …" Mali let out a string of curses that would have made the grumpiest tinker in Belldorn blush. Mali clicked the transmitter in her collar. "Arun! They're in the caves. We haven't seen a hint of them in the woods. It's the only thing that makes sense."

Arun's answer came in quiet static. "Understood. We will prepare the airships for any incursions."

"They aren't there yet," Samuel said. "We have time to get back."

Drakkar shifted in his saddle. "The Spider Knight is not wrong, Mali, but there is another path."

"What do you mean?" For the first time, an edge of worry shaped her words, and it unsettled Jacob more than he'd expected. "We've already covered *every* path. They aren't here!"

Drakkar gestured to the ground beneath their feet. "How well do you know the caves?"

"Well enough to know we might fall down a bottomless shaft. They'd have to be half mad to take armored crawlers underground."

"We do not ride on a crawler, Mali. We ride on mounts, sentient and with better vision than any of us have in the dark. Enter the caves in darkness, and let them lead us to our prey."

She glanced away from the Cave Guardian. "I can't ask my people to do that. I can send them to the city to wait."

"Ask them to volunteer." Samuel scratched at the back of Bessie's head.

"She doesn't need to ask," a voice said from just above them.

Jacob looked up to find another rider perched on the massive trunk of a fallen Forest Giant.

"The Spider Knights will follow," Samuel said. "I've seen spiders in the dark before. It's as natural to them as breathing."

Jacob didn't think Samuel was referring to Jumpers and Stalkers.

They'd both seen Widow Makers in the dark, and while they moved as well as any spider on the surface, none of those were mounts weighed down by armor and riders.

Mali stared at the rider above them before replying. "Ask for volunteers." She glanced at the map and looked at the rider again. "I first heard the crawlers almost two miles behind us. Turn the lines around and have them enter at the old copper mine. No crawler is getting through that at speed, and it may give us an element of surprise."

The soldier flipped his hand palm up and closed it into a fist. "It will be done."

Mali turned her mount and started leading the party directly into the woods. Shouted orders followed them down the line as more and more of the formation broke away. Some continued north, while others headed to Karn.

But a great many of the mounts followed to the west, plunging deeper into the forest at Mali's request. Jacob had already been dreading going back underground when they got to the Great Machine, and now his stomach knotted at the idea of catching the armored crawlers of the Children of the Dark Fire beneath the earth.

✧   ✧   ✧

MALI DIDN'T SLOW at the cavernous entrance to the abandoned mine. No one raised so much as a lantern in case that light might give them away. Instead, she rode through the archway with little more than a few words repeated into her transmitter.

"Guide your mounts always left. Even should you lose the path, your mounts will find an escape closer to Karn. It will keep you safe from the worst of the deadfalls."

Darkness closed in around them, and Jacob could just hear Alice muttering.

"The *worst* of the deadfalls? What exactly is a *good* deadfall?"

Jacob's first thought was that a good deadfall would clearly be one that caught a lot of prey for whoever set it up. His second thought was pondering the fact they'd be *anywhere* near one in the total darkness of the underground, relying solely on their mounts. He gripped the reins of his Tree Killer ever tighter, feeling his weight shift as they started down a steep incline.

The faint click of claws on stone was the only sound other than the shuffling of armor and weapons. The spiders were nearly silent, stepping with the pads of their feet when the footing didn't require their claws to dig into the cracks and crevices of the stone.

Jacob turned the volume up on the transmitter in his collar, but even at its highest setting, nothing but a low hum of static sounded across. There was no rhythm to it, no pattern. They were deep enough in the caves that the signal had been entirely cut off.

It was odd to think how dependent he'd grown on the transmitters. They couldn't summon Smith or Mary to swoop in with the Skysworn, no signal to call out to Jakon, or Eva, or anyone. Beneath the earth, they only had their allies.

There might have been dozens of riders behind them, but Jacob had not felt so alone in a very long time.

He couldn't be sure how much time had passed in the dark, having instead focused on the rhythm of his Tree Killer's strides. The shadows were absolute. He'd heard people describe the dark of a cave as being black as the night, but it was *far* darker than that.

The total absence of light played with his vision. Flashes of color and pulses of light danced before his eyes, but he knew they weren't really there. After a time, some of those specks of light didn't fade. In fact, he could have sworn he saw the outline of another rider eclipse it.

And then he understood. In the distance, the path glowed with them.

Dozens of Fireworms lined the wall, and in a small pool of water, one of the titanic forms of a full-grown adult rested in the dark.

They surged past the cluster of Fireworms, the largest of them raising its head from the pool to study the newcomers. But it wasn't the Fireworm that recoiled at the sight of Tree Killers and spiders. It was the mounts that gave the worm a wide berth.

It made a kind of sense in Jacob's mind, after hearing the story of the Stone Dogs and Samuel's rescue by Drakkar. The elder Fireworms were ferocious protectors, and their reputation apparently reached well beyond the caves where they spent their lives.

As slowly as the Fireworms had brightened the caves, their light disappeared faster when the path turned and dipped down an incline once more. The air grew cooler the farther they journeyed into the mines. It wasn't long before the close echo of claws on stone shifted, quieting to a great degree.

Jacob had little doubt that meant they'd reached a larger chamber in the mines, and it was infuriating not to be able to raise a light of any sort. But no one in their company did. They all charged into the black.

The shift came from nowhere, nearly slamming Jacob's face into the Tree Killer's saddle when they hit an incline so steep it might have been a wall. He leaned forward, hearing a few whispered curses behind him from other riders.

It only lasted for a few seconds before the path leveled out again, but this time, it wasn't darkness that waited in front of them. A great rumbling echoed around them in the narrowing tunnel. This time, Jacob *knew* the path had narrowed because lights stood out ahead, casting a long train of crawlers into silhouette.

They could only rush forward two mounts deep, which was going to give the armored crawlers an advantage. Almost as soon as Jacob had that thought, the Tree Killer beside Mali scuttled up onto the wall, followed closely by Samuel and Bessie. It gave them a height and numbers advantage, which he hoped would be enough.

Jacob met Alice's eyes. She gave him one sharp nod as she primed her wrist launchers. It was a good choice. She could fire an entire belt of bolts without having to reload or take her hands off the bridle. Aiming would be another problem, but if you had enough bolts, you didn't have to worry about that as much.

He'd been on the wrong side of an ambush before. He'd seen friends and allies fall at the hands of their enemies. Most of those hands had been guided by Mordair. Maybe in another time, another life, they could have been something more. But fate had long ago set things into motion. Battles and skirmishes that marched through the decades since the Deadlands War.

And now Mordair was coming for Karn. Coming for their new alliance with the aid of the Children of the Dark Fire. They would all pay a price for what their bastard king had wrought.

Mali raised her fist in the air, and Tree Killers surged across the ceiling, their riders strapped into heavy harnesses, wielding bolt throwers that would have looked more at home on an airship.

The first shot took the pilot of the rear crawler. The vehicle turned so suddenly the treads lost their grip, and the entire vehicle spun, slamming into the cave wall and blocking a third of the path. Stone cascaded down around the survivors, pelting them with rock as surely as the bolts launched from the riders who followed.

The open crawlers might have been good protection if they needed to escape an Acidwing. They were a death sentence beneath Mali's soldiers. Jacob's Tree Killer scurried over the third disabled crawler, casually spearing a survivor as it ran. The blank look on the man's cloaked face disappeared as fast as it had flashed in front of Jacob's eyes.

Drakkar lashed out with a collapsible spear, impaling another pilot.

She didn't die fast, but it didn't matter when a fireball erupted from the rear of the crawler. Shrill screams echoed up into the air, and for the first time, the forward crawlers took notice.

The alarm was subtle, a flashing of light like the signaling of a ship. It wouldn't reach the foremost of the armored crawlers as spread out as they were, but it reached enough to create a serious problem. Bolts whistled through the cave, sparking off stone and bringing down mounted riders as effectively as a cannon shot.

Mali signaled with her left hand, three splayed fingers, and the riders scattered. Whatever formation had been there before was lost as the mounts took to the walls and ceiling, leaving the Spider Knights and the Ancorans to churn across the stone and dirt.

Jacob understood they were the bait now. It was a smart decision for Mali to make. Bessie was more agile than the Tree Killers, and the armored spider mounts, while less mobile, could absorb more damage than those above.

One thing they couldn't afford to do was slow down. Their mounts moved in a natural weaving pattern, making it hard for any long-range weapon to lock on, but it didn't mean they weren't coming close.

A bolt pinged off the leg armor of Alice's mount and she leaned forward into the saddle. Her Tree Killer surged into a sprint, scuttling onto the wall just before it would have collided with the armored crawler, and Alice unleashed a hail of bolts into the compartment.

Jacob didn't need to see the inside as he sped past to know everyone in that crawler was dead. It slowed to a stop, a burial chamber for their attackers. The message had spread through the line of crawlers now. Some pulled to the side where the road flared out and the wall vanished against a great darkness. He would have been lying if he didn't feel a glimmer of satisfaction as one came too close to the edge of a chasm and plunged into it.

He racked the slide for the air cannon until it would barely move. There was enough ammunition hooked into his vest to last two dozen rounds. After that, he'd have to get creative, and Jacob cringed at the ideas that flashed through his mind.

But this wasn't a time for ideals and discipline and compassion. This was a time to act, or to die. Or, worse, watch his friends die. He had to fight the urge to look at Alice as that dark thought took root in his mind, and a hundred different scenarios played out in his head in the blink of an eye.

Jacob urged his mount to sprint. A simple command of two taps and a long drag behind the Tree Killer's head. They overtook Bessie in a flash, his mount swinging left, scampering between the wall and the next crawler. There wouldn't be much time to aim, and as soon as the thought entered his head, Jacob pulled the trigger.

The air cannon echoed through the mine, an absolute crack of thunder in the enclosed space. Blood and gore sprayed across the console of the armored crawler as the pilot slumped over, his helmet a ruin as the vehicle drifted to the right and ramped off the side into darkness, taking the screaming passengers into the abyss.

Bessie closed the gap, pacing close enough that Jacob could hear Samuel's shout. "Nice shot!"

The Spider Knight had far more grace than Jacob. He raised his halberd as Bessie pounced, her furry gray form slamming a crawler into the ground as Samuel struck with a violent thrust. Light caught on the metal of swords as they leaped away from the armored crawler. If Bessie had been hit, she didn't show it, instead passing in front of the crawler and angling for the next.

Drakkar followed close behind, hurling a collapsed spear through an armored side window in the crawler. As quick as he'd struck, the Cave Guardian retrieved the spear with a violent pull, collapsing it in one fluid motion that prevented any injury to his own mount.

There was a thrill in battle, an excitement unrivaled by almost anything else Jacob had experienced, but it was always pulled back down by the horror of what unfolded around him. The mounts might have been quick, and their foes might have had a difficult time aiming, but once there were enough projectiles hurtling through the air, some would find their mark.

A Tree Killer along the ceiling took a bolt to the head, and it crashed to the earth in the path of an armored crawler, a scream cut short as the treads drove the fallen rider and his mount into the stone floor.

Another shot clipped Mali's mount, and two legs spun off, trailing dark blue blood. Mali leaned into the saddle as the Tree Killer tried to compensate, shifting to the wall. The loss of legs wasn't only a death sentence, but it'd also slowed the bug down. Two more bolts took it in the chest, and Mali fell.

Alice raced alongside an armored crawler as it angled for Mali, still trying to free herself from the Tree Killer's complicated harness. Jacob watched, helpless, as Alice undid her own harness and leaned far to the side, risking getting crushed by her own mount's legs.

He saw the bolt launcher extend from the side of the armored crawler, but so did Samuel. Bessie hurdled Alice's mount, and the slash of a halberd sent the launcher clattering to the ground with a severed arm. In that same moment, Alice's Tree Killer rushed past Mali. Jacob heard the violent crack of leather on skin as Alice snared Mali from the dead mount, briefly dragging her along the ground. The Tree Killer lifted a leg in the air as it ran, giving Mali a chance to join Alice in the saddle.

The knot of dread didn't leave Jacob's chest. Adrenaline might have kept him engaged, focused, but the fact he could lose any of his friends at any moment was enough to keep that frisson of terror tempering whatever excitement might live beside it.

One thing was certain: they couldn't all remain behind the crawlers. Their position condensed them into a single target, but Jacob didn't know how to change their formation. He didn't know the signals. All he could do was get close to Alice and Mali and scream.

"We need to spread out!"

Mali nodded, flashing her arm out and giving a series of complicated signals. Her soldiers didn't hesitate, the clustered groups of riders breaking apart like snow swept from a stoop.

They wove between the Children of the Dark Fire's crawlers, giving them targets that, if missed, would land attacks on their own allies. But that didn't all go to plan. Some Tree Killers slowed at the wrong time, getting trapped beneath treads and hails of bolts. Others were lost to gouts of flame that looked like miniature explosions. That shouldn't have been enough to kill the mounts, but it *was* enough to disorient them, and the price was high.

A grim realization overwhelmed Jacob as the race through the mines continued. If the line of armored crawlers was as long as they'd seen in the photos, they'd never stop them in time. The front of the assault would already be nearing Karn, and they might be sprinting into the death of another city.

He bore down on the next target, readying a Burner for an attack. It was time to take a far greater risk than he wanted in that enclosed space. But Karn would not fall because they joined the alliance. He'd make sure of that.

Jacob's Tree Killer sprinted out past Alice and Drakkar, leaving Bessie and Samuel behind as he sped by even the foremost of their allies. He felt an impact on his saddle, glancing back to find a bolt stuck in the thick leather. It had been close. Too close.

He clicked the igniter for the Burner, locked it inside the shell of a firebomb, and hurled it into the armored carrier that had launched fiery attacks on the Tree Killers. Jacob spun and retreated, holding his hand out palm first, fingers splayed, before flipping it around.

Mali's soldiers didn't miss the signal. They scurried and turned back, taking shots at the armored crawlers as they raced forward. Everything slowed when the firebomb detonated. The darkness of the mine, illuminated only by the lanterns on the crawlers moments before, erupted into the raging blaze of a bonfire.

The fire formed a wall from floor to ceiling, only licking out into the chasm on the right where the dangling roots of a Forest Giant hung in columns of living tissue. As fast as the blinding ball had come, it dissipated in smoke and screams.

Hooded forms leaped out of the crawlers, holding their hands up and taking a knee on the stone.

"Run home or die," Mali shouted as she and Alice sprinted past the surrendering forces, mounting the wall to dash by the burning husk of an armored crawler. The rest of their allies followed, flowing around the Children of the Dark Fire.

Leaving them in that mine might give them time to regroup. Jacob wondered if it was too merciful of Mali to spare them. If it just meant they'd have to fight the Children of the Dark Fire's survivors again another day. But in that moment, what mattered was getting back to Karn.

And while the firebomb might have stopped some of the crawlers, it gave the foremost crawlers an advantage. Now Jacob and his allies had ground to make up, having paused for the fury of the firebomb, and he didn't know how much space was left in the tunnel for that to happen.

When they turned the next corner and saw daylight in the distance, he realized they were already out of time.

CHAPTER NINETEEN

"THIS IS IT!" Samuel shouted as Bessie scuttled along next to Jacob's Tree Killer, flanked by Mali and others from Karn. "Be ready for anything when we come out of this tunnel. *Anything!* Don't slow down. Don't stop to help anyone. Get to cover. Assess the battle. Got it?"

"Got it!" Jacob yelled back.

Drakkar raced beside them, another spear in his hand, his hood snapping in the wind that howled through the entrance to the mine. Broken vines hung between them and the daylight that waited beyond. Shadows of the forest dominated the view, but in the distance, Jacob could just make out the soaring towers of Karn and the airships that guarded the perimeter.

He hadn't forgotten how short that distance was. If the armored crawlers circled around to the west, they might circumvent the best-defended zone altogether. If they did, it would be up to Jacob and the others to run them down before they could do any significant damage to the city.

It was the last stray thought he had before they reached the entrance and exploded out into the forest, a stampede of Tree Killers and Jumpers that needed no direction. They followed the crawlers' tread marks, some diverting to the west, as Jacob had feared, but others heading straight toward Karn.

A shadow flew through the forest, and Jacob tried to understand what he was seeing—an armored crawler, upended and airborne, sailing through the woods until it shattered against a Forest Giant, sending splinters and metal shrapnel to rain down below.

Another silhouette stepped through the foliage, a towering form, designed by Charles, rebuilt by Jacob, an engine of destruction that unleashed the fury of its pilot on the armored column. But not even a Titan Mech could take down a force of crawlers that numbered so many.

Jacob cursed and shifted his path, heading straight for the Titan Mech as he unhinged another bomb. This one wasn't a firebomb. This one Charles had designed to be an explosive like few others. Jacob clicked the igniter, clipped the orb closed, and hurled it into the space between four crawlers in a tight formation.

One moment, they were exchanging fire with the Titan Mech. The next, they were gone, the air vibrating with the blast. Shrapnel and flames rained down through the woods, casting an eerie glow in the shadows of the forest as choking smoke rose above the ruined crawlers.

Jacob's mount leaped onto a tree and scuttled up to the first branch, following his commands to run down the Titan Mech. He froze when he saw who waited in the cockpit, clicking his transmitter and shouting at the man.

"Smith! What the hell are you doing here?"

"The Children of the Dark Fire were on the ground, Jacob. Everywhere. We tried strafing them from the Skysworn, but they had Bombardiers in the canopy. Firing blind against an opponent with a clear line of sight is not advisable."

"Bomb the edge of the woods."

Smith hesitated. "What?"

"Tell Kat to bomb the edge of the woods, *now!* The crawlers are circling west."

Smith cut out, and Jacob's focus on the Titan Mech shifted. He switched the dial in his transmitter and clicked the button. "Get everyone out of the forest. Get back into the city."

"We have them on the run!" Samuel called.

"Get out now or feed the Carrion Worms along with them!"

The Spider Knight cursed, and Jacob heard the calls go up nearby. Riders flashed signals from Tree Killers and spiders alike, and the fighting broke off all along the edge of the woods. He scanned the area for Alice and Mali, finding them on the far side of Smith's Titan Mech, sprinting back toward the city, almost inside the outskirts.

"Go!" Drakkar called as he passed Jacob.

He didn't need another reminder. The Tree Killer matched the pace of the Titan Mech beside them, and they hurtled across the open space between the forest and city, scarcely glancing backward as they ran.

Jacob didn't turn until they were halfway through the clearing, at least a quarter mile from the woods, but the bombs didn't drop right behind them. They crashed through the canopy as the first crawlers entered the western blocks of Karn.

The explosions didn't result in gouts of flame or burning embers being launched into the air. Instead, they looked like the white clouds of a glass fire extinguisher shattering across a blaze. The impact was no less violent. Armored crawlers turned to wreckage in the blink of an eye. The intensity of the blast sent some to smash into Forest Giants and a handful to barrel roll into the nearest towers.

Jacob wondered what it would take for the various farms to grow irritated enough that they would attack something on the ground. Apparently, more than the nearby battle. A chorus of shouts rose from inside the city, and he turned just in time to see the relentless rolling tide of Walkers, clad in armor and bristling with heavily armed soldiers.

These were not the weapons of Karn, but the Walkers led by Allie and Alana, leaders of Cave and Canopy. The Walkers were at home in the desert sands and stone, but the long hours spent training with Cave Guardians had made them more adaptable than Jacob could have imagined.

They surged across the streets, streaking over the smoking crawlers and closing on the survivors in the woods.

"Follow them!" Mali cried from the back of Alice's Tree Killer. And it wasn't only their company who moved to pursue the invaders. Every Spider Knight and soldier from Karn within earshot joined the charge, leaving churned earth in their wake as they plunged through the craters left by the bombs, the acrid stench of burning fuel and flesh choking the air around them.

Fallen trees peppered the forest floor, wreaking havoc on the treads of the armored crawlers, creating dead ends mired in splintered trunks and broken branches piled against the Forest Giants. As the Children of the Dark Fire fled into those spaces, the forces of Karn closed the trap.

There was no mercy in that moment. Not even those who tried to surrender were allowed to live as the defenders of Karn ran them down. It was an awful thing to see, but the leaders had chosen their path, and the soldiers at their command carried out their mission with ruthless efficiency.

Mordair's allies grouped together as they moved through the Gray Woods, forming larger and larger squadrons of survivors. At the rate Karn was chasing them down, they were going to have a terrible battle in the woods if the Children of the Dark Fire were allowed to regroup.

Alice guided her Tree Killer with Mali still in her saddle. They both fired bolts into clusters of cloaked soldiers, but as they rounded a dense copse of trees, the bulk of the survivors were waiting. They'd already had the time they needed to form ranks.

Armored crawlers faced outward, forming a protective circle as their riders ignited flamethrowers in the perpetual twilight of the deep woods.

It wasn't a clean fire. It spewed thick, caustic smoke into the air, choking their own allies as much as it burned the eyes of Karn's soldiers.

But it served another purpose. It hid the bolt launchers on the far side of the flames, and a hail of projectiles rained down on the Walkers. Mounts and riders scattered, but it wouldn't be enough to save the invaders.

Mali had spoken of the ambushes set in the woods. Nearly invisible sentries, guarding the roads and trails to Karn, had established an armed perimeter few could slip past. And while the Children of the Dark Fire might have found a way underneath, word had reached the sentries.

The forest canopy behind Mordair's allies churned, and two dozen Tree Killers sprinted between the branches, giving their riders a perfect angle on the exposed tops of the armored crawlers. But it wasn't only the Tree Killers that came at Karn's command. Their Bombardiers took aim at the ailing forces below and unleashed boiling jets of acid across the battlefield.

Jacob saw two more riders fall from their Walkers at the end of the battle. He hadn't realized who one of them was until Samuel screamed her name.

"Allie's down! Get her out of here, now!"

He could scarcely follow what was happening as Samuel fended off a surviving cultist with two quick swipes of his halberd. The Spider Knight didn't see what was coming behind him. Couldn't know a flamethrower was targeting his back as it inched closer.

Jacob raised his air cannon, focused, and gently squeezed the trigger. The tank of fuel for the flamethrower inside the armored crawler ruptured, and the flames took care of the rest. Heat washed over them all as a fireball billowed up into the canopy, dissipating in the wet leaves, though some embers still lingered.

The ground burned behind Samuel, and the Spider Knight stared at the blown-out husk of the crawler. He gathered himself and helped Drakkar load Allie onto the back of a Stalker. Jacob could see the two bolts that had found their mark. One in the neckline of her armor and another in an elbow joint. Depending on the angle, it might not be too severe. Judging by her limp form, he didn't have much hope.

Sentinels swept through the woods, scouring them for any survivors and bringing them to a swift end. Jacob wasn't surprised to find more Titan Mechs in Karn by the time they returned. A handful of exoskeletons patrolled the smaller alleys, and Jacob didn't miss the red stains along the blades of one.

He guided his mount back to the stables, only somewhat aware of Alice and Mali riding beside him. Mostly, he only heard the chants from the soldiers behind them. Cries of victory, a chorus of rejoicing that Jacob couldn't feel. They were alive, yes, but this was a tiny, tiny section of the forces at Mordair's disposal now. And in the end, they wouldn't be fighting in the woods they knew so well.

In the end, there might not be anything left to rejoice over.

✦   ✦   ✦

ALICE STOOD OUTSIDE the hospital with Drakkar and several Cave Guardians. There were at least as many dragonriders from Canopy there, and more of Karn's soldiers than she'd expected. Of course, they might not *all* be waiting on news about Allie. A number of injured had been taken to the hospital after the battle. They were the lucky ones. The rest would be burned soon.

Allie and Alana clearly shared a bond that had only been strengthened in the new alliances. So many of the Cave Guardians under Alana's leadership had family and distant relatives who had moved to Canopy in the city's earliest days. Now they were together once more, side by side with allies from Ballern and Belldorn, Bollwerk and Ancora.

Quiet conversations filled the air, but the weight of what had come in that battle settled like a clump of iron in water. Two fire brigades had been sent into the woods to ensure the flames did not spread from the burning armored crawlers. No prisoners returned to Karn. There were no prisoners to be taken. Either the people they'd spared in the mine had escaped, or they'd fallen to Karn's patrols.

Alice wasn't sure how to feel about that. There was something to be said for compassion, but to release so many back to a city where they would simply have to fight them again? She didn't know what the best answer was. She didn't think the kind of mercy Belldorn had shown to the Skyborn would work in Karn. The Children of the Dark Fire were different, conditioned to a degree the nobles of Ballern could have only hoped for.

Although they'd done more than hope for it, hadn't they? They'd been infiltrated by the Children of the Dark Fire, manipulated and corrupted and, in the end, turned against their own city.

Those spiraling thoughts only broke when Alana appeared at the door and raised her hand. She didn't say any words. She didn't need to. The whispers quieted as everyone faced her, Cave Guardians and dragonriders alike, waiting to hear Allie's fate.

"She will live."

It didn't bring back anyone else they'd lost that day, but there was relief throughout the crowd and a vibrant joy that echoed out among the dragonriders. Part of her thought Rin and Tatsu should have been with them in Karn. A larger part of her was glad they were helping rebuild Ballern and caring for the damage done to its people.

She put her arms around Drakkar when the Cave Guardian smiled at her. She was happy there was some good news for him, a solid friend they could rely on. The Cave Guardian soon exchanged grips with Jacob and Samuel as Alice tried to hold on to that bright moment.

The world had been smeared into shades of gray in the war with Fel. Enemies had become friends. Allies had become traitors. It wasn't only the shades of gray that worried Alice, and the delicate balance of a new alliance. It was the shades of red that stained the earth. Shades of red that drew a grim path to the funeral pyres. Shades of red that would lead to the Great Machine.

CHAPTER TWENTY

"THAT'S WHY I think Alice and I should do this alone." Jacob sighed and leaned on the map-covered table by Arun. "If we run into anyone, they won't think we're from Karn."

Mali grimaced and shook her head at Jacob. "Even with a guide, the chances of getting lost are great. I don't think we should let them leave with nothing more than a map and a compass."

Arun looked over the equipment Jacob had laid out on the table, from the grappling cannon to the thin ropes and hollow coil. "It is not our place to stop them, Mali. But we need you here."

"We should at least send them with a scouting party." Mali clenched her fists.

Alice reached out and placed her hand on Mali's forearm for a moment. "I appreciate what you're trying to do, Mali, but anyone from Karn could be recognized. They certainly wouldn't look as out of place as two Ancorans."

"She is of the old blood," Arun said. "That holds a great weight inside the Children of the Dark Fire. It could buy them precious moments, or an escape, should things grow complicated."

Alice spoke quietly. "Nothing like being the favorite of cultists."

"What did Kat and Archibald have to say?" Mali asked.

"It is not their place to make declarations on behalf of Karn, Mali." Arun offered a warm smile. "Regardless of what they might say, it is ultimately the decision of Jacob and Alice. We can offer equipment and mounts that may be of service in the woods, but their plan is sound."

"It's not safe."

"Little is in the Gray Woods."

Mali's rigid posture relaxed a hair, and her combative tone softened. "At least let me go over the map with you again. You don't want to wander into any of Karn's traps, either. Our soldiers don't know you, and they'll be on edge after the latest attack."

Jacob and Alice huddled around the table, listening to Mali describe the coordinates displayed along the punched edges. Small triangles detailed known permanent nests, and the direction they pointed indicated the level of the threat. It fascinated Jacob, as many of the nests near Ancora moved with the seasons. You might find Red Death in a shallow cave in the spring, but by winter, they would be deep beneath the earth, surfacing only to scavenge for their next meal.

Either the weather around the Gray Woods didn't have the same extremes as the mountainous terrain near Ancora, or the burrows dug into the Forest Giants provided far better insulation than he could have imagined. Regardless, knowing where a nest of Emerald Needles or Bombardiers resided was invaluable information.

They compared Mali's map to what they had from the control center. The topography added more detail to the terrain, even though it didn't have the details of the nests. But, combined, they could easily plot a path through the worst of the threats.

Mali tapped on a line to the far west. "This is a sheer cliff that drops down to a river. Avoid it because you won't have anywhere to run if you go that far."

Alice traced her finger along the same area on the control center map. Several lines grew close together. "These appear to show the cliff you're talking about. It should be easy enough to avoid so long as we follow the crest of the ridge to the west.

"I'm so glad we found these maps at the control center," Mali said. "Arun already has one of our cartographers creating an overlay. Most of the Children of the Dark Fire's patrols likely concentrate around those tunnels. It's going to make travel through the Gray Woods much safer for everyone from Karn."

"I'm happy it will help." Alice flashed a smile. "And I think *we* have our path through the woods. Staying along this ridge avoids almost all the nests. A good thing to know in case we lose the map or get separated."

"I don't see how you could possibly lose it. It's too large and unwieldy for that."

Memories crossed Jacob's mind, thoughts of the panicked flights through the caves of Ancora and the mad sprints in the desert around Midstream. It didn't matter how large something was; you could always lose it in the heat of a battle or the terror of an escape. The thought of getting separated from Alice in a situation like that made him shudder. It took him back to the underground bridge and the Water Beetle that had almost stolen his life in the river.

"Are you okay?" Alice's brow furrowed as she squeezed his arm.

"Fine, fine. It's nothing, really. Just remembering the river under Ancora."

She eyed him for a moment, but moved on. He was grateful for it. There were some memories that didn't need to be relived and sifted through over and over. And that moment, so close to death, was certainly one of them.

Mali held out a rough handwritten map with major landmarks noted. "This is in case you lose sight of the ridge. Tree Killers are normally drawn to higher ground, so once you reach the first rise, I don't think they'll lose the path."

"Thank you." Alice looked over the points and symbols, compared them to their own map, and then slid it into a pocket beneath the gray cloak she now wore. "And you're sure we need to wear these?" She flared the edge of the cloak to emphasize what she meant.

"It will be safer if you run into the Children of the Dark Fire. Use their blessing if you can't avoid any casual encounter."

"Be you blessed by the Dark Fire," Jacob muttered.

"Exactly," Arun said, some mild disgust in his voice. He gestured across the table. "Now, let's get you two your mounts."

✦　✦　✦

JACOB HAD SOMEWHAT expected Mary or Smith to protest their venture off into enemy territory alone, but the idea spoke more to their pirate roots than their sense of caution. Instead, the only argument had been that Smith wanted to take a closer look at the grappling cannon. Once he'd removed the housing, gone over every cog inside it in excruciating detail, and finally given his approval on it—regardless of the fact he'd seen it work before—they were off. And while Jacob and Alice made their way into the Gray Woods, Mary and Smith returned to helping lead some of the patrols around Karn.

Mali rode with them for a short time, holding her hand up to stop the trio when they reached the incline below the ridge. "Before you go on, I have a gift for both of you."

She guided her Tree Killer between Jacob and Alice, holding out a gray parcel wrapped in twine to each of them. At first, Jacob thought it was another cloak, but the idea fled as soon as he realized just how small the cube was.

"Should we open these now?" Alice asked.

"Please do."

She started untying the twine, and Jacob did the same. The fabric fell away to reveal a dark wooden box with a small hinge. Inside, nestled among padded crimson fabric, waited the metal-plated flame so many of the Children of the Dark Fire wore as a tattoo.

Jacob lifted it from the box, a chain trailing away from it as he raised it higher. "Do we … wear it?"

Mali offered a quick smile, as if she was trying to reassure him before she'd spoken a word. "Yes. Keep it tucked beneath your cloak. If you encounter any patrols, only reveal it then."

"Why not just keep it on display?" Alice turned the pendant between her fingers before slipping the chain around her neck.

"There are simple answers to that. If you keep it displayed and run into people who *aren't* part of that cult, it could end badly. Best to be cautious. If you *do* happen to see any Children of the Dark Fire, you'll notice very few display the Queen's Crest openly. Keep it hidden behind your cloak, close at hand, and you'll fit in better than keeping it displayed."

Alice nodded and closed the box, slipping it into a saddlebag on the side of her mount. "Thank you, Mali."

Their guide from Karn raised her fist to both of them. She left only after Jacob and Alice both exchanged the greeting of the Steamsworn. Mali didn't look back as she departed, leaving the Ancorans at the base of the ridge, alone in their march into enemy territory.

✧   ✧   ✧

JACOB WOULD HAVE preferred to ride on the back of a Jumper, but even Bessie and the more experienced mounts couldn't match the camouflage of the Tree Killers. The gray cloaks, with subtle patterns that might be mistaken for the bark of a Forest Giant, certainly helped them blend in, but it was still unsettling to think their survival could rely on a finely crafted piece of cloth.

"It's a rather beautiful symbol, isn't it?"

Jacob glanced at Alice to ask what she was talking about, but found her looking down at the metal-plated flame pendant. He pulled his own out from beneath the collar of his cloak, studying the wide curve of the metal and the rivets outlining each peak of the fire. There was an elegance to it, but the history that lingered behind it made his skin crawl.

"I hope you're not planning to get a tattoo," Jacob called back with mock concern.

Alice scoffed at that, slipping the pendant into her cloak once more. The chain was just short enough to keep the pendant from peeking out the bottom of the scarf-like wrap around her collar.

He swayed with the Tree Killer's stride as the mount sidestepped the broken stump of a long-dead Forest Giant. The falling tree had cut a swath through the canopy above them, and however many decades ago that had been, the surrounding foliage had almost entirely filled the void.

There was still enough light that the brambles on the forest floor had grown thick, showing thorns as long as Jacob's fingers and making him grateful for the measurable legs of the Tree Killers that kept them away from the worst of it.

They passed the shadow of the decaying stump in short order. The ridge cleared, the underbrush returning to moss and dirt in the heavier shadows of the Gray Woods. Dried and crumbling leaves crackled when the Tree Killers stepped into deeper collections and piles, but the mounts made little other noise.

It continued like that for a time, Jacob straining to hear anything that might be nearby in the woods or hidden in the canopy itself. There were a dozen nightmares that lived in the Gray Woods, and that was only what Jacob *knew* about. He didn't suspect he knew a fraction of the dangers that waited for them in the forest, but the idea of crossing Acidwings or wild Bombardiers was enough to keep him vigilant. That and the warning they'd received about the Shriekers.

"Relax." Alice's voice wasn't chiding or commanding. She simply gave him a suggestion.

His grip loosened on the reins and he took a slow breath, flexing his fingers as he tried to let the tension and stress bleed away. Charles had taught him that exercise years before when working with the most frustrating machines. It was a good policy to not keep chipping at a project until you threw it into a wall instead of regrouping and finding a workable solution.

All those thoughts flickered through his mind in the blink of an eye before he smiled at Alice. "Thanks."

"You looked like you were about to start a fight or cut those reins in half with your fingernails alone." He didn't miss the crease in her forehead that told him how concerned she was. It made him wonder just how intense his expression had been at that moment.

Smith had avoided him on more than one occasion when he was truly dug in at the workbench. Said he looked almost as scary as he'd seen the captain of the Skysworn on a bad day. That made Jacob laugh, but the sentiment had stuck with him.

He kept his breathing deep for nearly a minute, and it certainly helped to a degree. He didn't stare at every broad leaf that lifted in a breeze or freeze at every Pilly snuffling through the underbrush. The sounds of the forest grew more familiar as they went, but the thought of something waiting to ambush them never fully left his thoughts.

Jacob knew if anything attacked them on their way to the tunnels, it probably wouldn't be a bug. It was far more likely to be a scout from the Children of the Dark Fire. It didn't make him feel better, exactly, but he knew that people didn't camouflage nearly as well as Tree Killers, and staring into every shadow with a weight of dread wasn't necessary.

He laughed to himself, amazed at how well Alice knew him and how well she could change his darker thoughts with a few simple words. It was a priceless thing, and one he would always appreciate.

They rode in relative silence for another hour, the ridge climbing a bit more until the peak of it almost brushed the lowest branches of the nearby Forest Giants. His vigilance shifted to other distractions, namely the rumble in his stomach. Apparently, Mali's generous meal of eggs and jerky that morning was wearing down.

"Jacob."

He glanced over at Alice. "Yeah?"

"I'm getting hungry. You must be starving by now."

He couldn't stop the wide grin that crossed his face. "I was just thinking that. Do you want to stop and eat, or grab a snack while we're riding?"

"We have water and spiced jerky. Let's eat and ride." Alice started digging through the saddlebag nearest her pommel.

Jacob followed suit, drawing out an oiled sack of dried Tree Killer larvae. He felt a little odd riding on a Tree Killer's saddle while eating its young, but the salty scraps of meat tasted rich, finishing with a modicum of heat on the back of his tongue.

"This is so wrong," Alice muttered.

"Eating Tree Killer while riding Tree Killer?"

"No!" She shook her own sack of jerky at Jacob. "This is better than my mom's jerky. I'm both disturbed and happy about it."

"We'll have to compare it to your mom's jerky again when we get back to Ancora. Maybe she can finally abandon her quest to make the world's best jerky."

Alice gave him a flat look. "She may love making jerky, but that's ridiculous, Jacob. You do have a good idea, though. She'd love to try it. Maybe she'll come with us to visit Karn when the war is over. I think she'd like to see it."

"I'd like to try to get both our families out here. My dad would love the mines, I'm sure. We didn't see much running away underground, but we certainly saw enough of the old equipment down there to know they have an entirely different system."

"I'll wait for you in the city."

Jacob laughed and took a drink from his canteen. The Tree Killers slowed as they rounded the next copse of trees on the ridge, and he wasn't sure why until he saw what waited in the distance. A line of Scythe Beetles crossed their path, rummaging through the underbrush with their huge horns while their young followed close behind.

People might have been scared of those mighty beetles, but the Tree Killers obviously had a healthy respect for them, too. And Tree Killers were some of the most dangerous bugs Jacob had ever encountered, short of Widow Makers.

They waited for the last of the Scythe Beetles to leave the ridge before the Tree Killers started moving again without prompting. A few shadows crossed the breaks in the canopy where the shrubs around them grew thicker, but they were gone as fast as they'd appeared, never staying in sight long enough for Alice or Jacob to identify them.

And so it went, as one hour bled into another and the shadows shifted across the Gray Woods. They followed the wavy path of the ridge until the trees grew shorter, the underbrush thicker, and light started to break through the canopy with far more regularity.

"Look." Alice pointed to the northwest.

Through one of those larger gaps, Jacob could see the river. If they reached it, they'd know they'd gone off course. He slid the map and the compass from his pack, aligning the two to see if it was time to divert from the ridge.

"We went a little too far. We need to adjust course and keep a straight path."

"Not really a straight path through the woods, Jacob." She gave him a wry smile.

He glanced at the dense woods ahead of them and grimaced. "We can try."

"I'm with you."

And she was. It wasn't something Jacob even had to question. He knew for a fact she was with him. She'd been there with him since they were kids, and he'd try his best to do the same.

If they'd been on foot, diverting from the ridge would have taken an impossibly long time to get through the tangles of brambles and thick vines. The entire endeavor was made more worrisome as they descended, crossing into a bank of fog that cut their vision far too short.

The Tree Killers didn't seem to mind. They plodded forward through the dense vegetation, vines snapping as their mounts tore through them, and brambles leaving harmless scrapes along the exoskeletons.

Jacob watched the needle of the compass, holding their course as tight as he could while Alice followed the cleared path behind him. Every time his Tree Killer lashed out with its scythes to remove a cluster of vines, the saddle rocked and he lost track of the compass's reading.

Three times he had to adjust his course before the underbrush finally gave way and the clearing on the map came into view.

"I think this is it. We should be close to an entrance." He frowned at the coordinates, double-checked the compass, and nodded to himself.

Alice pulled up beside him in the clearing, the heavy fog giving everything an eerie cast. She pointed to their left. "That looks like a tunnel."

Jacob squinted into the fog for a time before he realized what Alice was pointing at. It wasn't a small access tunnel. It wasn't some cramped, claustrophobic thing that might fill him with terror like the dim tunnels beneath Ancora. This was large enough to walk a Titan Mech through and wide enough that four Tree Killers could enter it side by side.

They drew closer to it before he could clearly see the bars that kept unwanted visitors out. A huge grid of metal rose some twenty feet into the air, allowing a small stream to enter the tunnel, while a constant, overwhelming trail of steam billowed out of the upper third. So much that it rolled into the forest and created a blanket of fog that nearly blinded them.

But it didn't blind the guards standing in front of the gate.

"Halt!"

Jacob didn't miss Alice's muttered curse, but she was quick to recover.

She pulled her hood down to reveal her neat braid of brilliant red hair. "Be you blessed by the Dark Fire."

"And you, my lady. What brings you to the western tunnels?"

"I must apologize. My husband and I were scouting the woods, hoping to picnic by the river. Have we gone terribly off course?"

The guard walked closer, leaving three more to linger near the gate. "Husband, you say? And what is that accent, if I may ask?"

"We spent time in Fel." Jacob's heart pounded, but he kept his voice as even as he could. He didn't think he sounded much more stressed than any traveler caught off guard would. "Before moving to Belldorn when we were young. We were only recently liberated by Mordair."

"You've been in Karn?" the guard stood up a little straighter, his words hurried. "Do you have news of the battle there? We've lost touch with most of our units, and I'm hoping to hear word of my sister."

Jacob's heart sank. Even here, deep in enemy territory, before a man who would kill him if he knew who he was, he felt bad for the guard. It calmed his urge to grab his air cannon, but it didn't calm his urge to run from the gate. If they could see four guards, how many more were there in the fog?

Alice answered the guard before Jacob could say more. "It did not go well, I'm afraid. It moved into the mines, but we did encounter survivors.

They should be headed to the Great Machine."

"I will look for her there. Thank you." The guard's posture slumped, and he blew out a breath. After a moment, he gathered himself and pointed to the west. "You'll find the river not far from here. Follow the tunnel for a time and you'll see another entrance, though you may want to avoid it. The guards there are not pleasant."

Laughter rose from the other guards at that comment, falling silent when a chittering cry echoed in the distance.

The guard grimaced. "Shriekers are waking up." He glanced back at the gate before focusing on Alice. "Show your tattoos if you encounter any other guards."

Alice reached into her cloak. "We do not yet have tattoos, but we do carry the Dark Fire with us."

The guard inclined his head. "Good. That is a pendant fit for royalty, friends. Go in peace and be you blessed by the Dark Fire."

"And you."

As the Tree Killers strode away from the entrance to the tunnel, Jacob could just make out the conversation between the guards.

"They didn't have tattoos? Are they spies for the Children?"

"Could be, but I didn't ask."

"Only Children without tattoos I know of were in Dauschen, and you know what that bastard king did to them."

The rest of their conversation trailed off, muddled by the distance and a rumbling deep within the earth.

Jacob exchanged a look with Alice, and her furrowed brow told him she was just as confused as him. They didn't speak for a time, waiting until the river appeared in front of them, and the valley opened up beneath the lifting veil of the fog, the dark outline of a massive lake spreading in the distance.

"Strange thing to call someone you're sheltering," Alice said.

"I know. Bastard king? It doesn't sound like all of the Children of the Dark Fire are excited about Mordair's arrival."

"Maybe not, but if the guards out here know about him, it sounds like news of his arrival is widespread." Alice looked away and bit her lip. "One thing's for certain: they aren't as united as I'd feared."

CHAPTER TWENTY-ONE

While Jacob didn't think of the journey back to Karn as *relaxing*, exactly, it was certainly less nerve-racking than the journey out.

Once they were out of earshot of the guards, Jacob reached out to the Skysworn to let them know what had happened. A great deal of the time passed in silence as Alice and Jacob rotated positions, Alice taking lead along the top of the ridge for a while before Jacob would overtake her. It wasn't so much that they planned it, or even discussed it, but the Tree Killers themselves had a pattern of movement that cycled their positions.

From time to time, Jacob checked the compass and map, but it always showed the Tree Killers heading in the right direction. He wasn't sure if it was simply the path of least resistance, or if their mounts remembered the way they'd come, but it took some of the stress out of navigating.

"Do you want to live in the Lowlands when we get home?"

Alice's question caught him so off guard he barely registered it. "I'm sorry, what?"

"When we're back in Ancora. Do you want to live in the Lowlands again?"

Jacob frowned at the question. "I ... don't know. I guess I hadn't thought about it that hard. I'd like to help the Lowlands rebuild, be better than they were, even. But I don't know. It's ... it's what we saw in the Fall, really. How do we forget that?"

Alice turned in her saddle and gave him a small smile. "We don't, Jacob. No matter if we sail across the seas and never set foot in Ancora again, we won't forget what happened in the Fall."

"I suppose you're right. I do hope I can sleep better with Mordair's power buried alongside his legacy."

She glanced down at her reins, studying them before hooking them around the pommel. Her voice was quieter. "That's the question, isn't it? What happens when the war is over and we have to go home? How do you go live with your parents, knowing the things you've done? Knowing they've *seen* the things you've done?"

"I don't know." It was the simplest answer because it spoke to every conflicted thought he had.

The transmitter in his collar crackled to life with Mary's voice. "Are you two nearly back?"

Jacob exchanged a look with Alice—both of them clearly relieved for a break from the conversation—before clicking the button to respond. "On our way. Another fifteen minutes until we reach the stables? Maybe more."

"Good. When you arrive, head straight toward the Hall. A few of us will be waiting there, and you have some unexpected guests."

"Who?"

"Not over the transmitters. Skysworn out."

With that, Mary's voice fell quiet. Alice urged her Tree Killer closer to Jacob, so they didn't have to project their voices.

"You know what that means." Alice adjusted the reins in her hands. "Kat, or Archibald. Mary wouldn't be so secretive if it was someone with less authority."

"Could be Targrove or Theo? Or both?"

"I don't think so, Jacob. If it was Targrove, Mary probably would have said 'Theo's assistant.' It's such an easy misdirection, and so many people already know him as her assistant."

Jacob turned his attention back to the road. "That's a fair point. I guess we'll see when we get to the Hall."

It wasn't long before the shadowy woods grew lighter and the towers of Karn rose into the sky ahead.

✧   ✧   ✧

WITH THE TREE Killers returned to the stables, Jacob and Alice wandered to the northern side of the city, past the fountain that had grown to be a familiar sight, and into the alleys that would lead them to the Hall. Of course, they weren't really alleys, not so narrow as those of Ballern at least, and certainly nothing like the tight paths that had once turned the Lowlands into a maze with few equals.

There were times Jacob missed those tangled paths and narrow streets. Truly a haven for a young pickpocket looking for a place to escape. But the Lowlands had been changed forever. The Butcher had seen to that. And if his brother had his way, Mordair would turn another city, another people, into his weapons.

"What is it?" Alice frowned at him when he met her gaze.

"Just thinking about home. The Lowlands, you know? It'll never be quite the same, will it?"

She shrugged and her focus trailed up to the high towers behind the Hall. "But the people are still there, aren't they? Those who survived will build something new. It might never be the same, but it might be better than we could imagine."

"I hope you're right about that, Alice. I really do."

"Then help me. Come back to Ancora with me, and we can work with our parents and Baddawick and anyone else who wants to change it."

Jacob smiled and stepped around a small puddle in the cobblestone alley. "There's so much to see in the world, Alice."

She reached out and put her arm around his shoulders. "There is, and after we help make Ancora better than it was before, we can go see all of it. Leave it in the hands of better leaders. Better people."

He slid his hand around her waist and pulled her close, both of them stumbling with the awkward position before they drew apart. Holding hands instead. "I like how you think. I really do."

They walked the rest of the way to the Hall in relative silence, passing a few armed guards before the last opened the doors.

Stepping inside that space, their hands separated, arms falling to their sides as they took in the line of leaders standing there. Arun in the middle, flanked by Lady Katherine, dressed in a flight suit that wouldn't have looked out of place on a brig. Opposite her, wearing a dark gray jacket with matching pants, emblazoned with a Steamsworn Fist and a dozen medals, loomed Archibald, Speaker of Bollwerk.

But it wasn't only them. Mary stood to the side, Eva glowering at Kat for some as-yet-unknown reason, and Alana placed a series of markers in the corner of Arun's map.

The quiet conversations died when the others took notice of Jacob and Alice's arrival.

"What did you find?" Archibald wasted no time questioning them about their journey, and as every gaze at that table focused on them, Jacob couldn't help but feel intimidated by the power in the place. It was one thing to meet one of the leaders of the alliance by themselves, or with one other. It was something else to stand before so many figureheads who expected an immediate report.

Thankfully, as all the various scenarios of how Jacob could make a fool of himself flitted through his mind, Alice stepped in to give them exactly what they needed.

"The tunnel's there, wide enough for a few mounts to walk side by side, but the gate is guarded."

"How many?" Archibald's gaze narrowed.

"Four we could see, but those were all outside the gate. There could be any number of checkpoints inside, but the fog is so thick in the valley we couldn't see much."

Archibald focused on Alana. "What do you say?"

She moved one square marker away from the tunnel marked on the map. "Based on that, and the photographs from Mali's recent expedition, I think we have our translations."

"Translations for what?" Alice stepped closer to the table, leaning over the map before pausing and slowly raising her eyes to Mary and Smith. "The map we found?"

Smith gestured to the assembly of markers and notes strewn across the table. "It is the combination of the map from the control center and those of Karn. Topography, what appears to be an ancient channel for electrical lines not so different from the city lights, and perhaps most importantly—"

Alana cut him off. "A detailed log of guard stations and some patrols. We're sure it isn't comprehensive, based on our own assessments and those of Arun."

The leader of Karn inclined his head in agreement, slowly uncrossing his arms and reaching across the map. "From what you've told us here, the tunnel you found is the largest entry point, but it's also one of the most guarded."

Archibald snapped his hand out toward the map. "Then we need to get Alice and Jacob deeper inside."

"Who is to say those traps do not extend into the Great Machine itself?" Lady Katherine leaned forward, holding Archibald's gaze. "You cannot ask them to make a sacrifice you would not make yourself."

"Of course I can, my lady. That's all leaders ever do." Archibald's lips flattened, and he turned away for a time. The Speaker of Bollwerk let out a slow breath and tapped near the markers again. "This is our best chance."

"You're full of lies," Mary spat.

Archibald recoiled as if he'd been struck. "What—"

"It's your best bet to spare more of your ships, but you're asking these kids to sacrifice *everything*. I've seen you do it before. I know your games, Archibald. You can't use them until they're burned up like the Forgotten." Mary's voice fell to a hiss. "We *remember*."

Kat reached out for her arm, but the captain of the Skysworn pulled away.

"Mary." Alice waited for her to meet her gaze, but when she didn't, she almost snapped. "*Mary!*"

Slowly, Mary turned her eyes away from the Speaker of Bollwerk and focused on Alice.

"It's our choice."

The captain of the Skysworn closed her eyes and cursed. "This plan is a long fall from the docks without a glider, kid. And you know it."

Lady Katherine held her hand up for silence. "Perhaps there is another way. Sabotage may be the only way forward that prevents a full-scale battle at the Great Machine. And that feels like such an understatement. A loss there will create a cascade of Mordair's conquests. He is cornered, and we should expect the worst. Give them a war on three fronts. We need to slip in unexpected, like Ballern attempted to do in Belldorn."

Archibald inclined his head. "That is agreeable."

"They all died," Eva said, taking Mary's arm in a tight grip.

"*We* won't." Jacob's words brimmed with far more confidence than he felt.

"It will cost lives," Kat said, "and ships, but it will at least give Jacob and Alice time to get through the tunnels."

"They aren't going alone," Smith said, balling his fists.

"They have to. We can send multiple squads into the tunnels, but the more that go, the more likely they are to be detected. Fight with me in the skies, and keep Mordair's focus on the air."

Arun tapped another line near the tunnel. "If you mean to do this, you won't have a much better option than here. It's mostly collapsed, which means it may be impassible. But it also means the patrols will be fewer."

"How impassable?" Jacob asked.

"If I have read these correctly, a large stretch of the tunnel fell into the underground river. Some is still exposed to the forest above, and the rest is a maze of ravines."

"I built a grappling cannon. If there's enough clearance, we can span large gaps. Fifty feet without issue."

Arun grimaced as he studied the map. "A fall into those rivers is a death sentence, Jacob. Even if you survive the drop and the Water Beetles, it disappears under the earth for miles."

"I've been in underground rivers before." Jacob tried not to flinch at the memory of almost drowning beneath Ancora.

"Some rivers do not have the air pockets you need to survive." Alana crossed her arms as she spoke. "You need to stay out of them until divers have mapped the routes. And that is not an option so deep in enemy territory."

Arun traced his finger around the edge of the lake near the Great Machine and the few rivers documented nearby. "The Water Beetles of the west are not the same as those you may be accustomed to in the mountains." "They are fast, chaotic, and nearly invisible without adequate light. If you find yourself in the dark, and something catches the light, stay away until you know what it is. The Children of the Dark Fire have been known to lay traps with various creatures."

"Like Midstream is doing with the Tail Swords?" Mary asked.

Arun nodded. "Yes. But while the Children of the Dark Fire may have some control over the invaders, they are not living side by side with creatures that want nothing more than to devour them. Many of the bugs here are voracious, and it is best to use caution."

Mary walked around the table and put a hand on Alice's and Jacob's shoulders. "You two need to understand the risk. This isn't just reconnaissance. You'll be going farther into those tunnels than anyone in Karn ever has."

"At least anyone who isn't a spy." Arun tapped his chin. "That I am sure of."

Jacob didn't miss Mary's annoyed glance at the leader of Karn before she turned back to him and Alice.

"Tell me it's your decision," Mary said, "and I'll support you every step of the way. If you're doing this for your families, for your futures, I'll fight with you. Don't do it for … someone else."

"It *is* our decision." Alice wrapped her fingers in Jacob's.

Jacob squeezed her hand. "Don't doubt that. We lived through the Fall, Mary. We saw what Mordair's legacy will be if he comes to our home again. We lived under the Butcher long enough."

Alice nodded her agreement. "This is for our future."

Mary let her hands fall to her side and gave them both a small smile. "Then Smith and I are at your side. I don't care what's happening, you call us and we will find you. Remember that."

"We have much to discuss." Lady Katherine laced her fingers together as she leaned on the map. "Preparations must be made if this is to be a battle on three fronts, Archibald."

Archibald hesitated before responding. "It will begin with the fisherfolk. They already make to strike the northern docks."

Lady Katherine's eyebrow slowly rose. "At your behest?"

"At my lack of protest." He spread his fingers across the corner of the map.

"So be it. Let us do what we can in these final hours before we go our separate ways, Archibald. With Arun's help, and that of the Titan Mechs, perhaps we can create enough of a distraction without getting too many of our soldiers killed."

If there was one thing Jacob had learned in the conflict with Mordair, it was that war always cost more lives than one hoped.

CHAPTER TWENTY-TWO

O WEN PINCHED THE bridge of his nose as the arguing between Trevor and Fiona heated on the ocean liner's deck. "Please, Trevor, Fiona. Let's discuss this without casting so many insults."

"And you're taking orders from the Speaker of Bollwerk now?" Trevor asked as he spun to face Owen. "Do you really think he's an ally of the fisherfolk?"

Owen took a deep breath as heavy loads of metal clanged together toward the ship's bow. Snapping at Trevor at this point wouldn't do anyone any good. "No, Trevor. He asked if we would be willing to help, and I said we would. You don't have to be a part of this crew. You can take your boat and leave at any time."

Trevor scoffed at the idea. "Leave you lot out here alone? I can't let my entire customer base get themselves killed now, can I?"

"If that's what it takes for him to see reason," Fiona said, "then I guess it's a good thing most of his customers are going with us."

A few nearby fisherfolk grumbled their agreement, and Owen caught the obscene hand gesture one of them cast at Trevor. That broke the tension more than he'd expected, Fiona letting loose with a small laugh.

Trevor rubbed the back of his head and looked up at the sky. "Help me load my boat, would you?"

"My crew can take care of that." Natalia wiped her hands on an oily rag as she joined them. She tucked it into a stained pouch on her vest before buckling it closed. "Have the new cannons installed. It's not the prettiest job I've ever done, but it should give you quite an entrance."

"Thank you." Owen clasped his hands together. "Truly, thank you, Natalia."

She wiped her brow with the rough sleeve of her undershirt. "I understand why you're all afraid of Archibald. He's an ambitious leader, to be sure."

"We don't fight for Archibald."

Natalia gave Owen a small smile. "He fights for you, whether you realize it yet or not. If we lose this fight to Mordair, he'll kill every last survivor in Fel. Seen it before with the warlords, and I think you know the warlords are Mordair's people."

"Some of the warlords fought against Mordair," Trevor said. "I've met them! I remember Rana once—"

"Tried to murder a child?" Natalia spat on the deck. "Tell yourself what you have to, but try to remember a great deal of what Mordair told you was lies. Rana kidnapped a child princess of Midstream. Meant to kill her and the Ancorans. You've heard of *them*, haven't you? Rana caught a faceful of metal from the old blood instead. Remember that the next time you think a warlord is anything but an enemy."

Natalia didn't let Trevor respond. She turned her back on him, dismissing him entirely from the conversation as she spoke to Owen. "I trained the deckhands on the cannon. I can show you too, but it's simple enough if you've ever worked a ballista."

"I have."

"Good. Bit more explosive if the powder catches fire, so keep any torches and lanterns well away. I have to get back to the workshop. Archibald wants more of those Titan Mechs completed, and not even Frederick can keep up with the Speaker at this point." She traded grips with Owen before exchanging a nod with Fiona.

Owen called out to her as she started down the gangplank. "Thank you, Natalia! We're honored to fight with you."

She cast a look over her shoulder. "No one fights alone in this war and lives. Try to make sure your people remember that. Good luck."

"And to you." Owen raised a hand as she left.

Trevor waited until Natalia was well out of earshot before muttering to Owen. "Rana attacking kids. I've never heard that."

"He was a strong ally of Mordair." Owen rubbed his beard. "Would it surprise you so much?"

Trevor grimaced and looked at Fiona. "Help me hoist my boat? If we need an escape, she's as fast as anything else out there."

Much to Owen's relief, Fiona clasped Trevor on the shoulder and guided him in the direction of the ocean liner's port side. Most of the fisherfolk's vessels were anchored nearby, close enough the cranes mounted to the ship could reach out and pluck them from the sea.

Owen made his way toward the bow, but that wasn't his destination. He wanted to see what Natalia had wrought on the deck, and as he cleared the pilothouse, the cannons were plain to see. Side by side, the dual behemoth looked large enough for a person to climb inside.

Just behind those sizable cylinders was an armored dispenser for the powder bags, not so unlike the bait feeders they used on the docks of Fel. It was odd to see such a violently different use for essentially the same equipment.

Natalia had given him brief instructions earlier on the loading sequence, and it was easy enough to remember. Cannonball first, powder second, never more than three bags, lock the chamber. And that's all there was to bringing the weapon to bear.

But it was two cannons against a fleet of ocean liners. They wouldn't fire many rounds before their own ship went down. Even then, their escape might be doomed from the start. Should the worst happen, it wouldn't be an escape; it would be a dead man's charge down the throat of their forsaken king.

Owen clenched his fists and headed for the port side. It would be time to depart soon enough, and he needed to be sure everyone on that ship understood what they were about to do.

✧　✧　✧

THEY SAILED IN darkness. No light emanated from the ocean liner as they headed west, slipping through the night beneath the airship blockades riddling the sky. Owen knew it was a gamble, even with their departure from the northern docks. The inlets were well guarded, and Fel patrols had been sighted for miles to the north over the water.

It gave them a wide net, but the widest nets often had the largest holes. Adrenaline coursed through him at each sign of the airships patrolling above them. Not visible but for the beams of light they cast toward the eastern horizon, before vanishing when the lanterns were shielded once more. The airships themselves were nearly as invisible as the ocean liner on the Gray Sea below them.

But Owen and his crew sailed beneath the second blockade without issue, leaving those sweeping lights behind. It would have been impossible to clear those airships in the daytime, of that he had no doubt.

The waters of the Gray Sea stayed mercifully smooth in the early hours before sunrise. They made better time than Owen expected, and his heart pounded as he considered how soon they'd know if the plan was pure folly.

Static crackled through the transmitter in his collar, and a recently familiar but faint voice echoed around him. "Owen, are you there?"

"Yes, Bollwerk, I'm here." It was an odd thing to know what the Speaker of Bollwerk sounded like. Stranger still for the man to know Owen's name.

"Everything we discussed is moving forward. How soon do you expect to arrive?"

"If the seas continue to cooperate, we should be near the port in two hours, close to sunrise. If they don't, perhaps three."

"Good, that is good. You have assistance on the way. Once you draw their attention and the first of the airships return to the port, flee. There is no need to sacrifice your people."

Visions of Owen's family in Ancora flashed through his mind. There was every reason for him to make a sacrifice at the Great Machines. There was no reason more important than his family. But he also knew that wasn't what Archibald wanted to hear, so he said something else.

"As soon as the airships are in sight, we'll run."

"Excellent. Steel your crew, and yourself. Rough seas await."

The static faded from Owen's transmitter, and he sighed.

"That was Archibald?"

Owen slowly turned his head to find Trevor standing nearby. "It was. I didn't know anyone was listening."

"I didn't mean to. I … I heard voices and came to look and—"

Owen held up his hand to stop Trevor's rambling excuse. "It's fine, Trevor. You already know what we're doing here."

Trevor rubbed his hands together, running his fingertips over his knuckles. "I know. It's just … it's different here, Owen. It was one thing when we were talking about this in the bar back in Fel. But now … after what we saw on the docks?"

"That's why we can't stop." Owen's words hardened. "That's why we fight Mordair to the end. If we lose here. If *Archibald* and his allies lose here. Mordair will come back. You know that's true."

"We could leave Fel. You heard what Midstream offered, didn't you? It's spread all through the fisherfolk here. They invited us to their city."

"The desert, Trevor. No water. No fishing. It's no life for our people." Owen hesitated. He wanted to ask Trevor about the desert princess, but he wasn't sure it was the right time. Part of him knew it might be the *only* time. "Do you understand who made that offer to come to Midstream?"

"The Princess of Midstream herself, from what I hear! Who would have thought?"

Owen gave him a sad smile. "You know that's the girl Rana tried to kill? Kidnapped her. Cut her. Probably would have hung her from the wall. The Royal Guards themselves couldn't catch Rana and his accomplices. The Ancorans did."

Trevor recoiled. The creased brow and slack jaw wasn't the look of a man who learned he'd been mistaken. It was the look of a man who had served warlords in his bar, broken bread with people who were as bad as their own king, and likely spoken ill of Midstream on far more occasions than not.

"We all make mistakes, Trevor." Owen clasped his shoulder. "Try to make them right, and do not dwell too deep on past mistakes."

Trevor walked away, and Owen didn't miss the younger man wiping his eyes as he went. There wasn't much else he could say in that moment, so he let the barkeep wander off. It was good to get their thoughts in order before the coming battle. Good to say the things that should have been said ages before. The world changed as the days passed, and none of them would be quite the same when the war was done.

✧   ✧   ✧

Owen stood in the pilothouse beside their captain as they rounded the small islands that concealed the docks from their ship. It gave them, and their enemy, cover. On the far side of the island, as they traversed the shallow reefs through the only deep channel, he caught sight of the watchtower.

No audible order was given before the first ballista bolts took flight from the ocean liner's deck. The watchtower's supports splintered, bringing the entire structure to the sand in an instant. Whatever alarm they might have sounded was silenced forever.

Waves lapped at the massive ship's hull as they pushed onward, coming in view of Mordair's seagoing fleet and towering clouds of steam and soot rising from the distant Great Machine as the sun rose as well. The docks were built to fit as many ships as possible into the narrow bay. They weren't configured to allow those ships to bring their full armament to bear. Mordair had always favored flanking maneuvers, even making a spectacle of them during Fel's Celebration of the Sea. What a mockery that had been.

It didn't matter now. It only mattered that they had a clear line of sight to the sterns of a dozen ocean liners. A glance over his shoulder showed airships near the horizon. It would take time for them to be alerted, and again for them to reverse course and join the battle. Owen would make them pay for that mistake.

"Take us through the middle of the channel."

The captain raised an eyebrow. "We won't be able to turn back without giving them time to strike the ship."

Owen nodded. "Look at the land. Disable the ocean liners that can escape into the sea, and run us aground astern of the last of them."

Footsteps sounded outside the pilothouse, and Fiona swung the door open. "Ready to fire, Owen. Did I hear you say we're going to run aground? We'll be relying on our fishing vessels, if that's so."

"Yes. Tell the others. We can block the entire bay with a well-placed collision. Set explosives in the hull and tell everyone to prepare to deploy the starboard ships."

Fiona hesitated, and Owen knew why. Some of their ships were on the port side, and they wouldn't be going home. To most of the fisherfolk, losing their boat was akin to losing family. It was a hard sacrifice, but it was a choice that needed to be made.

"Understood."

The blade came fast, the captain unsheathing it and lashing out at Owen in moments. But the man had been too focused on the attack, too distracted from their course and the sudden rocking as they glanced off the reef. It likely saved Owen's life.

Fiona was on the captain in a heartbeat, Owen still trying to find his feet, patting the blood that ran from his neck. The man's wrist snapped in her iron grip, but he didn't get a chance to cry out. She stole his own blade from him and rammed it home in his throat.

She didn't stand again until the man stopped moving underneath her, ripping the blade out and releasing only a trickle of blood.

Fiona glared at him before taking the wheel and straightening their course. "Take the cannons, Owen. I don't know what the hell that was, but I'll keep us on course." She opened the horn and started shouting orders to the crew, biting off each word with an air of command that came naturally.

Owen patted at his neck again and closed his eyes. "Close. Too close."

"Three minutes, and we'll be in range, Owen."

That brought him back to the moment. He could worry about the betrayal later. It shouldn't have surprised him that some of the fisherfolk might still have loyalties to Mordair. And a king who promised wealth for that loyalty, well, he could corrupt a great many people.

✧   ✧   ✧

"BOLLWERK. IT'S BEGUN." Owen held a bundle of pull fuses for the cannons in his hand, the length of their ropes folded twice and still dangling almost to the ground as he released the button on his transmitter.

Trevor placed powder in the cannon before closing the breach and holding up a single finger. It was the signal they'd agreed on, and Owen stepped forward to insert one pull fuse in each barrel. The nearest had two bags of powder, and the second, three.

Power wasn't their main concern. Accuracy was, and Owen worried that with three bags of powder, the projectile's arc would be too long.

They planned to be in range of the ballistae before firing the first shot, and when the signal came, nothing quite felt real. Time slowed as Owen gritted his teeth and ripped the rope back on the pull fuse.

He remembered his father talking about the cannons in the old wars. How a friction primer used to ignite the exposed powder. But it was open to the elements, and rain or high waves could create a cascade of issues that could kill an entire crew.

Pull fuses weren't like that. Contained like an explosive themselves, the friction lit them like a match. A match with enough powder inside it to send a jet of flame into the cannon, and nearly knock Owen off his feet when the gun thundered to life.

He scrambled to his feet as fire and smoke billowed out from the end of the cannon, shaking the deck beneath him in the deafening blast. The projectile whistled through the air, shrieking like an enraged Mountain Walker before it crashed into the ocean liner's pilothouse.

Whatever element of surprise they'd had, it would be gone in short order. Owen ripped the fuse out of the second cannon, smoke trailing the thunder across the water in a gentle arc that ended in a gigantic clang. The stern of an ocean liner folded in on itself, raising the edge of its now-useless rudder above the water line.

Trevor worked to empty the first cannon of debris as Owen pulled open the second, scorching his hands on hot powder before dropping the next heavy shell into place and packing the powder behind it.

"Two bags!" he shouted.

"Two bags!" Trevor echoed.

Owen handed the man half the pull fuses and focused on the second cannon. With a third person to turn the massive geared wheel to aim, they'd fired another salvo in short order.

The ballistae joined in the frenzy, sending heavily armored timber soaring across the bay. Some landed on the decks, but many fell into the water. A handful of lucky shots tagged the heavy metal chains of the anchors to the ships' hulls, not even the metal of the stern able to stop the bolts entirely. It was almost as good as destroying the rudders.

By the fifth volley of shots from the cannon, with explosions of water and wood and metal rising up all along the ocean liners in the dock, Mordair's fleet returned fire. Only a handful of cannons had a decent angle on Owen's ship, but every impact rocked them as if the very sea had grabbed hold of their hull and shaken them within an inch of their life.

Gouts of water exploded over the side of the ocean liner, obscuring their aim and visibility altogether.

"Destroyers inbound!" Fiona shouted from the pilothouse.

Owen grunted. "You know what to do!"

She nodded and stepped back inside, angling the bow toward the last few destroyers.

"Get everyone to the ships, Trevor. Now!"

The barkeep threw the rest of his fuses to Owen. "You're ready to fire."

Owen slid two more fuses home as people ran past, including the man who had been aiming the cannons. The longer he waited, the farther off the cannons would be.

A ballista splintered when a round took it through the cables, cutting down two fisherfolk in the violent release.

Owen ripped the fuses out, firing both cannons at once. The dual projectiles screeched through the air beneath the first of Ballern's destroyers. Fel had another ship close behind, and once that vessel was fully in range, Owen knew they were out of time.

He turned to run when the cannon shots hit, rupturing the stern of another of Fel's ocean liners entirely. But the hull didn't merely implode. Water rushed in, and it must have reached the boilers. From one second to the next, half of Fel's docks were suddenly obscured behind superheated steam. The thunder of that ruptured ship hurt his ears nearly as much as the cannons he'd been standing by.

Everything sounded muffled in the aftermath, but Owen knew he had to run. He found himself beside Fiona as she almost threw him onto his fishing vessel. Two other fisherfolk were already onboard, though one was so bloodied Owen doubted she was alive.

He pulled the release, and the ropes let go, dropping them toward the sea far faster than he would have liked. The impact slammed him to the deck, sending sprays of water across them all, but he scrabbled to his feet, relieved to find the boiler still warm as he cranked the pressure as high as he dared and veered away from the ocean liner.

The massive ship held its course as the airships unloaded on it. Streaks of fire and ballistae rained down from Ballern's destroyer, joined by the cannons of Fel in short order.

It wasn't enough. The power it would take to stop something so large with so much momentum was beyond anything those weapons could do so quickly.

Owen bore down on the throttle, bouncing in the bay's waves as he streaked toward the relative safety of the outlying islands. Even from there, he could see the blockade closing on the bay, retreating from the perimeter they'd set.

Ashe turned the corner of the peninsula, skirting the forest's edge. A chill ran down his spine. A titanic form loomed in the sky, a floating city he'd seen before over Fel. Bollwerk's warship.

Clear of the inner reef, Owen watched as the battle in the harbor turned violently against Fel. The chainguns beneath Bollwerk's mighty warship hummed as they spun faster until fire burst forth in a rapid staccato, hurling death and destruction onto their enemy.

Even though he couldn't see through much of the steam and fog roiling in the distance, the high-pitched whine of projectiles echoed all around them, distant pops and pings eclipsing the roar of his own boiler. Until Owen's ocean liner reached the far side of the bay and collided with two of Fel's ships.

It wasn't spectacular. The ocean liners slowly forced into one another, metal screeching on metal as they pivoted in a slip that didn't have enough space to contain the collision. Figures appeared on the docks where the fog had thinned. Some running toward the ship, others away. Chaos ruled the ocean liners.

Until the explosives did their work. One moment, there were three intact ships involved in the collision, then the bow of the attacking ocean liner vanished, dark clouds exploding from port and starboard, sending shrapnel and superheated air to kill anything standing remotely close.

It looked like the nearest ocean liner had survived, until its stern floated backward, curling away from the bow, connected by a fragment of its superstructure. It would take time to sink, but it wouldn't go far. Flames and black smoke billowed into the air as more docks and ships caught fire.

The entire shoreline decayed into a hellish vision, figures running as fast as they could from the docks, some still engulfed in flames until they collapsed or fell into the sea. One thing was certain: Fel's hold on the seaward docks was finished. They wouldn't have a use for it other than securing the northern front for the Great Machines, and as Bollwerk's warship turned, Owen understood how foolish that would be.

Floating in the shadow of that behemoth vessel was the terrifying sight of a Belldorn Porcupine. Nothing so laden with metal should be able to float through the sky, yet it did. As Owen maneuvered between the last of the islands, the Porcupine unleashed a volley of cannon fire that could have brought down a city. Instead, it cut through two of Fel's destroyers before they could so much as flank the warship. No single fleet should have wielded that kind of power. The brigs followed nearby, their odd two-chambered forms scattering out between the airships of Fel and those who had betrayed Ballern.

Fire and smoke burned through the clouds, Bollwerk and Belldorn taking full advantage of the closed ranks Owen and his allies had baited Fel into. He saw a brig fall to the water in flames, and a cannon scored a hit on the Porcupines, but in that time, four destroyers crashed into the sea, with more drifting lamely to the north.

It was an absolute rout, but it had still cost lives. Several fisherfolk would never see their homes again, would never hug their families. But Owen would fight on. He'd see Mordair dead and his family protected, or he'd give his life trying to accomplish both.

He pushed forward on the throttle and sailed through the last strait, turning south to find a shielded inlet to dock in. They'd done what they could for now, but the battle had only begun.

CHAPTER TWENTY-THREE

MARY CURSED AS the Skysworn drifted over the canopy of the Gray Woods. It shouldn't have been all that surprising to see the Children of the Dark Fire regrouping in the outskirts of the city surrounding the Great Machine, but it was a terrible sight regardless.

She turned the dial on the transmitter and clicked the button. "Kat, we have a problem."

"I'm here. What is it?"

Mary frowned as she took in the view from the windscreen. "More armored crawlers outside the Great Machine, and I see several columns of Bombardiers. They aren't moving toward the docks."

"How close are you? Do *not* engage."

"Don't worry, we aren't *that* eager to die. The main blockades of airships have pulled back to the city itself. Still a good distance from the Great Machine, but the attack on the docks drew them in. You know what to do."

"I'll speak with Bollwerk. Keep the lines clear, Mary. I'm discussing our current strategy with Ballern."

Mary clicked off the transmitter and raised her voice. "Did you catch all that, Smith?"

"Yes. It sounds like Kat means to pull the Skyborn into the fight."

She ran her fingers through her hair and blew out a breath. "I don't know if that's the best idea. They're still in shock from Mordair's attack on Ballern."

"Some of them have seen war before." Smith's words were quiet.

Mary knew that was true, but how much of that horror had those serving in Fleet truly seen? And would they be ready to visit that kind of violence on their own people who had defected with Mordair? Too many chances for things to go wrong. She didn't mind playing the odds, but there were far too many unknowns to her liking.

The battle had already begun, and though she couldn't see more than small columns of smoke on the distant horizon, she knew that's where the attack had happened with the fisherfolk and Archibald's fleet. She switched the frequency and clicked the transmitter.

She kept her voice even. "Eva."

It didn't take long for her to respond. "I'm here. What's wrong?"

Mary smiled at the fact Eva had picked up something was wrong when all she'd said was her name. "Columns organizing outside of the Great Machine. Looks like they intend to move south again. Judging by their orientation."

"Understood. A moment." Eva might have intended to mute the transmitter, but she didn't, and Mary heard every word. "Ready the Skyriders. We have movement north of Karn. The alliance may not be willing to send the bombers over the woods, but that doesn't mean *we* can't."

Mary could barely make out someone else acknowledging the order. Deploying the Skyriders was a bold move, and one that might infuriate Kat. But there was a bigger concern on Mary's mind.

"Eva, you're going to leave the brigs short on crew. That kind of shortage could cost you in a battle."

"Let me worry about that, Mary." Her voice had that same false calm to it Mary had used. "Get your ship out of there. We'll be coming in above you, and I don't want you mistaken for one of those Dark Fire ships."

Mary squeezed the levers on the console. "Be careful."

"You don't know, do you?"

She pulled the horn open, making sure Smith could hear whatever Eva was about to say. Her voice always rose a little higher when she thought she knew something Mary didn't. It was both infuriating and endearing in the same breath.

"Both warships are closing from the east now, Mary."

She blinked. "What do you mean? Bollwerk?"

"Yes."

Mary's mind tried to reconcile the very *idea* of Archibald bringing both of his strongest airships across the Crystal Sea to fight over foreign land. She'd seen the lengths that man would go to in order to hoard the best defenses for Bollwerk year after year. Schemes and political maneuvering that turned her stomach every time she had to bear witness to it, much less be involved in it. But now he'd stripped the city of its greatest defenses. Sailed them across the sea for the chance to claim a better future for Bollwerk. It was a risk a good leader might take, and that was a strange thought to have about Archibald.

"But it's not just Bollwerk." Mary whispered that last thought out loud.

"Of course it's not! Kat split north and west. We only need to keep them out of the woods. If the bombers have a clear path, they'll make the strike."

"It could send them back into the city, Eva. Make it harder for the forward … scouts to get through." She didn't want to say who was making the run. Even the slimmest chance their transmission could be overheard was enough for her to avoid speaking about Jacob and Alice. Too much was pinned on the underground. Too much to risk in a casual exchange.

"Everything's a gamble now, Mary. Be safe." Eva ended the transmission with those words.

"Did you hear that, Smith?"

The pinging of metal on metal quieted. "I did. It sounds as though Eva has already coordinated this, Mary. It is of little surprise."

"What do you mean?" Mary leaned closer to the horn.

"The Titan Mechs and exoskeletons are not the only designs Frederick borrowed from Jacob. He has studied the gliders as well and has had plenty of time to implement some of the basic improvements into the Skyriders' equipment."

Mary watched the windscreen before circling off to the west to do a broader reconnaissance sweep. "Even if he *has* implemented some of those changes, they haven't had time to train on it. Not *nearly* enough time."

"It is one of my favorite things about Jacob's work, Mary. Perhaps more than Charles, or Targrove, everything he builds is intuitive. For the user, at least. Some of the paths he takes to reach a final design are anything but intuitive. It is quite remarkable."

"Have you *told* him that?"

"No. Not in so many words."

"Men," Mary muttered under her breath.

Smith didn't argue, but he was quick to change the topic. "We need to ensure the woods stay clear of Fel's warships."

"I think Archibald is seeing to that, Smith."

"Yes, until he is not. Fel will abandon the docks if his victory is swift. From there, I suspect they will reform the blockade in the Great Machine's airspace before pushing out again. We may not risk bombing the woods and jeopardizing Karn, but do you think Mordair will be so cautious?"

Mary cursed and shook her head. "No. No, I don't. Head to the gun pod to get a better view. We're climbing higher."

✦   ✦   ✦

SMITH SETTLED INTO the reclined seat beneath the hull of the Skysworn. There wasn't another view quite like it. Hanging in midair—eclipsing the lowest of the cloud banks—gave them a sweeping view of what was unfolding across the Gray Woods and beyond.

He held a telescope to his eye and watched Archibald's warship deliver devastation onto the sea docks where Mordair's fleet had once waited. If any of them were foolish enough to be there still, it was only a matter of time before they became food for the Carrion Worms.

Smith turned his attention back to the west, slowly sweeping his scope past the Great Machine and the diminishing forest in the distance. Nothing quite as grand as the Forest Giants waited around the Great Machine. Whatever had given rise to those mighty trees hadn't spread so far north. Or if it had, it certainly hadn't survived the coming of the Great Machine.

"Mary, look to the southwest of the Great Machine. Right at the forest canopy. Between the largest branches."

The string of curses that came over the horn told him she'd seen it. "What is that?"

"Airships, I believe. Better hidden than I would have expected, but not quite so discreet as Canopy."

"They aren't in the blockade."

"No, they are not. And if they have not joined the attack on the docks, I am afraid Mordair may have foreseen the attack."

"A trap to lure in the alliance fleet."

Smith grimaced and lowered the scope. "Yes."

The ship lurched, and the turbines whined as Mary urged the throttle forward. Smith wondered why she could possibly be heading closer to that mass of concealed ships before she veered west and held their path. They might have been hard to detect at their current altitude, but they certainly weren't invisible.

Mary's voice grew fainter, and a pop from the transmitter echoed over the horn before Smith heard her speak. "Kat, we have more airships hidden northwest of the Great Machine. Whatever you're engaged with at the docks is a fraction of the fleet."

"I would hardly call it a fraction, Mary. Archibald has identified twelve of Ballern's warships and several of Fel's."

"And how many does Fel have, Kat? Think about it. They're in the woods, well camouflaged and waiting."

Smith leaned closer to the horn and projected his voice so the transmitter might pick it up. "They likely plan to attack any forces that come for their ground assault. That is what I would do."

Silence reigned in the Skysworn before Kat responded. "They intend to lure us into a trap. We can turn that against them."

"Eva's taking the gliders into the front." Mary's words came out hurriedly, and Smith didn't miss the poorly hidden concern behind them. "They're planning to stop the columns before they get too deep into the woods so the bombers can hit them."

"Then we have bait for our trap." Kat's words became sharp. "Be sure our scouts are clear of the area. And make certain Eva understands what is coming."

Mary's voice grew louder, and Smith knew she was leaning into the horn. "Did you catch all of that?"

"I did. We need to support the brigs and the Skyriders. We can help evacuate if things do not go to plan."

"Smith, when was the last time *anything* went to plan?"

He let out a quiet laugh and climbed out of the gun pod.

CHAPTER TWENTY-FOUR

FURI LISTENED TO Lady Katherine's report as it echoed in the small room, stealing glances between Rin and Tatsu while Jakon's frown deepened. Guild members and enforcers stood around the outer edge of the room, too close for anyone to be comfortable.

Almost every bit of Furi screamed to fly out and join the battle at the Great Machine, but she couldn't leave Ballern undefended. Not in the aftermath of what Mordair had done. Not now.

"Skyriders will clear the way, but the plan is not without its risks."

"Risks?" Jakon's voice cracked as he leaned forward. "You're purposefully sending ships into an ambush. That is far beyond *risks*."

"We could use your help." Passion tinged Lady Katherine's words. "Any Skyborn who would join us. Any Stormborn who is not duty bound to stay in Ballern. You should know Archibald has sent both of his warships across the sea. In all my years, I have never known him to leave Bollwerk so undefended. He takes that risk for all of us."

Rin exchanged a look with Tatsu, who only offered a small nod. Tatsu leaned back in his seat.

Jakon pinched the bridge of his nose and rested his elbows on the table. "If there was ever a time for risks, I suppose this is it. You mean to bring down an empire, Kat. If you win, you will be celebrated for decades, perhaps longer, for your wisdom to join this battle. If you lose, you'll likely hang from the walls of Fel as Mordair burns his way through every city in the alliance."

"Yes, Jakon. It is why I ask all of my allies to fight with me. There are no half measures in this battle. Every warship between Bollwerk and Belldorn is now in the air. Ground defenses remain, but should our fleets be circumvented, our cities will fall. Take that as you will. I will fight, and die, with my people. I would not ask it otherwise."

"The riots on the docks could do serious damage if we leave." Rin laced his fingers together.

Jakon let out a long sigh. "Colt will keep the order. We might not like how he does it, but he wants revenge on Mordair. And we're the best shot he has at that."

But something had become painfully clear to Furi. A terrible truth she'd found hidden in the old books and manuscripts spread across Ballern and Belldorn. If they didn't fight for what they wanted, for what was *right*, they would lose everything. If they didn't stop the Children of the Dark Fire now, the endless tide of war would wash back over their city and burn it to the ground.

She closed her eyes, willing away tears as she almost growled the words. "We have to fight. We can't wait here. We *have* to fight. Any Stormborn, any Skyborn who means to join us, get to the docks and prepare the ships."

A tiny smile lifted the corner of Jakon's lips. "At once."

"More people are counting on you than you know." With that, Kat disconnected.

Jakon eyed the rest of the room. "Any Titan Mech not needed for the recovery, any exoskeleton, load it on the supply ships. We can be to the front in less than a day. With a bit of luck, that means we can join the battle outside the Gray Woods. With a little worse luck, we can help hold the line."

"That was Lady Katherine of Belldorn?" Abernathy asked, a brutish man with scars that spoke of a long life of fighting. He was the oldest of their guild and someone Furi had rarely seen without his henchmen close at hand.

Jakon inclined his head. "It was."

He shook his head, a kind of dazed smile on his face. "I'd like to meet her one day." He slapped his hand down on Tatsu's shoulder. "Now that I know she didn't kill and eat our sailors like the stories said."

Tatsu slowly turned to stare up at Abernathy. "What stories have *you* been listening to?"

The old man apparently found this to be the funniest thing he'd heard in a decade as the room filled with his cackling laughter.

✦   ✦   ✦

Furi had expected the remaining nobles to take issue with the idea of delaying the reconstruction. No matter how certain she was, Rin thought quite the opposite. So, when they met with Jakon and the surviving nobles, part of her wanted to smack the smirk off his face. The other part of her was thankful Rin had been right.

They didn't protest; they offered up their own guard to help load the supply ships. They helped coordinate where to land to give the Titan Mechs access, since the old loading docks had been destroyed in the collapse. The remaining supply ships weren't as versatile as those that had already left for the front, and the help was much needed.

They worked together with dust and dirt smeared across their clothes and boots. The fine silks of the nobility still peeked from the edges of their rugged tunics, picking up far more dirt and sweat than any delicate material would ever recover from. But Furi understood now that the nobles knew what would happen if Mordair returned. They might not be helping out of a sense of loyalty to Ballern, or especially to the Storm-born, but at least they helped. They understood they'd likely find a noose around their necks if the battle was lost.

It took most of the day to redirect everyone to the supply ships, but before night fell, the last of them rose into the air or left the docks. Only four warships had stayed behind to guard the city. Now, all that remained were the stationary defenses. A gamble, to be sure, but Jakon said it was their best course of action, and Furi trusted him more than anyone else she knew.

Even if the chef *did* think she was a fool for doing it.

The thought put a smile on Furi's face as she leaned into the copilot's seat on The Ray. "How do you like leading the Skyborn?"

She didn't miss the fluttering of his eyelashes as he tried not to snap at her. "Furi, I told you I'm no leader."

"Of course not." She glanced back at Rin and Tatsu. The former thoroughly absorbed in Furi's notes on the Great Machine and the latter snoring in the padded chair beside him.

Furi turned to the windscreen and smiled. "And here I thought that was Abernathy himself, hanging on your every word. He's not really the leader of the most powerful guild on the docks. You're probably right about that."

"Furi …" Jakon almost growled. "I'll turn this ship around."

"I think you'd throw me off this ship before you turned it around. And I think you'd make sure I had a glider pack on before you did it." She cast him a sly smile. "You're pretty nice for a pirate."

Jakon's scowl finally cracked into a low laugh. "You're going to be the death of me, kid."

✧   ✧   ✧

THEY SAILED IN silence for a time, the sun gradually replaced by the stars on the horizon. Jakon always said it was easier to navigate at night. Furi thought he'd lost his mind.

"But the stars *move*."

"So does the sun, Furi. But instead of a single point of reference, I have a sky filled with them."

Furi rubbed her forehead. "I guess. I need to study the sky more."

"I'm sure William or Alice could recommend a good book for that." He returned the same sly smile she'd given him earlier.

Furi bolted upright. "I should reach Alice on the transmitter."

"Now? For a book about the skies?"

"No, no, I mean to talk to her. Does she even know we left Ballern? I don't know what she's doing. It feels … weird?"

Jakon looked like he was about to say something, hesitated, and said simply, "I'm glad you have a good friend, Furi."

She gave him a short smile as she turned the dial for the transmitter, locking in the frequency she often reached Alice on. Furi clicked the button. "Are you awake?"

No answer came for a while, but the line crackled with static in the end. "Furi?"

"Hi, yes!" She could hear the exhaustion in Alice's voice. "Did I wake you?"

"No, no. Just a long day. Jacob and I tried to get to sleep early, but it's hard with everything going on. How's Ballern? Did you have any luck calming the docks?"

Furi rubbed her hands together. "We … aren't in Ballern."

"Really?" Alice immediately sounded more awake. "Where are you then?"

"I don't know, exactly."

Jakon cast her a sideways smile.

"But we should catch up with Bollwerk's ships in another hour, if I understand correctly." She eyed the chef. "Jakon tells me I should learn how to navigate using stars, and you might have a suggestion about a good book."

"I have lots of suggestions for good books, Furi, but I don't think any of them have a thing to do with navigating by the stars."

Furi returned Jakon's smirk. "That's okay. I don't need anything right now. Not that I could get to anything, mind you. I'm with Jakon, and you know there aren't many books here."

Jakon scoffed at that. "I have a fantastic selection of books, thank you very much. They just happen to be fiction, for the most part, several about pirates, of course, and quite a few of those *supposed* historical accounts from the Children of the Dark Fire."

"Did you hear all of that?" Furi asked.

"I … did. I feel as though I've missed a rather large part of your conversation, Furi."

She let a small laugh escape. "Rin and Tatsu are with us. There are several more friends joining us than I'd expected. Than I'd *planned*. We were going to stay in the city, keep watch over the docks, but that's not where we need to be. At least, I don't *think* it's where we need to be."

"Furi." Alice waited a short time, as if she was carefully choosing each word. "You are exactly where you need to be. I know how you feel. It's the same as Jacob and me when we left Ancora. It's … I felt like I'd abandoned my city, my family even. But I didn't. We do what we have to do, and what happens will happen."

Furi caught a wide smile on Jakon's face. Apparently, the chef agreed with Alice on that point.

"I do like the Ancorans," Tatsu muttered, only half awake in his seat behind Furi.

She focused her attention on the transmitter. "So you know where we'll be. If you need us, we'll be here. We all have our transmitters. I'll see you on the ground, Alice, or in the sky. For the Stormborn."

"I'm glad you're with us. To better days, Furi. For the Stormborn."

Jakon turned the transmitter's dial. "You had a good idea reaching out to our allies, Furi. We should probably tell a few more we're coming." He clicked the button. "Belldorn, this is The Ray."

Furi sat up a little straighter. She knew the codename for Lady Katherine, and even now, Jakon's audacity could take her by surprise.

"Ray, this is Belldorn. The hour is late."

"At least *you* aren't currently en route to rendezvous with a carrier across the Gray Sea with a navigator who doesn't believe in using the stars."

"Hey!" Furi snapped.

He flashed her a grin before Kat responded.

"I did not realize you would be departing so soon. Are there more allies joining you?"

"Yes. I don't know if anyone had reached out to you, and I wanted to be sure we weren't shot down on our approach. Four destroyers and several supply ships should reach the engagement at the northern docks in an hour, perhaps a bit more."

"That is welcome news. The docks are secured, so you may wish to direct the destroyers to join forces there. As to the supply ships, we need them on the ground. There is another offensive mounting against Karn. Plans are in motion, but support would be ideal."

"I'm not sure if you've spoken to anyone else about the supply ships, but they have several Mechs on board."

"Large or small?"

"Both, in fact. If that may change your deployment strategy."

Lady Katherine didn't answer for a moment. Her words were quicker when she did. "Direct them to the northern docks as well. We will push from both north and east to draw their focus and perhaps spare Karn any more casualties."

"Understood. You have my banner, Belldorn. You need only call upon it."

"Should you live through this battle, Ray, I would like to discuss several things the Skysworn has shared with me over the years. One particular issue with the forgery of a royal seal in the past four—"

Jakon reached out and turned the frequency, creating a burst of static before speaking loudly. "What was that? I'm afraid you're breaking up." He flipped the transmitter off, and Furi didn't miss his small cringe.

"You stole a royal seal?"

Jakon gave a slow shake of his head. "No, of course not. We … well, we may have had one forged so we could print our own papers for the docks." He hung his head and laughed. "One of the best jobs Mary and I ever worked together."

"That's a story I'd like to hear."

"Me too," Rin said before letting out a long yawn.

Furi didn't understand how the dragonriders could be so tired after Lady Katherine had just been speaking over the transmitter. It had her feeling more awake than she'd felt in days. They had a purpose and a focus, and that was a wonderful thing after the chaos of the Battle of Ballern.

If Furi had any say in it, she would keep Mordair from setting foot in her city ever again.

CHAPTER TWENTY-FIVE

I T HAD BEEN a long time since Gregory Mordair felt anything akin to nerves. But with his plans nearly complete and only one meeting remaining with the leaders of the Children of the Dark Fire, he couldn't help the unease in his gut.

Other encounters had been on his terms, with his own guard, but now only Patrice, garbed in crimson red, walked beside him through those halls many considered sacred. These were nothing like the bustling lower levels. Instead, the highest places of the Great Machine were reserved for leadership and worship.

Their first steps off the lift told him as much. Cloaked guards stood at attention before every hall branching off the walkway. He'd expected to find latticework floors similar to the docks in Ballern, but here, there was no trace of the supports holding them in place. No thick columns or exposed ironwork to betray the illusion of a floating floor.

The effect of the water flowing through troughs on either side of the path likely enhanced the trickery, and Mordair expected much of the structure was hidden beneath that water. A lowering spear brought his attention fully back to their situation. He didn't miss Patrice's hand slipping into her cloak, ready to eliminate the slightest threat, but the spear never crossed into the walkway; instead, it formed a barrier so they would not deviate from the path.

So it continued, guards crossing their spears to block the walkways, funneling them down the hall until, at last, they reached a pair of doors so plain and dark they might have been slabs of obsidian. They swung inward without prompting; only once opened could the guards within be seen.

There was no grand dais for a throne in that place, but it still held an authority Mordair wanted for his own. And with his lineage and the truth of what drove the Children of the Dark Fire, it would indeed be his, in time.

The lone cloaked figure seated there beckoned them closer. They crossed rings of polished stone and gems inlaid all along the floor, forming loops like the orbits of planets around the center. Only as they grew nearer could Mordair see the metal-plated flames that formed the Queen's Crest rising from the throne.

But that wasn't what froze Mordair in his tracks. It was Patrice's sudden grip on his arm as the cloaked figure lowered his hood and offered a broad smile.

"Lane!" Patrice hissed.

Pale blue eyes and an infuriating smile beamed back at her. "Welcome, friends. You stand at the heart of the Children of the Dark Fire, and I welcome you into our fold."

"Where are your leaders?" Mordair asked.

Patrice looked up at him, her eyebrows raised. "Don't you see? *Lane* is their leader, Gregory. He's been … all those weeks in training. Strategizing. You …"

Mordair rested his hand on the breathing mask clipped on his belt. "You are an excellent liar, Lane. A skill much needed while guiding an empire."

Patrice clenched her fists, staring as if willing Lane to meet her gaze, but the man kept his focus on Mordair. And Mordair appreciated that fact because while the leaders of the Children of the Dark Fire had been *his* goal, the king of Fel had apparently been their goal all along, hadn't he?

Lane stood. "In this place, I am not called 'king' or 'leader.' We are all one in the shadow of the Dark Fire, and we need no titles. What is … is. And what will be, will be. Come, friends. Walk with me that we might discuss the coming battles."

Mordair exchanged a look with Patrice when Lane turned his back on them. There was more than one unspoken question in that gaze. *Should we kill him now? What's our best option? Can you handle the guards?* But in the end, they followed Lane behind the small throne, admiring the precise metalwork it took to fit the pieces of the flame together, as opposed to engraving it in one large piece.

No guards trailed them as they entered a hallway on the fall wall, so dark it blended into the shadowy metal of the room itself. Only when Lane forced a lever up did the screens around a dozen braziers lift, and light flooded their path.

Lane called back over his shoulder. "We are alone in this place. Ask what questions you must, but we have more pressing matters than I would like. The attack you provoked on the docks has led to the sinking of your own fleet, Mordair. That is not the best terms to solidify our alliance."

"You risked exposing yourself in Ballern." Patrice's words weren't a question but a statement of fact.

Nevertheless, Lane answered as if it had been a question. "Yes. I don't send our missionaries into the world unchecked, Patrice. Nor do I journey unguarded. You may have detected the guards in the market and alleys, but what of the divers waiting in the sea? The archers posted behind the old arrow slits in the disused turrets. Many of which I lost in that ill-advised attack on the docks."

"People understand the threat of force." Mordair delivered his statement as if standing before a classroom. "It is the best way to maintain order."

Lane blew out a short breath. "There are times that is true. The coming of a new alliance not our own is certainly a time to employ force. We must now face the combined wrath of Bollwerk, Belldorn, and Karn."

"The Children of the Dark Fire face far more than that." Patrice didn't keep the venom from her voice. "You face those from Ballern who did not flee to your cult. You face Ancora and Cave, Midstream and Canopy. Your actions have resulted in an alliance unseen since the Deadlands War."

Lane inclined his head. "You make excellent observations. I would expect no less of an assassin. But how many of those cities now seek Mordair because of *your* hand, Patrice? I imagine it is quite a few of them. History comes in cycles. I suppose there is a kind of poetry at another cycle being triggered by an assassin."

Patrice's jaw flexed, and Mordair worried she might strike Lane down between one stride and the next. If she decided to do that after he had a better grasp of the power structure inside the Great Machine, it would be of little concern. But an attack now could put a great many plans in jeopardy. He supposed he could strike *her* down instead, though the battle would be fraught.

There was a small tremor of relief when she slowed her steps and took a deep breath. No attack, then. Not now, at least. Did Lane understand the danger Patrice posed? There were few assassins of her caliber, and to taunt her was to invite death herself into his breast.

Past the last of the braziers, a simple wood door stood before them. It didn't tower above all who approached it, but old stains and chips told of an age behind the wood. Something fit for a museum, or hoarded as a family treasure for some long-forgotten memory.

The plain door intrigued Mordair, but what waited beyond removed all thought of the wood from his mind. What waited beyond was the core of an empire, the power of a factory made wild, and a city born of bronze and steel.

"Welcome to the Great Machine, Gregory Mordair, heir to the lost bloodline."

He had seen Cave in the past. Spent time in their vast underground city. It was an impressive feat, but it was as to a child's drawing compared to what lay before him now. Each level of the Great Machine bore homes and shops, sloping away from their position in the center of the structure.

Following it farther down, some six distinct levels, large creatures milled back and forth, mingling with the residents there. Farms, he realized, in short order. There were no predatory bugs in that place. Instead, they were Pillies and Walkers, ideal for food and useful for carrying heavy loads.

Lane waited for Mordair and Patrice to turn away from that sight, and when they finally did, he smiled. "Beyond the residences await the factories. The equipment we use to manufacture our weapons is powered by the Great Machine. Be it water or steam, all our bounty comes from the Dark Fire. Now, please sit so we may discuss how to proceed. This war must end, and there are many of our people who do not believe you intend to end it. Convince them, and they will welcome you as the lost would welcome a messiah."

"And if he should fail?" Patrice asked.

"Let us not dwell on the darkest things." Lane bowed his head.

Mordair let out a low laugh. Lane might have been part of a cult, as much of a leader as the Children of the Dark Fire had ever had, but he knew how to threaten with the subtlety of an experienced noble. "Help me understand your defenses, and we will face the threat of our enemies as one. When they are done—when they are *burned*—all wars will end."

Lane laced his fingers together and eyed the pair. "You walk a path of trials, Gregory Mordair, and everyone around you suffers because of it. But your enemies are ours, and there are enough of us who understand that war has come to the Great Machine, no matter our desire to evade it."

Mordair withheld the smile that threatened to lift his lips. One step toward his place in this new hierarchy. One step toward dominating the last power that could oppose his rule. If all the Children of the Dark Fire could be made to follow, as he believed Lane soon would, every city within his realm would bow before the might of their alliance.

And the first bloody steps Mordair took in the Deadlands War would finally put Archibald where he belonged.

CHAPTER TWENTY-SIX

J ACOB ADJUSTED HIS gloves before wrapping the Tree Killer's reins around his forearm. It felt rushed to be venturing back into the field so soon after their scouting trip, but when the Speaker of Bollwerk and the Lady of Belldorn agreed on a course of action, there wasn't much anyone could do to resist that.

He glanced over at the cluster of Spider Knights, Samuel and Drakkar riding side by side as the Cave Guardian made a wide gesture with both hands from his Stalker's saddle. Memories of the Fall rose up, the escape from the Lowlands on the steambike with Charles, Bessie's mad scramble along the rooftops as the invaders crushed everything in their path.

Jacob had seen terrible things since the Butcher destroyed the Lowlands. Some of those visions he'd never truly escape. He knew that. But there were good things he'd found outside Ancora. Good friends and amazing stories. Nothing came without a price. If the Fall hadn't happened, he might never have ventured out to Bollwerk or Cave, might never have met Smith and Mary, Drakkar, Furi, or any of the people he trusted with his life.

The Tree Killer rocked to the side, pulling Jacob out of his thoughts as it stepped across an ancient tree stump. On the other side of the rotting expanse, he urged the Tree Killer closer to Samuel until the steps of his mount matched Bessie's.

"Not long now," the Spider Knight called out when he saw Jacob. "You're sure you have everything you need?"

Alice laughed at that. "Samuel, do you have any idea how many times Jacob packed and repacked his glider? I doubt he'd be able to fly with all the tools and gadgets he stuffed inside it."

"At least we'll be ready for anything!"

"Except gliding," Alice said flatly.

Samuel grinned at Jacob. "Sounds like you've learned a few things about being prepared. Close calls will do that to you. I've been there myself."

"Alice is right, though. I packed more Bangers into the glider than I should have."

Samuel raised an eyebrow. "I would have thought the cargo pockets would be plenty versatile for that."

"I do not believe that is what he's referring to." Drakkar leaned in his saddle when his Stalker took to the side of a hill. "He said he placed it in the *glider*. Not his pack."

Samuel's focus snapped back to Jacob. "Did you stuff explosives into the *wings*?"

"It sounds terrible when you say it like that," Jacob muttered.

Alice laughed under her breath. "Don't worry. He tested it. If he needs to deploy the glider, it'll just drop everything he placed by the wings. It won't do us any good, but at least he won't go cliff diving without water."

"That's a … colorful way to put it." Samuel stared at Alice for a moment, his brow crinkled as if he didn't quite know what else to say.

A quick series of flags rose farther into the ranks, echoed by more flag bearers closer to their position. Jacob hadn't spent as much time with Karn's infantry as Samuel and Drakkar had, and judging by the looks on their faces, he didn't think it was good news.

Jacob called out to Drakkar. "What happened?"

The Cave Guardian shook his head. "Nothing yet, but enemy soldiers have been sighted in the woods. I would suspect they are reconnaissance for Mordair and the Children of the Dark Fire, but I have been surprised before."

"You've been *surprised* before?" Samuel's voice rose. "So they're either scouts or assassins, practically the same thing."

Jacob didn't miss Drakkar's slight eye roll, which said a great deal coming from the Cave Guardian. Drakkar was more patient than almost anyone he knew, and if Jacob had to guess, this wasn't the first time the pair had engaged in that conversation.

"Drakkar." Alice waited for the Cave Guardian to return to flatter terrain where he could meet her gaze. "When we rode with Karn before, we split into smaller groups. Will that be the strategy here, too?"

"It seems unlikely. There is no true element of ambush now. It is well known that scouts from both forces are in the woods. Any sizable force would be detected, and a single Bombardier does not pose a threat to the operation."

"Poses a threat to me." Samuel rubbed his neck. "Poses a threat to anyone who gets boiled alive, doesn't it?"

"Of course, but if it were Carrion Worms, would you take a different approach?"

Samuel eyed Drakkar. "No, I guess I wouldn't."

"Even as long as their mandibles are, and the speed they can attack when provoked?"

The Spider Knight threw a hand up in the air. "Fine, you made your point. Let's just march to our doom already."

Jacob couldn't help but exchange a grin with Drakkar when Samuel looked down at his saddle to adjust the halberd strapped to it. Listening to Samuel complain was a bit like having a small piece of home at their side, but they both knew the Spider Knight often complained as he was bracing himself for a new trial. And a march into the shadowy woods outside Karn certainly qualified.

The flags changed again, and this time, the formation shifted. They didn't spread out into separate squads so much as move closer to the trees themselves. The arcing tangles of roots and fallen branches provided immediate cover, should any attack reach them.

Samuel looked up at Drakkar before focusing on Jacob and Alice. "You two should do what you need to do. We're almost to the ridge."

Alice pulled out a map she'd sketched into her notebook before placing a compass next to it. It wasn't as detailed as the map from Mali, but Alice had brought backups to her backup plans. The Tree Killer moved with enough grace and stability that she was still quick to get a bearing. "Samuel's right."

"Be well, Ancorans." Drakkar raised his hand and offered a smile. It wasn't the greeting of the Steamsworn, but the salutation of a friend.

"We'll see you again." The words came out harder than Jacob had intended. He tried to offset that fact with a jab at Samuel. "Try not to complain the entire time."

The Spider Knight smirked at him. "Try not to jump off any cliffs before you empty your pack."

Alice laughed as she pulled away to the northwest. "Be careful, both of you. And like Jacob said, we'll see you again."

THE COLUMNS MARCHING through the Gray Woods had a rhythm. A steady beat of claws and feet pounding the forest floor that was almost louder in its absence than it had been when they were in the middle of it. But as soon as they crossed over the first lower ridge, putting more distance and earth between them and the others, the woods grew quiet.

Occasional calls managed to find their way through the forest. But for the most part, Jacob would never have been able to tell there was a literal army marching less than a mile away. Of course, the longer they strayed from their original path, the more distance any sound had to travel.

He let his gaze roam, checking the lowest branches of the canopy and any shadow that could hide an ambush. It might have been more likely that an attack would focus on the main forces deeper in the woods, but ambushing stray soldiers was a sound strategy as well.

Jacob glanced down at his armor and blew out a breath, pulling the gray cloak out of his saddlebag that would disguise him as one of the Children of the Dark Fire. Alice had worn hers all day despite the rise in humidity, but the thick air made Jacob want to wear far less, even than the light cloak.

He had little doubt he'd be drenched in sweat by the time they reached the tunnels, but there were larger concerns. He only hoped when they found Samuel and Drakkar again, the pair would be no worse for wear.

✧   ✧   ✧

SAMUEL FROWNED AS the columns rolled back on themselves. He knew many Spider Knights were closer to the third set of flags. They'd slowed to a point that he and Drakkar had passed them by. Perhaps it was to help keep the eyes at the front of the lines fresh, or perhaps there was some other strategy preferred by Karn that he wasn't familiar with.

Drakkar pointed to the northeast. "Is that Alana?"

Samuel squinted against the low cloud of dust being churned up by the Stalkers and Tree Killers. To add to the mess, a handful of Walkers scurried through the dried leaves, kicking up even more detritus. The path cleared enough for him to see who Drakkar was pointing at.

Tight locs fell to the center of her back between the neatly shaved sides of her head. As she slowed, Samuel could just see the hint of the tattoos on her scalp.

"That's her." Samuel nodded. "It has to be."

Drakkar urged his Stalker forward, drifting to the other side of a Forest Giant as they lost sight of Alana and found her again on the opposite side of the massive trunk. "Alana!"

The leader of Cave turned toward her name, raising her fist in greeting as Drakkar caught up to her in earnest.

Drakkar held out his hand as if forming the Steamsworn Fist. "I did not realize you were riding with us today."

"Allie is leading the defenses in Karn. We wanted at least one of us on the front. There are a great many tactics we agree on, and some I think Karn would resist if left to their own devices."

"Have you heard from our brothers in Ancora?" Drakkar asked.

For a brief moment, Samuel had forgotten that a force of Cave Guardians had journeyed to Ancora, both to help defend the city and assist in the restoration of the Lowlands. He was glad of the changes that had come between Ancora and Cave, but he still remembered the awful things his father had once said about the underground city.

It wasn't a hatred of Cave exactly, but a distrust of its people that could be traced back to the Deadlands War. But it wasn't Cave who had betrayed Ancora. It was the Ancorans themselves in those darkest hours.

"Samuel?"

He glanced up when Drakkar called his name. "Sorry, what was that?"

Drakkar's brow furrowed, but he didn't say more about Samuel's distraction. "Alana spoke with Branddur. Apparently, Baddawick and Nora have been providing shelter and entertainment for the Cave Guardians."

"That's great. I'm glad to hear it."

Alana raised her finger, drawing both of their attention. "Perhaps more amusingly, Baddawick has been throwing more parties than he likely should be, forcing the Cave Guardians and Spider Knights to mingle with Parliament and the Lowlanders. It is a good strategy to build bonds on both sides of the walls."

Samuel grinned at Alana. "I always knew that old man was a politician at heart."

"I would never think to insult him with a label such as that." Drakkar placed a hand over his heart. "Now, as for Alana's politics in Cave …"

She narrowed her eyes. "You beg for favors with one hand and slap your benefactor with the other."

"You slapped someone?" Samuel asked, appalled.

Alana's stern expression cracked, and she didn't hide her laughter. "No, Spider Knight. It is only an expression. From another time, when Drakkar and I were many years younger."

"Younger than Rikken." A smile came and went across Drakkar's face. "Perhaps we can have days like that again. Without war upon our doorstep."

The flags ahead shifted, and no relay came before the first cries rose in the woods. The shouts reached them before the new pattern was raised.

"*Ambush!*"

It was a strange thing, hearing that cry as they moved through the forest. In the past, when Samuel had heard someone shout a similar warning, it was immediately followed by relentless fighting in the immediate area. Moving in columns with their allies, the warning here was not the same.

His halberd still came into his hand through instinct alone. Countless drills had instilled the memory in the very fiber of his muscles. The surge of adrenaline still coursed through his body, his fingertips tingling in anticipation as he waited for some shadow to move, some assassin to drop from the canopy, but none came.

Instead, there was the distant sound of conflict. The hammering ring of metal on metal and the faint screams of the dying as their column marched forward. The flags changed again, and their compatriots from Karn visibly relaxed as the red circle flew against a white background.

Samuel took several deep breaths to center himself. It was exhausting being that alert, on the verge of panic, and having nowhere to direct his energy. If he focused too hard, he'd jump at every sound, every movement, but his time in the Spider Knights had taught him better than that.

He picked up his crossbow and twisted the winch in the stock. The teeth of the mechanism grew taller as the gears inside turned, only lowering when the string was primed. He locked a bolt in place, pulling the leather strap of the safety tight across the release.

Only then did he let the crossbow hang from the saddle once more, turning his attention to Bessie. He ran his fingers through her hair in a familiar pattern, tracing a figure eight behind her eyes. It was familiar to them both, and a simple way to ground himself. Her stride relaxed in time, her body lifting a bit higher from the ground, every step no longer ready to launch her and her rider through the air.

They rode as one, and any tension Samuel felt was often reflected by the spider. That's how it was when you'd spent enough time with the same mount. Separate beings, but one unit. It was one of the secrets of the Spider Knights, a secret that made them deadlier than most.

Nearly a mile passed before they reached the site of the ambush. Invaders—bugs with so much bulk they could have charged *through* the Lowlands wall of Ancora—lay strewn across the forest floor. Bombardiers, their sides pierced and in some cases ruptured entirely, towered above the dead riders. The gray cloaks of the Children of the Dark Fire did little to hide the blood staining the earth and bodies.

A few had fallen to bolts, but the seared flesh and warped metals told of a different fate for many more. As horrible as the scene was, Samuel realized there weren't more than a dozen riders in that mass of corpses. Some of the Bombardiers hadn't been saddled, but they'd ridden into battle, regardless.

In the back of his mind, he wondered if the bugs had a hive mentality in the Gray Woods. Even separated from their own, were they so desperate to stay together that they had no thought of self-preservation? He glanced at Drakkar and Alana, the soldiers from Karn and Ballern and beyond. Were any of them really that different from those beetles?

It was a thought for another time, and preferably a time with far more drinks in hand.

The flags shifted, and Alana called out the orders.

"Clear to the front. If there are more ambushes, they haven't been detected yet, or the traps are still waiting. Keep your eyes wide and your teeth sharp."

Many of the Cave Guardians answered with a quick rap of fists on armor. Alana acknowledged them with a nod. She turned her focus to a small map in her hand, checking coordinates before projecting her voice again.

"We're within a mile of the forest's edge. You all know the plan. Push them back, hold, and escape into the woods before our reinforcements arrive."

Samuel knew their paths would intersect with two other columns of their allies. Nothing changed in the first half mile, but he could hear them soon after. Heavy thuds in the forest, not entirely dampened by the underbrush and trees around.

Within a quarter mile, there wasn't any question about what was making those sounds. Between the wide gaps in the Gray Woods, Titan Mechs marched, manned by pairs of pilots. Samuel had often seen them controlled by a single operator, but in battle, that wasn't the best option.

Like a destroyer deployed without its cannoneers.

Beyond those towering monstrosities were tight formations of smaller Mechs, the exoskeletons of Jacob's design. Jacob and Charles's design, Samuel thought. They didn't look much taller than a person, but their layered armor hissed like muted wind chimes as they marched.

The flags shifted again, the white and blue lowering before being replaced by a blood-red vision that made Samuel's heart stutter. It wasn't the flag of Karn, or Belldorn, not of Ancora or Bollwerk. Instead, the dark embroidery showed the outline of a Shadowwing, as if mocking the flags of Fel. Stormborn.

Drakkar stood in his saddle, braced against the stirrups as he pointed to the nearest of the flags before clapping his hands together in one sharp strike. The grin on the Cave Guardian's face sent a chill down Samuel's spine.

The shadows of the Gray Woods lightened as they reached the edge of the forest and the full expanse of their forces stepped into the light. There wasn't time to appraise the situation more than that. Clouds of smoke and dirt hurled into the air as the report of a Bombardier's blast echoed across the wide field.

The flags didn't change. They stayed with the bearers, leading the charge. Tree Killers and spiders alike surged forward. There was no way to direct the mounts then. All they could do was hold tight and attack when the time came. But that wasn't entirely true. There was something they could do. Something warriors and battle-worn soldiers had done for countless centuries.

Drakkar released a howl as he raised a spear to the skies. "For the Stormborn!"

The world screamed with him.

✧　✧　✧

ACCUSTOMED TO THE close-quarters combat of Cave and the ravines surrounding the underground city, and to the tight streets of Bollwerk and Belldorn, Drakkar was struck by just how far ahead he could see. It was something he'd only really experienced when he'd ridden through the clouds with the dragonriders.

Belldorn was the one place he'd seen forces like what waited for them in the narrow prairie between the Gray Woods and the city outside the Great Machine. But they were not all armored crawlers here. The Children of the Dark Fire marched forward on Bombardiers and Tree Killers, perhaps not as durable as metal machines but more agile and better armed, to be sure. Their enemies' mounts numbered in the hundreds across that field, with more stationed along the streets.

His Stalker surged with the frantic pace of his cohorts, the spider's claws digging deep furrows into the dirt and mud beneath churned-up grass as they sprinted toward the front line. Even from a distance, Drakkar felt a small relief in not being in that first wave. The front lines on both sides fell like so much wheat to be harvested, blood turning the ground into a slick pool of mud that sent many soldiers to their knees and their deaths.

The flags of the forward units lowered as their bearers collided with the enemy. There was a reason those signals were fastened to spears, and they did their work as well as any other. It was the last chance Drakkar had to appraise the field as a whole. Each company had their orders, knew what they were *supposed* to do, but many fled back into the woods at the carnage unfolding before them.

Limbs severed at the swipe of swords. Riders collapsed when whistling bolts took them in the chest and head. And then he was there, feeling the tug on his cloak as a bolt passed through it. Drakkar gritted his teeth as he caught the strike of a long halberd on his spear.

He escaped the blade, but it cut deep into his Stalker's leg, finding a space in the armor. The spider reeled, and the spear tip snapped off when the gap closed, the force flinging the haft into the attacker's face. Drakkar doubted the man could have survived the split wood embedded in his skull, but the Stalker reared back and lunged at the Tree Killer.

The bug's scythes broke with the force of the impact, and the Stalker's fangs found the rider. The strike came fast, and the Stalker forced its way deeper into the chaos. Drakkar landed a few blows with his spear before hurling it over the front line, putting down a nearby archer, who fell beneath the bloody battle.

He grabbed another of the collapsible spears, readying it for an immediate defense.

Swords rang off the Stalker's armor, but more than one found its mark, leaving trails of gore running down the beast's legs. His mount wouldn't last long. Drakkar needed to get away from the front, but he caught sight of Alana, a bolt in her shoulder. Her thick leather armor gave her some protection, but he had no idea how deep that bolt had gotten.

A blast of heat rolled by him, threatening to scald his face as the attack of a Bombardier thundered by. Two spiders died in the blast, but he didn't see Bessie's gray hair, and that would have to be enough for now.

Alana raised a spear and cried out as she hurled it past her spider's head, impaling an armored Walker swerving through the ranks. It reared up to strike, and Drakkar leveled his crossbow. The first bolt struck beneath the armored head, causing the Walker to jerk violently to the side.

He'd seen that kind of movement in the wild. When Walkers fought and attacked with such vehemence, they sometimes cracked their own chitin. The only thing that cracked now was the neck of its rider. She fell limply to the ground, lost in the rolling storm of legs and blood.

"Alana!"

She raised her fist in acknowledgment but didn't turn to look at Drakkar. That was the stuff of fledgling warriors and the dead. It was enough. That simple motion told him she wasn't mortally wounded. Her Stalker struck at the flailing Walker, silencing the beast once and for all before sprinting over the corpse.

It created a break in the lines of their enemy, and the mounted forces of their alliance surged through it, spreading the columns of the Children of the Dark Fire as they went. Some on both sides showed their lack of training, turning to engage the riders as they sprinted past.

But to do that was to expose their backs, and they were felled in short order. The columns from Karn continued pushing through, Tree Killers and Stalkers forcing the lines farther away, crushing the forwardmost soldiers from the Children of the Dark Fire into tight formations, until the Titan Mechs did their work.

It was a vision Drakkar wished he'd never seen. A Bombardier scooped up into the hands of a Titan Mech, its rider launching bolt after bolt to ping harmlessly off the canopy. The back of the Bombardier started to smoke, and the Titan Mech slammed it into the earth, crushing men and women and mounts before the Bombardier *ruptured.*

Flesh boiled in that wave of fluid. The concentrated attack turned into a cloud of superheated liquid. But their enemy wasn't the only casualty. The heat poured into the Titan Mech, filling it with steam before hydraulics snapped when their tolerances were breached.

He couldn't hear the pilots' screams. He could only watch as they clawed at the thick condensation on the glass before falling still. The Titan Mech slowly leaned to the side like a Forest Giant finally at the end of its long life. The impact when it fell crushed soldiers from every company beneath its mass, spraying mud and detritus and viscera across the lines.

And the lines broke. The forces of their enemy turned, and Karn's flags rose into the air once more. The Stormborn symbol no longer sailed above the battlefield. Instead, a square white flag with a red square in the middle signaled the retreat.

It wasn't immediate, as some of the skirmishes required far more focus. That in itself was enough to trigger more casualties and leave more bodies on the field. Drakkar tried not to dwell on that as he circled behind Samuel as the Spider Knight sprinted past, Bessie's armor covered in the red blood of the fallen.

Drakkar wove between Samuel and Alana, the intensity of his focus slowly bleeding away as they drew farther from the field of battle. At last, they stood at the outskirts of the Gray Woods, their mounts breathing heavily beneath them while others collapsed, unlikely to rise again.

He turned back to the woods ahead, the shadows a balm as they closed in around him.

✧　✧　✧

AFTER TENDING TO the spiders, Samuel checked over Drakkar's armor when the Cave Guardian removed his cloak to repair the worst of the cuts. "I don't think you need to worry about your cloak right now."

Drakkar harrumphed as he pulled a needle and thread out of a pouch at his belt. "I appreciate you caring for my Stalker. I didn't think she would survive those wounds. But I must tend to my cloak."

"You won't talk him out of that," Alana said from her position reclining on a cluster of tree roots. It didn't look like the most comfortable place to rest, but she didn't have any complaints. He supposed the bolt in her shoulder was probably far less comfortable.

Samuel whistled as he found a deep gash in the side of Drakkar's tightly wrapped leather breastplate. "You would have been feeling that if it'd hit you on the other side."

"I am feeling it well enough already." Drakkar glanced down at the cut.

"I don't see any blood. Unlike Alana over there."

"Calm yourself, Spider Knight." Alana smirked at him. "The medic is nearly here. Let them deal with those more wounded than I."

"Signs of movement in the far woods."

Samuel didn't see who had spoken, but Alana cursed in response.

"Where?" she asked.

"Northwest, near the clearing."

Samuel stood and stepped closer to the forest's edge. The man was pointing where he knew Jacob and Alice were headed. "That's the ridge Jacob and Alice have to cross." He cursed and clicked the transmitter in his collar. "The ridge is compromised. Are you receiving this?"

The transmitter crackled, and Alice's voice answered. "We haven't seen anything here."

"Close to the city. A line of trees is burned down like a fire line. I don't know if it's to expose any forces moving through or not. Be careful."

"We will."

Samuel raised a scope to his eye and tracked the ridge. He couldn't see anyone there, or any traps waiting, but it didn't mean the path was clear.

"Call Mary."

Samuel glanced at Drakkar, muttering to himself about how he should have thought of that. He switched frequencies. "Skysworn, over. We have a gap in the woods. Scouts could be detected."

"Understood." Mary's response came fast, but she didn't sound stressed. Maybe that was a good sign for the battle in the sky. "I'll get a message to Belldorn. Stay on ground frequencies unless something worse comes up."

"And now Lady Katherine will be aware of the vulnerability," Drakkar said. "You have done what you can. Jacob and Alice can take care of themselves."

Samuel grimaced. "I know that … it's just, I've looked after those two since we were *all* kids."

"You are all still kids to me."

The Spider Knight laughed under his breath. It broke the tension, even for only a moment, and he appreciated that more than he could say. All they could do now was wait for the next command. There were times waiting was worse than fighting.

✦ ✦ ✦

DRAKKAR STOOD WATCHING the medic as she worked on Alana's shoulder.

She winced when the medic tied off the bandage. "Thank you."

The medic didn't stop to say anything more, only moved to the next in a countless line of injured. Some she dismissed without treatment, others she demanded return to Karn. Far too many she left still and lifeless along the treeline, the blank stares and tears of their compatriots mingling in the bloodied soil.

Alana climbed to her feet as the first bombers darkened the skies. The Children of the Dark Fire hadn't retreated fully into the city. They reinforced the battlements, as if those could stop any attack Archibald and Kat and Arun would dare to use against them.

"May you rest in the shadow of the caves." Alana placed her hand over her heart, and what few Cave Guardians stood around her echoed the last of her words. "And may your spirit return to the darkness."

The bombers' bay doors opened. Black dots falling through the sky quickly grew into shaped charges the length of a barrel.

"For Ancora," Samuel whispered beside Drakkar.

The Cave Guardian put his arm around his friend as the first wave struck the ground. The earth itself shook with the blasts, the fountains of dirt and blood, metal and fire, darkening the sun as an endless staccato thunder threatened to deafen them all.

There were no half measures with Archibald. Drakkar knew that. He knew more about the Speaker of Bollwerk than Archibald likely realized. But there was a difference between *knowing* there are no half measures and seeing it unfold before him in a fiery death.

The second bomber hit the northern region, just outside the city proper, as the Children of the Dark Fire's forces tried to run. Drakkar took a deep breath when the first city block vanished in a cloud of stone and bodies. No one could have survived in those billowing clouds of flame and ash.

It was a victory in the moment, but Drakkar understood the darker side of what had happened. There would be no mercy from their enemy now. The same drive that burned in the heart of the Ancorans would take root in the Children of the Dark Fire. Another generation of war would come unless Archibald had truly muddled even Lady Katherine's sense of mercy.

But the bombs did not drop farther into the city. The screams of horror were not silenced in those streets, and nor were the screams of victory from his allies at the edge of the Gray Woods. The battle was not done. No matter how much he willed it otherwise, now they couldn't stop until Mordair himself had paid for his crimes.

The reports of the Porcupine's cannons crashed above them a second before the opposite side of the Gray Woods erupted in fire and dirt and splintered wood. Whatever threat had been waiting for Jacob and Alice would have far more to think about than marching into that clearing.

Samuel clicked the button on his transmitter. "Go. Now!"

CHAPTER TWENTY-SEVEN

S AMUEL DIDN'T HAVE to tell them twice. Jacob brushed the dirt from his cloak, the last explosion having been far too close for comfort. Even the wild Tree Killers in the branches above them scattered as small clumps of dirt and debris crashed through the canopy. With only a nod to Alice, they both urged their mounts forward, sprinting out of the forest and out into the clear-cut path the Children of the Dark Fire had carved.

He couldn't see the battlefield itself, only the curls and clouds of smoke rising from it, hidden behind the closest rise. They had been able to fool the guards once, but Jacob wasn't sure if they could do it again. Not when there was a blatant attack on the city.

That was a problem to solve when they encountered it. Even if they were taken, they were far from unarmed. Alice wore a pair of bolt gloves that looked like little more than riding gloves, and hidden beneath her vambraces were bolt throwers. Beyond that, they had the air cannons, Bangers, Burners, and enough compound bombs that Jacob worried that the weight of his pack might be too much in the end.

Instinct told them to avoid the clearing, but Alice signaled for Jacob to follow her, and they cut through the downed trees and underbrush, saving so much time that Jacob thought it may very well be worth the risk. The Tree Killer rose and fell beneath him, scampering over logs that would have been hard to climb on foot and leaving the battle farther behind them.

The reports of cannons and screams still reached them, but they were closer to whispers now as Jacob and Alice cleared the last stretch of open ground and plunged into the fog bank they'd seen before.

Alice had her head down, checking her map and compass before grumbling and stuffing it into her pack. She pulled out Mali's map with the inlaid compass and metal back, reading it before angling slightly to the southwest and striking off into a shallow stream. Cold water splashed around them, and Jacob's heart hammered when he saw the arched carapace surging along the streambed.

"Water Beetle!"

But he wasn't the only one who noticed. The Tree Killer lashed out with its scythe when the Water Beetle neared, impaling the slick body before flinging it out of the water entirely. The bug was nowhere near as large as the Water Beetle he'd encountered beneath Ancora, which was something to be thankful for. It cracked against the stone and did little more than flail its legs for a moment before falling still.

"Come on." Alice gestured for them to follow, and the Tree Killer obeyed without question.

The damp folds of Jacob's cloak slapped against his legs as he checked the rope coil holding the bolts for his own thrower. He'd opted for a more compact version that looked something like a blend of a spear gun and a crossbow. Most importantly, the bolts couldn't be dropped once they'd been loaded into the feeder, and that was only one advantage it had over a crossbow.

The fog thinned as they skirted the cliff above the river, following it until they reached the lake to the north. Alice slowed and pointed ahead.

"Jacob. What are those?"

He cursed when he found what she'd asked about. And he knew she knew *what* they were, but even he had no idea what they were capable of. Long, arced attachments that looked very much like wings, but ended in pontoons like those of the carrier, flanked the edges of a series of dark green airships. Sleek, armored gas chambers loomed above the decks. It was as if the great fin that declared a ship of Fel had been attached to either side.

Jacob clicked the transmitter in his collar. "Samuel, airships incoming! I don't know what they are. Heavy cannons, heavily armored."

"Understood. Thanks, kid. Where are you?"

"By the river, not far from the rendezvous." It wasn't really a rendezvous, but Jacob didn't want to say anything too exact over the transmitter. Not when they were this close to the enemy who might intercept it.

Alice had her own transmitter on and shouted into it. "Airships, Skysworn. Tell Kat, tell everyone. The Children of the Dark Fire launched their fleet. It's … tell *everyone*."

"How many?"

"A dozen at least. The fog is heavy, and I can't be sure."

"Received. Skysworn out."

More airships rose into the sky as the fog thickened, slowly closing over their view of what was coming for their allies. Their friends.

"We have to go back, Alice." He leaned forward, craning his neck to get a better view of the rising fleet. "We can't leave them to that."

Alice squeezed her eyes shut. "We have to, Jacob. They've already risked too much to get us clear of the woods. We can't turn back now." She checked the map and compass again, tracing a line with her finger. "Come on, we follow the shore and aim for the old access tunnels when we reach this bay on the map."

Jacob despised the idea of leaving their friends to fight against that fleet, even if there wasn't anything they could do from the ground, but he knew Alice was right. The only thing now was to focus on their task. The battle was *their* distraction and their best chance of finding their way into the Great Machine undetected.

They strode through the shallows of the lake while their friends waited for the onslaught above.

✧ ✧ ✧

Mary guided the Skysworn lower, piercing the cloud bank until she could see exactly what Jacob and Alice had seen. Even from above, the shadowy airships of the Children of the Dark Fire blended into the canopy of the Gray Woods. If it wasn't for their movement, they'd be all but invisible.

"Are you seeing this, Smith?"

His tinny voice sounded over the horn. "I am. This is not good, Mary. They are not as sizable as Fel's destroyers, but a compliment of both will be formidable."

Mary blew out a breath and clicked the transmitter. "Kat, we have eyes on the ships."

"Status?"

"You have ten minutes before a destroyer would be in range, but these aren't destroyers. Clear sign of long cannons. I've never seen anything quite like them."

"Movement in the north as well. Fel and Ballern's deserters are moving toward our forces at the docks."

Mary ground her teeth together. "We give up one position or split our forces. It's a risk, either way."

"Archibald has already made that decision. We stay divided. The remaining ships are deploying from the carriers. All hands, Mary." Kat's following words were muted, as if she hadn't intended anyone else to hear them. "I never wanted this."

Mary closed her eyes and bowed her head for a moment. "Neither did I, but it's the only way, isn't it?"

"If it was anyone but Mordair, perhaps it wouldn't be. Fight well, Skysworn. Let us end this forsaken war at last."

She turned the dial on the transmitter and clicked the button. "Eva."

The low hiss of static didn't change for a time, but the question came back hurried. "Mary, what is it?"

"Belldorn gave the order to deploy all ships. The Children of the Dark Fire and Fel are all in the air now. This is going to get rough."

"You always did have a gift when it came to understating things."

Mary didn't miss Smith's chuckle over the horn.

The Skysworn's captain pushed back in her chair and nodded to herself. "Be careful, will you? I don't know where you are, and I don't know if I want to know."

"I'll call if I need you, Mary. You know that. I love you."

"Love you too." The transmitter went dead, and Mary rapped her knuckles on the console. "We aren't engaging those warships yet, Smith. I don't want the Skysworn in their sights until we know what they can do."

"Agreed. Then shall we join our other compatriots?"

A small smile lifted the corner of Mary's lips as she changed the frequency. Once a pirate, always a pirate.

✧　✧　✧

THE SKYSWORN SETTLED in beside The Ray, both moving at speeds that would be hard for any sizable cannon to track. Mary could just see Jakon through the edge of the windscreen, and the pirate chef raised his hand in a two-finger salute.

Another face appeared next to him, far more excited as she waved with an energy Mary couldn't fathom. Furi sat in the copilot's seat, which likely meant Rin and Tatsu would be on the cannons. That was good. Jakon might have had the ability to deploy his cannons from the captain's chair, but The Ray was much like the Skysworn. For the best accuracy, you needed a cannoneer.

"We move in with the strikers," Jakon said. "Stay north of the battle, as they'll be focused on what's ahead of them."

"You don't have to convince me, Jakon. Just keep your cannons pointed at our enemy, yes?"

Jakon hesitated before his calm showed a crack. "That was *one* time, Mary! And I only *clipped* that warship. It barely had any holes in it at all."

Mary laughed under her breath. There were few things that could rile Jakon up, but reminding him of times when his aim hadn't been so good was certainly one of those things.

"Did you reach out to any other guild contacts?" Jakon asked.

"Just an old bartender. You know how that is. I think you met him a few times in Pirate's Cove." This time, Mary raised a scope to her eye. She wanted to see Jakon's face, and his slack-jawed expression didn't disappoint.

"I thought he was in Midstream."

"You never know with him. You know he has a lot of contacts from the old war. Not to mention his wife."

"Mary, what did you *do*?"

"I invited some friends."

Jakon's laugh came back across the transmitter. "A few smugglers from Ballern may show up, but I don't know what they can do against that cult's fleet. Though they're quite skilled at evading Ballern's destroyers. So that is something. But few have been tested against these numbers."

"They can do the same thing any of us can do, Jakon. We can buy time." But how much time did Jacob and Alice need to turn the battle inward? Draw the forces back inside the Great Machine? And if they did, and the sabotage failed, what then? They'd never make it out, and

Mordair might never pay for his atrocities.

Mary's knuckles whitened as she squeezed the levers on the console.

✧　✧　✧

FURI WATCHED THE Skysworn rise above them, drift farther out to sea, and come down on their starboard side. She didn't entirely understand why they'd switched positions with The Ray, but she trusted Jakon. A short time later, Furi focused her attention back on the map at her side.

Each fleet was marked out by magnets, both their allies and their targets. A handful of squares designated their allies on the ground, but most of the map was reserved for the airships, because *that* was their focus. More importantly, *that* was far more likely to kill them.

She served on enough missions with Ballern that she still expected signal flags to start the battle. There was a drill for battles they'd practiced dozens of times in Fleet that sat in the back of her mind like a kind of muscle memory. But individual missions were nothing like large-scale engagements. This wasn't a single line of warships. There were strikers above and below them, a Porcupine to the south, and one of Bollwerk's floating cities to the north.

Beyond that waited two of Ballern's destroyers, ships that held people Furi knew, had called friends, and who had now been dragged into Mordair's web by some foolish nobles and the Children of the Dark Fire. There was no signal flag here that started the engagement. No broadcast over the transmitters that told the cannoneers and artillery to open fire.

It was a single cannon shot fired from a Fel destroyer. Flames and smoke arced through the air, and no one spoke. There was a brief flash of sound across the transmitters, a call to evade, but it was lost to a hiss of static as one of the leading brigs took a hit to the bridge.

The airship crumpled in half, its gas chambers slamming together as the steel folded. One chamber failed, and the ship made a fiery descent into the water below.

That was as much of a signal as they got. Jakon forced the throttle forward, and The Ray soared into the cloud bank, the Skysworn flanking it.

Furi heard the battle unfold before she saw it. From one moment to the next, there was quiet, a great inhalation of everyone in the skies, and then there was only chaos. They punched through the far side of the cloud bank, nearly to the front lines of Fel's destroyers. Cannon fire and ballistae bolts roared through the air below them, leaving trails of smoke and violent plumes of flame and steam as they crashed into their targets and the sea below.

"Rin, Tatsu, get ready. Furi, keep an eye out for a command vessel."

Rin's voice came across the horn. "Cannons fully loaded. Ready to deploy."

"Remember to use the sights. Two marks up for every quarter mile. It doesn't have to be perfect for the large ships, but if you fire at a striker, you're going to miss. Let Mary handle anything small."

"Understood," Tatsu said.

Mary's voice echoed over the transmitter. "I'm flattered, Jakon."

Jakon barked out a laugh. "I'm trusting Smith and those chainguns of his."

Furi shifted pieces across her map as they moved, barreling past the front line of Fel's destroyers and diving beneath Ballern's. Bolts pinged off The Ray's armored hull, and Jakon threw the levers to the right, nearly rolling The Ray as they swooped beneath the Skysworn.

"A little warning!" Rin shouted between curses.

The ships shifted again, and Furi followed. She'd spent years in Fleet's classrooms. They hadn't taught her much about things that really mattered, but they *did* teach her the strategies of every enemy fleet in the hemisphere.

Belldorn's commanders always remained at the back of the formation. In theory, it gave them more protection, but it also made them vulnerable to a precise strike. Fel tended to cluster their forces around the command ship, so no matter which angle of attack their enemy used, it wasn't an easy target. Bollwerk was likely the smartest. They encased their leaders in the warships, floating armories that could take enough damage to drop four of Ballern's destroyers before they were disabled.

But what would the Children of the Dark Fire do? And would Mordair listen to them?

She moved the pieces again as Belldorn's brigs engaged with the destroyers from above. Fel and Ballern's warships shifted, constantly keeping one bank of cannons aimed at the enemy lines. All but one destroyer. A single vessel that barely moved position at all.

Furi hit the transmitter. "Single destroyer. Currently above the north shore. Bow pointed eastward."

"Got it." Mary's voice didn't sound right. She sounded cold, almost detached, and the Skysworn arced up into the air. "Follow me in, Jakon."

The pirate chef didn't hesitate, swinging The Ray in behind the Skysworn, holding a little to the port side, giving the cannons clearance. The Skysworn's gun pod swiveled, and its chainguns took aim as a small squad of strikers left the vicinity of the destroyer.

"That's the command ship." Jakon's grip tightened on the controls. "Rin, Tatsu. Aim for the last smokestack near the stern."

"Should we not attack the bridge?" Tatsu asked.

"Trust me."

Fire rippled across the first striker as explosive bursts left the chainguns of the Skysworn. Even at speed, at that distance, Furi could hear the buzz of those awful guns. The striker's cockpit imploded, and the sheer speed and air resistance tore the ship apart, sending it to the sea in a cascade of flame.

The second came in higher, avoiding the gun pod entirely. Sparks lit across the armored gas chamber of the Skysworn before the striker burst into a ball of smoke and debris, tumbling end over end as Mary veered around the last of them.

A third ailing striker managed to launch a series of rounds into The Ray, but Jakon didn't slow down.

"Hold on. Deploying cannons. Fire when you have the target."

The Ray's sides unfurled, unrolling banks of cannons as the destroyer's stern came into focus. The thick gray metal of the armored smokestack looked impenetrable, and Furi wondered just *why* Jakon didn't have Rin and Tatsu aiming at the bridge instead.

"Fire!" Rin shouted over the horn.

The cannons traded off, Rin and Tatsu each unloading round after round as the heavy cylinders shifted in their positions, dragged along by a mechanism not so different from the Skysworn's chainguns. But the effect as those cannons struck the destroyer was far, far different.

The first shots dented the smokestacks, crashing through the deck as smaller cannons were leveled at The Ray. A sweep of the Skysworn's chainguns sent those soldiers scrambling before the second round from The Ray's cannons punched through the base of the smokestacks, and the entire tower started to fall.

"Again!" Jakon shouted.

Furi gripped the armrests of her seat as they grew far too close to the destroyer, but Rin and Tatsu unleashed two more rounds before Jakon veered away, leaving a smoking crater in the aft deck. The destroyer still limped through the air.

But the Skysworn circled above it. A handful of tiny black dots fell from the deck of the Skysworn, and then both The Ray and the Skysworn slammed their throttles forward, hurrying out to sea.

Furi didn't understand why until the destroyer detonated. It wasn't compromised. It was finished. Fireballs and shrapnel erupted in the center of Fel's formation, tearing through strikers and damaging every nearby ship.

"Yes!" Furi shouted, watching the debris fall as their allies closed the distance on the surviving ships. Before she could say anything more, a line of shadows appeared on the horizon. Sleek airships that were like nothing she'd seen before, each with an armored pontoon jutting out either side of the hull supporting long cannons.

The distance played tricks on her eyes, and she wasn't sure how large the ships actually were, but judging by the string of curses being muttered by Jakon, it wasn't good. He clicked the transmitter.

"New warships behind Fel's destroyers. All ships: new threat behind Fel's destroyers. Cannons sighted." He glanced at Furi. "That must be what Jacob and Alice saw. I don't—"

Jakon didn't finish the thought before the first of those menacing guns opened fire. A short salvo hit a Ballern destroyer broadside. Furi leaned forward, aghast at the scale of damage in that single attack. The destroyer wasn't out of commission, but the smoke and flame rising for its starboard side looked like it had been in battle for hours, not the result of a single exchange.

A broken transmission crackled through the cabin. "Break formation. Give them no easy targets."

Furi had been in enough air battles to recognize when something had changed. The momentum stalled or reversed as some new variable barreled into the fray. So often, those battles would be between two warships in the end. A series of flanking maneuvers as they tried to target one another. This was nothing like that. The call to break formation turned the skies into further chaos. It wasn't merely the strikers and brigs that tore through the clouds at varying heights and angles. It was *everything.*

And with so many in the air, choking the sky, it was only a matter of time before some of them collided. For all that, with no clear target in sight, the Children of the Dark Fire set the skies aflame. Ship after ship unloaded their cannons into that field, popping strikers and imploding brigs like Pilly eggs.

The skies turned gray with smoke as ruined airships crashed onto the docks, the city, and the sea.

Lady Katherine's voice came alive in the cabin. "All ships, fire all cannons."

For most vessels, an order like that would be tantamount to a "fire at will" order. For the Porcupine near the center of the formation, it was a command to bury their enemy. Cannon fire turned the Porcupine into a cloud of acrid smoke and superheated metal. Round after round punched through the sky, and Furi wanted to close her eyes when she saw those salvos tear through their own allies as fast as they brought down two Ballern destroyers. It cost them a brig, but the long fin of a Fel warship shattered, and the gas chamber ruptured, sending it careening down into the city outside the Great Machine.

The longer they fought, the more the battle drifted inland until there wasn't a northern and a southern front. There was only the battle and the death it rained down from horizon to horizon. But the terror in Furi's heart faded. The adrenaline receded until there was only a cold drive to stay alive.

She heard Rin and Tatsu across the horn, shouting about reloads in the moments when their own cannons weren't firing. She saw bodies fall from the ailing ships, some aflame, others with parachutes that caught fire and failed as they fell.

Jakon pushed The Ray to its limits when two cannon shots grazed the hull, punching up through a cloud bank and arcing back down to give Rin and Tatsu a line of sight to another of those strange vessels of the

Children of the Dark Fire.

Before they fired again, Furi saw it. Bollwerk's warship, following the Porcupine deep into the enemy line. It was a mistake. She knew it. "They're going to get killed, Jakon."

He hadn't responded before the cannons exploded on the port side of the Porcupine, spiraling off into the water, bringing back violent memories of the end of the Nightingale. But those memories paled beside what happened to that mighty warship.

A sphere of fire and smoke surged out from the middle of the Porcupine, sending shrapnel and flame in every direction around it, setting other destroyers on fire and crushing the infantry battling below. It was an awful vision as that invincible warship met its end.

"Jakon!" Mary shouted over the transmitter. "Brig on your tail. Deserters!"

Furi screamed as the flak cannon hit their flank and blew out two of the windows, the metal folding in like a claw trying to snatch their lives away. The second explosion sent fragments of the deck into the air as Jakon dove in an effort to evade their attacker, but it put them in the path of a striker.

Jakon cursed. "Sorry, kid."

Furi closed her eyes.

And the striker vanished in a ball of black smoke. Jakon pulled up, and Furi stared out the window.

A ship of bronze and polished timber swept out of the cloud bank above them. The Skysworn jerked to the opposite side, diving away from the newcomer to avoid a collision.

"Mary, who is that?" Jakon asked.

"I don't know!"

Furi couldn't tell what it was, never mind *who* it was. Even as she wondered, the transmitter crackled to life.

"Skysworn, Ray, this is Targrove. Sorry to drop on top of you like that. Thought I had our trajectory a little farther out."

Furi could just make out Theo in the background, and she didn't envy Targrove those fiery words.

"Is that your ship?" Jakon stared at the polished copper that swept up above the gas chambers like the iridescent wings of a Dragonwing, a beautiful shine above the armored panels. "What did you do to it?"

"Mine? No, of course not! Why would I want so much … it doesn't matter. Pull your ships back. We're going to put an end to those destroyers. Jakon, disengage your target."

For only a second, Furi thought he was talking to her. But another voice sounded in the background, someone older and gruffer and entirely unfamiliar.

As she watched, the Skysworn pulled back in an impressive maneuver, gracefully twisting to the side in an elegant display that likely had Smith screaming in his harness.

It wasn't until the tail of Targrove's ship passed the windscreen that Jakon sat up straight. "Mary, is that … No, that's not possible. They all died in the Deadlands War. Just like … just like Targrove."

Furi stared out the windscreen as a chill ran down her spine.

CHAPTER TWENTY-EIGHT

Aᴸɪᴄᴇ ꜱᴛᴀʀᴇᴅ ᴜᴘ at the skies as much as she watched their path forward. A nightmare unfolded above them. Pieces of ships and sailors occasionally crashed through the nearby canopy, smoldering in the underbrush and the woods above.

The Fall was still the worst thing she'd ever witnessed, but the battle raging nearby might surpass it. They were on the far fringes of the conflict. What about their friends who were in the middle of that?

They passed well wide of the guarded tunnel they'd encountered before, holding to the edge of the lake except for the stretches of shore that had been overtaken by the forest. There, they had to cut back into the shadows of the Gray Woods before the tree line receded again.

"At least the woods aren't as dense here," Jacob said.

Alice adjusted her cloak and looked around at the smaller trees and choking underbrush. "I think you and I have very different understandings of *dense*."

Jacob glanced back at her before frowning at their surroundings. "I guess the trees *are* closer together. There aren't as many Forest Giants here."

"The underbrush could stop a train, Jacob."

They broke through the far side of the woods after crossing two creeks. In the distance, nearer to the mountains, several Forest Giants loomed on the other side of the lake.

Alice grinned at Jacob, who only rolled his eyes and continued on.

The thunder of the battle above had grown more distant, and while they found evidence of three different campsites along the shore, no one else obstructed their path.

If she tried, Alice could almost imagine the thunder above them to be a storm rolling into the Lowlands. It was a rare thing to get thunder that shook the earth in the mountains, but she had fond memories of watching the Pillies as they tried to hide from the noise.

She didn't know if she'd ever have days like that again with her mom, but she liked to think Ancora might rebuild those farms and stables soon. None of it would matter if they failed now. The distant cannon fire and dying screams would roll across the Crystal Sea until they reached the walls of Ancora itself.

Alice shivered and gripped the reins of her Tree Killer tighter. She focused on the map tucked into the edge of her saddle. Though she knew there was nothing more to learn from it, the map provided a calming distraction. Alice could have easily redrawn their path from memory, and the large boulder splitting the smaller river ahead told her exactly where they were.

"This is it, Jacob."

He slowed his mount and let Alice take the lead, nodding as she folded the map and slid it into her saddlebag. Even if a guard saw it, she doubted it would cause them trouble. The Mokuskrit Furi had helped scrawl on the map said their destination was the city outside the Great Machine. It would be an easy thing to explain away why they were off course when the river was noted as their best path.

She reminded herself of that fact as the Tree Killer's stride swayed from side to side. They rounded a narrow copse of trees, and there wasn't much question where the entrance to the underground was. No gate waited in the ruined building, no guards to deter any trespassers.

"Did it get hit in the battle?" Jacob glanced up at the sky before shaking his head. "We're too far away for that."

Alice slid off the Tree Killer's saddle before tying the reins to a low branch. "It looks like it collapsed from age. I don't see anything fresh. Moss everywhere, nearly a foot of fallen leaves. It's abandoned."

Jacob hopped down and hurried forward, pulling the air cannon off his back as he went. He peered from one side to the other in the u-shaped recess that might have been a door or a bay but was little more than a pile of rubble now. As Alice followed him into the building, jumbled stones threatened to roll their ankles. Though without a ceiling or an entire four walls, it was hard to call it a building anymore.

"Back left corner." Alice doubted she needed to remind Jacob where the access hatch was supposed to be, but they needed to remain focused. If there were guards waiting in that place, they would have seen them by then.

Jacob circled a rusty, mangled beam of metal, heading toward the rear corner of the structure before he froze. Movement shuffled through the fallen leaves, and his shoulders visibly relaxed when half a dozen young Jumpers scurried away into the prairie beyond.

He screeched when a *much* larger Jumper pushed up through the floor of the building, trailing a thick cluster of webbing with more than one Water Beetle trapped inside. The spider stopped and stared at the pair of Ancorans for a moment before letting the hidden door of webs and wood fall closed and following its offspring into the distance.

Jacob cursed under his breath. "*That* hatch?"

Alice breathed deeply before nodding. She slid her gloved fingers under the nearest length of wood and lifted. It wasn't nearly as heavy as she'd expected, and she almost threw the rotting door into the wall behind the hatch.

The sound of rushing water grew louder, and Alice's concern grew deeper. "Do you hear that?"

Jacob nodded. "Yeah. I heard it earlier, but I thought it was the river. I don't think it is. What should we do, Alice? If we go down, there's no coming back. We're committed until we find another exit or backtrack to this one."

"It's our best option." She stared into the darkness waiting below. Memories of the trap door to the catacombs in Ancora circled her mind. "Let's set the Tree Killers free. We don't need them giving away our arrival."

Jacob started toward the front of the building and hesitated. "If our transmitters get too wet, they may not work."

"We have a compass and a map. We can find our way back, Jacob." Leaves crunched beneath her boots as she stood up straight, following him to the clearing with their mounts.

They stripped the saddles and bags as fast as they dared, tying them onto their glider packs and leaving the Tree Killers with no visible indication they weren't wild bugs. Alice reached out and tapped the long face of the Tree Killer between the eyes five times.

The bug chittered and hummed before turning and walking away, heading back to Karn. Jacob's mount did the same, and they were soon left alone with only the thunder of the distant battle to keep them company.

Alice shivered as a cool breeze came in off the lake. "Come on, let's hurry." She clipped a lantern to her vest and led the way back to the open hatch. A quick turn of the igniter put a flame to the wick, and the reflector cast a ring of illumination into the darkness below.

The floor wasn't too far down. She counted ten ladder rungs sunk into the wall. "It's about ten feet to the bottom."

Jacob clicked the transmitter in his collar. "Skysworn. We're in."

✧   ✧   ✧

Samuel breathed out a sigh of relief when the banter picked up on the transmitter. The kids were in. They'd survived the skirmish in the woods or, if they were lucky, avoided it altogether.

Drakkar stood and wiped his forehead, glancing at another bandaged soldier as the medics loaded her onto a cart to be evacuated. "So many injured." He looked back toward the edge of the woods, where Alana raised a scope to her eye. Even without an aid for his sight, Samuel could see the burning ruins of several airships and countless bodies on the ground.

"So many dead." Samuel rubbed his hands together. "But they made it in, Drakkar."

"Let us hope we are able to do the same. The cost here is already too high, my friend. If we must push through the entire line of these warships, I fear the toll to be taken."

Samuel looked away from the Cave Guardian. He didn't want Drakkar to know he'd had the same thoughts in the back of his mind. They needed to focus on the moment, on their immediate battle, or they'd be among those dead in the field.

This wasn't a conflict to retreat from. This was a conflict that would echo down through the years, through the decades. Teachers like Miss Penny would be talking about this moment, Samuel knew. Just like they'd spoken of the Deadlands War when he'd been in those classrooms.

But as to what story would be told? That remained to be seen.

The shadows of the Dark Fire warships drifted nearby, and Samuel's stomach turned at the vision of the ruined Porcupine. It should have been indestructible. It had been anything but in the face of their enemy.

Alana hurried back to them. "The ground forces are returning to the city. I think they might be headed to shelter in the Great Machine itself, judging by the flow of the roads."

Samuel cursed. "That means more people could be in the way for

Jacob and Alice." He gritted his teeth and clicked his transmitter. "Mary, ground forces are retreating toward the Great Machine. We need to cut them off, or get our own troops in the front door. You know why."

"Not the best time, Samuel!" A boom of static crackled across the transmitter, echoed by a heavy cannon shot above them. Silence followed, and then one angry captain continued. "I'll get a message to Kat. Bombers incoming. Take shelter!"

"Bombers?" Samuel asked. "No …" He rushed to the outskirts of the forest, dodging soldiers and medics, both resting and hurrying to care for their wounded. He took a quick look at the sky, but nothing outside of the immediate battle caught his attention.

Again, his gaze swept the battle, looking beyond it this time, trying to focus on what Mary might have—

"Oh, gods."

Two wide shadows flickered through a break in the highest clouds. A series of brigs broke off from the battle and soared skyward to meet them, but Samuel knew how large those Fel bombers were. He'd seen them on drills when he'd taken a squad of Spider Knights into the hills around Dauschen to train.

The gas chambers were flanked by bomb bays stretching away from the hull like the wings of a glider. But those wings had no functional purpose outside of delivering a payload of utter destruction.

"Get everyone out of here!" Samuel screamed. "Bombers incoming!"

Some of the soldiers stared at him blankly, as if they had no idea what a bomber was or why they should be worried about it in that moment. But they had minutes, maybe less, before those airships would turn the battlefield to ash.

"They can level a city. Run!"

Alana stood beside him. "Move! Everyone, get deeper into the woods. Head west or south. Get out of their path!"

Samuel and Drakkar both sprinted to the medics, helping them strap down more patients so the Walkers could evacuate them. It wasn't much, and Samuel felt nauseous for whatever survivors might still be left in the field between them and the city, but there wasn't anything else to be done.

"Go!" Drakkar shouted. He grabbed Samuel's arm and spun him around. They sprinted to their mounts, untying the reins before hopping back into their saddles.

Bessie chittered at Samuel but didn't protest when he prodded her forward. They made it to the nearest road before cutting west, Drakkar following close on his bandaged Stalker when the first of the bombs shook the earth.

A quick glance showed him billowing clouds of fire and pitch-black smoke as the airships warred in the sky, and the forest started to burn behind them. The explosions grew closer as Samuel and his allies crashed through the underbrush and low branches strewn across the path.

By the third round of bombs, Samuel already knew they were losing soldiers. Fireballs tore through the forest around them, so close the heat felt like that from a freshly opened oven. The airships might have been slow compared to the Skysworn, but they couldn't outrun them on the ground.

Samuel braced himself as the seconds ticked past, knowing the next round of bombs would likely be the last thing any of them ever heard.

The first explosion came, followed by a series of relentless booms. But there was no heat. No fire to sear the flesh from their bones. It was a cold, thunderous thing that offered nothing but confusion until the light of the sun dimmed, and he saw the inferno above them.

Fire and darkness blotted out the sun as the first bomber was simply erased from the sky by its own payload. A detachment of brigs skimmed the surface of the Gray Woods before pulling up and angling for the next ship.

Bodies fell from that chaos, only to soar away on the wings of gliders, escaping the carnage that had devoured the bomber. The pieces slowly clicked together in Samuel's mind. Those weren't survivors leaping from the bombers. They were something else entirely.

"Skyriders!"

Samuel laughed as they vanished behind a cloud of debris. Bessie could have run faster, could have soared between the branches of the Forest Giants and left most of his allies to catch up. But he couldn't do that. He kept pace with Drakkar's Stalker, though he knew that lumbering beast would need to slow soon.

They could reach the lake and stop there. From what he remembered of the maps, it wasn't far and would be a good place to set up a new blockade in case more of the Children of the Dark Fire marched against them.

It would have to be enough for now, and he could only hope the others were still alive. He clicked his transmitter, unable to keep the disbelief from his voice. "Skysworn! Were those Skyriders? I saw the gliders!"

Mary's sharp response snapped back over the transmitter. "I'm going to kill Eva if she's not already dead."

Samuel grinned and leaned forward in Bessie's saddle. The battle was far from over, but Eva and her Skyriders had struck a devastating blow.

CHAPTER TWENTY-NINE

THE MESSAGE TO Samuel was likely the last message they'd send over the transmitter. At least until they either made it inside the Great Machine, or … best not to think about that. Jacob shook his head and followed Alice down the ladder. Rushing water echoed around them, and part of the dread in the back of his mind was replaced by curiosity.

Once their boots thudded onto the tile floor, he realized just how loud that water was. The only thing he'd heard like it before was the waterfalls beneath Ancora. And most of those, he'd been trying not to drown as he was ravaged by the currents.

Alice started to untie the Tree Killer's heavy saddle from her pack.

"Wait." Jacob held a hand out to her shoulder. "Do you have anything left in them?"

She shook her head.

"Look in the corner. Old foot lockers. We can hide them in there in case anyone comes through here."

Alice looked at the walls and ceiling before focusing on the lockers. "The only thing that's been through here in the last decade is bugs, Jacob. This place is a tomb."

She didn't argue about hiding the saddles, though. Instead, she kicked the lid of a foot locker open with her toe, the latch breaking off on a section of brittle metal. Nothing waited within but flakes of rust and a void. Alice dumped her saddle inside and gestured for Jacob's.

He dropped his in on top of it, and once the lid was closed, there were few signs of it having been disturbed. The only obvious indication that people had been there were footprints in the dirt, but even those were masked by the scrapes and drags and steps of the spiders who called the place home.

Jacob headed down a short hall that should give them access to the smaller maintenance tunnels. The water grew louder as Alice walked beside him.

"Two lefts and then …" Her voice trailed off.

There wasn't another left to be had. Another left would send them plunging some fifty feet into an abyss that held the roaring rapids they'd been hearing. Jacob tilted his lantern to get a better view, finding collapsed structural beams wedged between the walls twenty feet below them.

"I thought we'd get farther," he muttered as he turned his back on Alice. "Can you get the grappling cannon? We're going to need it if we want to get any deeper."

Alice sighed and tugged on the clasps before extracting the cannon. "Do you see how brittle that stone looks?"

Jacob grimaced. "I do. We'll have to see if it holds."

"You always did know how to reassure me."

He grinned at her as he primed the grappling cannon's firing mechanism. Jacob inched his way forward, testing the floor with every foot of progress before taking aim at an outcropping across the chasm. The trick with the grappling cannon was having to aim both sides at once.

"I should rebuild this so you can fire one side at a time."

"Not the best situation to be thinking about a redesign. How about we just focus on not firing at *me* for now?"

Jacob let out a quiet laugh. It was the first thing he'd done, making sure Alice was out of the target area. He braced himself with a wide stance, mounting the cannon on his shoulder before lining the target up in the scope. It wasn't really a scope, but that was the easiest name to remember. He thought Charles would likely have called the sights a reticle, but who wanted to explain a word like that every time they told someone to aim?

He pulled the trigger, and the cannon released a loud pop, not unlike a muffled bolt cannon. It wasn't as quiet as the one Charles had built, but so long as they were near the crashing chaos of the underground river, Jacob wasn't concerned about *any* noise they might be making.

The reverse side of the cable thudded into the wall well before the forward, the pulleys only tightening once the forward momentum ceased. The impact on each anchor should have deployed them, but they'd know soon enough.

Jacob relaxed and slid the grappling cannon back and forth, letting out a long exhale as the pulleys moved freely along the coil. It was a risk, using one huge cable across a complex system like that, but it made for a very compact gadget.

"Solid?" Alice asked.

Jacob leaned over and put all his weight on the line, nodding when nothing shifted or broke loose from the walls. "I'll go first. You remember the—"

"Lever forward goes forward. Lever back returns the line. Lever center and down releases the anchor, and we go swimming."

Jacob grinned at Alice. "Exactly." With that, he took a deep breath, stepped to the precipice, and let himself slide out over what amounted to an indoor gorge. Switching the lever forward, all the bound-up energy of one spring released, propelling him at a faster pace than he'd expected, but not so fast he risked hitting the far wall.

He muttered a curse when he realized he was hanging a good four feet above the floor. Still suspended, Jacob threw the lever back the other way before letting go. He dropped to the floor with enough force to make him cringe, worrying more of the rock might break away, but it held fast.

Alice caught the cannon at the other end of the line, sliding her arm into the wrist strap before pushing the lever forward. She zipped out over the darkness without hesitation, slowing to a stop just above him. "You might want to aim a little lower next time."

Before he could respond, she pulled the lever and dropped with the line, the near anchor snapping back into the cannon's housing as the far anchor whined and raced toward them. It whipped side to side as it grew close, but the tapered funnel did its work, keeping Alice's hands from getting hit.

She handed the assembly to him and took a deep breath. "Nice work."

"Thanks." He smiled and clipped the cannon into a wide loop on his belt. That done, he turned his attention to what waited behind them. It wasn't all stone and water there, though there was certainly both of those things. Instead, there was a ruined hallway and a floor he hoped would be solid enough to hold their weight.

The rushing river below might have masked most of the sound they were making, but that wasn't all it would mask.

"I don't like not being able to hear more." Jacob angled the lantern on his vest down a long hall that ended in a jumble of stone. "At least there aren't Widow Makers here."

Alice swatted his arm. "Not now, there aren't, but are you sure none of them nest here?" She pointed at the exposed ceiling above them.

Jacob flinched when the pale webs fluttering in the breeze caught the lantern light. Whatever had made them wasn't nearly so large as the spiders that lived beneath Ancora, but that didn't much matter if there were enough of them. He would have felt better if the remnants were as dusty as those in the walls of Fel, but that wasn't the case here.

"Let's keep going." He turned away and focused on the path ahead.

"We're probably in more danger of the floor collapsing into the river than any bugs in this place."

"Seriously, though, have I ever told you you're the *worst* at reassuring people?"

Jacob glanced back at Alice and didn't quite hide his smile when he found her scowling at him. "I think Samuel's a little worse at it than I am."

"He certainly complains about it more, but neither of you is exactly skilled at it."

"Good thing I don't want to be in Parliament."

Alice scoffed at that. "Oh, no, I think you'd do great. Casually mentioning how a problem could collapse an entire district if no one did anything would probably do wonders for the budget."

Jacob almost groaned as he turned the corner. Just the idea of going back to Ancora and sitting in meeting after meeting about city planning and the reconstruction of the Lowlands sounded like torture. Although, it would be nice if he had some input on the layout of the streets around Charles's old lab.

Something cracked beneath them, and Alice's hand shot out, pulling Jacob back a step. She held a finger to her lips and pointed to the broken floor that had long ago fallen into the river.

The lantern light caught on a shiny curve before it faded. Jacob moved the beam from side to side, trying to find it again, but whatever it was had moved. He started to turn away when the subtle glow caught his eye. Something, or some*one* else was there.

He inched forward, both out of an abundance of caution on the crumbling floor and for whatever measure of stealth they might have with lanterns in that place. He leaned closer to the edge as he unlatched the safety on his bolt thrower.

There was no sign of the shiny thing he'd seen earlier, only a narrow chasm that fell into darkness. But that darkness was spotted with the pale green luminescence of a thousand glowworms. He blew out a long breath and stepped back to Alice.

"Glowworms."

"I saw something else there. Did you? It was shiny, like metal, or reflective chitin."

Jacob nodded. "I saw it too, but whatever it was, it's gone now. We'll keep a watch for it, but we need to keep going. It's nearly half a mile to the next tunnel."

"And that's assuming it hasn't collapsed."

Jacob knew Alice was right. Seeing how much of the underground had crumbled, there was a real chance their planned path would be blocked or nonexistent. That was something they couldn't focus on yet. Some obstacles had to be tackled once they faced them. Depending on what had changed, the way forward might be very different indeed.

✧   ✧   ✧

THE WALL HAD provided an illusion, a sense that while the crevasse that dropped to the river was nearby, the wall itself was solid. So, when Jacob leaned on it as he reconfigured his glider pack, the ominous creaking sound caught them off guard.

"What the hell is that?" Jacob muttered, strapping the top of his pack closed before swinging it up onto his shoulders again.

Alice frowned and placed her hand on the wall. She hesitated for only a second. "Run!"

Jacob had learned a long time ago that when Alice screamed "Run" like that, the only thing to do was *run*. He could find out the reasons why later. Without even knowing why, his heart pounded as hard as his feet hit the cracked stone floor.

A horrible crash sounded behind them, but where the hall curved to the left ahead, there was no more path to walk. The only way through was over, and a glance backward showed him exactly what Alice had seen. The wall collapsed against stone, sending up a plume of dust and debris that chased them through the dark like a shadow.

"Jump!" Jacob shouted, flinging himself forward at nearly a full sprint. His boots caught on the edge of the cliff and slammed him onto the ground, stealing his breath. It didn't stop him from scrabbling to the edge as Alice followed him, the cloud of debris nearly engulfing her as she leaped from the opposite side of the cliff.

The floor beneath him cracked. He waited until Alice landed and grabbed her, throwing them both backward as the crack in the ancient tile grew wider, shearing off before thundering into the abyss below them.

Alice flicked the igniter on her lantern, the light lost in the chaos of the jump. She grabbed his arm as soon as they had enough light again, scattered as it was by the choking dust and dirt in the air. It would have to do. They had to move forward. Any part of the building could be as unstable as what they'd just gone through, ready to cast them down into a chasm they'd never survive.

The next room wasn't a room at all. The doorway opened onto an underground lake. Bulletin boards and ruined posters—fragments of the past—clung to the wall near the ceiling as if mocking their attempt to cross through the old, abandoned tunnels.

"I think I know why they don't guard these tunnels." Alice rubbed her hands together and flexed her fingers.

"Are you okay?"

She nodded. "Hit my fingers on the stone when I jumped. Thanks for pulling me in. I didn't realize the ground was cracking. Kind of distracted by the wall collapsing."

"Yeah, me too. It's …" Jacob rubbed his fingers through his hair and frowned at the small cascade of dust. The only good thing was the debris from the collapse wasn't as thick now. Dust lingered in the air, but not enough to block their view entirely.

"We need to get to the second floor." Jacob unhooked the grappling cannon and adjusted the scope. With any luck, they wouldn't be so far off the floor on the next jump. Considering how quickly the floor had fallen out from underneath them, he definitely wanted to minimize every drop.

A glance back showed Alice standing well to the side, nowhere near any part of the wall he planned to use for an anchor point. He nodded to himself, took aim, and pulled the trigger. The grappling cannon kicked on his shoulder, a small clang echoing out around them before the anchors thudded into the stone on either side.

He locked them in place and put his weight on the line again. "Ready?"

Alice went first, taking the grappling cannon out of his hands before hooking her arm through the wrist strap. One throw of the lever and she was off, a little bounce in the line as the pulleys whirred inside the housing. Her lantern rocked as she slowed, hanging close to the ground before she let go.

A small puff of dust and debris billowed up around her as she pushed the lever back, and the grappling cannon sped to Jacob. He did the same thing she had, with a little less concern in testing the lines now that Alice had made it over.

The dust cleared significantly as he rose to Alice's level, and he cursed when he realized just how low he'd anchored the line. A quick raise of his feet cleared the metal grate that formed the walkway, and he blew out a sigh of relief when the grappling cannon stopped.

"It feels solid." Alice tapped her foot on the grate beneath her boots.

Jacob threw the lever to retract the anchors and held his arm out to avoid any backlash. That done, he turned and followed Alice into the hall on the second floor.

What struck him first was the condition of this new area. It wasn't filled with nearly so much rust or cobwebs, as though it had been abandoned by everything that lived in the cave, not only the Children of the Dark Fire. Decay hadn't set into every corner, and the walkway didn't feel like it might crumble at any moment.

The tunnel took them straight ahead, with few paths branching off the entire time they walked forward. There were no winding turns or collapses to stop them at that point, but it still left the question of how they'd get back out once they'd sabotaged the Great Machine.

"Jacob."

He turned at Alice's whisper. "What is it?"

"Look at the supports." She pointed to a long metal rod sunk into the ceiling above.

Jacob didn't think much of it at first, but he narrowed his eyes when he saw the recess drilled into the stone. The support wasn't mounted to the ceiling at all, but something deeper, closer to the surface.

She stepped close to him. "They're like the Great Machine in the desert. I think we're getting close."

The idea sent a surge of adrenaline through him, and his fingertips tingled as he adjusted his lantern, trying to see just how deep in the stone the anchor might be. While he couldn't tell from their current position, he had little doubt they'd know more soon.

They continued on, leaving all semblance of walls and structure behind as the tunnel narrowed, giving the illusion that their lanterns had grown brighter. The path remained straight, most likely carved by some burrowing machine, like the miners sometimes used in Ancora.

The deeper they walked, the quieter the water grew, from a roar to a distant waterfall, and finally to something no louder than a faucet in the Highlands of Ancora. The quiet might have been reassuring in the dark, a sign they were truly alone in that place, but now they could hear their own footsteps. And Jacob knew if that was the case for them, any guards stationed nearby might have the same advantage.

He hadn't had a chance to speak that idea out loud when the lanterns reflected back at them, the relatively smooth stone of the corridor interrupted by a wide metal plate.

"Blocked." The word felt heavy on Jacob's tongue. This was their path forward. They'd followed the map, and it had been right every step of the way.

Alice hurried toward the barrier, and Jacob followed, not sure why she was so quick to run to the blockade. "Not a solid plate, Jacob. It's a door. An old hatch." She reached her fingers inside one of the riveted bands of metal, revealing a handle, but it only clicked when she squeezed it. The springs within released a squeak of protest. "Locked."

Jacob reached into a pocket on his vest, pulling out a small pouch of tools he hadn't used in some time. "Let me see."

Alice scooted to the side to give him access, holding her lantern at an angle so he could see the lock itself.

"It's an older one. Charles used to have a few like this around the workshop. He used them for parts, but I used them for practice." Jacob inserted the first hooked bar into the keyhole, applying gentle pressure with his thumb before following it with a pick crowned by a twisted wave on the end. It was a simple thing once he'd had enough practice. He could feel the tumblers as he worked back to front and then started again, inching the cylinder around.

"Jacob," Alice hissed.

"Almost got it."

"Water Beetles."

He frowned and glanced over his shoulder, slowly registering the new sound reaching them. Not the distant rush of water, but the scampering of a hundred chitinous feet. Black carapaces bounced their meager light around the tunnel as the walls appeared to pulse toward them.

Jacob cursed and focused on the lock. This wasn't a time for finesse and care. He pulled a third iron out of his picks and rammed it home, forcing the flexible filaments up and into the tumblers alongside the second pick. The lock squealed as the scurrying steps of the Water Beetles grew closer.

"Go!" Jacob rammed his shoulder into the door before sliding a hand into his pocket. He clicked the igniter on a Burner and let it drop to the floor. The heavy door was slow at first, and Jacob worried they'd never get it closed in time, even as they hurried through. The Burner burst to life, and the sudden gouts of flame caused the beetles to scatter around it, higher onto the walls.

The first of them reached the door as he leaned into it with all his might, the momentum and weight snapping two legs off as the beetle recoiled back into the tunnel. Jacob locked the door and blew out a breath, turning to find Alice with her bolt thrower armed and air cannon in hand.

She slowly relaxed, engaging the safety on both before stowing them away. "We got lucky, Jacob. No one said *anything* about those climbing the walls."

Jacob looked over his shoulder, trying to see if there was anything waiting in the shadows behind them. While he didn't see any movement, something else made him freeze in place. His arm snapped out and grabbed Alice's.

"Look at the far wall. Do you see it?"

"I can't see anything in this dark, Jacob. Not outside the lanterns. I don't know what …" Her voice trailed off, falling to a whisper. "Light."

Jacob gave one sharp nod. "This is it, Alice. This is the old maintenance hall listed on the map from the control center."

She slowly turned to look at him. "But it's still here. That map was so old. I can't believe they haven't done anything with this room since—" Alice stiffened and jumped back, taking a defensive posture.

Jacob swung hard with his elbow, having no idea what or who was behind him, and he almost screamed when he caught sight of glistening fangs in the dark. Memories of the Widow Makers in Ancora surged through his mind, but these spiders were nothing like those.

These were long-dead, hollow husks that had been sealed away in the old maintenance hall like a tomb. Littering the dusty floor beneath them were skeletons of people, most of their clothing having rotted away over the decades, even centuries, since the place had been abandoned.

"They aren't wearing cloaks." Alice stepped closer and angled her lantern at the bodies. "These are the people who came before, Jacob. Who ran the Great Machines before the Children of the Dark Fire drove them out?"

"They didn't drive them very far."

Jacob frowned at the dead spiders. "Do they look small to you?" He crouched and held his hand out. "They're a lot smaller, Alice. Half Bessie's size?"

She bent down, picked up an old locket, and pried it open. A long-faded photo sat inside, peeling at the edges, with a smiling child and mother, their clothes strange to Jacob's eye. Not leather, but knit so finely he couldn't see the stitching at that scale.

Alice closed it and put it back in the skeleton's hand. "They're from a different time altogether, Jacob. Early in the rise of the invaders. Maybe before they'd even crossed the Crystal Sea."

"Let's go, Alice. Let them rest."

Her gaze lingered on the skeletons before she nodded. They both shifted their steps, walking on the balls of their feet first like they did when sneaking around Ancora. Alice led the way toward the light of the far wall. Two things were clear when they reached it. First, the maintenance hall had been connected to the Great Machine, as detailed on the map.

The second, perhaps more disturbing fact was they could clearly see people in the distance through those rusted doors. Jacob crouched and reached for the lock. It had some age to it but less rust than the previous one he'd had to pick. This he could make quick work of. He almost laughed when he turned the lock in his hand.

"It has exposed screws. Hold on." It was faster to undo the screws than pick it, and soon Jacob had the backplate off and the guts of the mechanism torn out. The lock fell open in short order.

Alice muttered their next steps under her breath. They didn't discuss it. They already knew where they needed to go, and there wasn't much choice in the matter. "First hall, right, down to the staircase, north to the first boilers."

"Then it gets interesting."

"And pull out your pendant." She scowled at him as he pulled the door inward. A second lock on the opposite side resisted for a moment before the wooden brace it had been mounted on gave way. Aged wood pattered across their feet.

Jacob cringed at the sound, but as they slipped through the narrow opening, no one noticed them. In fact, the entire hallway was in deep shadow, the floor showing small drifts of dust that clearly hadn't been disturbed in quite some time.

That didn't change the fact that cloaked figures roamed the other end of the hall. And that was exactly where they needed to go. He pulled his pendant out and let it settle on his chest.

Alice flipped open the map case and leaned into Jacob. "If we read the layout correctly, we should be above the turbines here. I think that's what those huge cylinders were in the Deadlands, Jacob."

He stood a little straighter. "Not the turbines themselves, but the mounts and anchors above ground. I think you're right."

Alice tucked the map into her belt and pulled the hood of her cloak over her head. Jacob did the same, as many of the figures ahead of them wore their hoods in much the same fashion. Every step forward, Jacob braced for a shout, a sign they'd been detected or discovered, but the few glances he stole from underneath the hood showed him a very different scene.

The distant hiss and puff of boilers and valves sent jets of steam into the air, and the closer they got, the more humidity thickened the air around them. How the metal had survived that environment for centuries was beyond Jacob. He didn't understand how it could endure when even something as thick and rugged as a boiler would eventually fail.

Not a single person of the dozen they'd seen glanced down the hall at them. They were either so used to it being abandoned that they took no notice of the shadows moving through it, or the darkness was enough to shield them from prying eyes. Whatever the case, Jacob released a long sigh of relief when they turned the corner and started down the first hallway.

"Are you seeing this?" Alice gestured to the polished walls and clean floors that were a total reversal from the abandoned hall they'd entered through. "It's like we walked into the past, Jacob. This has to be what the Great Machine looked like in the Deadlands before it fell to ruin."

He had little doubt Alice was right. Everything they saw now—from the grooves in the wall and panels lining almost every inch of the corridor to the lengths of copper and bronze ducts and pipes they now glimpsed as they passed bulky windows and strange rectangular openings—was a window into the past.

"What are those for?" Alice asked, pointing at one of those same openings.

"I think it might be for ventilation. If the system broke down in a room, they could still cool the air, or potentially shut it off to choke a fire. It may be part of multiple systems. Remember the overlays we saw etched into those walls?"

Alice nodded and turned her attention back to the path ahead. "I haven't seen anyone through the windows on the right, have you?"

"No." He focused on the left, however, and the room opened into two floors, bustling with far more people than he'd expected. "If there are this many people here while there's a battle in their city, how many people are *normally* here?"

Alice didn't answer. She didn't need to. Because Jacob's question had a follow-up. One that gnawed at the back of his mind. How soon would those people return?

They reached the staircase soon after, and while Jacob's curiosity wanted to know what was above them, the logical side of his brain won out. The logical side being Alice, of course.

"Come on." She tugged on his sleeve and led the way down the latticework that formed the stairs. They weren't a smooth spiral like many he'd seen in Ancora, and Fel, but instead, each turn stopped at a wide landing before continuing down.

Descending a single level in that part of the Great Machine was a far different thing than a single level in an Ancoran home. It was different even than the higher levels of the machine itself, as here the stairs continued, thirteen steps, a landing, and thirteen more steps, for what felt like ages.

By the time they reached the next door and looked up, the towering stairwell gave the impression of a tall obelisk more than a simple set of stairs. The gleaming décor of the higher level was lost in this new place, and Jacob only hoped they wouldn't find another abandoned room behind that door. There were no windows here, no certainty of what waited beyond.

Alice put her hand on the door and slowly turned to Jacob. "It looks just like the ruins in the desert. The door, I mean. Look at the handles, even. Whoever designed this was consistent."

Jacob gave a slow nod. "Can't argue that."

Whatever fear of another abandoned, potentially bug-overrun room he had, the door whispered open. Long bars of light slowly flickered to life, reminding him of the city lights in Ancora, but somehow different, colder. The rhythmic thumping of something large and metal echoed in the background, but nothing in the room was responsible for it.

Banks of consoles sat to either side, the small black glass boxes set into them just as dark and lifeless as those in the Deadlands. Or at least, the first few were.

Alice froze as they passed the fourth bank, leaning over to study a pale green display embedded in the machine. "What is this?"

Jacob frowned at the series of lines that scrolled past, as though someone were writing them from inside the console itself. As though the lights from distant fireworks marched past in impeccable order.

"I think these are the monitors the manuals talked about, Alice. But how are they still working?"

She pointed at the silent banks on the far side of the room. "It doesn't look like a lot of them are."

"You're right." A dozen possibilities raced through his mind at once. Had those machines truly lasted through the decades? Did the Children of the Dark Fire have a better understanding of that ancient technology than anyone else? So much that they could repair it and maintain it centuries on?

He clenched his fists. As much as he wanted to know. As much as he *needed* to know, it was more important to put an end to Mordair's ambitions. To stop the creeping rise of a cult that devoured everything in its path.

"We have to stop them."

Alice reached out and grabbed his arm, pulling him toward the far wall. "We will, Jacob. That's why we're here."

"What if they know more about what really happened, Alice?" His words came out in a rush. "We could bury it all with the Great Machine. We might never really know."

"Maybe it's better that way. Maybe some things *should* be forgotten, Jacob. We know enough. We know they poisoned the world and tried to fix it. I doubt they could have known what they'd unleash. Does anyone need to know exactly how they did it?"

Jacob had a sudden memory of Charles in the Skeleton as he tore the pages out of those old books and burned them. Pages that detailed how to build ancient bombs that could deliver destruction on an unimaginable scale.

He followed when Alice pulled on his sleeve again, and they hurried to the opposite side of the room, passing more of the lit displays and scrolling lines they'd need the manuals to translate. But they didn't need to know how to operate the Great Machine. They only needed to know what parts of it to destroy, and that was information they already had. Information that haunted every tinker's nightmares.

Noise assaulted them as they pushed into the next room, the roar of enormous pistons and furnaces filling a hall that dwarfed any structure Jacob had seen, perhaps outside of the carriers or Bollwerk's warships. Great belts of powder and brick slowly worked their way across the room. Fuel, Jacob realized as he traced the path from boiler to boiler.

For a moment, he wondered how they could possibly feed each boiler equally, until he saw the gates along the conveyor. A small pocket would fill before triggering a door, leaving the rest of the fuel to continue on. A simple contraption it might have been, but those were often the most reliable when they needed to function for months or years.

Shadows moved on the far side of the room, revealing more workers in the area, and Jacob pulled Alice to the right, hurrying to stand behind a towering boiler that gave off enough heat to burn anything that got too close, much less touched it. He gestured to the map on her belt, and she pulled it out, opening the folded paper.

He tapped on a small square in the corner of the room. It wasn't where they'd originally planned to go, but it was opposite where he'd seen the Children of the Dark Fire. They might be able to pass as one of them, but they might not, and that was a risk he wasn't willing to take so deep into enemy territory. A skirmish could trigger an alarm, and that would be the end of them. Not just them. It could be the end of the war altogether.

Jacob took a deep breath and followed Alice. She had a sharper eye in the most stressful situations, and he didn't want to leave the smallest advantage unexplored. Even at a slow jog, he still cringed at every boot fall, no matter how unlikely it was to be overheard in that place. Their pace increased as they lost sight of the other Children of the Dark Fire behind the fourth furnace.

The corner of the room hadn't looked so far away on the map, or when he'd judged the distance with his own eyes. He'd been wrong. When they reached the wall, blessedly guarded by shadows and nothing more, they were both taking deep breaths.

It wasn't another staircase as he'd hoped, but a small access panel. A simple spring bolt held it closed, and Jacob made quick work of the locking mechanism with his picks. That done, the springbolt popped up, and Alice lifted the hatch.

A narrow ladder greeted them. Jacob didn't look much deeper than that as a pair of cloaks appeared at the far end of the corridor. Alice scurried through the hatch, taking the steps of the ladder two at a time before Jacob slipped in behind her. The cold metal bit into his fingers as he leveraged the hatch closed, an absolute contrast to the heat of the furnaces and boilers. They couldn't do anything to hide the open springbolt, but with any luck, it wouldn't be discovered for some time. Or ever.

Jacob wasn't sure what would be waiting for them beneath the heavy machinery of the previous level, but he had certainly expected more than what was there.

"It's just like the Deadlands." Alice made a sweeping gesture to the cavernous expanse before them. Several levels below, the deep earth teemed with life. Fireworms and glowworms formed separate colonies, the only reference for their size the titanic forms of their queens.

Even though Jacob knew how large those creatures were, they could have been the flame of a tiny candle at that distance. Where there had been Cutters choking the ground in the desert, here it was the worms and the sudden flashes of black chitin that rose and fell in the winding stream.

"It's an entire ecosystem *inside* the Great Machine." Alice leaned forward on the railing, her gaze roaming from the distant walls back to the lush foliage below them.

"More than one." Jacob pointed past the rocky terrain laden with worms. It ended in short bushes and trees that appeared no larger than a child's toys. They certainly weren't the towering giants that populated the Gray Woods, but he suspected they were much larger than they appeared.

He glanced up, and a slow smile crawled across his face. "Alice, look." He pointed to the metal lattice of the walkways above them. Some were high enough to be obscured by shadow, but those closest to them could be seen in the dimmer light of the underground.

"Those pipes are enormous." Alice stepped closer to him and raised a scope to her eye. "They're definitely connected. It looks like they get smaller and branch out in a dozen directions."

"I think they're one of the main junctions for the steam coming off the boilers." He took the scope from Alice when she offered it, studying a tangle of metal until a series of valves caught his eye. "I'm sure of it. That's our target." Jacob swept the scope to his right, following the largest pipe until it met with another junction. There, he could see the large wheels that controlled whatever valves had been installed on the platform. That wasn't why he frowned.

"What's wrong?"

Jacob lowered the scope and handed it to Alice. "I don't see a walkway connecting the two platforms. I don't see any walkway at all leading to the second platform. We may have to go up a level again because it's too far for the grappling cannon."

"Wait …" Alice leaned forward with the scope up to her eye once more, twisting the lens to adjust the focus. "Jacob, there are farms down there."

"With the bugs? That hardly seems safe."

"No, farther out. The river isn't just irrigation for the bugs or a supply for the boilers. The bigger problem is I can see a lot of workers down there. What if they have lookouts?"

"Then we'll have to move fast." Jacob squinted into the distance, barely able to make out anything that might be a person. That didn't mean their presence wouldn't draw attention. They'd just have to be even quieter than they'd planned.

Alice collapsed her scope and studied the platforms. "That's where we need to be."

Jacob nodded and started across the walkway. They could get to the first platform from the stairs, but after that, things looked to be a bit more complicated.

CHAPTER THIRTY

Jacob and Alice reached the first platform without issue, the stairs leading them to an elevated walkway and then out to the tangle of pipes. They still hadn't seen anyone near the valves or platforms, which gave them some hope they wouldn't.

He finished securing the charge to the valves on the platform. It was a technique Charles had taught him, even if the old tinker hadn't really expected Jacob to retain that knowledge. They'd used similar, though larger, charges to bring down Dauschen.

He clipped a tiny wire filament to it that was nearly invisible in the tangle of valves and pipes.

"I can't believe that's enough to destroy those valves, Jacob."

His gaze trailed up the mass of pipes and wheels, emergency releases, and hard angles used to control the flow of steam and power to the district. "Think of it like a heart, Alice. It doesn't need much damage to break it."

She turned and looked across the platform, eyeing the next. "And how many hearts does the Great Machine have?"

"Too many." Jacob activated the receiver mounted on the explosives. They'd need to destroy every relief valve if they meant to cause a major breach. Even that might not be enough, he knew. The Great Machine was a complicated structure, filled with fail-safes and redundancy that would awe any tinker.

But all designs had a flaw. He just needed to be sure he'd found the right one. If not, it would be up to Archibald and Lady Katherine to infiltrate the Great Machine and leave it in ruin. And how much time would that take? How many weeks, or months, to beat down the combined forces of Mordair and his allies?

"You have your transmitter?" Jacob asked.

Alice started to reach for her collar, then moved to the long leather pouch at her waist. She pulled out a cylinder that wasn't much larger than a collapsed scope, a heavy metal cage protecting the trigger.

"Good." Jacob patted his chest. He had one, too, because no matter what happened, he wanted to be sure at least one of them could set off the charges. Nothing they encountered would stop them. He wouldn't allow it. "Let's go."

Alice took a steadying breath and looked up, following the path of the ladder that rose straight into the ceiling. According to the map, it should take them out into the city above. They could follow the alleys then, like an exposed maintenance tunnel.

She reached for the first rung and started up, Jacob following close behind.

He glanced back, suddenly very thankful for the gliders they carried. A fall from the ladder to the platform would be serious. A fall beyond that would be like falling the height of three city walls to their death without a glider.

As they went, he had a sudden concern that the hatch would be locked from the other side, that he'd somehow have to shuffle around Alice to pick another lock. But those fears fled when Alice pulled a simple lever to the side, and the hatch clicked open.

Light flooded in, as well as noise. The noise of an armored city, housed inside the shell of their mechanical god. Voices and heavy machinery blended together in a cacophony of steam and people.

Jacob hurried out of the hatch right behind Alice. There wasn't anyone in the alley itself, but there were plenty of people nearby.

If there were still so many inside the Great Machine, what did that say about their forces outside? Were they like Ballern, forcing those seen as lower class to serve in their military?

Or more like Belldorn, where it was honorable, often celebrated.

Or perhaps like Ancora, where a great number served out of desperation and a chance to escape the Lowlands. Though that rarely happened. But even for the slightest chance, many would risk everything.

The hatch clicked closed behind them, and Alice led the way through the alley. They caught glimpses of the city there, the sheer scope and scale boggling Jacob's mind as the walls rose around them in that familiar trapezoid shape. But the desert ruins would have fit neatly inside the underground here. They'd built a city on top of the Great Machine, carrying its form through like some kind of mad crown.

It could have been Cave if it wasn't for the clean lines on the homes and stores and the smooth walls framing the streets. They couldn't all be the enemy. The families walking from store to store. The old women chatting as they carried small leather bags down the street. The group of kids rolling a cluster of Pillies through the gutter.

They reached the second hatch, and Jacob could barely stand to look at the people. These weren't the warriors outside. These weren't the pawns of Mordair sent to slaughter the Steamborn and the Skyborn. There were families here.

Alice gestured to the hatch. Jacob reached down, and the latch easily clicked open. He went down first, and Alice slipped in behind him, their eyes taking a moment to adjust to the dimmer light beneath the streets.

"Jacob, what are these bombs going to do?"

He closed his eyes as he stepped away from the ladder. "Cause the boilers to fail. Possibly collapse part of the structure, but I can't be sure about that."

"All these people?"

Jacob rubbed his forehead. "I know. I just … what else can we do?"

Alice squeezed her temples and shook her head. "I don't know. They're killing our friends outside right now. I don't think we can go back. We don't have another plan."

"No, we don't."

Jacob pulled a length of wire and a small, shaped explosive from his pack. He leaned into the webwork of valves and placed it at an angle that would cut the widest pipe before the emergency release. The sudden reduced pressure would cause far too much steam to be generated. Once the bombs were triggered, they'd have minutes before the boilers failed. If they were lucky.

"These are Mordair's people now, Alice. We have to think about Ancora. We have to think about our friends in Ballern and Canopy and Midstream. Everyone is at risk as long as the Children of the Dark Fire are still here. Maybe we can save some of them, but we can't stop because they might be in danger."

Alice looked away for a moment. "It turns my stomach, but I know you're right. We don't have any good choices."

Jacob engaged the receiver and pointed to the next platform. "We can use the grappling cannon here. The sound shouldn't carry to the workers down below." He pulled the device off his belt and took aim, carefully lining up the intake pipes as his target since they didn't have stone for an anchor.

He took a deep breath to settle himself and pulled the trigger, the anchor thudding into the metal behind him before the distant thump of the other anchor followed. Jacob slipped his arm into the strap and stepped over the railing, riding the line through the air until he crashed quietly into the railing of the far platform, grunting at the impact.

A flip of the lever sent the grappling cannon racing to Alice, and she joined him in short order, lifting her legs to avoid an impact with the railing. She retracted the anchors and engaged the safety before handing the cannon back to him.

Another charge set, and they moved to another platform. So it went for nearly two hours in the darker levels of the Great Machine. Another bomb, another trip on the grappling cannon, another hatch opened to race through the unsuspecting city above.

After the eighteenth charge was set, they had to breach the city again. Jacob cursed when he reached the top of the ladder. Every hatch had been unlocked until this one. Trying to keep himself stable on the ladder while working a lock above him proved challenging. In the end, after a few fumbles and one pick dropped into the river far below, the latch clicked open.

He stared into the face of a guard standing beside the hatch, the metal-plated flames of the Queen's Crest running the length of his forearms.

"Halt!"

✧   ✧   ✧

"I just got lost, that's all!"

Alice tried to understand why Jacob was yelling and holding his hand out, fingers splayed, and then he suddenly vanished from sight. Shouts and the sound of metal hitting metal echoed above her, and Alice's heart hammered in her chest.

She waited in shadow, listening to the yelling of what had to be guards.

"This is a secure area! How did you get here? What are you doing here? Are you here alone?"

"I swear I'm just lost. I'm inspecting the pipes today. First time alone, I swear!"

"Check the hatch."

There were two options Alice could see in that moment. Hide and wait for a chance to set the bombs off and hope they'd planted enough. Or fight and free Jacob so they could continue with the plan. Either way, they probably weren't getting away without a fight.

She hadn't fully made up her mind as she raced up the ladder. Hadn't fully considered what might be waiting outside the hatch. She'd heard three voices, which meant three targets and at least one guarding Jacob.

Alice unlocked the safety on her bolt thrower between one rung and the next. The hatch would be backlit. It gave her an advantage, and when a silhouette appeared in the square of light, two bolts found their home in short order.

She grabbed the guard's cloak and pulled, sending him down to crash against the railing and spiral off into the darkness below. She pulled her hood tight and crested the hatch.

"Did you see anyone else?"

The voice came from beside her, outside of her vision, but the cloak was translucent enough to see an outline. Alice turned on the woman, slamming her bolt glove into the guard's temple. She twitched as if trying to raise her spear before collapsing next to the hatch.

Alice's hood was down in a heartbeat, her bolt thrower spun up as she ground her teeth together, almost snarling as the last guard tried to ram a knife home into Jacob's neck.

Jacob threw the lever on his Biomech leg, snapping the stabilizers out the side and breaking the guard's ankle in two with the power behind them. He pushed the guard away, stumbling back a step and giving Alice a clear shot. Three bolts took the guard in the chest, and he went down on one knee. By the time he looked up, all he saw was Alice's fist before the bolt glove shattered his skull.

Jacob grabbed the guard's body and dragged them to the hatch, throwing him down while Alice rolled the last guard in after him. Her adrenaline started to wane, and her hands shook no matter how hard she rubbed them.

"Come on." She pulled on Jacob's vest after she closed the hatch. "We have to go. Someone's going to find that blood."

Jacob pulled her close and kissed her head before hurrying forward. "Thanks for that. I just … I froze. Six more charges. Let's hurry."

They moved at a fast pace, but they didn't run. Alice knew running would draw attention, and the last thing they needed was attention. But the area on the map didn't look the same as where they were now. The Children of the Dark Fire had turned the entire block into a secure area, and she worried they might not be able to reach the next hatch.

She whispered under her breath. "It should be here."

Jacob stared up at the wall beside them before following it down to the small door that waited in shadow. "No way to know what's on the other side, Alice. This could be it. We could go back the way we came."

She clenched her jaw. The encounter with the guards had jarred her more than she'd thought at first. She'd gone from wanting to sabotage as much of the Great Machine as they could to getting out alive. But they'd known the risks going in. They'd known the risk of every step they'd taken since they'd watched the Lowlands churned into ruins in the Fall.

"We go inside. Always forward." The words sounded cold, even to her.

Jacob pulled his lockpicks out of their pouch and went to work. Two heavy locks guarded the metal door, and Alice had to admit curiosity was strong in that moment. The top lock twisted in short order, opening with a heavy click. The second turned with little effort, and Jacob pushed his way inside.

The first thing she saw was the hatch no more than twenty feet in front of them, and relief flowed through her at the sight. But awareness crept in from all sides. The heat of the furnaces in the shadows and the ringing of metal on metal. The hissing flow of molten ore and unbearable heat.

They were surrounded by forges. Weapons hung in neat succession along the wall, spears and swords cast and forged by skilled metalsmiths. Farther in the distance of that cavernous building were unassembled frames of small airships and cylindrical structures that looked like they could only be cannons. A heavy door had a warning written in multiple languages. Alice could read two of them. No flames allowed.

"Weapons factory." Jacob pulled an explosive out of his pack and hurried to one of the largest boilers in the room. He fastened it with wire before walking over to the hatch.

Alice followed, stealing glances between the long rows of the assembly lines and forges. There weren't many workers at their stations, but there were enough that they might come to investigate if two people suddenly disappeared down a hatch. She waited until there was no one to be seen, then dipped below their line of sight.

Jacob gestured to the open hatch, and she slipped inside, taking the ladder down to the walkway.

✧　✧　✧

JACOB FINISHED SECURING another explosive, and Alice inserted the receiver before activating it. He pulled another out of his pack and eyed the walkway ahead.

"It looks well kept. I don't think we'll have an issue."

Alice glanced at him before returning her gaze to the extensive stretch of narrow metal that joined the next platform to their own. "At least we shouldn't have to go aboveground for a while. I'm still keeping one hand on the release for my glider."

Jacob flashed her a small smile. "Probably a good idea. Although it *is* a long enough drop, you'd have time."

"So reassuring."

He led the way across the narrow, lattice floor. The thin cable serving as a railing didn't bother him much, but the flex beneath every step grew a little unnerving at the halfway point. Similar to a timber plank that was a bit too long to support the weight it needed to, the metal walkway bent and flexed enough to challenge the sureness of his steps.

Soon, they were in the last quarter of the walkway, and the floor stabilized beneath their feet once more. Jacob let out a slow breath as he approached the tangle of pipes and valves.

"This one has a relay." He pointed to a spiral of metal. "Helps keep the pressure higher even when the boiler isn't as close."

"If the pressure isn't as high, will it still rupture? Do you think the explosives will be enough?"

He hesitated. "I don't know, Alice. I thought they would be, but actually seeing the distance between everything, I just don't know. We don't have another choice right now. We have to keep going forward."

"And we will." She reached out and squeezed his arm when he finished mounting the bomb. The receiver inserted, they headed off along another shaky walkway.

By the time they reached the last target, Jacob could make out more of the farms below them. What had seemed so impossibly far away was now right underneath them. He attached the explosive and grimaced at the workers below.

Of any targets among the Children of the Dark Fire, those bothered him most. People forced to work underground in dangerous conditions like the miners of Ancora. Like so many of those who had lived in the Lowlands before the Fall.

But Ancora would change. It had to change. "We have to do this."

Alice put a hand on his cheek and turned his face toward hers. She pulled him closer and kissed his forehead. "We do, Jacob. This is the path through the darkness. For all of Ancora."

JACOB TURNED THE last of the bombs in his hand, looking out at the remaining walkways that trailed farther into the Great Machine.

"What's wrong?" Alice squeezed his shoulder.

"What if this isn't enough? What if it doesn't even slow them down?"

"We'll know soon. No need to worry about that now. Remember when you thought a pair of bombs by the solid fuel could bring down a Great Machine?"

He glanced at her. "Yeah, but that was before I really understood how massive this machine is."

Alice flipped farther back in the pad of the map. "Going back the same way isn't an option. That leaves another access tunnel to the east."

"Which will dump us right in the middle of an airship battle."

A deep rumbling echoed up in the distance, and Jacob believed it was the sound of bombs hitting the earth nearby. And if they were, how much could those tunnels really take before they collapsed?

"*Or* we go up again. Try our luck in the streets and escape through the front door."

Jacob rubbed his chin. "Well, I doubt they'd be looking too closely at people *leaving* the Great Machine. We might need weapons or armor to blend in better."

"I don't think so. You saw those people on the streets before. They had cloaks, a few bags, nothing more. The workers in the factory carried even less."

"No, I don't remember that, but I trust you. I was focused on not getting caught again."

"Maybe paying attention to your surroundings a bit more would help with that." She smacked his arm and smiled. "Set that bomb, and let's go."

A few quick twists of wire held the last bomb in place. Alice slid the receiver home and activated it, giving them an entire network of active explosives.

There was no time to reconsider now. They had one chance to end the ambitions of Mordair and the Children of the Dark Fire.

Alice dusted off her hands and stepped toward the ladder. "If we're doing this, we should go now. If someone found that blood, the alarm could already have sounded. And I don't want to be anywhere near these walkways when those bombs go off."

"Agreed. If it's locked, we're going to a different platform. I'm guessing they're more particular about locking the hatches in protected areas."

Alice nodded and hurried up the rungs. Jacob followed, patting the pouch with the detonator stashed inside. The signal only had to reach one receiver, and the relays should do the rest. If they didn't … well, that was something he really didn't want to think about.

Alice pushed through the hatch with ease, a single unlocked springbolt the only barricade to entry. She checked the three sides without a hinge and then slipped into the streets. Jacob followed, finding Alice peering around the corner and into the alley behind them.

It could have been any street in Ballern, the way the brick had been smoothed and appeared lighter than anything in Ancora. An odd contrast to more of the metal and woodwork they'd seen in the other districts, but there were more than bricks that caught his eye.

"Mordair." Jacob stared at the procession of flags marching across an elevated walkway. So much pomp and for what? A message of war, a message of power? Had he already sunken his will so deep into the Children of the Dark Fire that they served him as a new master?

Alice grabbed Jacob's arm. "We can run, or we can hunt. But we can't stay here."

She was right, and he knew that. They needed to be far away from the bombs. The transmitters and receivers might have a range of miles, but the signals could be blocked if there was too much metal between them. That left few good places to trigger them, outside the walls near one of the tunnels or inside the walls a good distance from the explosives. There was no safe path forward, no guarantee they'd see daylight again, or home.

"We shelter, breach the walls, and then we hunt."

Alice studied his face, her eyes flicking back and forth as if tracing every line, every emotion she'd ever seen come across it. "I'm with you." She flipped to another page of the map, and in short order, they were off, weaving through the alleys of the Great Machine, listening to the unending rhythm of pistons and steam and power that permeated the very walls around them.

The farther they went, the more Jacob understood how different this Great Machine was from the ruins in the Deadlands. This wasn't merely a place to work and leave at the day's end, but an entire enclosed city.

The cost of what they were about to do weighed on him. It was one thing to kill the guards who would have killed them but quite another to put so many lives in danger. He tried to hide it, tried to keep a neutral expression anytime Alice looked at him, but he knew he was failing.

"Not much farther now." She pulled on his sleeve, guiding him out of an alley and onto the main street that crossed below the platform where they'd seen Mordair walking. The floor of the level above them loomed out over the walkway. Only a handful of residents still made their way through the Great Machine, ducking in and out of the few remaining open storefronts.

Alice chuckled under her breath as they passed a bookstore. The same wildly inaccurate tomes William had sold them in Ballern sat framed in the window. They were almost all history books there, and Jacob had little doubt they were just as fantastical as the others in Ballern.

If not more so.

But it reminded him of the families that lived inside those walls, the children who attended lectures and classes that raised them on that nonsense. It wasn't their fault they were so misled, but they'd suffer from this war. It didn't matter how generous Kat or Archibald were. Whoever survived always suffered for a time.

"We don't have a choice," Jacob said quietly.

Alice squeezed his arm. "I know, Jacob. I know. This is the heart of Mordair's scheme. It's time we tore it out." She gestured to the thick support beam that cut between two buildings. The narrowest slip of an alley curved to either side.

Jacob had to take his backpack off, careful to look for prying eyes before he stepped into the shadow of the beam. Alice followed, her breath loud in the enclosed space. If they leaned against the opposite side of the support, they were all but invisible from the street.

Alice had chosen well, Jacob knew. It would take far more than a few bombs to bring down a support like that. Of course, there was the chance of a chain reaction. He shook his head to clear that awful idea.

"What is it?"

He looked up and met her eyes. "It's … nothing."

"Jacob."

"Just, if there's a chain reaction. If the boilers failing does more damage than we expect. It might not be safe here."

"Everything is a risk. We knew that from the beginning. We knew that growing up in the Lowlands." She gave him a small smile. "We take the risks we have to."

He blew out a breath. "And this is something we have to do."

Alice pulled the detonator from her satchel. "Just remember, you didn't push the button."

"Alice?"

She lifted the wire safety and clicked the detonator.

CHAPTER THIRTY-ONE

"Take them on the left!" Owen roared, a broken spear in one hand and the long, hooked blade of his fishing knife in the other. Fisherfolk and their allies from Bollwerk followed his lead, rounding a crumbled stone wall on the far west side of the docks.

It wasn't the fight he'd expected. Not the faceless cloaks of the Children of the Dark Fire but sailors from Fel and Ballern standing in their way. People he could have called friends if their nobles hadn't ordered them across the sea to fight for an unworthy king.

Ballistae and cannons fired overhead, and more than a few in that battle were lost to falling debris, never knowing what had come from above. Still, the fighting continued, the fronts surging back and forth as they grew too close-knit for archers to take careful aim, but that still didn't stop them.

Trevor grunted as a bolt took him in the chest. The short hesitation from the impact left a hole in his guard, and two spears ran him through. His collapsing body broke the haft of one and gave Owen time to ram his knife home in the other's throat, pushing deeper through the lines.

Leaving Trevor on the field sent a wave of grief through him that quickly burned out in a surge of anger. Anger was dangerous in a battle. It made you lose sight of what was right in front of you as you tried to claw through every last one of your enemies.

A noble's guard fell at Owen's hand, another to Fiona's ax as she caught up to him. The noble, of course, was nowhere to be found, likely hidden behind the great armored walls of the Great Machine or stowed safely on some distant airship.

No matter the scene in front of them, no soldier could turn away when a section of the Great Machine erupted in a massive gray and white cloud, the wall blowing out in a deadly blast. Another explosion followed, sending debris and flames and ash into the sky, carving through the hull of a destroyer posted above.

The noise reached them a second later, a thunder like nothing Owen had ever heard. Louder than the collapse of the walls at Fel, greater than the cannons of a Porcupine. Debris peppered the field, arcing away from the smoldering expanse of a missing wall.

Anyone inside the surrounding city had to be dead. That was a calamity unleashed, a hellish vision of destruction like he could not imagine. Half the enemy lines broke, fleeing to the north, toward the ruined docks and woods that might provide some scant shelter.

Those nearest Owen pushed harder, bearing down on the remaining fisherfolk and warriors from Bollwerk. But a bizarre ship swept down in the gap left by the retreating lines. Its cargo doors opened some ten feet in the air before a small group of warriors leaped down, and the strange, winged vessel sped into the distance.

Owen's transmitter crackled and tried to reach him over the cacophony of the battlefield. He only caught a few words. "Berserkers ... out ... their way."

There were no berserkers remaining in the world. Owen knew that for a fact. They had all died in the Deadlands War. Twisted and tortured and left to expire in exile like the Forgotten themselves.

But there was no other word for the devils dropped onto that field of battle. Axes held high and metal arms wielding three swords mounted to braces, they cut through the Fel soldiers and Ballern dissidents like so many fish to be gutted.

He could see the ancient, wrinkled faces of those warriors. Men and women who shouldn't have been able to move like someone a fraction of their age. Shouldn't have been able to move with such strength and brutality.

There was no mercy left in those old souls. Owen hit the ground hard, tripped from the side, and dropped like a sack of grain. A bloody blade entered Owen's vision, hovering just short of his face.

"Stand down." The Red Hand held another sword to the throat of a Bollwerk guard. Owen didn't know her, only knew the crossbow patch on her shoulder. Elite. Archer. She shouldn't have even been on the front.

But he knew The Red Hand. He knew the face of evil. "Let me die. I'll not be a prop for your king and cult like my brother was."

The Red Hand glanced from Owen to the berserkers carving through her allies. "You're going the wrong way if you mean to stop this." She pushed the guard away and offered a hand to Owen.

With hesitation, he let her pull him to his feet.

"The code to the bunker at the airship docks. Six, Eleven, Four, Two. You'll find Ballern's traitors there, and the remaining munitions for the destroyers. Do as you will."

"What do you intend to do?" Owen's voice was little more than a growl.

The Red Hand grimaced and sheathed one of her blades. "Leave. I've made mistakes. If the fates spare me, I'll work to correct what I can."

"You spared the Ancorans."

The Red Hand dropped her sword into its sheath as the battle collapsed around them. "You know them."

Owen looked past The Red Hand and shook his head. Fiona had closed on her from behind, ready to strike, but now lowered her ax.

He couldn't deny the small satisfaction in his gut at the look of shock on the assassin's face. "You took my brother's life. Hung him from the wall. I suspect you've done worse."

She didn't argue it. Didn't try to deny it. "I have. May you find peace with the fisherfolk." The Red Hand turned and left without another word. No one on the lines tried to stop her. Perhaps the berserkers would have if they'd caught sight of her or had known who she was. But they were already carving a bloody path deep into the city, and exhausted though they might be, Owen and Fiona followed.

✧   ✧   ✧

Samuel didn't understand what he was seeing, what he was hearing. All the world was thunder in the distance and pain in his head. The Great Machine was burning. Great clouds of ash and fire rained down across the battlefield as a ripple of explosions tore out its heart.

"Jacob … Alice …"

He wiped blood from his eye before tearing a piece of linen from his undershirt and stuffing it under his helmet. It didn't feel like a deep cut, but head wounds could bleed like a river. The earth shook, and Bessie lurched from side to side, as unsure of what to do as Samuel himself was.

A long, narrow thing whistled by his ear and thudded into the chest of a cloaked figure. Samuel turned and found Drakkar at his side, readying another collapsible spear before he shouted at the Spider Knight.

"Move, soldier!"

Training had become habit, habit had become muscle memory, and Drakkar's order spurred him back into motion. Through the fog clouding his thoughts and the bodies crunching beneath every step Bessie took.

Though their god was damaged, still the Children of the Dark Fire marched through the burning city. Another line curling around the fiery remnants of a destroyer. But a tide moved through their ranks.

Golden metallic bodies and armor slashed their way through cloaks and blockades, leaving a spectacle of gore and terror behind them. Trailing them, following in their ranks, were the fisherfolk from Fel and a company of Bollwerk soldiers dressed in the drab grays and dark leather of their station.

"Who are they?" Samuel called out as Drakkar matched his pace, Bessie and the Stalker moving in sync as they both protected their riders and crushed through the line of cloaked enemies.

"Berserkers." Drakkar might have shouted the answer, but there was still a note of distaste, like a lingering horror from a long-forgotten nightmare.

Samuel lunged with his halberd, disarming one soldier and throwing another off balance. Two more fled into an armored crawler, only to have it burst into flames a moment later. Their screams grated against Samuel's ears. It was an awful way to meet one's end.

Beyond that, a Titan Mech lay across a building, arms splayed and canopy shattered, smoke and fire rising from the interior. Smaller exoskeletons moved nearby, crashing through walls and debris alike as they rejoined the main body of the alliance, struck out again, and circled back time after time.

Samuel's transmitter crackled and hissed, barely audible above the din of the battle. "Brigs clearing a path to the breach. All forces hold."

That answered one question he had. Kat was still alive. The Porcupine they'd seen folded in two wasn't hers. Small favors for the cost of that battle.

The shining golden warriors, the berserkers, slowed to a halt, circling back toward the front lines. What few Children of the Dark Fire remained on that city block fled at the sight of them.

Samuel braced himself as the berserkers turned onto their street, passing a series of collapsed homes before approaching on foot. He exchanged a glance with Drakkar, who only nodded before sliding off the saddle of his Stalker.

"A Cave Guardian!" the smallest of the berserkers said with a laugh. "What madness has overtaken this world? You hear stories from Targrove, but Targrove has always been a bit mad."

Samuel stared at the armored figure, only realizing much of the man's body wasn't armor at all. It was made of metal. More than Smith himself. Part of the berserker's torso remained flesh, covered in light leather armor, and most of his face except for a quarter of the lower jaw. It gave his smile a lopsided curve.

"Irvine's the name." He extended a hand to trade grips, but Drakkar didn't answer with his own.

He held out his fist, and Irvine stared at him for a moment before wrapping his fingers around Drakkar's in the greeting of the Steamsworn Fist.

"Perhaps not everything Targrove has told us was a lie." Irvine eyed Drakkar and inclined his head. "This is Pol, Rhona, Tavish, and Sheena."

"That's … not possible." Samuel stared slack-jawed at the group.

Irvine slowly turned to face him. "An Ancoran! A Spider Knight, no less. What strange tides ripple through the years."

A line of brigs unloaded their flak cannons through the city. There was no talking as the reports and explosions tore through the ranks of the Children of the Dark Fire. The slow retreat devolved into a screaming exodus as they fled back into the Great Machine itself, showing the alliance exactly where the building had been breached.

"We don't have time for this." Rhona stepped up beside Irvine. Her metal-clad fingers clicked on his shoulder. "Mordair is here, and I'm not leaving until I see him in pieces."

Irvine smiled at her. "It's been too long since we fought together."

"We fight every day, Irvine. You always burn the toast."

Irvine glanced between the Cave Guardian and the Spider Knight as a bulky silhouette stepped up behind them.

"Owen." Samuel looked over the bloodied form and those of his allies. "Do you know who these people are?"

"Berserkers from the Deadlands War. Rebuilt by Targrove, from my understanding."

Rhona sighed and gestured to the other berserkers as if unwanted guests had lingered too long, and not as though they were on the doorstep of a bloody battle.

"They're the Forgotten."

Rhona froze and slowly turned to Samuel. "How do you know that name?"

"Charles von Atlier was a friend of ours." Drakkar's answer silenced the berserkers for a time, leaving screams and cannons to fill the void.

When Rhona started to speak, a series of explosions ripped through the city, leaving a deafening chaos in its wake. Only when it quieted again, and another of Fel's mighty destroyers crashed into the nearby woods, did she resume.

"You? Cave befriended *Atlier*?" Rhona's lips curled back in disbelief.

Drakkar let out a small laugh. "Perhaps we should save this discussion for a more opportune time."

Rhona gave a nod of her head. "As you get older, Cave Guardian, you'll learn that waiting is not always the best course of action. Time catches us all." She raised her fist, and her voice wasn't her own. It took on a booming echo that rose from the transmitters. "To the walls!"

"The Forgotten!" Mary shouted into the transmitter. "What the hell, Targrove? I've met Tavish before. I've *run contraband* for Tavish before. How … why … *how?*"

"Sometimes the past wishes to be left in the past, Mary. I promise you can ask me anything you want when this battle is done. You know nearly all of this old man's secrets now. The rest I leave to Theo."

Smith grumbled over the horn as something hissed and popped belowdecks. "Run contraband, Mary? I have worked on their biomechanics in Pirate's Cove. I had no clue as to the extent of their work."

"That was intentional." Targrove had a light note of amusement in his words, which was a strange thing as they punched through another cloud bank while evading a squad of strikers. "I always made sure they only had their legs or arms maintained by an outsider. The rest I saw to myself, though Pol is a skilled Biomech tinker himself."

The transmitter crackled. "The Forgotten?" Jakon laughed. "Well done, old man. I had no idea. Not the slightest."

Targrove released an exasperated sigh. "Jakon's on this frequency, too."

"Of course he is!" Mary snapped. "We never changed frequencies."

Theo's chuckle barely came over the transmitter. "Oh, don't you give me that look, Targrove. We've earned a life without secrets in our old age."

A loud thunk echoed over the horn. "Lines are repaired. Forward chainguns are reloaded."

"Finally," Mary muttered. She pulled hard on the controls, both rising and slowing. "You be the bait, Targrove."

"I'm here too!" Theo squawked. "You want to get the old man shot out of the sky? That's fine. We've had a good life. But I'd rather like to get back to The Fish Head with George. He owes me soup."

The strikers streaked out of the clouds one after the other, still holding formation. It would take them time to realize only one of their targets was ahead of them. Mary pressed the button for the forward guns as she centered the trio in her windscreen.

Sparks flew across the sterns before the first exploded in a glorious cloud of steam and debris while another careened down to the sea. The third jerked to the south, racing away from the Skysworn, but not before Theo turned their cannons on it. One shot sailed wide, leaving a smoldering streak all the way to the ruined docks. The second crashed through the canopy, folding the striker into so much falling debris.

Mary blew out a breath and pulled around, heading back to the line of brigs as they reformed closer to the Great Machine. Smoke rose from the damage on Archibald's warship in the distance, but it showed no signs of slowing. Destroyers ringed the docks, and not a single Fel vessel was left in the sky beside them.

They'd pushed the defenses of the Great Machine well behind it, and with the damage suffered to the structure itself, Mary suspected a great many of those commanders would flee the battle. The consequences they would face if Mordair triumphed were likely overshadowed by the immediate threat of the alliance's fleet.

The shadows of Belldorn, Bollwerk, and Ballern's warships fell like a funeral shroud around the Children of the Dark Fire. Now, they only needed to cut off the head.

CHAPTER THIRTY-TWO

J ACOB HUDDLED WITH Alice against the heavy supports of the Great Machine as the clouds of debris and smoke settled around them and slowly left through the gaping holes in the walls and ceiling. He'd miscalculated. The explosions should have torn the floors out and destroyed the boilers, but they'd done far more than that.

He raised the leather of his vest away from Alice, trying to see her face in the dim light of the suddenly quiet machine. While the machine itself might have grown silent, the screams of the people who lived there clawed at his ears.

Alice squinted and blinked, leaning forward to look out into the street as best as she could. "I guess it worked."

"Yeah. I think we got lucky. That could have dropped this entire district into the underground."

Jacob couldn't make out what most of the screams were around the Great Machine, but one cut through the chaos. A high-pitched warning as someone sprinted past the end of the alleyway.

"The gates are down! Water Beetles! The gates are down!"

"Water Beetles?" Jacob asked. "We're so elevated here. Who has to worry about Water Beetles?"

"The farmers?" A pained look crossed Alice's face as she looked away. "They probably don't need to worry about anything now."

More people ran past the alley, and Jacob pulled Alice to her feet. They made their way forward, the dust and debris creating a cloudy twilight with the fires and sunlight of the collapsed walls. It wasn't only the citizens running through the streets now, but bloodied soldiers and mounts from outside the Great Machine.

"We need to get out of here." Jacob squeezed Alice's hand tighter, and they slipped into the streets, only to freeze when they saw what was barreling toward them.

Fire glinted on black chitin as Water Beetles scurried along the streets, faster and more agile out of water than they had any right to be. That made the choice of which way to run an easy one, and the pair sprinted off to the right, racing by abandoned restaurants and small markets embedded in the walls.

"Jacob, they're throwing their cloaks."

He glanced back without slowing. Sure enough, the Children of the Dark Fire were tossing cloaks into the path of the stampeding beetles. That caused some of them to dash off the side of the street and fall to the lower levels while others slowed down and tried to shake themselves free.

Jacob would have thrown his own if it wasn't tied to his glider pack. Short of cutting it off, there wasn't an easy way to remove it, and that certainly wasn't anything he'd be trying at a sprint. He glimpsed something else ahead of them, a winding staircase that didn't need the power of the Great Machine to run a lift.

But they wouldn't get there in time. Every block they passed, a glance back showed him the tide of beetles surging over citizens and their brethren alike, a churning mass of black chitin and blood.

He didn't think about the consequences as he drew the bomb from a pouch on his thigh. Didn't think about anyone other than Alice in that moment. He could buy them time, or they could die with their enemy in the wave of beetles.

The igniter clicked on the Burner. The shell clicked closed in his hands, and he dropped it on the ground as they sprinted. Five seconds, maybe more, if they were lucky.

"Go!" Jacob screamed as he grabbed Alice and dove behind the last building before the staircase.

Even in the chaos of the Great Machine, the compound bomb detonated like a thunderclap, its fireball brightening the cavity of the dead god as surely as the shrapnel tore through beetles and people alike. He didn't want to look back as they mounted the stairs, ears ringing from the cataclysmic boom.

But the spiral forced that vision on him again and again. The pools of blood. The screaming faces. There was no undoing that, but the beetles had met their match. They stumbled and collapsed or surged in the other direction before the inevitable crush pushed them past that gory scene.

"Mordair." Alice's words were more a growl than anything else. "He's still here."

Jacob looked up. Two levels above them, Mordair's guard stood stunned, watching the chaos unfold below them. A guard of four. What were four more lives to bring an end to a tyrant?

Alice's steps slowed. "If we run at him, they'll be ready for us. Slow. Steady. We belong here as much as anyone on that walkway."

But Jacob noticed one thing as they climbed higher inside the Great Machine. A shift from the simple cloaks and grimy walkways of the lower levels to ornate garb and an air of nobility that made his skin crawl. They'd be spotted in a moment in their current clothes if they stepped onto that walkway.

He reached out and gently pulled Alice's shoulder to him. "Listen, we stick out. Unless you think you can hit him with a bolt from here, they're going to see us. And *we're* going to be more exposed than they are."

Before he finished speaking, the group on the walkway turned and started toward the far end, where a pair of doors waited. They swung in to reveal two more soldiers before whispering closed behind the entourage.

Alice grabbed Jacob's hand and led him into the dark shadow of a nearby storefront. No light came from the windows, and none reached them in the small alcove.

"Then we blend in, Jacob. Open it."

He frowned at her before looking over her shoulder. It wasn't any storefront she'd stopped at, but a shop that sold gilded cloaks and garb befitting the leaders of the Children of the Dark Fire. He didn't ask anything else, only leaned down and waited for his eyes to adjust a little better.

In moments, he had the tensioner in place and worked through the tumblers. One disengaged after another before he repeated the process, and the bolt clicked open.

The heavy clang of boots on metal sounded nearby. Jacob and Alice slipped inside, stepping farther into the darkness where no one would see them without entering the shop.

"Get your pack off." Alice shrugged out of hers even as she told Jacob to do the same.

There weren't racks and racks of identical cloaks, like the small tailor shops they'd seen on the lower levels. These were intricate, emblazoned with crests and flames, both embroidered and pounded into the leather.

Jacob set his glider pack down and the first cloak he grabbed reached the floor. He picked up a shorter one and pushed his arms into it. "It's heavy."

"Not as heavy as our gliders."

"Fair." He moved to the boots next, knowing his muddy leather would be a dead giveaway to anyone paying attention. Wrapping the cloak around him would hide the rest of the caked-on filth, but not the boots.

Alice slipped her feet into riding boots with silver accents along the toes. They matched the flowing leather of her new cloak, embellished with its own bits of silver and gold.

"Let's go."

Jacob nodded as he finished tying the boots, annoyed at how comfortable they were compared to those he'd gotten in Ancora. That didn't matter now. All that mattered was getting to Mordair, and this would help.

He racked the slide for the air cannon and slipped it back into his glider pack. Alice did the same with the handheld cannon, releasing the safeties for her bolt thrower and bolt gloves one after the other.

The glider packs might have looked somewhat out of place as they returned them to their shoulders and headed to the front of the store again, but there were a thousand excuses they could have for wearing them. In a hurry to rescue their valuables, protect family heirlooms, preserve an ancient book.

More people had reached the highest level of the Great Machine now, making it easier to blend in as they crossed the walkway to the towering black doors. Screams and cries echoed up from the lower floors, and a glance showed him the river had overtaken most of the farms far below. Beetles swarmed the walls, blocked by the levels above, except where they found the stairs.

It was only a matter of time before the Great Machine would be overrun if the Children of the Dark Fire didn't quell that tide.

"Whatever happens, Alice. I love you."

She reached out and squeezed his hand. "I love you, too."

Jacob clicked the transmitter on the collar of his leather vest. "Mordair's on the highest level of district four. Behind the black doors." He turned the volume down completely.

"Was that to Mary?"

Jacob nodded. "If we don't end this, someone else will." He slipped his hand into a pouch on his vest. A Banger might not do much on its own, but the compound bomb in his other hand would change that fact.

"The instant that goes off, we go in." Alice reached up and knocked on the door.

Jacob waited until the door cracked open.

"Do you have an appointment with the lords, young ones?"

The igniter clicked in Jacob's hand before he nestled it into the shell beneath his cloak.

"In fact, I do." Alice pulled her hood down and exposed her hair.

"Old blood?"

Five seconds was the longest Jacob was willing to wait. Five seconds could get them both killed, but it gave them the best chance of clearing the doorway. The compound bomb thudded against the stone floor and disappeared through the gap in the towering door.

There were no raised voices as Jacob and Alice whirled away to either side of those heavy doors. No warning before the bomb detonated and shrapnel pinged against the door and shouts erupted from inside. The air cannon came smoothly into his hands.

Alice grabbed the nearest door before it could shut, pulling it open so Jacob could slip past into the hot cloud of smoke and the acrid stench of failed metal. The nearest guards were dead, their bodies torn and burned to ruin by the explosion, cloaks left to smolder like funeral shrouds on a pyre.

But the room was bigger than Jacob had expected, far too big for one compound bomb to kill everyone inside it. It had more in common with a great hall than a throne room, but the distance hadn't spared the others from the sound.

Jacob pulled the trigger on the air cannon, and a cloaked form with their hands over their ears collapsed. He tried to find Mordair in the chaos, but the king of Fel was nowhere to be seen. Alice followed, bolts cutting through the air with a rapid series of snaps as two archers raised crossbows, one managing a sloppy shot that shattered against the door behind them.

They moved to the wall, keeping to the shadows as best they could, though with the smoke-obscured sconces near the center table, the dark couldn't conceal them entirely. Jacob's air cannon thundered again, blowing spirals of gray away from the barrel as another guard fell.

He primed the air cannon as Alice fired the remaining bolts in her thrower, the spinning wheel along her wrist spitting them across the room like a hailstorm.

Shadows moved by the table, and Jacob ran after Alice to circle them, smoke trying to claw the air from his lungs. If their targets had time to collect themselves, he didn't want to think about what might happen.

But they weren't the only ones circling the room. Alice yelped behind him, and Jacob spun to face her. A bloodied hand dug its nails into her shoulder, but a ferocious punch landed Alice's bolt glove squarely on the woman's forehead. There wasn't any delay when the springs thudded home. Only a crack of bone before the body collapsed like a marionette.

The distraction had done its work. Jacob grunted when something took him in the side, looking down to find a bolt stuck in a vest pouch. He dove forward, putting the table between him and the archer, snapping the bolt off and landing awkwardly on his air cannon.

The lack of pain told him it hadn't penetrated his vest. Alice slid in beside him, her air cannon raised before it thundered close to Jacob's ear. He winced away from the boom but didn't miss the scream on the other side of the massive table as bolts tore through the archer's ankles.

"Move and you die."

The voice was immediately behind them. Jacob didn't need to aim. He only changed the angle of his air cannon and blew a hole through the man's chest without looking.

Alice rose to a crouch, sliding to her right and silencing the screaming archer with another shot from the air cannon. "No one here!"

If they weren't there, then they had to be by the throne. Jacob lunged forward, seeing a glint of metal. A ring of spikes on the breathing mask of Gregory Mordair.

By the time he fired, Mordair had pulled one of the Children of the Dark Fire into the path of the air cannon. "Sorry, Lane." He let the body collapse, and a swift kick sent Jacob's air cannon spiraling across the room.

Mordair reached down for him, but Alice tackled the older man from behind, hammering a bolt into his back, but Mordair caught her chin with a hard elbow. Alice stumbled, dazed, before falling to the ground and shaking her head, clearly stunned by the impact.

Jacob pulled the lever for the stabilizer in his foot as he lashed out with a savage kick. Mordair's shin should have broken, should have bent, but it only clanged as heavy armor turned the attack away.

"You should have been buried in Dauschen!" Mordair roared as he raised the tip of a spear into the air.

Alice's air cannon echoed through the room. Mordair stumbled forward, grasping his thigh before flinging a knife at Alice's prone form. It caught the edge of her cloak, and she snarled as she freed it and hurled it at the king of Fel.

The doors of the throne room buckled and crashed to the floor. Armored Biomechs stormed through the doorway, and the color fled from Gregory Mordair's face.

"Impossible." He stumbled a step before three bolts took him in the thigh, sending him down onto a knee. "Tavish! I saw you die in the desert!"

The Biomech stepped over Jacob. "We spent too long in the shadows." Tavish wrenched Mordair's head back. "A mistake we will atone for. Sparing these children any more blood on their hands."

Mordair sneered and started to respond before the spring-loaded swords mounted to Tavish's arm leaped forward. The thud was audible. The gasp, wet. Mordair crumpled to the ground, only his breathing mask remaining in Tavish's hand.

The old Biomech watched the fallen king for a time before he turned and held the mask out to Alice. "I took your kill. It's only right you keep the trophy. The memory is enough for me."

Alice didn't argue with Tavish. She took the breathing mask and stared at it as much as Jacob stared at her. She looked up at him after a while. "They're still fighting outside. We need to stop them." She winced and rubbed her jaw.

"Rhona, have a look at them, would you? I see more than one wound here." Tavish gestured to Jacob and Alice.

"We need to stop them," Alice whispered before tears welled up in her eyes. Jacob pulled himself back to his feet, retracting his stabilizers as he made his way to Alice.

He sat down close by, reaching his arms around her as he felt the tears flow down his own cheeks.

"We have to stop them."

"Battles are like that." Rhona rubbed her fingers together and put her hand on Tavish's shoulder. "It takes time for them to die down. But it is good to lay some of them to rest."

More boots crashed into the room, shouts and cries and cheers blending into a mad cacophony to rival the worst battles Jacob had ever been in the middle of, or the greatest Festival he'd ever set foot in. Confusion set in when someone screamed his name, and heavy armor tackled him and Alice onto the ground. But the look on Rhona's face was more annoyance than concern.

Jacob didn't understand until he caught sight of Samuel's bloodied smile and the cloak of the Cave Guardian behind him.

"Drakkar! Samuel!" Alice's voice hitched as she dragged them both into an embrace.

"We have to go." Samuel pulled them tighter before standing up and offering a hand to Jacob. He took it as Drakkar helped Alice up, Mordair's breathing mask still clutched in her fist.

"Tavish, is everyone clear?" Samuel looked around, as if taking count of the faces in the room. "Irvine?"

Tavish shook his head, wiping the blood from his swords before snapping them back onto his arm. "Afraid we lost him to the beetles. He'd be glad to know it wasn't a spear that took him down."

Samuel cursed under his breath and gestured to a hulking pair nearby. "Can you take up the rear guard? We need to get to the first floor and out on the battlefield."

"Owen!" Jacob shouted as he reached out and slapped the man on the shoulder. "How?"

"Long story, son. I'd rather tell you when we're back in Ancora if it's all the same to you. These Biomechs are a big part of it, I can tell you that."

Jacob looked at the Biomechs, trying not to stare at the metal hoses and bronze plates that protected the mechanical parts of their bodies. "Who are you?"

Samuel blew out a breath and laughed. "Meet the Forgotten, kid. Or at least some of them."

"We avoided this war as long as we could." Tavish put his arm around Rhona's shoulder. "It always comes back if you don't end it."

"How?" It was the only question he could choke out.

"Targrove, of course," Alice said before focusing on the Forgotten. "You knew Charles, too, didn't you?"

Tavish smiled. "Knew a lot of folks, miss. But yes, we knew Atlier.

Targrove told us of Atlier's *mad* apprentice. Never expected to meet the tinker who could bring a Titan Mech to life. Not even Charles could get that quite right."

Samuel grabbed Jacob and Alice. "You two with me. The rest of you get out and get to the north. The docks are secured."

Tavish pointed to the banners in the room. "Grab the Queen's Crest and that Fel abomination. You want to end a battle? I'll show you how to end a battle."

CHAPTER THIRTY-THREE

J ACOB CLUNG TO Alice while she held fast to Samuel. Bessie's saddle wasn't made for three people, but if anyone knew how to make it work, it was the Spider Knight. Bessie scuttled down the side of the spiral staircase, leading them into the fighting below as a new banner unfurled from the walkway above.

A Queen's Crest on a white background, two blood-red lines on either side.

Bessie pounced onto the lower floor, crushing a Water Beetle in the process, the others with no recourse but to scamper away from her. Jacob thought his leg muscles might catch fire trying to ride the spider without a proper saddle. He hunched forward, legs over Alice's thighs as he held on for all he could.

Mercifully, they reached solid ground, and the cries of the battle inside the Great Machine lessened. Cloaked forms threw down their weapons or spun to fight Water Beetles side by side with their enemy. One simple flag had turned the tide in that place in an instant.

Part of Jacob was relieved. Another part of him marveled at how obedient the Children of the Dark Fire were to a flag of surrender. A cloth hung in the air that tamped down their battle cries and hostility like the pull of a lever. The thought of that kind of control was terrifying. To see it laid out before him was nauseating.

Bessie punched through the crowd in the breached wall, taking her riders out into the burning city at a sprint. Ruined buildings smoldered around the blast site, black smoke still climbing into the sky, obscuring the small skirmishes in the air.

"Skysworn, I've got them. Headed southeast through the city. We'll be into the craters soon enough."

Jacob couldn't hear the staticky reply that came across the transmitter. But by the time they cleared the city proper and entered the terrible vision of the battle that had come before, Jacob understood why Samuel had simply said "craters."

Bessie danced along the rims of the craters, never dipping more than a furry claw or two over the edge as she turned and shot to the north, keeping her riders remarkably well balanced. Fires burned in the homes and shops of the city around the Great Machine, but they also burned in the forest on both sides of the fire line.

It would be days before that kind of inferno would burn itself out, and the damage it might do in the meantime was unimaginable.

A shadow swept down from the clouds, copper and brass accents showing new dents and scars from the recent battle, but the Skysworn still flew. The loading ramp opened in the hull as the ship turned away from them, and Samuel guided Bessie ever closer.

Samuel shouted over the distant boom of cannon fire and the slow rumble of a falling tower. "Get that mask and banner to Kat."

"What about you?" Alice reached up to his shoulder.

"I'm staying with Drakkar. There's more to be done here, and I'm not leaving any of them behind. He'd do the same for me."

"We should stay with you."

Samuel shook his head. "No, you go. I'll see you again. I promise."

Jacob slid backward when Bessie crouched, giving him a decent angle to dismount. He reached up to Samuel and traded grips before Alice slid down, too. They hurried to the Skysworn as Bessie wheeled around.

Smith stood at the top of the ramp, his sleeve bloody. Jacob suspected the Skysworn hadn't been sitting by the wayside.

"Good to see you two. Get inside before Mary leaves us all behind."

As soon as they were both on the ramp, Smith started raising it, causing Jacob to stumble as the angle of the ground changed beneath his boots. "Glad to see you're still in the air."

Smith nodded to him as Alice crushed the older tinker with a hug. "Get to the cabin. Mary. We're in. Go!"

The Skysworn turned as it rose, tossing Alice into the wall as they hurried through the corridor. Soon enough, they were at the hatch to the deck, struggling against the wind until they pushed through the cabin door.

Mary cast a smile over her shoulder. "Happy to see you both. We need to get you to Kat."

"What for?" Jacob asked.

"To fly that banner, of course. Samuel told me all about it."

"Did he tell you about this?" Alice raised the blood-streaked breathing mask of Mordair.

Mary almost snarled. "Good riddance. Get in your jump seats."

Jacob pulled his seat up from the floor and flopped down into it, thankful for an actual seat and not the half-on, half-off craziness of the ride there. He let his glider pack fall to the floor next to Alice, frowning at the blood streaked across it.

"Hold tight. Heading to the Porcupine."

That was all the warning they had before the Skysworn shot into the clouds above. In the dark of the cloud bank, Jacob noticed the damaged windows. Two of them were cracked and a high-pitched whistling told him there was more damage to the ship than dents and cracks.

They exited the far side of the clouds, and the sea opened up in the distance. Mary angled to the northwest, not quite following the shore but staying clear of the distant fight beyond the Great Machine.

Mary clicked the button for the transmitter. "Kat, we're almost there. Do you have a place for us to dock on that thing?"

"No. I'd recommend landing lines and wheels."

"Understood."

Smith's voice sounded over the horn. "The winch has not been repaired, Mary. That shot we took to the bow will require parts."

Mary hung her head and cursed.

Jacob exchanged a look with Alice. She bent over and picked up her glider. "I think I have another way."

He nodded in agreement and started tying the banner to the cargo pouch at the base of his pack. Alice did the same with the breathing mask, and a vision of the Butcher flashed through his mind. Memories of the makeshift throne room in Ancora, and the sickening crack of a monster's ribs.

"Are you sure about this?" Mary asked.

Jacob watched the view change in the windscreen before he nodded. Ships burned along the ground, and others limped through the sky, but three monstrosities loomed over it all. The Porcupine with its countless cannons, and beyond that, Archibald's warships.

One of those titanic forms would have been enough to frighten the strongest fleets. Two of them flanked by a Porcupine was madness.

"Aim for the upper deck behind the turret with four cannons. It's closest to the bridge." Mary clicked the transmitter again. "Kat, they're coming in from the top. Tell your guards to stand down. They'll be on gliders."

"Understood."

Mary turned to look at the pair. "I'm going to need stories later. Lots and lots of stories."

Alice unfastened her belt and stepped forward to hug Mary around her seat. "And we'll need to hear yours, too."

The captain of the Skysworn smiled at the Ancorans. "Now, get off my ship."

Jacob gave her a two-finger salute and pulled the door open. It felt odd not tying off to the safety line, but when he intended to jump overboard anyway, it didn't seem necessary. With the explosives deployed and the compound bombs used, the glider shouldn't have any issues with the weight of their cargo pouches. He leaned on the railing and blew out a breath.

"You see the turret?" Alice pointed toward midship, slightly closer to the stern.

"I see it. I hope it's bigger than it looks from here."

Alice patted him on the back. "I'm sure it's bigger than that alley you tested the gliders in."

Jacob blinked.

"What was it you said the first time you used a glider?" Alice grinned at him as she took a step back. "Cock-a-doodle-doo!"

He didn't even have a chance to laugh before she was up and over the railing. All he could do was follow, leaping into the sky and pulling the lever for the glider. The sudden resistance wasn't as brutal as usual, the momentum of the Skysworn already putting them in the right direction.

Jacob guided his glider to the north before diving a bit and pulling up, the extra boost of speed helping him catch up to Alice. It was difficult not to smile there, above the battles, away from the world if for only a moment. They'd done what they needed to. They could go home to Ancora soon. And that was worth almost any price.

Alice adjusted her flight path as they approached the deck, using the same dive and pull up maneuver as Jacob, then snapping her wings closed. She sprinted to a stop, hands on her hips as she caught her breath.

Jacob landed close behind her. Not quite so graceful as he tripped, stumbled, and stopped himself on a nearby railing.

"Jacob, Alice, with me."

He turned to find Kat waving to them from a doorway. They both tucked their glider wings in and followed. The four-cannon turret wasn't merely *close* to the bridge, as the bridge itself almost sat on top of it.

Jacob and Alice found themselves standing on the control deck by a large round table, maps and notes sprawled across it with pins and a compass seemingly laid out at random.

"Arun? Mali?" Alice frowned at the pair standing there.

"I'm so glad you survived." Mali hurried over and squeezed Alice's arms. "We heard about the bombing and sent more soldiers to the front. Karn wasn't as well protected as we wanted, but …"

"But to lose this battle was to doom Karn." Arun reached forward in greeting, exchanging grips with Jacob and then Alice once Mali stepped away from her.

"May I?" Kat held out her hand.

Alice glanced down at her side and nodded, untying the leather cord that secured the breathing mask. She held out the spiked mask and Kat took it, a brief crease in her brow before she turned it over and back again.

"He could have been imprisoned, you know." Kat handed the mask to Alice. "Mordair could have been paraded before Ancora's Parliament and hung from the walls."

Alice grimaced. "I'd rather be able to live with myself. He's dead. Let his memory be a lesson." She dropped the mask onto the floor. It clanged against the plating and rolled to the side before settling across a dirty streak of blood.

"A martyr either way." Arun blew out a long breath and bent down to retrieve the mask. "I understand your distaste for this relic. Truly, I do. But you should return to Ancora with it. Do not bury the atrocities of the past. Do not honor them, but do not forget what has come before."

Alice hesitated, then took the mask and tied it back onto her pack.

Jacob shrugged out of his glider and opened the cargo pouch, pulling out the tightly rolled banner and handing it to Kat.

She unrolled a corner and looked to Arun. "Is this it?"

He nodded. "That is indeed their flag of surrender. Fly it as a signal, and what remains of the fleet should stand down."

"Take it to the signal bearers, please." She offered the bundle to Arun.

"Come, Mali. Let us see this done."

"Have you heard from Eva?" Alice asked. "I forgot to ask Mary. That was terribly rude of us, Jacob."

Kat laughed, casting a broad smile at the pair of Ancorans. "Eva is fine, and I'm sure Mary will forgive you such a small oversight. Likely before she forgives Eva for deploying with the Skyriders."

Heavy boots clanged on the floor behind them, followed by someone gasping for breath. Jacob turned to see what the commotion was, somewhat confused by the appearance of a very disheveled Archibald.

"It's true. You made it back. Mary said … I just … it's over?"

Jacob had never seen the man so uncomposed, so hopeful for something to be true. He'd seen compassion from Archibald in the past, but this unguarded moment made him more human than Jacob had seen the Speaker of Bollwerk before.

Alice untied the loop at her waist and raised the breathing mask. Archibald closed his eyes.

"It's been so long. I wasn't sure it would ever end."

Kat clicked the transmitter. "Mary, we're done here. Can you send lines down for Jacob and Alice?"

"No. Winch is broken. Hold on."

The transmitter went dead for nearly a minute as Archibald turned the mask in his hands before giving it back to Alice.

"Kat, Jakon will be there shortly. He'll drop lines at the middeck and rendezvous with us at the carrier."

"Understood, Mary. I'll be sure Eva follows as soon as she is able. Archibald, what do you mean to do?"

The Speaker of Bollwerk rubbed his hand over his mouth. "You and I should not accept their surrender. Delegate to one of your commanders. I will do the same. Leave enough of your fleet here to make a statement, but take the rest back to Belldorn, Kat. We have rebuilding of our own to do."

"Agreed, but I intend to move some of my tinkers to Ballern for a time. That city is in dire need, much like Ancora was when you reached out to them."

Archibald eyed Kat for a moment before nodding. "A good choice. Bollwerk will send aid as well. The survivors here will need help, too. It may be our only chance to forge a relationship with them." His voice took on some of the regal tone Jacob was used to hearing. A bald decisiveness that had been lost, if only for a minute. "Jacob, Alice, return to Ancora. Take proof of what has happened here. I've little doubt Baddawick will already know what transpired, but proof will be needed for some. When we are done, Lady Katherine and I will visit Ancora together. It is time to present a united front and grant our allies their due."

"Well past time." Lady Katherine inclined her head to Archibald.

✧　✧　✧

IT WAS NEARLY an hour before The Ray hovered above the deck and started dropping a line with a pair of wheels attached. It wasn't just any set of wheels, though. They were the same Charles had designed, able to take a Burner and climb with little effort from the person activating it.

Jacob held them in his hand as he looked out to the burning city and forest beyond. Several of the remaining ships of the Children of the Dark

Fire now flew white banners from their signal flags. Others had landed, their sailors disembarking and abandoning the destroyers. A fleet of fire brigades had deployed, running tanks of water from the lake and sea to the worst of the flames.

No one fired on them, and Jacob had no idea whose fleet they belonged to. Perhaps that was how it always should have been.

Jacob and Alice stood silhouetted by the burning remains of a long-forgotten god. They watched the fires for a time, their allies marching below them as they made for the remaining skirmishes in the city. Alice reached out and took Jacob's hand, pulling him away from that vision of the inferno below. He followed without protest.

They left the ruins behind.

CHAPTER THIRTY-FOUR

Alice stepped over the railing of The Ray's loading ramp before helping Jacob over the edge. She grunted when someone tackled her in a hug and laughed when she realized it was Furi.

"Told you they wouldn't die." Rin leaned against the wall before he slapped the lever for the lines, the winch pulling the cable back onto its spool.

"You said nothing bad would happen to Ballern too!" Furi snapped.

"Well … well, this was different."

Alice squeezed her tighter before letting go.

"Tastsu and Jakon are in the cabin." Furi hugged Jacob and started dragging him toward the corridor. "Come on, we have to decide what we're doing now." She regaled them with a dozen ideas as Jacob and Rin awkwardly exchanged grips, all the while Furi insisting they get to the cabin.

"So we can go back to Ballern and help with the reconstruction, or we can stay here in case they need us. But Archibald and Kat already have so many ships I don't know if that's necessary. But I also want to go see William in Belldorn! Can you imagine how he must be feeling? Seeing the Crown Library for the first time?"

"Still haven't made a decision?" Jakon cast a smile over his shoulder as they stepped into the plush cabin of The Ray.

Furi scowled at him before taking a seat beside Tatsu. The dragonrider stood, hesitated, and then embraced Jacob.

"I am glad to see you two alive. Once the bombing started, we weren't sure what happened."

Jakon pulled away from the Porcupine once he'd gotten the signal over the horn. "I'd say I've been in worse battles, but that would be an outright lie. First things first. Furi, we have to get to the carrier and drop these two off. As angry as Mary can get over a barrel of pickled eggs, I don't want to be dragging her friends off on another adventure."

They took their seats in the cabin, Tatsu and Furi in the plush upholstered chairs, while Jacob and Alice shared a padded bench against the wall. Rin pulled up a jump seat, and it didn't seem to bother the dragonrider one bit.

Alice leaned forward and grabbed Furi's hand. "You'll come to Ancora, won't you? When you're done restoring Ballern?"

"It's … it's a long journey, Alice. I don't think I can afford that kind of travel."

Jakon cast a glance over his shoulder before focusing on the windscreen. "Don't worry, kid, I'll take you. Knowing Archibald, he'll plan some extravagant event to celebrate the new alliance between all our cities. That's not something I'm going to miss. He might do it in Bollwerk, but we can get to Ancora quick enough from there."

Furi squeezed Alice's hand before letting it go. "We'll be there."

Another hour in the air and The Ray slowly settled onto the deck of the carrier. A number of brigs had returned as well, though several looked as if they'd never take to the sky again. The scale of the damage on two nearby destroyers was a sight to behold.

Most of the fleet would need extensive repair, and Alice wondered how many of them would have to remain near Karn for the time being. She supposed it wasn't too large an issue. They had carriers now, and if they seized Ballern's carrier with the defeat of the Children of the Dark Fire, every city could benefit from a new era of trade and transportation.

Maybe it was a wild hope, but it was one she held on to.

Jakon clapped his hands together as the group gathered in the cargo hold. "We need to refuel, and then I can get you three back to Ballern. Jacob, Alice, it's been a pleasure. And you'll note I've docked us right beside that junker known as the Skysworn."

"Watch it, pirate."

Alice turned to find Mary and Eva walking up the ramp to The Ray. "Eva!"

She pounced on her, embracing the woman as though she were a long-lost sister. "I'm so glad you're here."

"Sore, but alive."

Alice stopped squeezing her quite so tightly. She offered a sheepish grin. "Sorry."

Mary squared off with Jakon, eyeing the pirate with her hands on her hips. "I can't believe I have to say this again, but thank you."

Jakon laughed and threw his arms out wide. "What madness is this?"

Mary stepped closer and hugged the captain of The Ray. "I guess it could be worse. It could be Archibald I have to hug."

Jakon smiled and patted Mary's back. "To new adventures, my friend."

She muttered into his shoulder. "I'd prefer to sleep. Thank you very much." She pulled away and turned to Furi and the dragonriders. "I'll be seeing the three of you around Ballern, I hope."

"For a while at least," Tatsu said. "We still have a city to care for in Canopy as well. I suspect you will be most welcome there."

"Come visit," Rin said, exchanging grips with Mary. "And tell Smith to come too."

"I will."

With that, they took their leave and headed to the Skysworn.

A pair of lengthy and creative strings of curses greeted them as Smith and Frederick pulled a cracked boiler out of the Skysworn.

"You're just lucky we had some old junk on this carrier that used them," Frederick said.

Smith squatted down and dropped the metal scrap onto the deck. "I do appreciate the help. And tell anyone in the barracks I am sorry for the cold showers."

"Oh, yes, I'm not taking the blame for that."

Smith laughed and clasped Frederick on the shoulder.

"Smith."

He turned at the sound of Mary's voice. "Jacob, Alice, good to see you again. Are you coming with us, Eva?"

But her answer was lost to the sudden shout of Frederick. "Jacob! We couldn't have won without you. The Titan Mechs were critical in the taking of the city. And the—"

"Thanks, Frederick." He offered a weak smile to the older tinker. "I'd rather not think about it right now."

Alice glanced at Jacob. She worried how he might feel about the Titan Mechs being deployed in force like they were. It was a necessary thing, but it didn't change the fact his hands had been involved. He'd need time to process that, and she'd be there to help him through it. He'd do the same for her.

Frederick clasped Jacob's shoulder. "Know you did well." He turned his attention to Smith. "Don't forget about your reduced capacity. You'll need to refuel before you reach Ancora."

"If my calculations are correct, we already have our destination."

"And if you're wrong?" Mary asked.

"We will be revisiting the sands of the Deadlands earlier than anticipated."

"Great."

Frederick took his leave with a laugh.

"We need to go." Mary glanced up at the Skysworn. "You'll have to make any other repairs in the sky, or wait until we get to Ancora."

Eva pulled Mary into a hug. "I'll see you in Ancora as soon as I can get there."

Mary kissed her gently and leaned her forehead on Eva's. "If you aren't, I'll come find you. So long as you don't show up with the Skyriders and I have to kill you. Also, assuming Smith can fix our list of repairs as fast as he says he can."

"Do you doubt the legendary airship mechanic?" Eva laughed and stepped back from Mary. "Go, I'll see you soon. And no gliders for now." She winked at Mary before heading down the road between the Skysworn and The Ray, leaving in the opposite direction of Frederick.

Mary took a deep breath as she watched her walk away. "Let's get out of here, and you can tell me all about these *calculations.*"

Smith grinned and followed Mary up the loading ramp.

✧   ✧   ✧

JACOB WAS THANKFUL Smith had let him and Alice sleep for a few hours after a long shower and some quick stitches. The cuts surprised him, as he hadn't noticed the damage on his shoulder until he stepped into the water and the pressure dug into the wounds.

Alice wasn't much better, her ribs showing a patch of lacerations that would likely turn into a nasty bruise in the coming days. But she hadn't needed stitches, so that was some good news.

They crawled into their bunk and were asleep in minutes, the gentle bumps and shakes of the Skysworn lulling them away from consciousness. Smith, on the other hand, had quite the opposite effect as he banged a long pry bar on the bulkhead.

"Jacob, I need you in the engine room. Wake up and join me when you can."

He started to flop back down, but Alice shoved him toward the edge of the bed.

"Go," she muttered into her pillow. "I'll be up in a minute."

He laughed at that and kissed her briefly before swinging his legs out, his Biomech foot cracking against the frame. Jacob rubbed his eyes, slipped his shoes on, and grabbed his leather vest from the wall. He needed to clean it more, but at least there wasn't much blood crusted to it.

Smith held out a mug that smelled rich and dark. "Eva's blend. Don't drink it too late in the day unless you plan on staying up until sunrise."

Jacob sipped at the coffee and sighed. "That's good. That's great, actually."

It wasn't long before they'd walked the length of the corridor and stepped into Smith's workshop. The only time Smith really called it the engine room was when something was broken, which always amused Jacob, and quite annoyed Mary for some reason.

"Normally, I would not swap out a valve while the system is under pressure, but we need the thrusters if we intend to reach our destination."

Jacob nodded and took a deeper drink, the coffee cool enough that he didn't have to worry about burning himself.

"I have the system prepped, but I need another set of hands. With the thrusters inactive, I believe we will be able to remove the valve without issue."

"As long as you vented the secondary release."

Smith's eyes widened. "Of course I did, Jacob. Why not sit and finish your coffee?"

He took a seat as the older tinker leaned into the tangle of pipes and shutoffs before shuffling to the side. In short order, a hissing blast sent steam billowing along the workshop's ceiling, and Jacob couldn't help but smile into his coffee.

Smith sighed as he slid back out and into the light of the engine room. "It has been a long day." He flipped open the horn. "Mary, we are about to replace the valve. Please be sure—"

"Not to engage the thrusters, yes, Smith. I am aware. If you tell me one more time, I might do it just to be rid of your nagging."

Jacob bit his lips before downing the rest of his coffee. "I'm ready."

"A long day, Jacob. A very long day." Smith gestured to the access panel open at the ground and handed him a wrench nearly the length of his forearm. "If you can loosen the lower bolts, I will take care of the upper set."

Jacob crouched down and crawled underneath the lowest pipes. "Anything I should be worried about burning me down here?"

"Not that low, no. Do not reach above the valve, and you will be fine."

The first valve Jacob found didn't fit the wrench, so he moved to the next. But that one was quite a bit larger than he'd expected, with the wheel itself looking nearly as large as a boat wheel.

"Smith? Are we changing this huge valve?"

As if in answer, one of the pipes above Jacob's head lifted away, revealing an exhausted-looking tinker. "Unfortunately, yes. I tried to use a smaller valve in the past, but it did not go well."

Jacob smiled at what he suspected was a tremendous understatement. He reached for the first bolt, fitting the head of the wrench in place before pulling it toward him. It took a good deal of effort to break it free, and Smith had two bolts loose in the time Jacob finished one.

Once he found a rhythm, it wasn't hard to pry each bolt free and spin the nut off the opposite end with his fingers. Two more came loose in short order before Smith leaned in and grabbed the valve wheel. Jacob twisted the final bolt before shifting to the side as he spun the nut off. It clinked against the floor of the Skysworn.

"Last bolt coming out now." Jacob shuffled farther away as he pulled the bolt out, just in case the heavy valve decided to break free of Smith's grip.

But Smith didn't have a problem lifting it out and setting it on the ground. He returned a moment later with a new valve in hand, fresh gaskets shining on either side of it. In moments, Jacob had three bolts shoved through their mounts, and Smith could finally let go.

They finished the installation, and Jacob wasn't unhappy to be crawling back out from beneath the array of pipes. He frowned at the soot and grease on his forearms.

"I need another shower."

"In time. For now, help me repair the braces in the hold. We took a strong hit that damaged two ribs, and I want to reinforce them before engaging the thrusters."

And so it went, even after they had the supports repaired. Smith and Jacob moved on to less critical repairs, finishing one after another, though there was external damage that would require the Skysworn to be docked.

Mary didn't seem to be too concerned about that. She only gave a brief warning to grab a seat once Smith told her the ship was ready for the thrusters. Jacob laughed from his jump seat as Smith braced himself on his workbench.

They stayed to monitor the new valve as the Skysworn soared through the clouds. Only after an hour did Smith give his approval, and Jacob finally made his way back for another shower.

✧   ✧   ✧

JACOB'S DAMP HAIR felt good in the breeze as he almost crawled across the deck of the Skysworn. It wasn't the most comfortable thing to do without a pair of goggles on, but he knew the ship well enough to follow the safety lines with his head down.

He only unclipped when he reached the cabin door, relieved to close out the howling winds behind him before pulling up a jump seat and sitting down beside Alice.

"Did you see where we are?" Alice beamed at him.

Jacob frowned and leaned to the side, looking out the windscreen at what waited on the horizon. It wasn't the towers of a city like Belldorn or Bollwerk, but a familiar sight in the expansive desert of the Deadlands.

"Midstream?"

"Yes! Gladys has no idea we're coming. I'm so excited to see her."

Mary tapped a pair of gauges on the console. "We weren't going reach Ancora without refueling, so I thought this was as good a stop as any."

"Not to mention Bollwerk might not be the most welcoming place right now." Alice crossed her arms and looked out the window.

"It's not so bad. Lady Grey did a lot of work getting the factions to talk to each other again. I think Bollwerk is past the worst of it, but I don't know how it's affected their dock workers. Another reason to aim for Midstream."

Mary pulled a scope down and swept it across the horizon. "Looks like they've made good progress at the docks. I see several ships at the new structure." She paused. "Not all from Bollwerk, either. Interesting. Alright, get yourselves strapped in. I'm cutting the thrusters in ten."

Jacob exchanged a look with Alice. They were already strapped in since the flight hadn't exactly been what he would have called smooth. Smith had a bit more work to do on the stabilizers, but the tinker was well aware of that fact.

Mary waited a little longer than she said she would before cutting the power to the thrusters. Jacob grunted as he slammed into the harness, the inertia swinging the nose of the Skysworn up.

Alice winced and rubbed at the bruised ribs on her right side. In the meantime, Smith gave a status update from his workshop, and Jacob was happy to hear the new valve hadn't leaked, much less blown out.

He focused on the windscreen as they grew closer to Midstream. There weren't many airships there, but he recognized one of Belldorn's supply ships not far from a Bollwerk destroyer. Archibald had kept his word and more.

Mary angled for one of the lowest bays, keeping the others open for more stable ships as the Skysworn drifted into it, nudging against the spring-loaded docking clamps much like what had been installed in Ancora. She blew out a long breath and leaned back in the captain's chair.

"I want this ship refueled in two hours, Smith. You hear that? I want to be sleeping in Ancora tonight."

"As do I, Mary. Let me find out what the situation is on the ground."

She turned to face Jacob and Alice. "You two, go get some food or say hi to Gladys. I'm sure she'll be thrilled to see you. We'll get the ship ready to go. Be back here in three hours and we can have you home before sunrise."

They didn't need any more prompting than that. Jacob and Alice hopped up from the jump seats and made their way out onto the deck. The winch for the lines might have been broken, but the plank still worked just fine. Jacob led the way to the docks, and from there, headed down the short flight of stairs to the ground.

"Where do you think she is?" Jacob asked.

"Let's try George's. If she isn't there, I bet someone can tell us."

They set off into the city.

✧   ✧   ✧

GEORGE'S HOUSE MIGHT have been empty, but Jacob could clearly hear voices nearby. He followed Alice out into the street and east toward Targrove's workshop, which still remained in place and had expanded far enough that it nearly touched the homes behind it.

Two tinkers worked on a long length of tread, but they were the only people Jacob had seen since they stepped off the docks. He thought about asking them where Gladys might be, but he didn't want to interrupt.

Alice had no such worries. "Excuse me, do you know where we could find Gladys or George?"

The nearest tinker raised her goggles and blinked at the pair. "You must be the Ancorans. Most of the city is down in the river. It's tradition after a big rain moves through."

"Thank you." Alice took Jacob's hand and dragged him toward the next intersection. They turned left, heading north through the last city block, the sound of voices growing louder as they went.

Jacob paused at the edge of the street, staring out at the bizarre sight of actual water running through the normally dry bed. It wasn't deep, or dangerous, other than the Tailswords, of course, but it was still odd to see so many gathered there.

They wandered closer, skirting a small cluster of Tailswords, which only confused Jacob more. Large troughs of Sweet-Flies had been set out around them, and the creatures slowly dipped their claws into them as if they were no more dangerous than a Pilly at Festival.

Gladys stood near the center of the river, flanked by George and Rikken. Drakkar's son wrung out his cloak, and Jacob suspected the Cave Guardian regretted not removing it beforehand.

"So we give thanks the rains have come again, and our wells will not dry." Gladys raised her arms, and the gathered crowd clapped politely. "Harvest any cacti you find that won't survive the deluge. We can prevent excessive rot and loss if we act quickly.

"We have good news from the battlefront in the west. Mordair has fallen, and with him, the greatest threat to Midstream. Those of you from Fel are welcome to remain here as long as you like. Or you may return to the gray city and travel between our realms in peace."

"She sounds so old," Alice whispered.

"I'd bet a fair amount of coin George wrote that."

Alice elbowed him in the stomach. "Maybe the part about Mordair. But I wouldn't be so sure."

An older woman hushed them and turned back to Gladys.

"So please join us in the feast today. Take what you like as we have a great bounty and a …" Gladys trailed off.

"Uh oh," Alice whispered.

George stepped up beside her. "Princess, what is—"

"Alice!" Gladys squealed as she pushed George away, hopping off the underwater dais and splashing down into the waters as she wove through the crowd.

Rikken gestured helplessly as his quarry escaped. He took a step to follow her, but George stopped him with a shake of his head and a hand on his shoulder.

For a moment, Jacob couldn't see where Gladys was, only the small ripple as people in the audience moved to the side before the desert princess suddenly appeared. She left a trail of water behind her, and a line of amused citizens.

She didn't slow down as she reached Alice, plowing into her at full speed as she threw her arms around her. There weren't many people who could withstand that sort of impact was Jacob's last thought as Alice fell over into him, and they all three went down in a tangled heap.

Gladys grabbed them both and didn't let go. At first, Jacob didn't realize she was sobbing, but Glady's grip grew tighter as she held onto them.

"I thought you were gone! We heard about the bombers, and Belldorn even lost a Porcupine. Rikken got word a bunch of dragonriders from Canopy died in the attack, and people thought it was a bomber that breached the Great Machine. But it was you, wasn't it? I thought you were gone."

Alice wrapped both her arms around Gladys and held her close there in the sand. Jacob wiped his eyes and rubbed the desert princess's back. He saw Alice's lips quiver as she tried to speak.

It was only then he noticed the tears in the eyes of Midstream's citizens. They cared for the desert princess, perhaps more than even she understood. Jacob knew Gladys loved the residents of Midstream just as much, and it was why she'd be a great leader. He had little doubt her stories would grow as they were whispered in the bars and alleys of Midstream. She was there when Rana fell. She was there when unrest came to Bollwerk. And she rebuilt their homes after the attack by Mordair.

George's voice rose above the crowd, sounding from the horn Gladys had used. "As our princess said, please join us for the feast. You will find everything you need in the tents on the eastern side of the city. Join us. Break bread with us. And know we count you as more than allies. You are our friends from now until the sands part and we are returned to them."

It was Helena who broke the silence that followed. A spear raised in the air. "For Midstream! For the Stormborn!"

It wasn't only the citizens of Midstream who answered that cry. It was citizens of Fel and Cave, Bollwerk and Ancora, outsiders who had only used the desert village as a stopping point in their long travels. But they answered with a roar.

Part of Jacob worried about the proximity to the Tailswords, but those deadly beasts had apparently been settled by the enormous troughs of Sweet-Flies. They barely stirred as the cheers echoed across the desert and let all pass as they made their way to the east.

✧   ✧   ✧

IT DIDN'T TAKE much convincing to make the decision to stay in Midstream for the night. Mary and Smith were just as exhausted, and Alice was glad they could still see reason. Aside from that, she couldn't stand the idea of leaving without spending at least a little more time with Gladys.

She reached for another steamed bun in an etched decorative tin at the head of the table. Jacob sat to her right, looking impressively uncomfortable in the flickering torchlight of the evening, while Gladys was on her left with Rikken, followed by George.

Alice had to admit it was a little odd being seated at the head table with Gladys, George, and the rest of those guarding the princess, but the strangest thing about it was how casual all of Midstream's citizens were. They stopped by the table to chat with their princess as if enjoying her company like an old friend.

It wasn't like that in Ancora. Members of Parliament were rarely seen outside of a few regular businesses they frequented, and even then, they expected a modicum of solitude. Archibald reminded her of that kind of leadership, distant and aloof. Almost unconcerned with the finest details of caring for a city, but that wasn't quite the case with Archibald.

Regardless, Gladys was an entirely different leader. Maybe it was her youth, or an unbridled compassion to preserve the city her family had fought so hard to protect.

"Are you okay, Alice?" Gladys frowned at her.

Alice smiled. "I am, thank you. Just thinking about Ancora. You know my mom is getting involved with Parliament now?"

"I didn't! That's exciting. Do you think she'll do good?"

"I think she can handle it. She's done stressful things her entire life."

Gladys paused and gently squished a steamed bun between her fingers. "No, Alice, I mean … do you think she'll do *good?*"

Alice blinked at the desert princess. "Yes. I do. We lost everything in the Fall. She won't want that to happen to anyone ever again." She took a bite of the steamed bun and sighed at the salty crunch of the filling.

Gladys elbowed Rikken. "Would you just ask them already?"

Rikken sat up straighter. "It is an impropriety, Princess."

Gladys rolled her eyes in a most un-princess-like fashion. "Did either of you see Drakkar? Was he okay?"

Jacob leaned forward and stared at Rikken. "How is that … that's a perfectly reasonable question, Rikken. And yes, we saw him. He's fine! He's probably listening to Samuel complain about a thousand different things right now."

Alice couldn't help but chuckle at Jacob's rather blunt but likely accurate assessment.

"Thank you." Rikken relaxed a hair and picked up a small sphere of fried potatoes. "I'll be glad to see him again. I heard about some of the dragonriders, and I know he was with many of them. It was … I was worried."

"You can speak your mind here." Gladys gestured to him with a half-eaten steamed bun. "George might want us to be a little more formal, but that's only on rare occasions."

The Royal Guard raised an eyebrow. "It is my punishment for raising you in a restaurant full of cooks and barkeeps."

Gladys snorted. "Cooks and *assassins*, you mean?"

George glanced away before a wide smile crossed his lips. "Only a few of them, Princess, only a few."

The feast went deep into the night. So far that the reflections on the Tailswords' eyes looked like stars across the desert, and the sky itself shone in brilliant constellations. Alice would be sad to leave Midstream in the morning, but she was glad to listen to the desert princess tell tales of the constellations and the long-forgotten warriors who roamed the sky.

One, in particular, wore a cracked mask and would watch over Midstream until the end of time. Alice sat there beside Gladys and Jacob, wanting to be home, but also feeling like she was already there.

✧   ✧   ✧

WITH MIDSTREAM BEHIND them, the realization of what came next caused Jacob's heart to leap. They were going home. They'd be walking the streets of Ancora well before dinner, and that was a hard thing to reconcile with the battle they'd so recently survived.

Something else gnawed at the back of his mind. "We should have stayed to help. They were still fighting in some pockets when we left."

Mary glanced over her shoulder. "Jacob. I'm going to tell you this once. I understand why you feel that way. I understand why you think you should have fought until the skin on your hands blistered and grew raw. But you would have gotten yourself killed, or your friends killed, or Alice killed. You did more than anyone could have asked of you, and yet you still ask more of yourself. Don't do that. Don't forget the good you did for the tiny chance that you could have done some sliver more." Her voice fell to little more than a whisper. "It'll eat you alive."

Alice leaned over and kissed his cheek. "She's right. I've thought the same thing, but if we weren't alive, we couldn't help rebuild Ancora. And that's something I intend to do, Jacob. That's a fight I want to be here for. We can make our home better than it has ever been."

The Bull's Horn rose outside the windscreen, a gateway out of the plains before the Ridge Mountains. Cave wasn't far south of their current position, but Jacob couldn't take his eyes away from the mountains. They were home, standing in defiance of whatever dared journey into their crags and hills.

He squeezed Alice's hand as they drifted past mountain peaks higher than the Skysworn before Mary adjusted their angle and soared above the lowest mountains, continuing to the east before resuming a path north. The hour passed in heartbeats before they saw it. The clean, bright walls of a city reborn.

Ancora.

Jacob didn't try to stop the tears that flowed at the sight of their home. No more was it surrounded by the aged timber of the Lowlands wall. Now, stone protected the city in its entirety, the way it always should have.

Crenellations adorned with long spikes, some the equal of a Cave Guardian's spear, lined the top of every wall. The rough blocks had been sealed away behind smooth stone, leaving little purchase for any invader to climb, though even if they could, few had the ability to pass over the crenellations without dire injury.

Mary whistled as she wheeled the Skysworn to the east, coming around the far side of the wall and revealing just how expansive the docks would be when they were completed. The new wall left almost no space between the cliffside and its foundation. The extra measure of land didn't seem like a tremendous amount until Jacob realized the entire wall was like that.

It wouldn't entirely make up for the property that was lost to the new docks, but if more homes were built like Alice's mom's in the Lowlands, they could easily handle the old population numbers of the city. It would likely be years before Ancora was that large again, but the way forward filled Jacob with an optimistic warmth.

Mary guided the Skysworn into a low bay, gently bumping against the docking clamps before tapping on the horn. "We're in, Smith. Power down." She turned her seat and eyed Jacob and Alice. "Where are you two going?"

Jacob's mind raced. Where indeed? The Wildhorse? Alice's mom's? The stables?

"Bat's house." Alice beamed at Mary. "We're going to find Jacob's parents." She grabbed his arm and dragged him out the cabin door, Mary's laughter following them.

For the first time in a long time, the weight of the glider pack didn't burden their shoulders. And for the first time in an even longer time, Jacob wasn't worried about running through a city almost entirely unarmed. They crossed the gangplank and scurried down a spiral staircase to the ground.

Jacob didn't see any dockhands as they raced away from the Skysworn, but he knew they'd be around and Smith would have whatever help he needed. They passed another set of pylons buried in the stone, a base for a new spike of the airship docks, the faint chalk outline of the future structure marked in flags.

He wondered why the cranes weren't working on it if they'd gone so far as to draw up the schematics, but the answer was revealed in short order. Two cranes hummed along the stone streets near the cliff, raising more of the multi-story tenements. There was a lot to be done, but the structure already towered over the flattened streets and the buildings below.

"Good thing you built those Titan Mechs." Alice grinned at him. "I imagine it would have taken quite a bit longer to start rebuilding the Lowlands like that."

"How tall are they making those?" Jacob didn't respond to her comment directly. She was right, and he knew it, but he'd never forget what those Mechs had done on the battlefield. There was only so much horror that could be forgotten. "Four stories?"

"I think so. They'd be able to fit the entire city in a few blocks of space, Jacob. I can't wait to see it done!" Her pace increased to a jog, and they headed toward the gates to the Highlands.

Jacob heard the guards talking as they passed. He waved at them but didn't slow down when he heard their names.

"I'm telling you, that was Jacob and Alice."

Alice glanced back. "I think that was Nora."

The name was enough to get Jacob to stop, his boots skidding on the stones like he was trying to outrun the city guards. Sure enough, the guards hurried over to them, pulling their helmets off to reveal two very familiar faces.

"Nora!" Jacob said. "Cage! What are you two doing guarding the gates?"

Cage gestured toward the wall. "The gates? Who cares about the gates! What are *you* doing here?"

"It's like Baddawick said, isn't it?" Nora stepped closer. "It's done?"

Cage stood a little straighter.

"There's a lot to figure out still." Jacob rubbed his hands together. "I think Bollwerk and Belldorn are going to keep a presence there for quite a while. It's just—"

"Mordair's dead." Alice's words fell like a hammer.

Nora's shoulders slumped as she leaned her head back, releasing a long sigh as if a heavy weight had been lifted from her shoulders.

Cage cursed and clenched his fists. "Finally. Baddawick said … but … it's something else when you hear it from the people who were there. Did you see the body? He's a cunning bastard."

"We killed him." It wasn't the entire truth, but it was perhaps what Cage needed to hear.

Cage froze before reaching out to both of them, a hand on each of their shoulders. "You cannot even imagine how many lives you saved. Do not be burdened by what had to be done. I know those are hollow words. I've heard them a dozen times myself, but give yourselves time."

"We saw Owen," Jacob said. "He was okay."

Cage's hands fell to his sides. "I am glad of it. He's the last family I have left. What did your parents say?"

"I haven't seen them yet. I haven't even talked to them." He glanced up the street. "They're probably so worried."

Nora swatted Cage away from the pair with a few soft slaps on his arms. "Gods, go, see them. We didn't mean to keep you. We'll see you both soon!"

Jacob hesitated before nodding, taking Alice's hand as they jogged up the sidewalk, passing the hospital and the sweets shop before coming to the main drag with Bat's house.

He muttered under his breath. "Samuel's house."

Alice laughed and squeezed his hand. "We'll remember to call it that one of these days."

Jacob slowed down at the door to the workshop, but it didn't feel right to sneak in on them. Instead, they walked to the thick wood of the front door, lifting the heavy knocker and letting it fall with a loud thud against the metal plate.

Footsteps sounded, the locks clicking open before the door creaked inward. The man inside could only stare at them for a moment. No sound came to his lips as tears gathered in the corner of his eyes.

"Dad."

"They're home!" Those were the only words any of them spoke as his dad dragged them both into the front room.

Jacob cried into his father's shoulder as his mother raced into the room to join them. They didn't need words in that moment. They only needed each other. An embrace that felt lost since the start of his father's illness, since before the Fall.

The four of them stayed in that place, one arm around the next as the tears flowed. There was darkness in the world. There always would be. But a few would always stand against the shadows.

CHAPTER THIRTY-FIVE

Six Months Later

JACOB PULLED THE buckle of his new leather apron tighter. It wasn't the most formal thing to wear to a meeting with the Speaker of Bollwerk and the Lady of Belldorn, but the flimsy shirts and slacks so popular among the Highlanders had never felt comfortable to him.

"Jacob, we need to go." Alice tapped her fingernail on the doorframe to their room at Samuel's house. "Archibald strikes me as the type to hold a grudge if we miss his speech. And it's going to be pretty obvious since we're supposed to be standing *next to him*."

"I know. I know. I think I'm ready." He held his arms out to the side and did a slow turn. "Well?"

"You look less dirty than usual. It's perfect."

He blinked at that and then registered Alice's new dress. A simple gray fabric at first glance, but intricate patterns had been woven into it, giving the illusion of sashes hanging over either shoulder. He caught sight of a Steamsworn Fist and a Stormborn Shadowwing in the patterns and couldn't hide his smile.

"What?"

"You look amazing. I love your dress."

She flashed him a short grin. "Now grab your boots and let's go."

He stared down at his naked toes. Clearly, more sleep was in order.

✧   ✧   ✧

JACOB KNEW ARCHIBALD liked to make an impression, but he hadn't expected the Speaker to build a temporary stage that flanked the new airship docks. Samuel gestured to them from the side by the stairs, begging them to hurry without saying a word. Baddawick stood nearby, taking a long sip from a flask before hiding it in his vest.

Alice hurried up the stairs, and Jacob followed as Archibald walked up the far side. He offered the pair a nod as they took their seats beside Theo and a very grumpy-looking Targrove. A hush came over the crowd, so much so that Jacob could hear every click of Archibald's shoes on the wooden stage.

On the opposite side of the stage, and slightly forward, sat Lady Katherine with Allie, Alana, and Gladys. Jacob's first instinct was to run over to the group and greet them, but there would always be time for that later. He suspected Archibald wouldn't be overly happy about being interrupted either, so he leaned back and waited. It was only then that the true scale of the crowd set in.

This was no mere gathering of Ancorans. There were more people stretched from the stage to the new homes in the north to fill the city twice over. Owen, Hefina, Vaughn, and a handful of fisherfolk sat beside people from Cave, who in turn were surrounded by those who lived in Midstream, Fel, and even Ballern.

Jacob smiled when he spotted his parents in the fourth row, seated with Alice's mom and a few others from the new Parliament. But he almost jumped out of his seat when he saw Furi waving from her seat next to Rin.

He elbowed Alice and pointed to Furi, where she'd caught his eye on the other side of the stage. Alice grinned and waved back. Standing guard opposite Samuel were Drakkar and George. So many of their friends in one place. They'd have to leave Ancora and visit them all again. Talking over the transmitter and sending letters just wasn't enough sometimes.

Archibald leaned in close to the podium, positioning himself before the wide panel of an oversized transmitter. "My friends, I welcome you all to an Ancora reborn." His voice echoed as the speakers boomed from one end of the city to the other.

Cheers and applause rose, but it was a polite thing. Nothing like the war cries of the Stormborn as they faced down the Children of the Dark Fire, as they fought for vengeance for their homes. Archibald still gave the crowd time to quiet before continuing.

"A great number of you have expressed concern for what comes next. Some fear the mercy shown to the survivors of the Children of the Dark Fire, and others do not truly believe Gregory Mordair is dead." Archibald raised Mordair's breathing mask from beneath his cloak and set it on the podium.

Many in that place might have known that style of mask as Mordair's, but the Ancorans knew it as something else. The Butcher had worn one nearly identical to it, and both of those brothers had brought horrors down on their city.

"This will stand as proof of his end. To be mounted in Parliament, not as a trophy, but as a warning to all who approach with ill intent. Ancora is stronger than it has been in ages. There are still wounds here, yes, and I am sad to tell you they will linger as long as many of you will live.

"That is not as unwelcome as it sounds. You will carry forward, teaching the next generation of Ancorans the value of caution. The value of questioning those who may not have your well-being at heart. And the importance of maintaining an alliance that will extend far beyond the aftermath of the Deadlands War.

"I do not say this alone, friends." Archibald spread his arms wide, encompassing everyone seated on that stage. "I have with me the leaders of most cities in our alliance, and while not all could attend, I see many of you made the journey to Ancora. It is not only my voice that pledges to this new alliance, to the Stormborn."

At that word, the crowd grew louder, shouting their support for Archibald, their distrust of Archibald, and their hopes all at once. The Speaker of Bollwerk hung his head, not hiding the smile on his face.

"I only ask you for time, my friends. Then, I will welcome your judgments. Let our friends speak who have pledged themselves to the alliance, and those who have not, let us speak the oath together. An oath from a different time, but perhaps an oath we very much need."

Archibald gestured to Lady Katherine, who stood and joined him at the podium.

She leaned toward the transmitter. "I am the Lady of Belldorn. Our city lies across the Deadlands and past the Dragonwing Mountains. We will do anything we can to protect our city and all the people under the flag of the Stormborn. From Karn to Ancora, Ballern to Cave, we stand with you."

Kat waited for the crowd to quiet before she gripped the sides of the podium and raised her voice. "We are *all* Stormborn now!"

There were no speakers that could overpower the roar of that crowd. No gesture to silence them. No orders to put away the banners that appeared in the air, emblazoned with the Shadowwing. The world had shifted, and perhaps for the first time, in that moment, Jacob understood.

Lady Katherine stood waiting until the shouts and cries finally quieted enough for her to speak again. "You are all welcome in Belldorn. Do not hesitate to visit our fair city. The leaders of Canopy and Cave can tell you more."

She stepped away to applause as Allie and Alana took the podium together.

Allie raised her hand in greeting. "I'm sure fewer of you are familiar with Canopy. But we are of the same blood as Cave, and of Ballern.

Outcasts of both cities, united in our exiles, even if some of those exiles were self-imposed. If you wish to see a city in the treetops, visit us in Canopy."

Alana smiled and leaned forward. "I see many faces I have come to know in Cave. We gave you shelter, and you returned the favor for our detachment of Cave Guardians. Know that the hidden city is open to you now. And I hope your gates will remain open to us, for I dearly miss Brandurr's cooking."

She waited for a small chorus of laughter to die down. "There is a new airship dock being built near Cave. Soon there will be a route of supply ships that journey from Cave to Canopy to Belldorn on a regular schedule, thanks to the generosity of Archibald. Please, come and visit us. We have a long history with the Steamsworn, and we would be happy to share that history with you."

Gladys hesitated when Alana gestured for the desert princess. She blew out a breath and hopped up, making her way to the podium.

Alana smiled and faced the crowd one last time. "Now, please welcome our youngest leader. Ruler of the desert city of Midstream, Princess Gladys."

Jacob choked back a laugh when Gladys's nerves turned to obvious annoyance at the use of her formal title. She composed herself in short order, offering a bow to both of the leaders at the podium before returned to their seats.

"Hi." Gladys's voice echoed around the crowd, and they responded with the same abbreviated "Hi." Gladys smiled at that. "There's another route opening for the airships. You can visit Bollwerk, Midstream, and Fel along the northern route, and of course, you have the railway to reach Dauschen. Fel needs new leadership, and Archibald has offered to provide whatever help they need in establishing that.

"The fisherfolk will be instrumental, though they had no desire to join us on the stage. Please know they are wonderful people who helped protect my friends. I say this as a target of Mordair. When he was king of Fel, he guided warlords to attack Midstream. I wouldn't have survived if it wasn't for two Ancorans." She gestured to Jacob and Alice.

"Now I'm still here, and I can welcome you to our city. If you ask nicely, I might be able to get the Royal Guard to fix you some soup."

A small pocket of cheers went up with that, a telling sign of who had tried George's soup, and who hadn't.

Archibald stepped up beside Gladys. "Thank you, Gladys."

She bowed and returned to her seat, George flashing her a thumbs up from just offstage.

"Of the last four people I have to introduce, they are all of them Steamsworn, and two of them are Biomechs. Some have heard the tales of Theo, the great tinker from Belldorn. Many more of you likely know tales of her husband, Targrove. A man who created Biomechs and designed systems that have saved the lives of countless people since the Deadlands War.

"Most of you know he died there. Taken by the war he tried to end. A handful of you know that was a myth. So I introduce you now to the mentor of Charles von Atlier, one of the greatest tinkers who ever lived, Targrove."

The old tinker stepped up to the podium, stunned silence greeting him as he looked back at Theo. She smiled and inclined her head, as if giving him permission. And perhaps it was indeed that, because both their lives would change with the revelation he was still alive.

"I am who Archibald says I am. I fought in the Deadlands War, poisoned bodies with toxic metals because I didn't know better. I caused more death and despair in my life than I can ever atone for. But I'm trying. If you have any questions about those days, I'll answer what I can. My memories are old, and I may not have the answers you want to hear, but I was there when the world went wrong.

"And I'm glad to be here now when so many of you are trying to set it right." He paused and glanced down at the podium. "You'll see more Biomechs in Ancora this week than you have likely ever seen. I urge you to welcome them. Speak to them. They have a deep history with this city, as many of you know them as the Forgotten."

An audible intake of breath was the crowd's response to those words, and Jacob knew the feeling. The idea that any of them could still be around, that berserkers could have been treated and healed and carried on through the decades. It was all too much to take in.

"Truth is, none of us would be here if it weren't for these two." Targrove held a hand out to Jacob and Alice. "Apprentice to *my* old apprentice, and his wise counsel. If it wasn't for Alice digging into long-forgotten journals and finding discrepancies in the history between Belldorn and Ballern, this war might have been lost before it started in earnest. The Butcher might have slain you all, and Mordair would have lit the pyre. So thank them when you see them. The road might have been much worse without them."

Cheers and applause went up, and Jacob heard more than one person shout Alice's name. He found a pair screaming both their names, wearing the armor of Spider Knights, but without their helmets, he could see Reggie and Bobby as clear as day.

Theo raised an eyebrow at Targrove and wheeled her chair closer to the podium, raising her voice to the transmitter. "Targrove also thanks you for your generous welcome and did not intend to be rude by failing to acknowledge it."

He cringed at the round of laughter in the crowd.

"Now, I believe Archibald has a few more words."

The Speaker bowed to the group before taking the podium again. "For the rest of you. If you would have it, I propose to make the oath of the Steamsworn now the oath of the Stormborn. They are two hands of the same body, and I see it as a union of our past and our future. Say aye, should you agree."

The stage shook with the crowd's response: a long, unified "Aye."

"Then speak the words with me, those of you who would become Stormborn. Those of you who would become Steamsworn. Those of you who are already both."

Tears welled in Jacob's eyes as Archibald spoke. Alice clenched her fists, not wiping away the moisture that reached her cheeks. She spoke along with them. As did Gladys and everyone else on that stage. They all made the pledge again to become Steamsworn.

Through the black, we ride once more
Within the flames, our fortunes told
The gates of Hell lie broken wide
Within the steam, no hold abides

Feared and cast upon the stones
We fight to save the sacred lives
When all is done, and all are safe
Find me in that Steamsworn grave

Archibald nodded at the end, leaning close to the transmitter. "Welcome to the Stormborn."

The crowd hung silent for a time before Smith stood in the second row and raised his fist to the sky. "For the Stormborn!"

And the world thundered its reply.

✧　✧　✧

LATE THAT AFTERNOON, Jacob and Alice found themselves in Brandurr's restaurant, a steaming plate of Sea Claw set in front of them that no mortal could hope to eat in one sitting.

"I'm going to finish this entire plate." Alice cracked into her next claw and ran it through the dipping sauce. Not the clear butter Jacob was used to seeing in Cave, but a thick creamy thing with a lot of tang and a little crunch.

To say the place was crowded didn't capture the sheer volume in Brandurr's. Every seat at the bar was taken. Every open space along the wall where someone could so much as lean was occupied. Ancora had seen several new restaurants and bars arrive in the past months, but with the influx of people for Archibald's speech, the city felt more like Cave when it was filled with refugees.

It didn't hurt that a dozen Cave Guardians were in Brandurr's at that very moment. Drakkar and Rikken swapped plates, sampling the various fares from Brandurr while Alice leaned over and snatched up a fried dumpling.

Even with the crowds, Jacob's anxiety spiked when someone slapped him on the shoulder. He turned to find a spray of wild white hair held back by a strap filled with lenses.

"Baddawick! I thought you'd be at the Wildhorse."

The old man shook his head. "No, no, my staff can handle any crowd that strolls in. Besides, I think the busiest restaurants are here in the Lowlands now. It's a nice change from the chaos after the Fall." He raised his voice as Brandurr hurried by behind the cooktop. "Could use a bit more metal in the décor, though!"

Brandurr scowled at Baddawick but broke down with a laugh when the old man winked at him.

"Alice." Baddawick waited for Alice to turn around, her fingers coated in oil and grease from the perfectly fried Sea Claw.

"Hmph?"

"When you and Jacob are done here, could you bring him by the

Wildhorse? The back room. There are a few old berserkers who would like to speak with you both."

"Mmhmph." She hadn't quite finished chewing her latest bite. "I will. What do they want to see us for?"

"Have you been by Charles's old workshop today?"

Alice shook her head. "I haven't. I don't think Jacob has, have you?"

He finished chewing the last bite of fried scrambler, and had to admit the deep fried dish was growing on him. "No, I haven't been."

Baddawick smiled. "Good, that's good. Come see us at the Wildhorse before you go there, please. There's a … well, I'll let them tell you." He patted them both on the shoulder before taking his leave, stopping by Smith and Mary's table, where Eva and Lady Katherine had huddled close together, laughing with a Cave Guardian, Jakon, and a small group from Ballern.

"Where did Furi and Rin go?" Jacob asked. "I haven't seen them since the speech."

"I'm sure they'll find us before they leave." Alice dragged another chunk of Sea Claw through the dipping sauce, eyed it as if she might be having second thoughts about finishing the plate, and then downed it anyway.

"You know, we promised our parents we'd come to dinner tonight."

Alice blew out a breath. "Exactly. We'd *come* to dinner. We didn't say anything about actually *eating* dinner. Now leave me to my food." She frowned. "Now help me finish my food."

Jacob grinned at her and picked up one of the larger remaining Sea Claws. The shell cracked between his fingers, perfectly cooked and prepped by Brandurr and his staff, which was no small thing in the chaos of that restaurant.

As soon as one order went out, another was dropped onto the cook-top. It was a mesmerizing dance and would put some of the factories to shame.

Fifteen more minutes and Alice finally made it through the last of the Sea Claw. They thanked Brandurr and walked over to Drakkar.

"My friends, Brandurr's cooking is good, but it is not *that* good."

"Good thing my guards are too drunk to drag you out of here."

Drakkar laughed at Brandurr's quip and turned back to Jacob and Alice. "I am glad to see you both in your home again. Do you know where you intend to stay?"

"Samuel offered to let us live there for a while longer. I think we might."

Alice nodded in agreement. "It gives my mom a little more room, too. Her new place is hers, which … I don't know what I'm trying to say."

Drakkar smiled and gestured to Rikken. "I know exactly what you are trying to say. Distance is good as we get older. That is simply how it is in Cave. You still live in the same city, along the same rivers or woods, or the sea. It is not bad to have your space."

"Tell that to Mom," Rikken muttered.

"Yes, well, she will come around, Rikken. Do not be overly concerned. You found a calling in Midstream, and we people of Cave follow our callings."

They said goodbye to the pair with a few quick hugs before heading out. Even the streets by Brandurr's restaurant teemed with people. Two pubs had opened in the adjacent buildings, and they appeared to be no less crowded.

Jacob and Alice took the short road north to the new lift, riding it to the upper level of the Lowlands, where they could see the stage and the docks again. The space was nearly empty, and Jacob smiled when he noticed something else.

"They're putting up Cork nets. By the airship docks."

Alice looked toward the far wall and smiled. "I don't think I'd survive a game of Cork right now. So much Sea Claw."

Jacob laughed and put his arm around her as they made for the gates of the Highlands. They stood wide open now, and he hoped they'd never close again.

✧   ✧   ✧

THE LOWLANDS MIGHT have been busier overall, but that didn't mean there wasn't a crowd at the Wildhorse. The bright melodies of a piano and the low hiss of the mechanical tables mixed with the buzz of conversation.

It wasn't hard to spot the patrons who had never been in that place before. The wide eyes and wider smiles as the tables opened and flared, launching trays back to the bartenders as casually as ever. It was a spectacle performed with such nonchalance one might think it was an everyday occurrence. Of course, for those who worked at the Wildhorse, that's exactly what it was.

"Jacob? Alice! Oh my goodness!"

Jacob turned toward the voice and froze. "Miss Penny?"

Their teacher swept them both into a ferocious hug. Alice squeezed her back at least as hard, laughing and grinning at the woman.

"How are you?" Alice asked. "It feels like it's been so long!"

"I rather hoped you two would be back in school by now." She took a step back, wiping tears from her eyes. "You still have a year left, you know."

Jacob smiled and scratched the back of his head. "I didn't know the school had been rebuilt."

"It wasn't. All the students come to the Highlands now. It's what I've been working on since, well, you know. I'm surprised your father didn't mention it. He and Baddawick helped a great deal." Miss Penny sighed and smiled at the pair. "The entirety of the library is open to everyone now too. It's … some things are better than they've been in many years." She squeezed both of their shoulders. "I don't mean to keep you, but it's so good to see you both."

"We'll come by the school," Alice said. "I have to tell you all about the Crown Library in Belldorn. That's something you should see for yourself."

"Maybe … with the new airships? Maybe I will, Alice."

Alice leaned in and hugged her again, waving as they headed deeper into the Wildhorse.

Jacob and Alice wove between the tables and servers, ducking into the far walkway that took them toward the piano. They passed the spot where they'd once had their picture taken, the tables where they'd plotted with Charles and Ambrose, and even the back room where Baddawick had rallied their allies.

Beyond that, tucked behind a door nearly hidden but for its polished brass handle, a small group gathered at a long, heavy wood table. Some of the faces Jacob knew. Baddawick and Targrove and Theo, of course, but also Tavish and Rhona, a great deal of their biomechanics concealed beneath armor and cloaks.

Two others at least their age sat on the opposite side of the table, their biomechanics stretching up their necks, with the woman's framing her eye. Jacob almost smiled at the lenses mounted to that sliver of metal. A sure sign of a tinker.

"Jacob!" Baddawick opened his arms wide and gestured to the table. "Please, take a seat. Tavish and the others wanted to meet you in a less … hectic place."

"The battlefield or the bar?" Alice asked.

Tavish let out a slow laugh. "I have heard good things about you two. Many good things."

Jacob slipped into a seat across from Theo while Alice sat opposite

Targrove.

Baddawick joined them at the head of the table. He clicked a button, and several compartments opened, glasses rising from inside, filled by a gentle waterfall that smelled nothing like tea. It cut off before the rim of the glasses passed the outlet, the coaster sealing the holes in the table that had appeared.

"Take it easy on that now. It's an old recipe. Bit strong, but we have our traditions. Well, at least they do." Baddawick nodded to the Forgotten.

Tavish gestured to the pair they hadn't formally met. "This is Pol."

The man with the biomechanics in his neck inclined his head, the metal sliding over itself like the scales of a Fire Lizard.

"Pol isn't the most talkative of us. And this is Sheena."

She tipped her glass to them.

"We have a tradition, as Baddawick mentioned. When we lose one of our own." Tavish reached for the glass and raised it. He gave two nods before the four spoke as one.

"The Forgotten will never be."

They each sipped their drink, Tavish closing his eyes for a moment.

"Now, join us, if you would, in a toast to Irvine. I know you did not know him, but we drink to Charles as well and all who were taken by this damned war. Let it end."

Jacob took a sip of his drink with the others, trying his best not to cough as it burned his tongue and throat, and warmth spread through his stomach.

Pol turned the glass in his hand and sighed. "It's been too long since we were here and not nearly long enough. Irvine was glad to see you again, Targrove."

"I was glad to see him, too. There are far fewer old friends at our age."

Pol snorted a laugh. "I never thought Biomechs would be allowed in Ancora. We were always monsters to the people here. Better off dead in the eyes of most."

"That was the Butcher." Theo drummed her fingers on the table.

"We should have come back." Sheena took a deep drink from her glass. "We left our work to be finished by these young ones."

"Bah," Rhona dismissed the idea with a wave of her copper hand, the springs and pistons framing the withered fingers within. "Atlier lived here for decades and never killed Newton. Who's to say we would have been any more proactive?"

"Ancora's different now." Alice took a small sip of her drink. "Things are changing, and the Fall … the Fall changed everything. Lots of people here know Jacob's a Biomech. None of them have even been rude since we got back from across the Crystal Sea. And it's been months now."

Tavish blew out a breath. "You put an end to one scary story and replaced it with another. And so it goes down the years. One nightmare traded for another. Children here won't grow up to fear Biomechs now, but they will remember the stories of the Children of the Dark Fire. They'll question and poke and prod until they're satisfied. Hopefully, they won't uncover a monster."

"I'll be the monster to some of them." Jacob turned the glass of pale amber liquid. "I'll be the one they tell stories about, like Cave told stories about Charles. But they'll be right about me. I built the machines that killed their families."

Targrove laughed and leaned forward in his chair. "Son, we've all done terrible things. It took most of us years to understand that. You're already a better person than me. It is not the time to dwell on such things." He turned his gaze to the Forgotten. "Do you need more? Do you need to see Charles's journals to understand? He ignited a change in this city, one the Butcher unwittingly turned into a revolution."

Pol inclined his head. "I admit, there is perhaps more weight to the claims than I first thought. It would be nice to spend more time in Ancora. To see what has changed and what has persisted through the decades."

Tavish stood and gestured to the door. "Come, all of you. There is something by Charles's workshop we would like you to see."

NO ONE SAID much as they walked through the Highlands. A few citizens were not subtle about their double takes as the Biomechs wandered by. The city might have become more tolerant of them, more accepting, but it was still an odd thing to see such brilliant metal embedded in flesh.

Jacob reached for Alice's hand as they passed through the gates. He cast a smile at the group of Forgotten, their hoods down and cloaks gathered behind them. There was nothing hidden on them now, and the extent of their biomechanics shone in the late afternoon sun.

Perhaps the thing that fascinated him most was the quiet clockwork of Tavish's left knee. A heavy glass window showed the coil inside, spinning and expanding like the mainspring of a clock. He wondered if Tavish had to wind it or if it was more like a mechanical watch that wound itself with momentum or some other movement. That seemed most likely, as what tinker would want to have to remember to wind their knee?

Jacob almost laughed at the thought as they made their way down the hill. His mind sobered at the memories of what had stood in that place, each storefront and home, one after another, all lost to the Fall. But ahead of them, at the top of a winding street, the odd cone shape of Charles's workshop waited in silence.

The roof had been well repaired, and Jacob was about to comment on it, ask if Targrove or the Forgotten had something to do with it, or if perhaps it was Ambrose as a favor to the memory of Charles. All thoughts of the hammered tin roof fled when he noticed the canvas tarp standing beside it.

A strong breeze caused the hem to flutter, revealing the lower edge of a pedestal carved from pale stone and embellished with dark metal.

"Did you have to make it so … large?" Targrove asked.

Theo glanced up at him from her wheelchair, an eyebrow raised. "You saw it on the ship already. Are you just mad no one made one for you?"

Their steps slowed as they reached the top of the hill, standing close to the front door.

"You're sure you tied that rope right?" Sheena asked.

Pol scowled at her. "Since when have I not known how to tie a rope?"

"Since we lost a sail in Pirate's Cove trying to escape *someone's* bar tab."

Pol pursed his lips. "That's … fair. How was I supposed to know that bottle was so expensive? Three months' wages. Ridiculous."

Targrove laughed and patted Pol's shoulder. "Tavish, if you would."

"You know he would have hated this." Tavish smiled up at the tarp. "That amuses me more than I can tell you." He pulled a length of rope, each knot opening with a whirl and twist of the braid until the tarp was free. Tavish slowly dragged it down, bundling it in his arms as he went.

Alice gasped when the pedestal was revealed, engraved with a Steamsworn Fist and a single name.

Charles von Atlier

To all things an end

Atop that pedestal sat a sculpture that stole Jacob's breath. A younger Charles. He could see the man he knew, the start of the beard and the lenses etched into the edge of the bronze goggles perched on his forehead. But there was something different, something almost optimistic in the smile on his face, and the fist extended as if to greet every Steamsworn who might visit that place.

Alice squeezed him tighter as they all looked up into the face of their fallen friend.

Targrove turned to them with tears in his eyes. "Charles would be so proud of you."

✧   ✧   ✧

JACOB GLANCED BACK at the statue of Charles as they started up the hill that would take them past the airship docks.

"What do you all think will happen now that the Great Machine has been destroyed?" Alice asked.

Tavish exchanged a glance with Theo. "I think we need to study those manuals you all found. But it would seem the atmosphere itself will change, given enough time."

"But it will be slow, right?" Jacob couldn't help but think of some of the things that wouldn't survive a violent change in the atmosphere, and Bessie was at the top of that list.

"I imagine so. After all, there is at least one more beneath the Silver Gulf, is there not?"

It was a reassuring thought, but there were other questions he had. He almost laughed when Alice voiced one of them.

"We still don't know who built them. I think we know *why*, but who were they, though?"

"We've always had theories," Rhona said. "Irvine used to think they were built by the cities across the Silver Gulf. That they *knew* what would happen with the invaders, so they sent the entire experiment to another continent first."

Alice frowned at that. "Even if that was true, they had to know the changes would reach them, eventually. Wasn't that the point of building the Great Machines?"

Targrove harrumphed. "You live long enough, you'll come to understand a great many people in power don't care about issues that don't affect their own lives. A problem for their great-grandchildren is no problem at all. Irvine's theory wouldn't surprise me if it were true."

"Ancora will be better than that. We'll all be better than that."

"I hope you're right, Alice. I truly hope you're right."

A small roar went up close to the airship docks. The area by the stage was fully clear now, and Jacob could see at least four fields set up for Cork. As they grew closer, he could make out more of the players' details. Some of them were young, not even ten years, if Jacob had to guess, and others looked old enough to be of the Forgotten.

That was how he wanted to be if he lived that long. Still playing Cork with the younger kids.

Alice cursed. "Are you joking? Is that Archibald?"

Jacob flinched like he'd been slapped. "Surely not." Take away the cloak, the regal vest, and leave nothing but a pale undershirt and black pants. He almost fell over with laughter. "Come on, we have to see this!"

They hurried forward, finding Lady Katherine standing beside a miserable-looking Archibald.

"If I was ten years younger …" Archibald took a deep breath.

"Ten?" Lady Katherine scoffed. "Try forty."

Archibald scowled at her and bounced the Cork ball in his hand. "You two ready?"

"We should have bet more than a crate of strawberries."

It was only then Jacob realized who their opponents were. Reggie and Bobby stood on the opposite side of the field, guarding their nets.

"Go Reggie!" Alice shouted, cupping her hands around her mouth.

Archibald pulled back and threw a Cork with an impressive curve. It would have gotten by Bobby if he'd been any slower, but he wasn't. He snatched the ball out of the air and tossed it to Reggie.

Reggie leaned his entire upper body into his throw, bringing his arm forward like a whip. It flashed forward between Archibald and Lady Katherine, and though she managed to get a fingertip on it, the bell still sounded on the net, and the crowd cheered.

"Well done, boys." Lady Katherine offered them a small bow.

"It was an honor, my lady. Perhaps we'll see you in Belldorn."

"Please do come visit. I would love for someone to teach our kids the finer points of Ancoran Cork." She walked to the sidelines and gathered up her overcoat in one arm.

"You want a real challenge?" Alice shouted. "For all the strawberries."

Bobby scanned the crowd until he saw her, and a wide smile spread across his face. "Ah, the Festival champions!"

"You're not still working for a hustler, are you?" Alice cocked an eyebrow. "Some of us have good memories."

Archibald's mouth dropped open just a hair before he broke down into laughter and followed Kat off the field.

"Let them through!" Reggie gestured to them. "Let's have a proper match, shall we?"

It was that moment, stepping back onto the Cork field, feeling the light weight in his hands as he stared down two of his friends, that Jacob thought things might truly get better. Maybe there was still a light in the shadows. Maybe he and Alice could help spread some small hope. Maybe there was more worth fighting for.

Jacob faked his throw, casting the Cork to Alice. She caught it at the peak of its arc, her feet leaving the ground as she released it with absolute ferocity. It looked low, but the spin kept it moving, skimming outside Bobby's reach before it slammed into the net, sounding the bell.

It was a good start to the game and the first time Jacob had felt so at home since the end of the war.

Alice grinned at him. "Just like old times."

Jacob leaned forward and gave her a quick kiss. "Even better."

They left the war behind.

Also by Eric R. Asher

Shop ebooks, audiobooks, and paperbacks at ericrasherstore.com

The Theme Park at the End of the World

The Steamborn Series

Steamborn

Steamforged

Steamsworn

Skyborn

Skyforged

Skysworn

Stormborn

Stormforged

Stormsworn

The Vesik Series
(Recommended for Ages 17+)

Days Gone Bad

Wolves and the River of Stone

Winter's Demon

This Broken World

Destroyer Rising

Rattle the Bones

Witch Queen's War

Forgotten Ghosts

The Book of the Ghost

The Book of the Claw

The Book of the Sea

The Book of the Staff

The Book of the Rune

The Book of the Sails

The Book of the Wing

The Book of the Blade

The Book of the Fang

The Book of the Reaper

Dreams of the Forgotten Dead

Garden Gnome Graves

The Vesik Series Box Sets

Box Set One (Books 1-3)

Box Set Two (Books 4-6)

Box Set Three (Books 7-8)

Box Set Four: The Books of the Dead Part 1

Box Set Five: The Books of the Dead Part 2

Mason Dixon: Monster Hunter

Episode One

Episode Two

Episode Three

Episode Four

Want to receive an email when one of Eric's books releases?
Visit ericrasher.com to get started.

About the Author

Eric is a former bookseller, cellist, and comic seller currently living in Saint Louis, Missouri. A lifelong enthusiast of books, music, toys, and games, he discovered a love for the written word after being dragged to the library by his parents at a young age. When he is not writing, you can usually find him reading, gaming, or buried beneath a small avalanche of Transformers. For more about Eric, see: www.ericrasher.com

Enjoy this book? You can make a big difference.

If you've enjoyed this book, I would be very grateful if you could take a minute to leave a review on the platform of your choice. It can be as short as you like. Thank you for spending time with Jacob and Alice.